FIFTY FAMOUS STORIES *for* GIRLS

Selected & edited
by
LEONARD GRIBBLE
Editor of
"FIFTY FAMOUS STORIES FOR BOYS" ETC.

BURKE PUBLISHING COMPANY

First published 1949
Reissued 1952
Third impression October 1953

Made and printed in Great Britain for
Burke Publishing Co., Ltd., 55 Britton Street, E.C.1.
by A. Wheaton & Co., Ltd., Exeter.

INTRODUCTION

HERE is a book for girls designed along the same lines as *Fifty Famous Stories for Boys*. Each story has been selected because it is of interest for girls, because it contains characters who are worth meeting, and because many of the books from which the stories have been taken are ones which readers will want to turn to again. That is as it should be. Some of the characters in the following stories are among the most famous in the realm of literature. They are friends worth making, and it is good to have them on one's bookshelf, so that at any time they can be brought out and enjoyed.

Most of the stories are tales to be read more than once. Some even improve with reading, which might seem a strange thing for me to say, but is a truth you can find out for yourselves.

The stories are of all kinds. There are adventure stories, because girls like adventure stories in which girls play a part. There are school stories, and stories set in other lands. Tales of other days jostle stories about girls who would be easily recognizable if met in the street. There are even some stories which might be described as tearful and a little sad. But it is good to remember that there are sad things that can be appreciated and even enjoyed for themselves, just as gay and jolly things can be enjoyed and appreciated. Some of the stories are narratives of what really happened, and the bravery they recount is something for which all girls can feel a just pride in their sex.

Naturally a few fantasies appear, and tales for the younger girl readers as well as stories for those who like a wider scope for their reading and have an ear for a nicely turned phrase and sentence.

All the stories have been very popular, and the popularity they achieved has been due solely to their worth as stories. Furthermore, they are all in the words of the famous authors who penned them, and each has been especially introduced, so that before commencing to read the reader knows something of the characters' background and the general setting of the various stories. In some cases, in order to preserve the story value, the stories have been cut, but in no case have words been added to the original text.

Not long ago I asked a girl who receives a copy of *Best Children's Stories of the Year* whenever it comes out which kind of story she preferred. I had asked the same question of a boy, who had replied very readily, "Oh, stories in which things happen." The girl thought for a moment, then she said, "I prefer stories in which people do things because they feel about them."

I was very pleased with her answer.

The two answers were, in fact, very much the same. It is people's feelings that are important and make them do things. Anger, indignation, pity, admiration, hope, love, ambition—these are the feelings which result in actions.

Well, in the present book, most of the heroes and heroines feel quite strongly about things, and as a result there is plenty of action, and quite a number of things happen that wouldn't have taken place had they felt less strongly. When one understands this one can understand the character better, and only when the characters portrayed by an author are correctly understood does the reader get the fullest enjoyment from a story.

Which is something to remember when reading the stories in this book.

LEONARD GRIBBLE

CONTENTS

To
ALL GIRLS
who like a
good story

THE SCAPEGOAT

By CHARLOTTE BRONTË

At Gateshead Hall, where little Jane Eyre lives the life of a poor relation in her aunt's home, the child is treated as a scapegoat by relatives and servants alike. In every way she is humiliated and made to feel an intruder. Her cousin John Reed bullies her continuously, until one fateful day the scapegoat rebels. Not that rebellion helps her. She is promptly banished to a little-used room which her childish fancy peoples with phantoms. This story is taken from "Jane Eyre."

THERE was no possibility of taking a walk that day. We had been wandering, indeed, in the leafless shrubbery an hour in the morning; but since dinner (Mrs. Reed, when there was no company, dined early) the cold winter wind had brought with it clouds so sombre, and a rain so penetrating, that further out-door exercise was now out of the question.

I was glad of it; I never liked long walks, especially on chilly afternoons. Dreadful to me was the coming home in the raw twilight, with nipped fingers and toes, and a heart saddened by the chidings of Bessie, the nurse, and humbled by the consciousness of my physical inferiority to Eliza, John, and Georgiana Reed.

The said Eliza, John, and Georgiana were now clustered round their mamma in the drawing-room. She lay reclined on a sofa by the fireside, and with her darlings about her (for the time neither quarrelling nor crying) looked perfectly happy. Me she had dispensed from joining the group, saying, "She regretted to be under the necessity of keeping me at a distance; but that, until she heard from Bessie, and could discover by her own observation, that I was endeavouring in good earnest to acquire a more sociable and childlike disposition, a more attractive and sprightly manner—something lighter, franker, more natural as it were—she really must exclude me from privileges intended only for contented, happy, little children."

"What does Bessie say I have done?" I asked.

"Jane, I don't like cavillers or questioners; besides, there is something truly forbidding in a child taking up her elders in that manner. Be seated somewhere; and until you can speak pleasantly remain silent."

A small breakfast-room adjoined the drawing-room—I slipped in there. It contained a book-case; I soon possessed myself of a volume, taking care that it should be one stored with pictures. I mounted into the window-seat: gathering up my feet, I sat cross-legged like a Turk; and, having drawn the red moreen curtain nearly close, I was shrined in double retirement.

Folds of scarlet drapery shut in my view to the right hand; to the left were the clear panes of glass, protecting, but not separating me from the drear November day. At intervals, while turning over the leaves of my book, I studied the aspect of that winter afternoon. Afar, it offered a pale blank of mist and cloud; near, a scene of wet lawn and storm-beat shrub, with ceaseless rain sweeping away wildly before a long and lamentable blast.

I returned to my book.

Each picture told a story: mysterious often to my undeveloped understanding and imperfect feelings, yet ever profoundly interesting—as interesting as the tales Bessie sometimes narrated on winter evenings, when she chanced to be in good humour; and when, having brought her ironing-table to the nursery-hearth, she allowed us to sit about it, and while she got up Mrs. Reed's lace frills, and crimped her night-cap borders, fed our eager attention with passages of love and adventure taken from old fairy tales and older ballads.

I was then happy—happy at least in my way. I feared nothing but interruption, and that came too soon. The breakfast-room door opened.

"Boh! Madam Mope!" cried the voice of John Reed; then he paused: he found the room apparently empty.

"Where the dickens is she?" he continued. "Lizzy! Georgy!" (calling to his sisters) "Joan is not here. Tell mamma she is run out into the rain—bad animal!"

"It is well I drew the curtain," thought I; and I wished fervently he might not discover my hiding-place. Nor would John Reed have found it out himself; he was not quick either of vision or conception; but Eliza just put her head in at the door, and said at once:

"She is in the window-seat, to be sure, Jack."

And I came out immediately, for I trembled at the idea of being dragged forth by the said Jack.

"What do you want?" I asked, with awkward diffidence.

"Say, 'What do you want, Master Reed,' " was the answer. "I want you to come here"; and seating himself in an armchair, he intimated by a gesture that I was to approach and stand before him.

John Reed was a schoolboy of fourteen years old—four years older than I, for I was but ten; large and stout for his age, with a dingy and unwholesome skin; thick lineaments in a spacious visage; heavy limbs and large extremities. He gorged himself habitually at table, which made him bilious, and gave him a dim and bleared eye and flabby cheeks. He ought now to have been at school, but his mamma had taken him home for a month or two, "on account of his delicate health." Mr. Miles, the master, affirmed that he would do very well if he had fewer cakes and sweetmeats sent him from home; but the mother's heart turned from an opinion so harsh, and inclined rather to the more refined idea that John's sallowness was owing to over-application, and, perhaps, to pining after home.

John had not much affection for his mother and sisters, and an antipathy to me. He bullied and punished me, not two or three times in the week, not once or twice in the day, but continually; every nerve I had feared him, and every morsel of flesh on my bones shrank when he came near. There were moments when I was bewildered by the terror he inspired, because I had no appeal whatever against either his menaces or his inflictions. The servants did not like to offend their young master by taking my part against him, and Mrs. Reed was blind and deaf on the subject. She never saw him strike or heard him abuse me, though he did both now and then in her very presence; more frequently, however, behind her back.

Habitually obedient to John, I came up to his chair. He spent some three minutes in thrusting out his tongue at me as far as he could without damaging the roots. I knew he would soon strike, and while dreading the blow, I mused on the disgusting and ugly appearance of him who would presently deal it. I wonder if he read that notion in my face; for, all at once, without speaking, he struck suddenly and strongly. I tottered, and on regaining my equilibrium retired back a step or two from his chair.

"That is for your impudence in answering mamma a while since," said he, "and for your sneaking way of getting behind curtains, and for the look you had in your eyes two minutes since, you rat!"

Accustomed to John Reed's abuse, I never had an idea of replying to it; my care was how to endure the blow which would certainly follow the insult.

"What were you doing behind the curtain?" he asked.

"I was reading."

"Show the book."

I returned to the window and fetched it thence.

"You have no business to take our books; you are a dependant, mamma says; you have no money; your father left you none; you ought to beg, and not to live here with gentlemen's children like us, and eat the same meals we do, and wear clothes at our mamma's expense. Now, I'll teach you to rummage my bookshelves: for they *are* mine; all the house belongs to me, or will do in a few years. Go and stand by the door, out of the way of the mirror and the windows."

I did so, not at first aware what was his intention; but when I saw him lift and poise the book and stand in act to hurl it, I instinctively started aside with a cry of alarm—not soon enough, however; the volume was flung, it hit me, and I fell, striking my head against the door and cutting it. The cut bled, the pain was sharp; my terror had passed its climax; other feelings succeeded.

"Wicked and cruel boy!" I said. "You are like a murderer—you are like a slave-driver—you are like the Roman emperors!"

"What! what!" he cried. "Did she say that to me? Did you hear her, Eliza and Georgiana? Won't I tell mamma! but first——"

He ran headlong at me; I felt him grasp my hair and my shoulder; he had closed with a desperate thing. I really saw in him a tyrant—a murderer. I felt a drop or two of blood from my head trickle down my neck, and was sensible of somewhat pungent suffering. These sensations for the time predominated over fear, and I received him in frantic sort. I don't very well know what I did with my hands, but he called me "Rat! rat!" and bellowed out aloud. Aid was near him: Eliza and Georgiana had run for Mrs. Reed, who was gone upstairs; she now came upon the scene, followed by Bessie and her maid Abbot. We were parted; I heard the words:

"Dear! dear! What a fury to fly at Master John!"

"Did ever anybody see such a picture of passion!"

Then Mrs. Reed subjoined:

"Take her away to the red room, and lock her in there."

Four hands were immediately laid upon me, and I was borne upstairs.

I resisted all the way—a new thing for me, and a circumstance which greatly strengthened the bad opinion Bessie and Miss Abbot were disposed to entertain of me. The fact is, I was a trifle beside myself, or rather *out* of myself, as the French would say. I was conscious that a moment's mutiny had already rendered me liable to strange penalties, and, like any other rebel slave, I felt resolved, in my desperation, to go to all lengths.

"Hold her arms, Miss Abbot: she's like a mad cat."

"For shame, for shame!" cried the lady's maid. "What shocking conduct, Miss Eyre, to strike a young gentleman, your benefactress's son! Your young master!"

"Master! How is he my master? Am I a servant?"

"No; you are less than a servant, for you do nothing for your keep. There, sit down, and think over your wickedness."

They had got me by this time into the apartment indicated by Mrs. Reed, and had thrust me upon a stool: my impulse was to rise from it like a spring; their two pair of hands arrested me instantly.

"If you don't sit still, you must be tied down," said Bessie.

"I will not stir."

In guarantee whereof, I attached myself to my seat by my hands.

"Mind you don't," said Bessie: and when she had ascertained that I was really subsiding, she loosened her hold of me; then she and Miss Abbot stood with folded arms, looking darkly and doubtfully on my face, as incredulous of my sanity.

"She never did so before," at last said Bessie.

"But it was always in her," was the reply. "I've told Missis often my opinion about the child, and Missis agreed with me. She's an underhand little thing. I never saw a girl of her age with so much cover."

Bessie answered not; but ere long, addressing me, she said:

"You ought to be aware, Miss, that you are under obligations to Mrs. Reed: she keeps you. If she were to turn you off, you would have to go to the poor-house."

I had nothing to say to these words; they were not new to me; my very first recollections of existence included hints of the same kind. This reproach of my dependence had become a vague singsong in my ear; very painful and crushing, but only half intelligible. Miss Abbot joined in:

"And you ought not to think yourself on an equality with the Misses Reed and Master Reed, because Missis kindly allows you to be brought up with them. They will have a great deal of money, and you will have none; it is your place to be humble, and to try to make yourself agreeable to them."

"What we tell you is for your good," added Bessie, in no harsh voice. "You should try to be useful and pleasant, then perhaps you would have a home here; but if you become passionate and rude, Missis will send you away, I am sure."

"Besides," said Miss Abbot, "God will punish her. He might strike her dead in the midst of her tantrums, and then where would she go? Come, Bessie, we will leave her; I wouldn't have her heart for anything. Say your prayers, Miss Eyre, when you are by yourself, for if you don't repent something bad might be permitted to come down the chimney and fetch you away."

They went, shutting the door and locking it behind them.

The red room was a spare chamber, very seldom slept in—I might say never, indeed, unless when a chance influx of visitors at Gateshead Hall rendered it necessary to turn to account all the accommodation it contained; yet it was one of the largest and stateliest chambers in the mansion. A bed, supported on massive pillars of mahogany, hung with curtains of deep red damask, stood out like a tabernacle in the centre; the two large windows, with their blinds always drawn down, were half shrouded in festoons and falls of similar drapery; the carpet was red; the table at the foot of the bed was covered with a crimson cloth; the walls were a soft fawn colour, with a blush of pink in it; the wardrobe, the toilet-table, the chairs, were of darkly polished old mahogany. Out of these deep surrounding shades rose high, and glared white, the piled-up mattresses and pillows of the bed, spread with a snowy Marseilles counterpane. Scarcely less prominent was an ample, cushioned easy chair near the head of the bed, also white, with a footstool before it, and looking, as I thought, like a pale throne.

The room was chill, because it seldom had a fire; it was silent, because remote from the nursery and kitchens; solemn, because it was known to be so seldom entered. The housemaid alone came here on Saturdays to wipe from the mirrors and the furniture a week's quiet dust.

My seat, to which Bessie and the bitter Miss Abbot had left me riveted, was a low ottoman near the marble chimney-piece; the bed rose before me; to my right hand there was the high, dark wardrobe with subdued, broken reflections varying the gloss of its panels; to my left were the muffled windows; a great looking-glass between them repeated the vacant majesty of the bed and room. I was not quite sure whether they had locked the door, and when I dared move I got up and went to see. Alas! yes; no jail was ever more secure. Returning, I had to cross before the looking-glass; my fascinated glance involuntarily explored the depth it revealed. All looked colder and darker in that visionary hollow than in reality, and the strange little figure there gazing at me, with a white face and arms specking the gloom, and glittering eyes of fear moving where all else was still, had the effect of a real spirit. I thought it like one of the tiny phantoms, half fairy, half imp, Bessie's evening stories represented as coming out of lone, ferny dells in moors, and appearing before the eyes of belated travellers. I returned to my stool.

Superstition was with me at that moment; but it was not yet her hour for complete victory: my blood was still warm; the mood of the revolted slave was still bracing me with its bitter vigour; I had to stem a rapid rush of retrospective thought before I quailed to the dismal present.

All John Reed's violent tyrannies, all his sisters' proud indifference, all his mother's aversion, all the servants' partiality, turned up in my disturbed mind like a dark deposit in a turbid well. Why was I always suffering, always browbeaten, always accused, for ever condemned? Why could I never please? Why was it useless to try to win anyone's favour? Eliza, who was headstrong and selfish, was respected. Georgiana, who had a spoiled temper, a very acrid spite, a captious and insolent carriage, was universally indulged. Her beauty, her pink cheeks and golden curls, seemed to give delight to all who looked at her, and to purchase indemnity for every fault. John, no one thwarted, much less punished; though he twisted the necks of the pigeons, killed the young pea-chicks, set the dogs at the sheep, stripped the hothouse vines of their fruit, and broke the buds off the choicest plants in the conservatory; he called his mother "old girl," too; sometimes reviled her for her dark skin, similar to his own; bluntly disregarded her wishes; not unfrequently tore and spoiled her silk attire; and he was still "her own darling." I dared commit no fault. I strove to fulfil every duty; and I was termed naughty and tiresome, sullen and sneaking, from morning to noon, and from noon to night.

My head still ached and bled with the blow and fall I had received. No one had reproved John for wantonly striking me; and because I had turned against him to avert further irrational violence I was loaded with general opprobrium.

"Unjust!—unjust!" said my reason.

What a consternation of soul was mine that dreary afternoon! How all my brain was in tumult, and all my heart in insurrection! Yet in what darkness, what dense ignorance, was the mental battle fought! I could not answer the ceaseless inward question—*why* I thus suffered; now, at the distance of—I will not say how many years, I see it clearly.

I was a discord in Gateshead Hall; I was like nobody there; I had nothing in harmony with Mrs. Reed or her children. If they did not love me, in fact, as little did I love them. I know that had I been a brilliant, careless, exacting, handsome, romping child—though equally dependent and friendless—Mrs. Reed would have endured my presence more complacently; her children would have entertained for me more of the cordiality of fellow-feeling; the servants would have been less prone to make me the scapegoat of the nursery.

Daylight began to forsake the red room; it was past four o'clock and the beclouded afternoon was tending to drear twilight. I heard the rain still beating continuously on the staircase window, and the wind howling in the grove behind the hall; I grew by degrees as cold as a stone, and then my courage sank. My habitual mood of humiliation, self-doubt, forlorn depression, fell damp on the embers of my decaying ire. All said I was wicked, and perhaps I might be so: what thought had I been but just conceiving of starving myself to death? That certainly was a crime; and was I fit to die? Or was the vault under the chancel of Gateshead Church an inviting bourne? In such vault I had been told did Mr. Reed lie buried; and led by this thought to recall his idea, I dwelt on it with gathering dread. I could not remember him; but I knew that he was my own uncle—my mother's brother—that he had taken me when a parentless infant to his house; and that in his last moments he had required a promise of Mrs. Reed that she would rear and maintain me as one of her own children. Mrs. Reed probably considered she had kept this promise; and so she had, I dare say, as well as her nature would permit her; but how could she really like an interloper not of her race, and unconnected with her, after her husband's death, by any tie? It must have been most irksome to find herself bound by a hard-wrung pledge to stand in the stead of a parent to a strange child she could not love, and to see an uncongenial alien permanently intruded on her own family group.

A singular notion dawned upon me. I doubted not—never doubted—that if Mr. Reed had been alive he would have treated me kindly; and now, as I sat looking at the white bed and overshadowed walls—occasionally also turning a fascinated eye towards the dimly gleaming mirror—I began to recall what I had heard of dead men, troubled in their graves by the violation of their last wishes, revisiting the earth to punish the perjured and avenge the oppressed; and I thought Mr. Reed's spirit, harassed by the wrongs of his sister's child, might quit its abode—whether in the church vault, or in the unknown world of the departed—and rise before me in this chamber. I wiped my tears and hushed my sobs, fearful lest any sign of violent grief might waken a preternatural voice to comfort me, or elicit from the gloom some haloed face, bending over me with strange pity. This idea, consolatory in theory, I felt would be terrible if realized: with all my might I endeavoured to stifle it—I endeavoured to be firm. Shaking my hair from my eyes, I lifted my head and tried to look boldly round the dark room. At this moment a light gleamed on the wall. Was it, I asked myself, a ray from the moon penetrating some aperture in the blind? No; moonlight was still, and this stirred; while I gazed it glided up to the ceiling and quivered over my head. I can now conjecture readily that this streak of light was, in all likelihood, a gleam from a lantern carried by someone across the lawn; but then, prepared as my mind was for horror, shaken as my nerves were by agitation, I thought the swift-darting beam was a herald of some coming vision from another world. My heart beat quick, my head grew hot; a sound filled my ears, which I deemed the rushing of wings: something seemed near me; I was oppressed, suffocated: endurance broke down; I rushed to the door and shook the lock in desperate effort.

Steps came running along the outer passage; the key turned, Bessie and Abbot entered.

"Miss Eyre, are you ill?" said Bessie.

"What a dreadful noise! It went quite through me!" exclaimed Abbot.

"Take me out! Let me go into the nursery!" was my cry.

"What for? Are you hurt? Have you seen something?" again demanded Bessie.

"Oh! I saw a light, and I thought a ghost would come." I had now got hold of Bessie's hand, and she did not snatch it from me.

"She has screamed out on purpose," declared Abbot, in some disgust. "And what a scream! If she had been in great pain one would have excused it, but she only wanted to bring us all here: I know her naughty tricks."

"What is all this?" demanded another voice, peremptorily; and Mrs. Reed came along the corridor, her cap flowing wide, her gown rustling stormily. "Abbot and Bessie, I believe I gave orders that Jane Eyre should be left in the red room till I came to her myself."

"Miss Jane screamed so loud, ma'am," pleaded Bessie.

"Let her go," was the only answer. "Loose Bessie's hand, child: you cannot succeed in getting out by these means, be assured. I abhor artifice, particularly in children; it is my duty to show you that tricks will not answer. You will now stay here an hour longer, and it is only on condition of perfect submission and stillness that I shall liberate you then."

"Oh, Aunt, have pity! Forgive me! I cannot endure it—let me be punished some other way! I shall be killed if——"

"Silence! This violence is all most repulsive": and so, no doubt, she felt it. I was a precocious actress in her eyes; she sincerely looked on me as a compound of virulent passions, mean spirit, and dangerous duplicity.

Bessie and Abbot having retreated, Mrs. Reed, impatient of my now frantic anguish and wild sobs, abruptly thrust me back and locked me in, without further parley. I heard her sweeping away.

THIN ICE

By LOUISA M. ALCOTT

The March sisters—Jo, Meg, Beth, and Amy—behaved as most sisters do. They quarrelled occasionally about things that seemed important at the time, and then made up with tearful forgiveness and regrets. But Jo had a temper which was hard to control at times, and once Amy hurt her in a way she found it difficult to forgive. As a result something happened that filled the older sister with remorse. Both Amy and Jo learned a great lesson. This very human story is taken from "Little Women."

"GIRLS, where are you going?" asked Amy, coming into their room one Saturday afternoon and finding them getting ready to go out, with an air of secrecy which excited her curiosity.

"Never mind; little girls shouldn't ask questions," returned Jo, sharply.

Now if there *is* anything mortifying to our feelings when we are young it is to be told that, and to be bidden to "run away, dear" is still more trying to us. Amy bridled up at this insult, and determined to find out the secret, if she teased for an hour. Turning to Meg, who never refused her anything very long, she said, coaxingly, "Do tell me! I should think you might let me go too; for Beth is fussing over her dolls, and I haven't got anything to do, and am *so* lonely."

"I can't, dear, because you aren't invited," began Meg; but Jo broke in impatiently, "Now, Meg, be quiet, or you will spoil it all. You can't go, Amy; so don't be a baby and whine about it."

"You are going somewhere with Laurie, I know you are. You were whispering and laughing together on the sofa last night, and you stopped when I came in. Aren't you going with him?"

"Yes, we are; now do be still, and stop bothering."

Amy held her tongue, but used her eyes, and saw Meg slip a fan into her pocket.

"I know! I know! You're going to the theatre to see the *Seven Castles!*" she cried; adding, resolutely, "and I *shall* go, for Mother said I might see it; and I've got my rag-money, and it was mean not to tell me in time."

"Just listen to me a minute, and be a good child," said Meg soothingly. "Mother doesn't wish you to go this week, because your eyes are not well enough yet to bear the light of this fairy piece. Next week you can go with Beth and Hannah, and have a nice time."

"I don't like that half so well as going with you and Laurie. Please let me; I've been sick with this cold so long and shut up, I'm dying for some fun. Do, Meg! I'll be ever so good," pleaded Amy, looking as pathetic as she could.

"Suppose we take her. I don't believe Mother would mind, if we bundle her up well," began Meg.

"If *she* goes *I* shan't, and if I don't Laurie won't like it; and it will be very rude, after he invited only us, to go and drag in Amy. I should think she'd hate to poke herself where she isn't wanted," said Jo crossly, for she disliked the trouble of overseeing a fidgety child when she wanted to enjoy herself.

Her tone and manner angered Amy, who began to put her boots on, saying in her most aggravating way, "I *shall* go; Meg says I may; and if I pay for myself, Laurie hasn't anything to do with it."

"You can't sit with us, for our seats are reserved, and you mustn't sit alone; so Laurie will give you his place, and that will spoil our pleasure; or he'll get another seat for you, and that isn't proper, when you weren't asked. You shan't stir a step, so you may just stay where you are," scolded Jo, crosser than ever, having just pricked her finger in her hurry.

Sitting on the floor, with one boot on, Amy began to cry, and Meg to reason with her, when Laurie called from below, and the two girls hurried down, leaving their sister wailing—for now and then she forgot her grown-up ways, and acted like a spoilt child. Just as the party were setting out Amy called over the banisters in a threatening tone, "You'll be sorry for this, Jo March; see if you ain't!"

"Fiddlesticks!" returned Jo, slamming the door.

They had a charming time, for *The Seven Castles of the Diamond Lake* were as brilliant and wonderful as heart could wish. But, in spite of the comical red imps, Jo's pleasure had a drop of bitterness in it. The Fairy Queen's yellow curls reminded her of Amy, and between the acts she amused herself with wondering what her sister would do to make her "sorry for it." She and Amy had had many lively skirmishes in the course of their lives, for both had quick tempers, and were apt to be violent when fairly roused. Amy teased Jo, and Jo irritated Amy, and semi-occasional explosions occurred, of which both were much ashamed afterwards.

Although the oldest, Jo had the least self-control, and had hard times trying to curb the fiery spirit which was continually getting her into trouble. Her anger never lasted long, and, having humbly confessed her fault, she sincerely repented, and tried to do better. Her sisters used to say that they rather liked to get Jo into a fury, because she was such an angel afterwards. Poor Jo tried desperately to be good, but her bosom enemy was always ready to flame up and defeat her, and it took years of patient effort to subdue it.

When they got home they found Amy reading in the parlour. She assumed an injured air as they came in, never lifted her eyes from her book, or asked a single question. Perhaps curiosity might have conquered resentment, if Beth had not been there to inquire, and receive a glowing description of the play. On going up to put away her best hat, Jo's first look was towards the bureau; for in their last quarrel Amy had soothed her feelings by turning Jo's top drawer upside down on the floor. Everything was in its place, however, and after a hasty glance into her various closets, bags, and boxes, Jo decided that Amy had forgiven and forgotten her wrongs.

There Jo was mistaken, for the next day she made a discovery which produced a tempest. Meg, Beth, and Amy were sitting together, late in the afternoon, when Jo burst into the room, looking excited, and demanded, breathlessly, "Has anyone taken my story?"

Meg and Beth said "No" at once, and looked surprised; Amy poked the fire and said nothing. Jo saw her colour rise, and was down upon her in a minute.

"Amy, you've got it!"

"No, I haven't."

"You know where it is, then!"

"No, I don't."

"That's a fib!" cried Jo, taking her by the shoulders and looking fierce enough to frighten a much braver child than Amy.

"It isn't. I haven't got it; don't know where it is now, and don't care."

"You know something about it, and you'd better tell at once, or I'll make you," and Jo gave her a slight shake.

"Scold as much as you like, you'll never get your silly old story again," cried Amy, getting excited in her turn.

"Why not?"

"I burnt it up!"

"What! My little book I was so fond of, and worked over? Have you really burnt it?" said Jo, turning very pale, while her eyes kindled and her hands clutched Amy nervously.

"Yes, I did. I told you I'd make you pay for being so cross yesterday, and I have, so——"

Amy got no further, for Jo's hot temper mastered her, and she shook Amy till the teeth chattered in her head, crying, in a passion of grief and anger:

"You wicked, wicked girl! I never can write it again, and I'll never forgive you as long as I live!"

Meg flew to rescue Amy, and Beth to pacify Jo; but Jo was quite beside herself, and, with a parting box on her sister's ear, she rushed out of the room up to the old sofa in the garret, and finished her fight alone.

The storm cleared up below, for Mrs. March came home, and, having heard the story, soon brought Amy to a sense of the wrong she had done her sister. Jo's book was the pride of her heart, and was regarded by her family as a literary sprout of great promise. It was only half a dozen little fairy tales, but Jo had worked over them patiently, putting her whole heart into her work, hoping to make something good enough to print. She had just copied them with great care, and had destroyed the old manuscript, so that Amy's bonfire had consumed the loving work of several years. It seemed a small loss to others, but to Jo it was a dreadful calamity, and she felt that it never could be made up to her. Beth mourned as for a departed kitten, and Meg refused to defend her pet; Mrs. March looked grave and grieved, and Amy felt that no one would love her till she had asked pardon for the act which she now regretted more than any of them.

When the tea-bell rung, Jo appeared, looking so grim and unapproachable that it took all Amy's courage to say meekly:

"Please forgive me, Jo; I'm very, very sorry."

"I shall never forgive you!" was Jo's stern answer; and from that moment she ignored Amy entirely.

No one spoke of the great trouble—not even Mrs. March—for all had learned by experience that when Jo was in that mood words were wasted, and the wisest course was to wait till some little accident, or her own generous nature, softened Jo's resentment and healed the breach. It was not a happy evening; for, though they sewed as usual, while their mother read aloud, something was wanting, and the sweet home peace was disturbed. They felt this most when singing-time came; for Beth could only play, Jo stood dumb as a stone, and Amy broke down, so Meg and Mother sung alone. But, in spite of their efforts to be as cheery as larks, the flute-like voices did not seem to chord as well as usual, and all felt out of tune.

As Jo received her good-night kiss, Mrs. March whispered gently:

"My dear, don't let the sun go down upon your anger. Forgive each other, help each other, and begin again to-morrow."

Jo wanted to lay her head down on that motherly bosom and cry her grief and anger all away; but the tears were an unmanly weakness, and she felt so deeply injured that she really *couldn't* quite forgive yet. So she winked hard, shook her head, and said gruffly, because Amy was listening:

"It was an abominable thing, and she don't deserve to be forgiven."

With that she marched off to bed, and there was no merry or confidential gossip that night.

Amy was much offended that her overtures of peace had been repulsed, and began to wish she had not humbled herself, to feel more humbled than ever, and to plume herself on her superior virtue in a way that was particularly exasperating. Jo still looked like a thunder-cloud, and nothing went well all day. It was bitter cold in the morning. She dropped her precious turn-over in the gutter, Aunt March had an attack of fidgets, Meg was pensive, Beth *would* look grieved and wistful when she got home, and Amy kept making remarks about people who were always talking about being good, and yet wouldn't try when other people set them a virtuous example.

"Everybody is so hateful; I'll ask Laurie to go skating. He is always kind and jolly, and will put me to rights, I know," said Jo to herself, and off she went.

Amy heard the clash of skates, and looked out with an impatient exclamation.

"There! She promised I should go next time, for this is the last ice we shall have. But it is no use to ask such a cross-patch to take me."

"Don't say that. You *were* very naughty, and it *is* hard to forgive the loss of her precious little book; but I think she might do it now, and I guess she will, if you try her at the right minute," said Meg. "Go after them; don't say anything till Jo has got good-natured with Laurie, then take a quiet minute and just kiss her, or do some kind thing, and I'm sure she'll be friends again with all her heart."

"I'll try," said Amy, for the advice suited her; and, after a flurry to get ready, she ran after the friends, who were just disappearing over the hill.

It was not far to the river, but both were ready before Amy reached them. Jo saw her coming, and turned her back. Laurie did not see, for he was carefully skating along the shore, sounding the ice, for a warm spell had preceded the cold snap.

"I'll go on to the first bend and see if it's all right before we begin to race," Amy heard him say, as he shot away, looking like a young Russian in his fur-trimmed coat and cap.

Jo heard Amy panting after her run, stamping her feet and blowing her fingers as she tried to put her skates on; but Jo never turned, and went slowly zig-zagging down the river, taking a bitter unhappy sort of satisfaction in her sister's troubles. She had cherished her anger till it grew strong and took possession of her, as evil thoughts and feelings always do, unless cast out at once. As Laurie turned the bend he shouted back:

"Keep near the shore; it isn't safe in the middle."

Jo heard, but Amy was just struggling to her feet, and did not catch a word. Jo glanced over her shoulder, and the little demon she was harbouring said in her ear:

"No matter whether she heard or not; let her take care of herself."

Laurie had vanished round the bend, Jo was just at the turn, and Amy, far behind, was striking out towards the smoother ice in the middle of the river. For a minute Jo stood still, with a strange feeling at her heart, then she resolved to go on; but something held and turned her round, just in time to see Amy throw up her hands and go down, with the sudden crash of rotten ice, the splash of water, and a cry that made Jo's heart stand still with fear. She tried to call Laurie, but her voice was gone; she tried to rush forward but her feet seemed to have no strength in them, and for a second she could only stand motionless, staring with a terror-striken face at the little blue hood above the black water. Something rushed swiftly by her, and Laurie's voice cried out:

"Bring a rail; quick, quick!"

How she did it she never knew; but for the next few minutes she worked as if possessed, blindly obeying Laurie, who was quite self-possessed, and, lying flat, held Amy up by his arm and hockey stick till Jo dragged a rail from the fence, and together they got the child out, more frightened than hurt.

"Now then, we must walk her home as fast as we can; pile our things on her, while I get off these confounded skates!" cried Laurie, wrapping his coat round Amy, and tugging away at the straps, which never seemed so intricate before.

Shivering, dripping, and crying, they got Amy home; and, after an exciting time of it she fell asleep, rolled in blankets, before a hot fire. During the bustle Jo had scarcely spoken, but flown about, looking pale and wild, with her things half on, her dress torn, and her hands cut and bruised by ice and rails and refractory buckles. When Amy was comfortably asleep, the house quiet, and Mrs. March sitting by the bed, she called Jo to her and began to bind up the hurt hands.

"Are you sure she is safe?" whispered Jo, looking remorsefully at the golden head, which might have been swept away from her sight for ever under the treacherous ice.

"Quite safe, dear; she is not hurt, and won't even take cold, I think; you were so sensible in covering and getting her home quickly," replied her mother cheerfully.

"Laurie did it all; I only let her go. Mother, if she *should* die, it would be my fault"; and Jo dropped down beside the bed in a passion of penitent tears, telling all that had happened, condemning her hardness of heart, and sobbing out her gratitude

for being spared the heavy punishment which might have come upon her.

"It's my dreadful temper! I try to cure it; I think I have, and then it breaks out worse than ever. Oh, Mother, what shall I do? What shall I do?" cried poor Jo in despair.

"Watch and pray, dear; never get tired of trying, and never think it is impossible to conquer your fault," said Mrs. March, drawing the blowzy head to her shoulder, and kissing the wet cheek so tenderly that Jo cried harder than ever.

"You don't know; you can't guess how bad it is! It seems as if I could do anything when I'm in a passion; I get so savage I could hurt anyone, and enjoy it. I'm afraid I *shall* do something dreadful some day, and spoil my life, and make everybody hate me. Oh, Mother, help me; do help me!"

"I will, my child, I will. Don't cry so bitterly. But remember this day, and resolve with all your soul that you will never know another like it. Jo, dear, we all have our temptations, some far greater than yours, and it often takes us all our lives to conquer them. You think your temper is the worst in the world, but mine used to be just like it."

"Yours, Mother? Why, you are never angry!" and for the moment Jo forgot remorse in surprise.

"I've been trying to cure it for forty years, and I have only succeeding in controlling it. I am angry nearly every day of my life, Jo; but I have learned not to show it, and I still hope to learn not to feel it, though it may take me another forty years to do so."

The patience and the humility of the face she loved so well was a better lesson to Jo than the wisest lecture, the sharpest reproof. She felt comforted at once by the sympathy and confidence given her. The knowledge that her mother had a fault like hers, and tried to mend it, made her own easier to bear, and strengthened her resolution to cure it, though forty years seemed rather a long time to watch and pray, to a girl of fifteen.

"Oh, Mother, if I'm ever half as good as you I shall be satisfied!" cried Jo, much touched.

"I hope you will be a great deal better, dear. You have had a warning; remember it, and try with heart and soul to master this quick temper before it brings you greater sorrow and regret than you have known to-day."

"I will try, Mother; I truly will. But you must help me, remind me, and keep me from flying out. It's so comfortable to say all I think to you, and feel so safe and happy here."

"My Jo, you may say anything to your mother, for it is my greatest happiness and pride to feel that my girls confide in me, and know how much I love them."

Jo's only answer was to hold her mother close, and in the silence which followed the sincerest prayer she had ever prayed left her heart without words; for in that sad, yet happy hour she had learned not only the bitterness of remorse and despair, but the sweetness of self-denial and self-control, and, led by her mother's hand, she had drawn nearer to the Friend who welcomes every child with a love stronger than that of any father, tenderer than that of any mother.

Amy stirred and sighed in her sleep, and, as if eager to begin at once to mend her fault, Jo looked up with an expression on her face which it had never worn before.

"I let the sun go down on my anger; I wouldn't forgive her, and to-day, if it hadn't been for Laurie, it might have been too late! How could I be so wicked?" said Jo, half aloud, as she leaned over her sister, softly stroking the wet hair scattered on the pillow.

As if she heard, Amy opened her eyes and held out her arms, with a smile that went straight to Jo's heart. Neither said a word, but they hugged one another close, in spite of the blankets, and everything was forgiven and forgotten in one hearty kiss.

DAUGHTER OF THE DOONES

By R. D. BLACKMORE

On a cold winter's day, John Ridd, the young son of an Exmoor farmer who had been killed by the wild and lawless Doones, goes fishing and finds a stream that leads him to the secret Doone stronghold. There he has a mishap. When he comes to he finds a little girl sitting by him. She is Lorna, daughter of the chief of the outlaw clan. It is she who tells him of a secret way to leave the valley when the searching Doones have gone. This story is taken from "Lorna Doone," which tells of many adventures shared by Lorna and John.

BEING resolved to catch some loaches, whatever trouble it cost me, I set forth without a word to anyone, in the forenoon of St. Valentine's Day, 1675–6, I think it must have been. The winter had been long, and snow lay here and there, in patches in the hollow of the banks, like a lady's gloves forgotten. And yet the spring was breaking forth, as it always does in Devonshire, when the turn of the days is over; and though there was little to see of it, the air was full of feeling.

I doffed my shoes and hose, and put them into a bag about my neck; and left my little coat at home, and tied my shirt-sleeves back to my shoulders. Then I took a three-pronged fork firmly bound to a rod with cord, and a piece of canvas kerchief, with a lump of bread inside it; and so went into the pebbly water, trying to think how warm it was. For more than a mile all down the Lynn stream, scarcely a stone I left unturned, being thoroughly skilled in the tricks of the loach, and knowing how he hides himself.

When I had travelled two miles or so, conquered now and then with cold, and coming out to rub my legs into a lively friction, and only fishing here and there because of the tumbling water; suddenly, in an open space, where meadows spread about it, I found a good stream flowing softly into the body of our brook. And it brought, so far as I could guess by the sweep of it under my kneecaps, a larger power of clear water than the Lynn itself had; only it came more quietly down, not being troubled with stairs and steps, as the fortune of the Lynn is, but gliding smoothly and forcibly, as if upon some set purpose.

I found it strongly over-woven, turned, and torn with thicket-wood, but not so rocky as the Lynn, and more inclined to go evenly. There were bars of chafed stakes stretched from the sides half-way across the current, and light outriders of pithy weed, and blades of last year's water-grass trembling in the quiet places, like a spider's threads, on the transparent stillness, with a tint of olive moving it; and here and there the sun came in, as if his light were sifted, making dance upon the waves, and shadowing the pebbles.

The place grew thicker and thicker, and the covert grew darker above me, until I thought that the fishes might have a good chance of eating me, instead of my eating the fishes.

For now the day was falling fast behind the brown of the hill-tops; and the trees, being void of leaf and hard, seemed giants ready to beat me.

Then says I to myself: "John Ridd, these trees, and pools, and lonesome rocks, and setting of the sunlight, are making a gruesome coward of thee. Shall I go back to my mother so, and be called her fearless boy?"

I girt up my breeches anew, with each buckle one hole tighter, for the sodden straps were stretching and giving, and mayhap my legs were grown smaller from the coldness of it. Then I bestowed my fish around my neck more tightly, and not stopping to look much, for fear of fear, crawled along over the fork of rocks, where the water had scooped the stone out; and shunning thus the ledge from whence it rose, like the mane of a white horse, into the broad black pool, softly I let my feet into the dip and rush of the torrent.

How I went carefully, step by step, keeping my arms in front of me, and never daring to straighten my knees, is more than I can tell clearly, or even like now to think of, because it makes me dream of it. Only I must acknowledge, that the greatest danger of all was just where I saw no jeopardy, but ran up a patch of black ooze-weed in a very boastful manner.

Here I fell very piteously, and was like to have broken my knee-cap, and the torrent got hold of my other leg, while I was indulging the bruised one. And then a vile knotting of cramp disabled me, and all of my body was sliding. But the fright of that brought me to again, and my elbow caught in a rock-hole; and so I managed to start again, with the help of more humility.

Now being in the most dreadful fright, I laboured hard with both legs and arms, going like a mill, and grunting. At last the rush of forked water drove me into the middle, and I stuck awhile with my toe-balls on the slippery links of the pop-weed, and the world was green and gliddery, and I durst not look behind me. Then I made up my mind to die at last; for so my legs would ache no more, and my breath not pain my heart so; only it did seem such a pity, after fighting so long to give in, and the light was coming upon me, and again I fought towards it; then suddenly I felt fresh air, and fell into it headlong.

When I came to myself again, my hands were full of young grass and mould; and a little girl kneeling at my side was rubbing my forehead tenderly, with a dock-leaf and a handkerchief.

"Oh, I am so glad," she whispered softly, as I opened my eyes and looked at her; "now you will try to be better, won't you?"

I had never heard so sweet a sound as came from between her bright red lips, while there she knelt and gazed at me; neither had I ever seen anything so beautiful as the large dark eyes intent upon me, full of pity and wonder. And then, my nature being slow, and perhaps, for that matter, heavy, I wandered with my hazy eyes down the black shower of her hair, as to my jaded gaze it seemed; and where it fell on the turf, among it (like an early star) was the first primrose of the season. And since that day, I think of her, through all the rough storms of my life, when I see an early primrose. Perhaps she liked my countenance; and indeed I know she did, because she said so afterwards; although at the time she was too young to know what made her take to me. Not that I had any beauty, or ever pretended to have any, only a solid healthy face, which many girls have laughed at.

Thereupon I sate upright, with my little trident still in one hand, and was much afraid to speak to her, being conscious of my country-brogue, lest she should cease to like me. But she clapped her hands, and made a trifling dance around my back, and came to me on the other side, as if I were a great plaything.

"What is your name?" she said, as if she had every right to ask me; "and how did you come here, and what are these wet things in this great bag?"

"You had better let them alone," I said; "they are loaches for my mother. But I will give you some, if you like."

"Dear me, how much you think of them! Why, they are only fish. But how your feet are bleeding! oh, I must tie them up for

you. And no shoes nor stockings! Is your mother very poor, poor boy?"

"No," I said, being vexed at this; "we are rich enough to buy all this great meadow, if we chose; and here my shoes and stockings be."

"Why, they are quite as wet as your feet; and I cannot bear to see your feet. Oh, please to let me manage them; I will do it very softly."

"Oh, I don't think much of that," I replied; "I shall put some goose-grease to them. But how you are looking at me! I never saw anyone like you before. My name is John Ridd. What is your name?"

"Lorna Doone," she answered in a low voice, as if afraid of it, and hanging her head, so that I could see only her forehead and eyelashes; "if you please, my name is Lorna Doone; and I thought you must have known it."

Then I stood up, and touched her hand, and tried to make her look at me; but she only turned away the more. Young and harmless as she was, her name alone made guilt of her. Nevertheless I could not help looking at her tenderly, and the more when her blushes turned into tears, and her tears to long, low sobs.

"Don't cry," I said, "whatever you do. I am sure you have never done any harm. I will give you all my fish, Lorna, and catch some more for mother; only don't be angry with me."

She flung her little soft arms up, in the passion of her tears, and looked at me so piteously, that what did I do but kiss her. It seemed to be a very odd thing, when I came to think of it, because I hated kissing so, as all honest boys must do. But she touched my heart with a sudden delight, like a cowslip-blossom (although there were none to be seen yet) and the sweetest flowers of spring.

She gave me no encouragement, as my mother in her place would have done; nay, she even wiped her lips (which methought was rather rude of her), and drew away, and smoothed her dress, as if I had used a freedom. Then I felt my cheeks grow burning red, and I gazed at my legs and was sorry. For although she was not at all a proud child (at any rate in her countenance), yet I knew that she was by birth a thousand years in front of me. They might have taken and trained me, or (which would be more to the purpose) my sisters, until it was time for us to die, and then have trained our children after us, for many generations; yet never could we have gotten that look upon our faces, which Lorna Doone had naturally, as if she had been born to it.

Here was I, a yeoman's boy, a yeoman every inch of me, even where I was naked; and there was she, a lady born, and thoroughly aware of it, and dressed by people of rank and taste, who took pride in her beauty, and set it to advantage. For though her hair was fallen down, by reason of her wildness, and some of her frock was touched with wet, where she had tended me so, behold her dress was pretty enough for the queen of all the angels! The colours were bright and rich indeed, and the substance very sumptuous, yet simple and free from tinsel stuff, and matching most harmoniously. All from her waist to her neck was white, plaited in close like a curtain, and the dark soft weeping of her hair, and the shadowy light of her eyes (like a wood rayed through with sunset), made it seem yet whiter, as if it were done on purpose. As for the rest, she knew what it was, a great deal better than I did; for I never could look far away from her eyes, when they were opened upon me.

Now, seeing how I heeded her, and feeling that I had kissed her, although she was such a little girl, eight years old or thereabouts, she turned to the stream in a bashful manner, and began to watch the water, and rubbed one leg against the other.

I for my part, being vexed at her behaviour to me, took up all my things to go, and made a fuss about it; to let her know I was going. But she did not call me back at all, as I had made sure she would do; and so I turned round again, and came back to her, and said, "Lorna."

"Oh, I thought you were gone," she answered; "why did you ever come here? Do you know what they would do to us, if they found you here with me?"

"Beat us, I dare say, very hard, or me at least. They could never beat you."

"No. They would kill us both outright, and bury us here by the water; and the water often tells me that I must come to that."

"But what should they kill me for?"

"Because you have found the way up here, and they never could believe it. Now, please to go; oh please to go. They will kill us both in a moment. Yes, I like you very much"—for I was teasing her to say it,—"very much indeed, and I will call you John Ridd, if you like; only please to go, John. And when your feet are well, you know, you can come and tell me how they are."

"But I tell you, Lorna, I like you very much indeed. I never saw anyone like you; and I must come back again to-morrow, and so must you, to see me; and I will bring you such a maun of things—there are apples still, and a thrush I caught with only one leg broken, and our dog has just had puppies——"

"Oh, dear, they won't let me have a dog. There is not a dog in the valley. They say they are such noisy things——"

"Only put your hand in mine—what little things they are, Lorna! —and I will bring you the loveliest dog; I will show you just how long he is."

"Hush!" A shout came down the valley; and all my heart was trembling, like water after sunset, and Lorna's face was altered from pleasant play to terror. She shrank to me, and looked up at me, with such a power of weakness, that I at once made up my mind to save her or to die with her. A tingle went through all my bones and I only longed for my carbine. The little girl took courage from me, and put her cheek quite close to mine.

"Come with me. I can carry you easily; and mother will take care of you."

"No, no," she cried, as I took her up: "I will tell you what to do. They are only looking for me. You see that hole, that hole there?"

She pointed to a little niche in the rock, which verged the meadow, about fifty yards away from us. In the fading of the twilight I could just descry it.

"Yes, I see it; but they will see me crossing the grass to get there."

"Look! look!" She could hardly speak. "There is a way out from the top of it; they would kill me if I told it. Oh, here they come; I can see them."

The little maid turned as white as the snow which hung on the rocks above her, and she looked at the water, and then at me, and she cried, "Oh, dear! oh, dear!" And then she began to sob aloud, being so young and unready. But I drew her behind the withy-bushes, and close down to the water, where it was quiet, and shelving deep. Here they could not see either of us from the upper valley, and might have sought a long time for us, even when they came quite near, if the trees had been clad with their summer clothes. Luckily I had picked up my fish, and taken my three-pronged fork away.

Crouching in that hollow nest, as children get together in ever so little compass, I saw a dozen fierce men come down, on the other side of the water, not bearing any firearms, but looking lax and jovial, as if they were come from riding and a dinner taken hungrily. "Queen, queen!" they were shouting, here and there, and now and then: "Where the pest is our little queen gone?"

"They always call me 'queen,' and I am to be queen by and by," Lorna whispered to me, with her soft cheek on my rough one, and her little heart beating against me: "oh, they are crossing by the timber there, and then they are sure to see us."

"Stop," said I; "now I see what to do. I must get into the water, and you must go to sleep."

"To be sure, yes, away in the meadow there. But how bitter cold it will be for you!"

She saw in a moment the way to do it, sooner than I could tell her; and there was no time to lose.

"Now, mind you never come again," she whispered over her shoulder, as she crept away with a childish twist, hiding her white front from me; "only I shall come sometimes—oh, here they are, Madonna!"

Daring scarce to peep, I crept into the water, and lay down bodily in it, with my head between two blocks of stone, and some flood-drift combing over me. The dusk was deepening between the hills, and a white mist lay on the river; but I, being in the channel of it, could see every ripple, and twig, and rush, and glazing of twilight above it, as bright as in a picture; so that to my ignorance there seemed to be no chance at all, but that the men must find me. For all this time, they were shouting, and swearing, and keeping such a hallabaloo, that the rocks all round the valley rang; and my heart quaked, so (what with this and the cold) that the water began to gurgle round me, and lap upon the pebbles.

Neither in truth did I try to stop it, being now so desperate, between the fear and the wretchedness; till I caught a glimpse of the little maid, whose beauty and whose kindliness had made me yearn to be with her. And then I knew that for her sake I was bound to be brave, and hide myself. She was lying beneath a rock, thirty or forty yards from me, feigning to be fast asleep, with her dress spread beautifully, and her hair drawn over her.

Presently one of the great rough men came round a corner upon her; and there he stopped, and gazed awhile at her fairness and her innocence. Then he caught her up in his arms, and kissed her so that I heard him; and if I had only brought my gun, I would have tried to shoot him.

"Here our queen is! Here's the queen, here's the captain's daughter!" he shouted to his comrades; "fast asleep, by God, and hearty! Now I have first claim to her; and no one else shall touch the child. Back to the bottle, all of you!"

He set her dainty little form upon his great square shoulder, and her narrow feet in one broad hand; and so in triumph marched away, with the purple velvet of her skirt ruffling in his long black beard, and the silken length of her hair fetched out, like a cloud by the wind, behind her. This way of her going vexed me so that I leaped upright in the water, and must have been spied by some of them, but for their haste to the wine-bottle. Of their little queen they took small notice, being in this urgency, although they had thought to find her drowned; but trooped away, one after another, with kindly challenge to gambling, so far as I could make them out; and I kept sharp watch, I assure you.

Going up that darkened glen, little Lorna, riding still the largest and most fierce of them, turned and put up a hand to me; and I put up a hand to her, in the thick of the mist and the willows.

She was gone, my little dear (though tall of her age and healthy); and when I got over my thriftless fright, I longed to have more to say to her. Her voice to me was so different from all I had ever heard before, as might be a sweet silver bell, intoned to the small chords of a harp. But I had no time to think about this, if I hoped to have any supper.

I crept into a bush for warmth, and rubbed my shivering legs on bark, and longed for mother's fagot. Then, as daylight sank below the forget-me-not of stars, with a sorrow to be quit, I knew that now must be my time to get away, if there were any.

Therefore, wringing my sodden breeches, I managed to crawl from the bank to the niche in the cliff, which Lorna had shown me.

A MAD TEA-PARTY

By LEWIS CARROLL

After following the White Rabbit down the hole that brought her into a strange wonderland, the adventurous Alice was shown a piece of magic mushroom. When she ate one side of it she grew taller; when she ate from the other side she became smaller. She still had some of the mushroom when she set out to visit the house of the March Hare, not sure in her mind whether she should have chosen, instead, to visit the Hatter. As it turned out, she met both—and found them to be very disturbing creatures. This story is from "Alice's Adventures in Wonderland."

ALICE came in sight of the house of the March Hare. She thought it must be the right house, because the chimneys were shaped like ears and the roof was thatched with fur. It was so large a house, that she did not like to go nearer till she had nibbled some more of the left-hand bit of mushroom, and raised herself to about two feet high. Even then she walked up towards it rather timidly, saying to herself, "Suppose it should be raving mad after all! I almost wish I'd gone to see the Hatter instead!"

There was a table set out under a tree in front of the house, and the March Hare and the Hatter were having tea at it. A Dormouse was sitting between them, fast asleep, and the other two were using it as a cushion, resting their elbows on it, and talking over its head. "Very uncomfortable for the Dormouse," thought Alice; "only, as it's asleep, I suppose it doesn't mind."

The table was a large one, but the three were all crowded together at one corner of it. "No room! No room!" they cried out when they saw Alice coming. "There's *plenty* of room!" said Alice, and she sat down in a large armchair at one end of the table.

"Have some wine," the March Hare said in a kindly tone.

Alice looked all round the table, but there was nothing on it but tea. "I don't see any wine," she remarked.

"There isn't any," said the March Hare.

"Then it wasn't very civil of you to offer it," said Alice angrily.

"It wasn't very civil of you to sit down without being invited," said the March Hare.

"I didn't know it was *your* table," said Alice. "It's laid for a great many more than three."

"Your hair wants cutting," said the Hatter. He had been looking at Alice for some time as if eager to find out all about her, and this was his first speech.

"You should learn not to make personal remarks," said Alice severely; "it's very rude."

The Hatter opened his eyes very wide on hearing this. But all he *said* was, "Why is a raven like a writing-desk?"

"Come, we shall have some fun now!" thought Alice. "I am glad they've begun asking riddles—I believe I can guess that," she added aloud.

"Do you mean that you think you can find out the answer to it?" said the March Hare.

"Just so," said Alice.

"Then you should say what you mean," the March Hare went on.

"I do," Alice hastily replied; "at least—at least I mean what I say—that's the same thing, you know."

"Not the same thing a bit!" said the Hatter. "Why, you might just as well say that 'I see what I eat' is the same thing as 'I eat what I see'!"

"You might just as well say," added the March Hare, "that 'I like what I get' is the same thing as 'I get what I like'!"

"You might just as well say," added the Dormouse, who seemed to be talking in his sleep, "that 'I breathe when I sleep' is the same thing as 'I sleep when I breathe'!"

"It *is* the same thing with you," said the Hatter. And here the talk ceased, and the party sat silent for a minute, while Alice thought over all she could remember about ravens and writing-desks, which wasn't much.

The Hatter was the first to break the silence. "What day of the month is it?" he said, turning to Alice. He had taken his watch out of his pocket, and was looking at it uneasily, shaking it every now and then, and holding it to his ear.

Alice thought a little, and then said, "The fourth."

"Two days wrong!" sighed the Hatter. "I told you butter wouldn't suit the works!" he added, looking angrily at the March Hare.

"It was the *best* butter," the March Hare meekly replied.

"Yes, but some crumbs must have got in as well," the Hatter grumbled: "you shouldn't have put it in with the bread-knife."

The March Hare took the watch and looked at it gloomily. Then he dipped it into his cup of tea, and looked at it again. But he could think of nothing better to say than his first remark, "It was the *best* butter, you know."

Alice had been looking over his shoulder to have a good look at it: "What a funny watch!" she remarked. "It tells the day of the month, and doesn't tell what o'clock it is!"

"Why should it!" muttered the Hatter. "Does *your* watch tell you what year it is?"

"Of course not," Alice replied very readily; "but that's because it stays the same year for such a long time together."

"Which is just the case with *mine*," said the Hatter.

Alice felt very puzzled. The Hatter's remark seemed to have no meaning in it, and yet it was certainly English. "I don't quite understand you," she said, as politely as she could.

"The Dormouse is asleep again," said the Hatter, and he poured a little hot tea on his nose.

The Dormouse shook his head impatiently, and said, without opening his eyes, "Of course, of course; just what I was going to remark myself."

"Have you guessed the riddle yet?" the Hatter said, turning to Alice again.

"No, I give up," Alice replied: "what's the answer?"

"I haven't the slightest idea," said the Hatter.

"Nor I," said the March Hare.

Alice sighed wearily. "I think you might do something better with the time," she said, "than waste it in asking riddles that have no answers."

"If you knew Time as well as I do," said the Hatter, "you wouldn't talk about wasting *it*. It's *him*."

"I don't know what you mean," said Alice.

"Of course you don't!" the Hatter said, tossing his head. "I dare say you never even spoke to Time!"

"Perhaps not," Alice replied; "but I know I have to beat time when I learn music."

SOLD

"Ah! that accounts for it," said the Hatter. "He won't stand beating. Now, if you only kept on good terms with him, he'd do almost anything you liked with the clock. For instance, suppose it were nine o'clock in the morning, just time to begin lessons: you'd only have to whisper a hint to Time, and round goes the clock in a twinkling! Half-past one, time for dinner!"

("I only wish it was," the March Hare said to himself in a whisper.)

"That would be grand, certainly," said Alice: "but then—I shouldn't be hungry for it, you know."

"Not at first, perhaps," said the Hatter. "But you could keep it to half-past one as long as you liked."

"Is that the way *you* manage?" Alice asked.

The Hatter shook his head. "Not I!" he replied. "We quarrelled last March—just before *he* went mad, you know—" (pointing with his teaspoon at the March Hare) "—it was at the great concert given by the Queen of Hearts, and I had to sing

"Twinkle, twinkle, little bat!
How I wonder what you're at!

You know the song, perhaps?"

"I've heard something like it," said Alice.

"It goes on, you know," the Hatter went on, "in this way:

"Up above the world you fly,
Like a teatray in the sky.
Twinkle, twinkle——"

Here the Dormouse shook himself, and began singing in his sleep "*Twinkle, twinkle, twinkle, twinkle*——" and went on so long that they had to pinch him to make him stop.

"Well, I'd hardly finished the first verse," said the Hatter, "when the Queen bawled out, 'He's murdering the time! Off with his head!'"

"How very savage!" cried Alice.

"And ever since that," the Hatter went on in a sad tone, "he won't do a thing I ask! It's always six o'clock now."

A bright idea came into Alice's head. "Is that the reason so many tea-things are put out here?" she asked.

"Yes, that's it," said the Hatter with a sigh: "it's always tea-time, and we've no time to wash the things between whiles."

"Then you keep moving round, I suppose?" said Alice.

"Just so," said the Hatter: "as the things get used up."

"But when do you come to the beginning again?" Alice ventured to ask.

"Suppose we change the subject," the March Hare said, yawning. "I'm getting tired of this. I vote the young lady tells us a story."

"I'm afraid I don't know one," said Alice, rather alarmed at the idea.

"Then the Dormouse shall!" they both cried. "Wake up, Dormouse!" And they pinched him on both sides at once.

The Dormouse slowly opened his eyes. "I wasn't asleep," he said in a hoarse, feeble voice. "I heard every word you fellows were saying."

"Tell us a story!" said the March Hare.

"Yes, please do!" pleaded Alice.

"And be quick about it," added the Hatter, "or you'll be asleep again before it's done."

"Once upon a time there were three little sisters," the Dormouse began in a great hurry; "and their names were Elsie, Lacie, and Tillie; and they lived at the bottom of a well——"

"What did they live on?" said Alice, who always took a great interest in questions of eating and drinking.

"They lived on treacle," said the Dormouse, after thinking a minute or two.

"They couldn't have done that, you know," Alice gently remarked; "they'd have been ill."

"So they were," said the Dormouse; "*very* ill."

Alice tried a little to fancy to herself what such a strange way of living would be like, but it puzzled her too much, so she went on: "But why did they live at the bottom of a well?"

"Take some more tea," the March Hare said to Alice, very earnestly.

"I've had nothing yet," Alice replied in an offended tone, "so I can't take more."

"You mean you can't take *less*," said the Hatter. "It's very easy to take *more* than nothing."

"Nobody asked *your* opinion," said Alice.

"Who's making personal remarks now?" the Hatter asked in great glee.

Alice did not quite know what to say to this: so she helped herself to some tea and bread and butter, and then turned to the Dormouse, and repeated her question. "Why did they live at the bottom of a well?"

The Dormouse again took a minute or two to think about it, and then said, "It was a treacle-well."

"There's no such thing!" Alice was beginning very angrily, but the Hatter and the March Hare went "Sh! sh!" and the Dormouse sulkily remarked, "If you can't be civil, you'd better finish the story for yourself."

"No, please go on!" Alice said very humbly: "I won't interrupt you again. I dare say there may be *one*."

"One, indeed!" said the Dormouse. However, he agreed to go on. "And so these three little sisters—they were learning to draw, you know——"

"What did they draw?" said Alice, quite forgetting her promise.

"Treacle," said the Dormouse, without thinking at all this time.

"I want a clean cup," said the Hatter. "Let's all move one place on."

He moved on as he spoke, and the Dormouse followed him: the March Hare moved into the Dormouse's place, and Alice rather unwillingly took the place of the March Hare. The Hatter was the only one who got any advantage from the change: and Alice was a good deal worse off than before, as the March Hare had just upset the milk jug into his plate.

Alice did not wish to offend the Dormouse again, so she began very carefully: "But I don't understand. Where did they draw the treacle from?"

"You can draw water out of a water-well," said the Hatter; "so I should think you could draw treacle out of a treacle-well—eh, stupid?"

"But they were *in* the well," Alice said to the Dormouse, not choosing to notice this last remark.

"Of course they were," said the Dormouse; "—well in."

This answer so puzzled poor Alice that she let the Dormouse go on for some time without stopping him.

"They were learning to draw," the Dormouse went on, yawning and rubbing his eyes, for he was getting very sleepy; "and they drew all manner of things—everything that begins with an M——"

"Why with an M?" said Alice.

"Why not?" said the March Hare.

Alice was silent.

The Dormouse had closed his eyes by this time, and was going off into a doze. But, on being pinched by the Hatter, he woke up again with a little shriek, and went on: "—that begins with an M, such as mouse-traps, and the moon, and memory, and muchness—you know you say things are 'much of a muchness'—did you ever see such a thing as a drawing of a muchness?"

"Really, now you ask me," said Alice, very much puzzled, "I don't think——"

"Then you shouldn't talk," said the Hatter.

This piece of rudeness was more than Alice could bear. She got up in great disgust, and walked off. The Dormouse fell asleep at once, and neither of the others took the least notice of her going, though she looked back once or twice, half hoping that they would call after her. The last time she saw them, they were trying to put the Dormouse into the teapot.

"At any rate I'll never go *there* again!" said Alice as she picked her way through the wood. "It's the stupidest tea-party I ever was at in all my life!"

Just as she said this, she noticed that one of the trees had a door leading right into it. "That's very curious!" she thought. "But everything's curious to-day. I think I may as well go in at once." And in she went.

Once more she found herself in the long hall, and close to the little glass table. "Now, I'll manage better this time," she said to herself, and taking the little golden key, she unlocked the door that led into the garden. Then she set to work nibbling at the mushroom (she had kept a piece of it in her pocket) till she was about a foot high. Then she walked down the little passage. And *then*—she found herself at last in the beautiful garden, among the bright flower-beds and the cool fountains.

THE ARRIVAL OF TOPSY

By HARRIET BEECHER STOWE

Augustine St. Clare, a rich landowner in the Southern States of America in the days when Negroes were slaves, presents his cousin Miss Ophelia with a little bundle of bright-eyed mischief—Topsy. Very soon poor Miss Ophelia is utterly distracted, and the other Negro girls in the St. Clare home —Dinah and Rosa and Jane—find no good in the new-comer. Topsy, however, discovers a friend in St. Clare's little daughter Eva. This story is taken from "Uncle Tom's Cabin."

ONE morning, while Miss Ophelia was busy in some of her domestic cares, St. Clare's voice was heard, calling her at the foot of the stairs.

"Come down here, cousin; I've something to show you."

"What is it?" said Ophelia, coming down, with her sewing in her hand.

"I've made a purchase for your department—see here," said St. Clare; and, with the word, he pulled along a little negro girl, about eight or nine years of age.

She was one of the blackest of her race; and her round, shining eyes, glittering as glass beads, moved with quick and restless glances over everything in the room. Her mouth, half open with astonishment at the wonders of the new mas'r's parlour, displayed a white and brilliant set of teeth. Her woolly hair was braided in sundry little tails, which stuck out in every direction. The expression of her face was an odd mixture of shrewdness and cunning, over which was oddly drawn, like a kind of veil, an expression of the most doleful gravity and solemnity. She was dressed in a single filthy, ragged garment, made of bagging; and stood with her hands demurely folded before her. Altogether, there was something odd and goblin-like about her appearance—something, as Miss Ophelia afterwards said, "so heathenish," as to inspire that good lady with utter dismay; and, turning to St. Clare, she said:

"Augustine, what in the world have you brought that thing here for?"

"For you to educate, to be sure, and train in the way she should go. I thought she was rather a funny specimen. Here, Topsy," he added, giving a whistle, as a man would call the attention of a dog, "give us a song, now, and show us some of your dancing."

The black, glassy eyes glittered with a kind of wicked drollery, and the thing struck up, in a clear, shrill voice, an odd negro melody, to which she kept time with her hands and feet, spinning round, clapping her hands, knocking her knees together, in a wild, fantastic sort of time, and producing in her throat all those odd guttural sounds which distinguish the native music of her race; and finally, turning a somerset or two, and giving a prolonged closing note, as odd and unearthly as that of a steam-whistle, she came suddenly down on the carpet, and stood with her hands folded, and a most sanctimonious expression of meekness and solemnity over her face, only broken by the cunning glances which she shot askance from the corners of her eyes.

Miss Ophelia stood silent, perfectly paralysed with amazement.

St. Clare, like a mischievous fellow, as he was, appeared to enjoy her astonishment; and, addressing the child again, said:

"Topsy, this is your new mistress. I'm going to give you up to her; see, now, that you behave yourself."

"Yes, mas'r," said Topsy, with sanctimonious gravity, her wicked eyes twinkling as she spoke.

"You're going to be good, Topsy, you understand?" said St. Clare.

"Oh, yes, mas'r," said Topsy, with another twinkle, her hands still devoutly folded.

"Now, Augustine, what upon earth is this for?" said Miss Ophelia. "Your house is so full of these little plagues now, that a body can't set down their foot without treading on 'em. I get up in the morning, and find one asleep behind the door, and see one black head poking out from under the table, one lying on the door-mat—and they are mopping and mowing and grinning between all the railings, and tumbling over the kitchen floor! What on earth did you want to bring this one for?"

"For you to educate—didn't I tell you? You're always preaching about educating. I thought I would make you a present of a fresh-caught specimen, and let you try your hand on her, and bring her up in the way she should go."

"Well, I'll do what I can," said Miss Ophelia; and she approached her new subject very much as a person might be supposed to approach a black spider, supposing them to have benevolent designs toward it.

"She's dreadfully dirty, and half naked," she said.

"Well, take her downstairs, and make some of them clean and clothe her up."

Miss Ophelia carried her to the kitchen regions.

"Don't see what Mas'r St. Clare wants of 'nother nigger!" said Dinah, surveying the new arrival with no friendly air. "Won't have her round under *my* feet, *I* know!"

Miss Ophelia saw that there was nobody in the camp that would undertake to oversee the cleansing and dressing of the new arrival; and so she was forced to do it herself, with some very ungracious and reluctant assistance from Jane.

When arrayed at last in a suit of decent and whole clothing, her hair cropped short to her head, Miss Ophelia, with some satisfaction, said she looked more Christian-like than she did, and in her own mind began to mature some plans for her instruction.

Sitting down before her, she began to question her.

"How old are you, Topsy?"

"Dunno, missis," said the image, with a grin that showed all her teeth.

"Don't know how old you are! Didn't anybody ever tell you? Who was your mother?"

"Never had none!" said the child, with another grin.

"Never had any mother! What do you mean? Where were you born?"

"Never was born!" persisted Topsy, with another grin, that looked so goblin-like, that, if Miss Ophelia had been at all nervous, she might have fancied that she had got hold of some sooty gnome; but Miss Ophelia was not nervous, but plain and business-like, and she said with some sternness:

"You mustn't answer me in that way child; I'm not playing with you. Tell me where you were born, and who your father and mother were."

"Never was born," reiterated the creature, more emphatically;

"never had no father nor mother, nor nothin'. I was raised by a speculator with lots of others. Old Aunt Sue used to take car on us."

The child was evidently sincere; and Jane, breaking into a short laugh, said:

"Laws, missis, there's heaps of 'em. Speculators buys 'em up cheap, when they's little, and gets 'em raised for market."

"How long have you lived with your master and mistress?"

"Dunno, missis."

"Is it a year, or more, or less?"

"Dunno, missis."

"Have you ever heard anything about God, Topsy?"

The child looked bewildered, but grinned as usual.

"Do you know who made you?"

"Nobody, as I knows on," said the child, with a short laugh.

The idea appeared to amuse her considerably; for her eyes twinkled, and she added:

"I 'spect I grow'd. Don't think nobody never made me."

"Do you know how to sew?" said Miss Ophelia, who thought she would turn her inquiries to something more tangible.

"No, missis."

"What can you do?—what did you do for your master and mistress?"

"Fetch water, and wash dishes, and rub knives, and wait on folks."

"Were they good to you?"

"'Spect they was," said the child, scanning Miss Ophelia cunningly.

Miss Ophelia began with Topsy by taking her into her chamber the first morning, and solemnly commencing a course of instruction in the art and mystery of bed-making.

Behold, then, Topsy, washed and shorn of all the little braided tails wherein her heart had delighted, arrayed in a clean gown, with well-starched apron, standing reverently before Miss Ophelia, with an expression of solemnity well befitting a funeral.

"Now, Topsy, I'm going to show you just how my bed is to be made. I am very particular about my bed. You must learn exactly how to do it."

"Yes, ma'am," said Topsy, with a deep sigh, and a face of woeful earnestness.

"Now, Topsy, look here: this is the hem of the sheet, this is the right side of the sheet, and this is the wrong; will you remember?"

"Yes, ma'am," says Topsy, with another sigh.

"Well, now, the under sheet you must bring over the bolster—so—and tuck it clear down under the mattress nice and smooth—so—do you see?"

"Yes, ma'am," said Topsy, with profound attention.

"But the upper sheet," said Miss Ophelia, "must be brought down in this way, and tucked under firm and smooth at the foot—so—the narrow hem at the foot."

"Yes, ma'am," said Topsy, as before; but we will add, what Miss

Ophelia did not see, that, during the time when the good lady's back was turned, in the zeal of her manipulations, the young disciple had contrived to snatch a pair of gloves and a ribbon, which she had adroitly slipped into her sleeves, and stood with her hands dutifully folded, as before.

"Now, Topsy, let's see you do this," said Miss Ophelia, pulling off the clothes, and seating herself.

Topsy, with great gravity and adroitness, went through the exercise completely to Miss Ophelia's satisfaction; smoothing the sheets, patting out every wrinkle, and exhibiting, through the whole process, a gravity and seriousness with which her instructress was greatly edified. By an unlucky slip, however, a fluttering fragment of the ribbon hung out of one of her sleeves, just as she was finishing, and caught Miss Ophelia's attention. Instantly she pounced upon it. "What's this? You naughty, wicked child—you've been stealing this!"

The ribbon was pulled out of Topsy's own sleeve, yet was she not in the least disconcerted; she only looked at it with an air of the most surprised and unconscious innocence.

"Laws! why, that ar's Miss Feely's ribbon, an't it? How could it 'a got caught in my sleeve?"

"Topsy, you naughty girl, don't you tell me a lie—you stole that ribbon!"

"Missis, I declar for 't, I didn't; never seed it till dis yer blessed minnit."

"Topsy," said Miss Ophelia, "don't you know it's wicked to tell lies?"

"I never tells no lies, Miss Feely," said Topsy, with virtuous gravity; "it's jist the truth I've been a-tellin' now, and an't nothin' else."

"Topsy, I shall have to whip you, if you tell lies so."

"Laws, missis, if you's to whip all day, couldn't say no other way," said Topsy, beginning to blubber. "I never seed dat ar—it must 'a got caught in my sleeve. Miss Feely must have left it on the bed, and it got caught in the clothes, and so got in my sleeve."

Miss Ophelia was so indignant at the barefaced lie that she caught the child and shook her.

"Don't you tell me that again!"

The shake brought the gloves on the floor from the other sleeve.

"There, you!" said Miss Ophelia, "will you tell me now you didn't steal the ribbon?"

Topsy now confessed to the gloves, but still persisted in denying the ribbon.

"Now, Topsy," said Miss Ophelia, "if you'll confess all about it, I won't whip you this time."

Thus adjured, Topsy confessed to the ribbon and gloves, with woeful protestations of penitence.

"Well, now, tell me. I know you must have taken other things since you have been in the house. Now, tell me if you took anything, and I shan't whip you."

"Laws, missis! I took Miss Eva's red thing she w'ars on her neck."

"You did, you naughty child! Well, what else?"

"I took Rosa's yer-rings—them red ones."

"Go bring them to me this minute, both of 'em."

"Laws, missis! I can't—they's burnt up!"

"Burnt up?—what a story! Go get 'em, or I'll whip you."

Topsy, with loud protestations and tears and groans, declared that she could not. "They's burnt up—they was."

"What did you burn 'em up for?" said Miss Ophelia.

"'Cause I's wicked—I is. I's mighty wicked, anyhow. I can't help it."

Just at this moment, Eva came innocently into the room, with the identical coral necklace on her neck.

"Why, Eva, where did you get your necklace?" said Miss Ophelia.

"Get it? Why, I've had it on all day," said Eva.

"Did you have it on yesterday?"

"Yes; and what is funny, Aunty, I had it on all night. I forgot to take it off when I went to bed."

Miss Ophelia looked perfectly bewildered; the more so as Rosa at that instant came into the room with a basket of newly ironed linen poised on her head and the coral ear-drops shaking in her ears.

"I'm sure I can't tell anything what to do with such a child!" she said in despair. "What in the world did you tell me you took those things for, Topsy?"

"Why, missis said I must 'fess; and I couldn't think of nothin' else to 'fess," said Topsy, rubbing her eyes.

"But, of course, I didn't want you to confess things you didn't do," said Miss Ophelia, "that's telling a lie, just as much as the other."

"Laws, now, is it?" said Topsy, with an air of innocent wonder.

"La, there an't any such thing as truth in that limb," said Rosa, looking indignantly at Topsy. "If I was Mas'r St. Clare, I'd whip her till the blood run. I would—I'd let her catch it."

"No, no, Rosa," said Eva, with an air of command, which the child could assume at times; "you mustn't talk so, Rosa. I can't bear to hear it."

Eva stood looking at Topsy.

There stood the two children, representatives of the two extremes of society. The fair, high-bred child, with her golden head, her deep eyes, her spiritual, noble brow, and prince-like movements; and her black, keen, subtle, cringing, yet acute neighbour. They stood the representatives of their races. The Saxon, born of ages of cultivation, command, education, physical and moral eminence; the Afric, born of ages of oppression, submission, ignorance, toil, and vice!

Something, perhaps, of such thoughts struggled through Eva's mind. But a child's thoughts are rather dim, undefined instincts; and in Eva's noble nature many such were yearning and working, for which she had no power of utterance. When Miss Ophelia expatiated on Topsy's naughty, wicked conduct, the child looked perplexed and sorrowful, but said sweetly:

"Poor Topsy, why did you steal? You're going to be taken good care of now. I'm sure I'd rather give you anything of mine than have you steal it."

It was the first word of kindness the child had ever heard in her life; and the sweet tone and manner struck strangely on the wild, rude heart, and a sparkle of something like a tear shone in the keen, round, glittering eye; but it was followed by the short laugh and habitual grin. No! the ear that has never heard anything but abuse is strangely incredulous of anything so heavenly as kindness; and Topsy only thought Eva's speech something funny and inexplicable —she did not believe it.

But what was to be done with Topsy? Miss Ophelia found the case a puzzler; her rules for bringing up didn't seem to apply.

She instituted regular hours and employments for her, and undertook to teach her to read and to sew.

In the former art, the child was quick enough. She learned her letters as if by magic, and was very soon able to read plain reading; but the sewing was a more difficult matter. The creature was as lithe as a cat, and as active as a monkey, and the confinement of sewing was her abomination; so she broke her needles, threw them slyly out of windows, or down in chinks of the walls; she tangled, broke, and dirtied her thread, or, with a sly movement, would throw a spool away altogether. Her motions were almost as quick as those of a practised conjuror, and her command of her face quite as great; and though Miss Ophelia could not help feeling that so many accidents could not possibly happen in succession, yet she could not, without a watchfulness which would leave her no time for anything else, detect her.

Topsy was soon a noted character in the establishment. Her talent for every species of drollery, grimace, and mimicry—for dancing, tumbling, climbing, singing, whistling, imitating every sound that hit her fancy—seemed inexhaustible. In her play-hours, she invariably had every child in the establishment at her heels, open-mouthed with admiration and wonder—not excepting Miss Eva, who appeared to be fascinated by her, as a dove is sometimes charmed by a glittering serpent.

Topsy was at first despised and contemned by the upper servants. They soon found reason to alter their opinion. It was very soon discovered that whosoever cast an indignity on Topsy was sure to meet with some inconvenient accident shortly after—either a pair of ear-rings or some cherished trinket would be missing, or an article of dress would be suddenly found utterly ruined, or the person would stumble accidentally into a pail of hot water, or a libation of dirty slop would unaccountably deluge them from above when in full gala dress—and on all these occasions, when investigation was made, there was nobody found to stand sponsor for the indignity. Topsy was cited, and had up before all the domestic judicatories, time and again; but always sustained her examinations with most edifying innocence and gravity of appearance. Nobody in the world ever doubted who did the things; but not a scrap of any direct evidence could be found to establish the suppositions, and Miss Ophelia was too just to feel at liberty to proceed to any length without it.

The mischiefs done were always so nicely timed also, as further to shelter the aggressor. Thus, the times for revenge on Rosa and Jane, the two chambermaids, were always chosen in those seasons when (as not unfrequently happened) they were in disgrace with their mistress, when any complaint from them would of course meet with no sympathy. In short, Topsy soon made the household understand the propriety of letting her alone; and she was let alone accordingly.

Topsy was smart and energetic in all manual operations, learning everything that was taught her with surprising quickness. With a few lessons, she had learned to do the proprieties of Miss Ophelia's chamber in a way with which even that particular lady could find no fault. Mortal hands could not lay spread smoother, adjust pillows more accurately, sweep and dust and arrange more perfectly, than Topsy, when she chose—but she didn't very often choose. If Miss Ophelia, after three or four days of careful and patient supervision, was so sanguine as to suppose that Topsy had at last fallen into her way, could do without overlooking, and so go off and busy herself about something else, Topsy would hold a perfect carnival of confusion, for some one or two hours. Instead of making the bed, she would amuse herself with pulling off the pillow-cases, butting her woolly head among the pillows, till it would sometimes be grotesquely ornamented with feathers sticking out in various directions; she would climb the posts, and hang head downwards from the tops; flourish the sheets and spreads all over the apartment; dress the bolster up in Miss Ophelia's night-clothes, and enact various scenic performances with that—singing and whistling, and making grimaces at herself in the looking-glass; in short, as Miss Ophelia phrased it, "raising Cain" generally.

On one occasion Miss Ophelia found Topsy with her very best scarlet India Canton crape shawl wound around her head for a turban, going on with her rehearsals before the glass in great style —Miss Ophelia having, with carelessness most unheard of in her, left the key for once in her drawer.

"Topsy," she would say, when at the end of all patience, "what does make you act so?"

"Dunno, missis—I 'spects 'cause I's so wicked!"

"I don't know anything what I shall do with you, Topsy."

"Law, missis, you must whip me; my old missis allers whipped me. I an't used to workin' unless I gets whipped."

"Why, Topsy, I don't want to whip you. You can do well, if you've a mind to; what is the reason you won't?"

"Law, missis, I's used to whippin'; I 'spects it's good for me."

Miss Ophelia tried the recipe, and Topsy invariably made a terrible commotion, screaming, groaning, and imploring, though half an hour afterwards, when roosted on some projection of the balcony, and surrounded by a flock of admiring "young 'uns," she would express the utmost contempt of the whole affair.

"Law, Miss Feely whip!—wouldn't kill a skeeter, her whippin's. Oughter see how old mas'r made the flesh fly; old mas'r know'd how!"

Topsy always made great capital of her own sins and enormities, evidently considering them as something peculiarly distinguishing.

"Law, you niggers," she would say to some of her auditors, "does you know you's all sinners? Well, you is—everybody is. White folks is sinners too—Miss Feely says so; but I 'spects niggers is the biggest ones; but Lor! ye an't any one on ye up to me. I's so awful wicked there can't nobody do nothin' with me. I used to keep old missis a'swarin' at me half de time. I 'spects I's the wickedest crittur in the world"; and Topsy would cut a somerset, and come up brisk and shining on to a higher perch, and evidently plume herself on the distinction.

Miss Ophelia busied herself very earnestly on Sundays, teaching Topsy the catechism. Topsy had an uncommon verbal memory, and committed with a fluency that greatly encouraged her instructress—only now and then she would oddly transpose some important words, and persist in the mistake, in spite of very effort to the contrary.

In this way Topsy's training proceeded for a year or two—Miss Ophelia worrying herself, from day to day, with her, as a kind of chronic plague, to whose inflictions she became, in time, as accustomed as persons sometimes do to the neuralgia or sick headache.

GINGER'S STORY

By ANNA SEWELL

When the young black horse was bought by Squire Gordon of Birtwick and named Black Beauty he was given a stable companion who had had a very exciting career. Ginger tells her story of wrongs and ill-usage to the dark newcomer, and explains with becoming modesty how she came by her unenviable reputation. This story is taken from "Black Beauty."

I USED to stand in the stable, and my coat was brushed every day till it shone like a rook's wing. Early in May there came a man from Squire Gordon's, who took me away to the Hall. My master said, "Good-bye; be a good horse, and always do your best." I could not say "Good-bye," so I put my nose into his hand; he patted me kindly, and then I left my first home.

Squire Gordon's park skirted the village of Birtwick. It was entered by a large iron gate, at which stood the first lodge; and then you trotted along on a smooth road between clumps of large old trees. Soon you passed another lodge and another gate, which brought you to the house and the gardens. Beyond this lay the home paddock, the old orchard, and the stables. There was accommodation for many horses and carriages; but I need only describe the stable into which I was taken. This was very roomy, with four good stalls. A large swinging window opened into the yard; this made it pleasant and airy.

The first stall was a large, square one, shut in behind with a wooden gate; the others were common stalls—good stalls, but not nearly so large. My stall had a low rack for hay and a low manger for corn; it was called a loose box, because the horse that was put into it was not tied up, but left loose to do as he liked. It is a great thing to have a loose box.

Into this fine box, clean, sweet, and airy, the groom put me. I never in my life was in a better box, and the sides were not so high but that I could see through the iron rails at the top all that went on.

The man gave me some very nice oats, patted me, spoke kindly, and then went away.

When I had eaten my corn, I looked round. In the stall next to mine stood a little fat grey pony, with a thick mane and tail, a very pretty head, and a pert little nose.

Putting my head up to the iron rails at the top of my box, I said, "How do you do? What is your name?"

He turned round as far as his halter would allow, held up his head, and said: "My name is Merrylegs. I am very handsome. I carry the young ladies on my back, and sometimes I take our mistress out in the low chair. They think a great deal of me, and so does James. Are you going to live next door to me in the box?"

"Yes," I replied.

"Well, then," he said, "I hope you are good-tempered; next door to me I do not like anyone who bites."

Just then a horse's head looked over from the stall beyond. The ears were laid back, and the eye looked rather ill-tempered. This tall chestnut mare, with a long, handsome neck, looked across to me and said, "So it is you who have turned me out of my box. Is it not a very strange thing for a colt like you to come and turn a lady out of her own home?"

"I beg your pardon," I said, "I have turned no one out. The man who brought me put me here, and I had nothing to do with it. And as to my being a colt, I am turned four years old, and am a grown-up horse. I never yet had words with horse or mare, and it is my wish to live at peace."

"Well," she said, "we shall see. Of course, I do not want to have words with a young thing like you."

I said no more.

In the afternoon, when she went out, Merrylegs told me all about the mare.

"The thing is this," said Merrylegs. "Ginger has a bad habit of biting and snapping; that is why she is called Ginger. When she was in the loose box, she used to snap very much. One day she bit James in the arm and made it bleed, and so Miss Flora and Miss Jessie, who are very fond of me, were afraid to come into the stable. They used to bring me nice things to eat—an apple, or a carrot, or a piece of bread; but after Ginger stood in that box they dare not come, and I miss them very much. I hope, if you do not bite or snap, that they will now come again."

I told him I never bit anything but grass, hay, and corn, and could not think what pleasure Ginger found in it.

"Well, I don't think she does find pleasure in it," said Merrylegs; "it is just a bad habit. She says no one was ever kind to her, and so why should she not bite? Of course it is a very bad habit; but I am sure, if all she says be true, she must have been very ill-used before she came here. John and James do all they can to please her, and our master never uses a whip if a horse behaves himself; so I think she might be good-tempered here.

"You see," he said, with a wise look, "I am twelve years old; I know a great deal, and I can tell you there is not a better place for a horse all round the country than this. John is the best groom that ever was; he has been here fourteen years; and you never saw such a kind boy as James is. So it is all Ginger's own fault that she did not stay in that box."

A few days after this I had to go in the carriage with Ginger. I wondered how we should get on together; but except for laying her ears back when I was led up to her, she behaved very well. She did her work honestly, and did her full share; and I never wish to have a better partner in double harness.

When we came to a hill, instead of slackening her pace, she would throw her weight right into the collar, and pull away straight up. We had both the same sort of courage at our work; and John had more often to hold us in than to urge us forward. He never had to use the whip with either of us. Then our paces were much the same, and I found it very easy to keep step with her when trotting. This made it pleasant, and master always liked us to keep step well, and so did John. After we had been out two or three times together we grew quite friendly and sociable; this made me feel very much at home.

I was quite happy in my new place, and if there was one thing that I missed, it must not be thought I was discontented. All who had to do with me were good, and I had a light, airy stable, and the best of food.

What more could I want? Why, liberty! For three years and a half of my life I had had all the liberty I could wish for; but now, week after week, month after month, and no doubt year after year, I must stand up in a stable night and day except when I am wanted; and then I must be just as steady and quiet as any old horse who has worked twenty years. I must wear straps here and straps there, a bit in my mouth, and blinkers over my eyes.

Now, I am not complaining, for I know it must be so. I mean only to say that for a young horse, full of strength and spirits, who has been used to some large field or plain where he can fling up his head, toss up his tail, gallop away at full speed, and then go round and back again with a snort to his companions—I say it is hard never now to have a bit more liberty to do as he likes.

Sometimes, when I have had less exercise than usual, I have felt so full of life and spring that when John has taken me out to exercise I really could not keep quiet. Do what I would, it seemed as if I must jump, dance, or prance; and many a good shake I know I must have given him, especially at the first, but he was always good and patient.

"Steady, steady, my boy," he would say; "wait a while, and we'll have a good swing, and soon get the tickle out of your feet." Then, as soon as we were out of the village, he would give me a few miles at a spanking trot, and bring me back as fresh as before, only clear of the fidgets, as he called them.

Spirited horses, when not enough exercised, are often called skittish, when in fact it is only play; and some grooms will punish them, but our John did not; he knew it was only high spirits. Still, he had his own ways of making me understand by the tone of his voice or the touch of the rein. If he was very serious and quite determined, I always knew it by his voice, and that had more power over me than anything else, for I was very fond of him.

I ought to say that sometimes we had our liberty for a few hours; this used to be on fine Sundays in the summer-time. The carriage never went out on Sundays, because the church was not far off.

It was a great treat to us to be turned out into the home paddock or the old orchard; the grass was so cool and soft to our feet; the air was so sweet, and the freedom to do as we liked—to gallop, lie down, roll over on our backs, or nibble the sweet grass—was so pleasant. Then, as we stood together under the shade of the large chestnut-tree, was a very good time for talking.

One day, when Ginger and I were standing alone in the shade, we had a long talk. She wanted to know all about my bringing up and breaking in; so I told her.

"Well," she said, "if I had had your bringing up I might have as good a temper as you; but now I don't believe I ever shall."

"Why not?" I said.

"Because it has been all so different with me," she replied. "I never had anyone, horse or man, that was kind to me, or that I cared to please; for in the first place I was taken from my mother as soon as I was weaned, and put with a lot of other young colts; none of them cared for me, and I cared for none of them. There was no kind master like yours to look after me, talk to me, and bring me nice things to eat.

"The man that had the care of us never gave me a kind word in my life. I do not mean that he ill-used me, but he did not care for us more than to see that we had plenty to eat and were sheltered in the winter.

"A footpath ran through our field, and very often the big boys passing through would fling stones to make us gallop. I was never hit, but one fine young colt was badly cut in the face, and I should think it would leave a scar for life. We did not mind the boys, but of course it made us more wild, and we settled it in our minds that boys were our enemies. We had very good fun in the meadows, either galloping up and down and chasing each other round and round the field, or standing still under the shade of the trees.

"But when it came to breaking in, that was a bad time for me. Several men came to catch me, and when at last they closed me in at one corner of the field, one caught me by the forelock, another took me by the nose, holding it so tight I could hardly draw my breath, and a third, grasping my underjaw in his hard hand, wrenched my mouth open; and so by force they got on the halter and put the bar into my mouth.

"Then one dragged me along by the halter, and another flogged me behind. This was the first experience I had of man's kindness; it was all force. They did not give me a chance to know what they wanted. I was high bred, with a great deal of spirit, and, no doubt, was very wild and gave them plenty of trouble; but then it was dreadful to be shut up in a stall, day after day, instead of having my liberty. I fretted and pined and wanted to get loose. You know yourself, it's bad enough when you have a kind master and plenty of coaxing; but there was nothing of that sort for me.

"There was one—the old master, Mr. Ryder—who, I think, could soon have brought me round, and have done anything with me; but he had given up all the hard part of the trade to his son and to another experienced man. My master came only at times to oversee.

"His son was a strong, tall, bold man called Samson; and he used to boast that he had never found a horse that could throw him. There was no gentleness in him as there was in his father, but only hardness; a hard voice, a hard eye, and a hard hand. I felt from the first that what he wanted was to wear all the spirit out of me, and just make me into a quiet, humble, obedient piece of horse-flesh. 'Horseflesh!' Yes, that is all that he thought about"; and Ginger stamped her foot as if the very thought of him made her angry.

Then she went on: "If I did not do exactly what he wanted he would get put out, and make me run round with that long rein in the training-field till he had tired me out. I think he drank a good deal, and I am quite sure that the oftener he drank the worse it was for me.

"One day he had worked me hard in every way he could, and when I lay down I was tired, miserable, and angry; it all seemed so hard. The next morning he came for me early, and ran me round again for a long time. I had scarcely had an hour's rest when he came again for me with a saddle and bridle and a new kind of bit.

"I could never quite tell how it came about. He had only just mounted me on the training-ground, when something I did put him out of temper, and he jerked me hard with the rein. The new bit was very painful, and I reared up suddenly: this angered him still more, and he began to flog me.

"I felt my whole spirit set against him, and I began to kick, and plunge, and rear as I had never done before; we had a regular fight. For a long time he stuck to the saddle and punished me cruelly with his whip and spurs; but my blood was thoroughly up, and I cared for nothing he could do if only I could get him off.

"At last, after a terrible struggle, I threw him off backwards. I heard him fall heavily upon the turf, and, without looking behind me, galloped off to the other end of the field; there I turned round and saw my persecutor slowly rise from the ground and go into the stable. I stood under an oak-tree and watched, but no one came to catch me.

"Time passed; the sun was very hot, the flies swarmed round me and settled on my bleeding flanks where the spurs had dug in. I felt hungry, for I had not eaten since the early morning; but there was not enough grass in that meadow for a goose to live on. I wanted to lie down and rest, but with the saddle strapped tightly on my back there was no comfort, nor was there a drop of water to drink. The afternoon wore on, and the sun got low. I saw the other colts led in, and I knew they were having a good feed.

"At last, just as the sun went down, I saw the old master come out with a sieve in his hand. He was a very fine old gentleman with quite white hair, but I should know him by his voice amongst a thousand. It was not high, nor yet low, but full, clear, and kind; and when he gave orders it was so steady and decided that everyone, both horses and men, knew that he expected to be obeyed.

"He came quietly along, now and then shaking about the oats that he had in the sieve, speaking cheerfully and gently to me: 'Come along, lassie, come along, lassie; come along, come along.' I stood still and let him come up.

"He held the oats towards me and I began to eat without fear; his voice took all my fear away. He stood by, patting and stroking me whilst I was eating, and seeing the clots of blood on my side he seemed very vexed. 'Poor lassie, it was a bad business, a bad business!' Then he quietly took the rein and led me to the stable.

"Just at the door stood Samson. I laid my ears back and snapped at him. 'Stand back,' said the master, 'and keep out of her way; you've done a bad day's work for this filly.' He growled out something about a vicious brute. 'Hark ye,' said his father, 'a bad-tempered man will never make a good-tempered horse. You've not learned your trade yet, Samson.'

"Then he led me into my box, took off the saddle and bridle with his own hands, and tied me up. Calling for a pail of warm water and a sponge, he took off his coat, and while the stableman held the pail, he sponged my sides for some time so tenderly that I was sure he knew how sore and bruised they were. 'Whoa! my pretty one,' he said; 'stand still, stand still.' His very voice did me good and the bathing was very comforting.

"The skin was so broken at the corners of my mouth that I could not eat the hay, for the stalks hurt me. He looked closely at my mouth, shook his head, and told the man to fetch me a good bran mash and put some meal into it. How good that mash was! so soft and healing to my mouth. He stood by, stroking me and talking to the man all the time I was eating. 'If a high-mettled creature like this,' said he, 'can't be broken in by fair means, she never will be good for anything.'

"After that he often came to see me, and when my mouth was healed the other breaker, Job, went on training me. As he was steady and thoughtful, I soon learned what he wanted."

The next time that Ginger and I were together in the paddock she told me about her first place.

"After my breaking in," she said, "I was bought by a dealer to match another chestnut horse. For some weeks he drove us together, and then we were sold to a fashionable gentleman, and were sent up to London. I had been driven with a bearing rein by the dealer, and I hated it worse than anything else; but in this place we were reined far tighter, the coachman and his master thinking in this way we looked more stylish. We were often driven about in the Park and other fashionable places. You, who never had a bearing rein on, don't know what it is; but I can tell you it is dreadful.

"I like to toss my head about, and hold it as high as any horse; but you can fancy how it would feel if you tossed your head up high and were obliged to hold it there for hours together, not able to move it at all, except with a jerk still higher; and all this time your neck was aching till you did not know how to bear it.

"Besides this, you have two bits instead of one; and mine was a sharp one. It hurt my tongue and my jaw, and the blood from my tongue coloured the froth that kept flying from my lips, as I chafed and fretted at the bits and rein. It was worse when we had to stand by the hour waiting for our mistress at some grand party or entertainment; and if I fretted or stamped with impatience, the whip was laid on. It was enough to drive one mad."

"Did not your master take any thought for you?" I said.

"No," said she, "he cared only to have a stylish turn-out, as they call it. I think he knew very little about horses; he left that to his coachman, who told him that I was of an irritable temper, and that I had not been well broken to the bearing rein, but that I should soon get used to it.

"However, *he* was not the man to do it; for when I was in the stable, miserable and angry, instead of being soothed and quieted by kindness, I only got a surly word or a blow. If he had been civil, I would have tried to bear it. I was willing to work, and ready to work hard too; but to be tormented for nothing but their fancies angered me. What right had they to make me suffer like that? Besides the soreness in my mouth and the pain in my neck, the bearing rein always made my windpipe feel bad; and if I had stopped there long, I know it would have spoiled my breathing.

"I grew more and more restless and irritable; I could not help it. Then I began to snap and kick when anyone came to harness me. One day, as they had just buckled us into the carriage and were straining my head up with that rein, I began to plunge and kick with all my might. I soon broke a lot of harness, and kicked myself clear; so my stay there was ended.

"Soon I was sent to Tattersalls' to be sold. Of course, I could not be warranted free from vice; so nothing was said about that. My handsome appearance and good paces soon brought a gentleman to bid for me, and I was bought by another dealer. He tried me in all kinds of ways and with different bits, and soon found out what I could bear. At last he drove me quite without a bearing rein, then sold me as a perfectly quiet horse to a gentleman in the country.

"He was a good master, and I was getting on very well, but his old groom left him and a new one came. This man was as hard-tempered and hard-handed as Samson; he always spoke in a rough, impatient voice, and if I did not move in the stall the moment he wanted me, he would hit me above the hocks with the stable broom or the fork, whichever he might have in his hand. Everything he did was rough, and I began to hate him; he wanted to make me afraid of him, but I was too high-mettled for that.

"One day when he had aggravated me more than usual, I bit him; this of course put him in a great rage, and he began to hit me about the head with a riding-whip. After that, he never dared to come into my stall again, either my heels or my teeth were ready for him, and he knew it. I was quite quiet with my master, but of course he listened to what the man said, and so I was sold again.

"The same dealer heard of me, and said he thought he knew of a place where I should do well. ''Twas a pity,' he said, 'that such a fine horse should go to the bad for want of a real good chance'; and the end of it was that I came here not long before you did. I had now made up my mind that men were my natural enemies, and that I must defend myself. Of course, it is very different here; but who knows how long it will last? I wish I could think about things as you do; but I can't after all I have gone through."

"Well," I said, "I think it would be a real shame if you were to bite or kick John or James."

"I don't mean to," she said, "while they are good to me. I did once bite James pretty sharp, but John said, 'Try her with kindness,' and instead of punishing me as I expected, James came to me with his arm bound up, and brought me a bran mash and stroked me; and I have never snapped at him since; and I won't again."

I was sorry for Ginger, but of course I knew very little then, and I thought most likely she made the worst of it. However, I found that as the weeks went on she grew much more gentle and cheerful, and lost the watchful, defiant look that she used to turn on any strange person who came near her. And one day James said, "I do believe that mare is getting fond of me, she quite whinnied after me this morning when I had been rubbing her forehead."

"Ay, ay, Jim, 'tis the Birtwick balls," said John; "she'll be as good as Black Beauty by and by; kindness is all the physic she wants, poor thing!" Master noticed the change too, and one day when he got out of the carriage and came to speak to us, as he often did, he stroked her beautiful neck. "Well, my pretty one, well, how do things go with you now? You are a good bit happier than when you came to us, I think."

She put her nose up to him in a friendly, trustful way, while he rubbed it gently.

"We shall make a cure of her, John," he said.

"Yes, sir, she's wonderfully improved; she's not the same creature that she was. It's the Birtwick balls, sir," said John, laughing.

This was a little joke of John's; he used to say that a regular course of the Birtwick horse-balls would cure almost any vicious horse. These balls, he said, were made up of patience and gentleness, firmness and petting: one pound of each to be mixed with half a pint of common sense, and given to the horse every day.

THE ALPINE PASTURE

By JOHANNA SPYRI

Heidi, a little orphan, has come to live with her grandfather in his hut on an alpine slope. The life is new and strange to her, and she awakens to all the pleasure of a day to be spent with young Peter, the goat-herd, up in an alpine pasture. With Peter will go her grandfather's two sleek goats, Schwänli and Bärli, and she will pick brighter flowers than she has seen in the valley, and before they all descend at evening she will see the magic of the alpenglow, when the light of the setting sun on the mountain snows seems to set the peaks and crags aflame.

This story is taken from "Heidi."

HEIDI was awakened by a loud whistle, and as she opened her eyes a yellow sunbeam, shining through the opening, fell on her bed, and turned it, and all the hay that was spread about the loft, to glistening gold. She looked about her with astonishment, and could not make out where she was.

Soon she heard her grandfather's deep voice, and it all came back to her; how she came there, and that now she lived with her grandfather.

She sprang up and soon had on all her clothes of the day before; and they were few enough. She ran out of doors. There stood Peter with his goats; and her grandfather brought out his from the stall, that they might join the flock. Heidi bade both him and the goats a good-morning.

"Would you like to go with them to the pasture?" asked the old man.

The child could only jump for joy, she was so delighted.

"First, however, you must wash and make yourself clean; or the sun will laugh at you, while he is shining so brightly up there, and sees you all dirty and black. Look there—everything is ready for you." He pointed to a big tub of water that stood in the sun before the door. Heidi splashed and rubbed herself till she shone again. Her grandfather in the meanwhile went into the hut, and soon called to Peter, "Come here, goat general, and bring your knapsack."

Peter obeyed in surprise, and opened his bag, in which was his poor little dinner.

"Wider, wider," said the old man, and put in a big piece of bread and another piece of cheese. Peter opened his eyes as wide as ever he could, for the pieces were each twice as large as his own.

"Now the mug goes in, too, for the little one can't drink as you do from the goats themselves; no, indeed. And you must milk this twice full at noon; for the child will go with you, and stay till you come back in the evening. Now, take care that she does not fall off the cliffs."

Heidi was soon ready, and came running to say, "Now can the sun make fun of me, grandfather?"

In her fear of the laughter of the sun, she had rubbed her face, neck, and arms so roughly with the coarse towel she found by the tub that she was as red as a lobster, as she stood there before him.

He laughed a little, but said soothingly, "No, he will find nothing to make fun of now. But do you know something? In the evening, when you come home, you must go into the tub all over, like a fish; for when you go about like the goats you will get very black feet. Now go on your way."

And on they went, climbing joyfully. The wind had swept the last trace of cloud from the sky, which was of a wonderful dark blue. The green alp was covered with blue and yellow flowers, and their wide-open petals seemed laughing back at the sun, while everything shimmered and shone.

Heidi scampered hither and thither, shouting for joy. Now it was a whole group of red primroses; one place was perfectly blue with lovely gentians; and here and everywhere the tender blossoms of the yellow buttercups nodded and laughed in the sunlight. Carried away with delight by all the beckoning, glistening flowers, the child forgot the goats, and Peter also. She was running now forwards, now back again; first on this side, then on that side; for here they were like red, and there like yellow sparkles, and she was tempted in every direction. She gathered great handfuls of flowers and stuffed them all into her apron; for she must carry them home with her, and place them in the hay in her bedroom, to make it look as it did on the alp.

Poor Peter was obliged to keep his eyes about him to-day; and those round eyes, that were not in the habit of moving very quickly, had enough to do. For the goats were like Heidi: they ran about everywhere, while Peter must whistle and shout and swing his stick to bring together all the wanderers.

"Where have you got to now, Heidi?" he called out, somewhat angrily.

"Here," came back the reply from—somewhere.

Peter could see no one; for Heidi sat on the ground behind a little mound that was covered with the sweetest-smelling prune flowers, and the whole air was perfumed. Heidi had never breathed anything so perfectly delicious. She seated herself among the bushes, and drew in the scent in long, full-drawn breathings.

"Come here now," shouted Peter. "You must not fall over the precipices; your grandfather has forbidden it."

"Where are the precipices?" asked the child, but did not stir from her seat; for with every breeze the sweet perfume was wafted to her nostrils.

"Up there, aloft. We have still a good bit to climb, so come along. Up there, at the very top, sits and screams the old eagle!"

This stirred the little girl. She jumped up, and ran towards her companion, with her apron full of flowers.

"Now you have picked enough of these," said he, "else you will be always stopping; and, besides, if to-day you pick them all, to-morrow you will find no more."

This last reason convinced Heidi; moreover, she had stuffed her apron so full that there was not room for another flower, and to-morrow she must see them again.

She now kept along with Peter; and the goats, too, went in better order, for they scented the sweet herbs from their pasture on the heights afar, and pushed forward without pausing.

The pasture where Peter usually stopped and made his resting-place for the day lay at the foot of the peak, which rose steep and naked towards the sky, clothed from its base with scrub trees and bushes. On one side of the alp the great rocks were divided by steep clefts and chasms, and the old man was quite right to warn them against that danger.

As they now had reached the highest point, Peter took off his knapsack and placed it carefully in a little hollow where it would be sheltered from the wind, which blew often in strong gusts up so high on the mountain. This Peter knew very well, and did not mean to see his knapsack, with the nice dinner, go rolling down the hill-side. Having put this in a place of safety, he stretched himself his full length on the sunny turf, to rest after the steep ascent.

Heidi had also tucked her apron into the same hollow with the knapsack, having rolled it up with all the flowers in it; then she seated herself beside Peter, and looked about her on every side. Below lay the valley in the full glow of the morning sun; before her was a huge white snowfield rising toward the dark blue heaven; to the left, an enormous mass of rocks was piled up, on each side of which stood a pillar of rock, bald and jagged against the blue sky. Heidi thought the pinnacles were looking down at her; and she sat there as still as a little mouse, and looked and looked on every side. All was still; only a light, soft breeze stirred the blue harebells and the shining yellow buttercups that grew all about and stood nodding to her on their slender stalks. Peter had fallen asleep after his exertions; and the goats climbed here and there, and up into the bushes.

Never had the child been so happy in all her life. She drank in the golden sunlight, the fresh air, the sweet perfume of the flowers, and longed for nothing but to stay where she was for ever.

Thus a long time passed; and Heidi gazed at the needles of rock above her so steadfastly that they seemed to her to have faces, and to be returning her gaze like old friends, when suddenly she heard above her a loud, sharp scream. As she looked up a huge bird, such as she had never seen before, circled overhead; with wide-spread wings it soared through the air, and in great sweeps came back again and again, screaming loud and piercingly over Heidi's head.

"Peter, Peter! wake up!" cried Heidi aloud. "See, the eagle is here. Look, look!"

Peter roused himself at her cry. The children gazed at the bird, which rose higher and higher, disappearing at last in the blue air over the grey rocks.

"Where is he now?" asked Heidi, who had watched the bird with breathless interest.

"In his home up there."

"Oh, how beautiful to live up there! But why does he scream so?"

"Because he must."

"Let us climb up there to see his home," suggested Heidi.

"Oh, oh, oh!" cried Peter; and each "oh" was louder than the last. "Even the goats are not able to climb up there."

After this Peter began to whistle and call so loudly that Heidi did not know what had happened; but the goats knew well enough, and all came running and jumping, and were soon all gathered on the green field. Some nibbled at the sweet grass, others ran here and there, while some stood opposite each other a little way apart, and butted playfully with their horns. Springing to her feet, Heidi ran in amidst the goats, for she found it a new and indescribable pleasure to see the dear little creatures gambolling together so happily. She too jumped from one to another to make herself acquainted with each separately, for each had its own peculiarities, and looked and behaved differently.

While Heidi played with the goats Peter had fetched the knapsack, and arranged the four parcels in a square on the grass, the big ones on Heidi's side, and the little ones on his; then he filled the mug with fresh milk from Schwänli, and placed it in the middle of the square.

Then he called to Heidi to come. But he had to call again and again, longer than to the goats; for the child was so delighted with the thousand movements and pranks of her new playfellows that she saw and heard nothing further. Peter understood how to make himself heard. He shouted so very loud that he could have been heard up on the rocks, causing Heidi to run as fast as she could; and then the table looked so very inviting, that she hopped about for joy.

"Stop dancing about. It's time to eat," said Peter, seating himself and beginning.

"Is the milk for me?" asked Heidi, as she took her seat, surveying the four corners and the centre ornament with pleasure.

"Yes," he replied, "and the two biggest packages are yours also. When you've emptied the mug you can have another one full from Schwänli; and when you've finished it's my turn."

"And where do you get your milk?" asked the little girl curiously.

"From my goat, from Snail. Do begin."

Heidi began at last, with the milk; and when she had emptied the mug Peter rose and filled it again. Heidi broke some of her bread into it, and then handed the rest of it to Peter. It was a big piece, twice as large as his, which he had already eaten, together with the rest of his dinner. She gave him also her big lump of cheese, saying, "You have it all; I have had enough."

Peter stared at Heidi with his big eyes in speechless astonishment; for never in his life had he been able to say what she had just said, nor to give anything away. He hesitated a little, for he could not believe that she was in earnest; but the child held her pieces towards him again, and when he did not take them she at last laid them on his knee.

When he saw that she was serious he took his present, nodded for thanks and pleasure, and made forthwith the heartiest meal that had fallen to his share since he first tended the goats. While he ate Heidi watched the flock.

"What are all their names, Peter?" said she.

He knew them, and could carry them in his head easily enough, for he had little else there. So he began and named them one after the other without hesitating, and pointed at each with his finger as he spoke. To this lesson Heidi gave all her attention, and soon could also name them all; for each had its peculiarity, which was easily learned with a little trouble.

There was the big Turk with his strong horns, who was for ever butting the others; so that they generally scampered away when he came towards them, and would have nothing to do with such a rough comrade. Only the bold and slender Thistlebird did not avoid him, but struck out sharply, once, twice, sometimes six times, until the great Turk stood still in astonishment, and did not try again soon; for Thistlebird stood always ready for battle, and had sharp horns, too.

And often Heidi ran to the little white Snowball, who was always bleating beseechingly, and took its head between her hands to comfort it. Even now the child sprang towards it again, for she heard its wailing cry; she put her arm round the little creature's neck, saying, "What ails you, Snowball? Why do you call for help so piteously?"

The animal nestled confidingly against the little girl, and was quiet again; and Peter called out from his seat, explaining Snowball's trouble between each two mouthfuls.

"She does that because her old one does not come with us any more. She was sold to Mayenfeld the day before yesterday, and will not come any more."

"Who is the old one?" asked Heidi.

"Its mother," was the reply.

"Where is the grandmother?" asked the child.

"Has none."

"Or the grandfather?"

"Has none."

"Oh, you poor little Snowball!" said Heidi tenderly, pressing the goat softly to her side. "But now don't cry so any more. I will come every day with you, then you will not be lonely; and if you are feeling very bad you may come to me."

Snowball rubbed her head trustingly on Heidi's shoulder, and bleated no more.

Suddenly the lad sprang to his feet, and was after the goats with great leaps; and Heidi after him, for something must have happened, and she could not stay behind.

Away went Peter through the flock towards the side of the alp, where the rocks rose up steep and naked, and where a heedless goat might easily fall and get its legs broken, while climbing. He saw that the giddy Thistlebird had strayed in that direction, and he ran after her only just in time, for she had reached the very edge of the precipice. As he was about to seize her, he tripped and fell, catching her only by the leg as he came down; but he held her fast, though she bleated with surprise and anger to find herself held, and unable to go on with her frolicsome amusements, while she persisted in pressing forward.

Peter called loudly for Heidi; he was unable to rise, and seemed to himself almost pulling the little goat's leg off, she was so determined to go on. In a trice Heidi was there, saw the danger of his situation and of the goat's. Pulling quickly a sweet-smelling herb, she held it under Thistlebird's nose, saying soothingly, "Come, come, little goat; come and be good, Thistlebird. See, now you might have fallen and broken your leg, and that would have hurt you."

The goat turned quickly about to nibble at the herb held out by Heidi, and was quite content. Peter, having regained his feet, hastened to seize the string that hung from her collar, while Heidi took the collar from the other side; and they led the wanderer between them to rejoin the rest of the flock, which was peaceably feeding below.

Once Peter had his goat in safety again he raised his stick and was about to whip her soundly, while Thistlebird drew back in alarm, for she saw what was coming. Heidi, however, screamed out in terror. "No, Peter, no! You must not strike her. See how frightened she is!"

"She deserves it," said he angrily, and was about to strike, but the child seized him by the arm, calling out, "You must let her alone!"

Her companion stood staring in surprise at her commanding tones and flashing eyes, while he involuntarily dropped his arm, saying, "So, then, she may go, if you will give me some of your cheese to-morrow." He felt that he must have something to console him for his fright.

"You may have it all, to-morrow and every day, for I do not care for it," said Heidi, "and a big piece of bread also, as I gave you to-day. But you must promise me not to strike Thistlebird nor Snowball, nor any of the goats."

"It's all the same to me," said Peter. That was his equivalent for a promise, and he let the offender go. Away sprang the happy goat with great leaps, in amongst the others.

Almost unheeded the day had passed, and now the sun was beginning to sink behind the mountain. Heidi sat quietly on the ground, gazing at the harebells and bluebells, as they shone in the golden light, observing how the grass took a golden hue, and how the rocks above began to shimmer and flash, when suddenly she started to her feet, shouting, "Peter, Peter! it is burning, it is on fire! All the mountains flame, and the great snow yonder, and the sky. Look, look! The highest peak is glowing. Oh, the beautiful fire! Now look, Peter, it has reached the eagle's nest. See the rock! See the pines! Everything burns!"

"It's always like that, but it's no fire," said Peter kindly.

"What is it then? cried Heidi, and ran about in all directions to look; for she could not see enough of it standing still, it was so beautiful everywhere. "What is it, Peter? What is it?" she asked again.

"It comes of itself," explained the lad.

"Look, look now!" she screamed in the wildest excitement. "Just this minute it is all as red as roses. Look at the snow and those high, pointed rocks! What are they called?"

"Mountains have no names," was the answer.

"Oh, the lovely, rosy snow! And all over the rocks are roses. Oh, now they are growing grey! It is going! It has all gone, Peter!"

Little Heidi threw herself on the ground, looking as unhappy as if there were an end to all beauty in the world.

"It will be just so again to-morrow," said the lad. "Get up. We must go home now."

So, whistling the herd together, they set out on their homeward track.

"Will it be so every day, always when we go up to the pasture?" asked the child, longing for an assuring reply, as she descended with the goatherd.

"Generally," he said.

"But certainly to-morrow?"

"Yes, to-morrow, of course."

This promise quieted the child, who had to-day received so many new impressions, and through whose little head such a multitude of thoughts was running, that she scarcely spoke a word until the hut came in sight, and she discerned her grandfather sitting on his bench outside, waiting for the goats.

Then she ran to him quickly, with Schwänli and Bärli at her heels.

Peter called out, "Come again to-morrow. Good night." He was very anxious for Heidi to go again. And the child ran to him, gave him her hand, promising to go to-morrow, and bidding good-bye to the departing goats. She put her arm about the neck of little Snowball, saying, "Good night, Snowball. Sleep well. Don't forget that I am going with you again to-morrow, and you must not bleat so sadly again."

The goat looked at her with friendly eyes, and then sprang joyfully after the others.

Then Heidi came back under the pine-tree, calling out before she could reach her grandfather, "Oh, it was so beautiful! The fire, and the roses on the rock, the blue and yellow flowers. Look what I have brought you."

She shook out all the flowers from her apron, before her grandfather.

But how the poor little flowers looked! The child did not recognize them. They were like hay—not one was open.

"What is the matter with them, grandfather?" cried she, frightened. "They did not look like that when I got them."

"They want to be out in the sun, and not in your little apron," said the old man.

"Then I will not bring any more. But why did the eagle scream so?" she asked anxiously.

"Now you must go and wash yourself, while I go to the goat's stall to fetch the milk. Afterwards we will go into the hut for supper, and then I will answer your questions."

Heidi told him all that had happened during the day: how beautiful it was, and particularly about the fire at sunset, and begged her grandfather to explain it to her, for Peter knew nothing whatever about it.

"Yes," said her grandfather, "the sun does that when he says good-night to the mountains. He casts his most beautiful beams across them, so that they will not forget that he is coming again in the morning."

This pleased the little girl, and she could scarcely wait until the morrow, she was in such haste to go again to see the sun bid good-night to the mountains. But first she must go to sleep. She slept through the whole night soundly in her little hay bed, and dreamed of pink mountains covered with roses, in the midst of which Snowball jumped gaily about.

THE SHEPHERD GIRL OF NANTERRE

By CHARLOTTE M. YONGE

This is the touching story of the pious and fearless shepherd girl Geneviève, who, because of her good deeds and thought for the city she loved, later became the patron saint of Paris. When reading the story of La Esmeralda and Quasimodo, elsewhere in this book, it will be interesting to reflect that the Cathedral of Nôtre-Dame was actually started in Geneviève's lifetime. This story is taken from "A Book of Golden Deeds."

FOUR hundred years of the Roman dominion had entirely tamed the once wild and independent Gauls. Everywhere, except in the moorlands of Brittany, they had become as much like Romans themselves as they could accomplish; they had Latin names, spoke the Latin tongue, all their personages of higher rank were enrolled as Roman citizens, their chief cities were colonies where the laws were administered by magistrates in the Roman fashion, and the houses, dress, and amusements were the same as those of Italy. The greater part of the towns had been converted to Christianity, though some Paganism still lurked in the more remote villages and mountainous districts.

It was upon these civilized Gauls that the terrible attacks came from the wild nations who poured out of the centre and east of Europe. The Franks came over the Rhine and its dependent rivers, and made furious attacks upon the peaceful plains, where the Gauls had long lived in security, and reports were everywhere heard of villages harried by wild horsemen, with short double-headed battle-axes, and a horrible short pike, covered with iron and with several large hooks, like a gigantic artificial minnow, and like it fastened to a long rope, so that the prey which it had grappled might be pulled up to the owner. Walled cities usually stopped them, but every farm or villa outside was stripped of its valuables, set on fire, the cattle driven off, and the more healthy inhabitants seized for slaves.

It was during this state of things that a girl was born to a wealthy peasant at the village now called Nanterre, about two miles from Lutetia, which was already a prosperous city, though not as yet so entirely the capital as it was destined to become under the name of Paris. She was christened by an old Gallic name, probably Gwenfrewi, or White Stream, in Latin Genovefa, but she is best known by the late French form of Geneviève. When she was about seven years old two celebrated bishops passed through the village, Germanus, of Auxerre, and Lupus, of Troyes, who had been invited to Britain to dispute the false doctrine of Pelagius. All the inhabitants flocked into the church to see them, pray with them, and receive their blessing; and here the sweet childish devotion of Geneviève so struck Germanus that he called her to him, talked to her, made her sit beside him at the feast, gave her his especial blessing, and presented her with a copper medal with a cross engraven upon it. From that time the little maiden always deemed herself especially consecrated to the service of Heaven, but she still remained at home, daily keeping her father's sheep, and spinning their wool as she sat under the trees watching them, but always with a heart full of prayer.

After this St. Germanus proceeded to Britain, and there encouraged his converts to meet the heathen Picts at Maes Garmon, in Flintshire, where the exulting shout of the white-robed catechumens turned to flight the wild superstitious savages of the north—and the Hallelujah victory was gained without a drop of bloodshed. He never lost sight of Geneviève, the little maid whom he had so early distinguished for her piety.

After she lost her parents she went to live with her godmother, and continued the same simple habits, leading a life of sincere devotion and strict self-denial, constant prayer, and much charity to her poorer neighbours.

In the year 451 the whole of Gaul was in the most dreadful state of terror at the advance of Attila, the savage chief of the Huns, who came from the banks of the Danube with a host of savages of hideous features, scarred and disfigured to render them more frightful. The old enemies, the Goths and the Franks, seemed like friends compared with these formidable beings, whose cruelties were said to be intolerable, and of whom every exaggerated story was told that could add to the horrors of the miserable people who lay in

their path. Tidings came that this "Scourge of God," as Attila called himself, had passed the Rhine, destroyed Tongres and Metz, and was in full march for Paris. The whole country was in the utmost terror. Every one seized their most valuable possessions, and would have fled; but Geneviève placed herself on the only bridge across the Seine, and argued with them, assuring them, in a strain that was afterwards thought of as prophetic, that, if they would pray, repent, and defend instead of abandoning their homes, God would protect them. They were at first almost ready to stone her for thus withstanding their panic, but just then a priest arrived from Auxerre, with a present for Geneviève from St. Germanus, and they were thus reminded of the high estimation in which he held her; they became ashamed of their violence, and she led them back to pray and to arm themselves. In a few days they heard that Attila had paused to besiege Orleans, and that Aëtius, the Roman general, hurrying from Italy, had united his troops with those of the Goths and Franks, and given Attila so terrible a defeat at Chalons that the Huns were fairly driven out of Gaul. And here it must be mentioned that when the next year, 452, Attila with his murderous host came down into Italy, and after horrible devastation of all the northern provinces, came to the gates of Rome, no one dared to meet him but one venerable Bishop, Leo, the Pope, who, when his flock were in transports of despair, went forth only accompanied by one magistrate to meet the invader, and endeavour to turn his wrath aside. The savage Huns were struck with awe by the fearless majesty of the unarmed old man. They conducted him safely to Attila, who listened to him with respect, and promised not to lead his people into Rome, provided a tribute should be paid to him. He then retreated, and, to the joy of all Europe, died on his way back to his native dominions.

But with the Huns the danger and suffering of Europe did not end. The happy state described in the Prophets as "dwelling safely, with none to make them afraid," was utterly unknown in Europe throughout the long break-up of the Roman Empire; and in a few more years the Franks were overrunning the banks of the Seine, and actually venturing to lay seige to the Roman walls of Paris itself. The fortifications were strong enough, but hunger began to do the work of the besiegers, and the garrison, unwarlike and untrained, began to despair. But Geneviève's courage and trust never failed; and finding no warriors willing to run the risk of going beyond the walls to obtain food for the women and children who were perishing around them, this brave shepherdess embarked alone in a little boat, and guiding it down the stream, landed beyond the Frankish camp, and repairing to the different Gallic cities, she implored them to send succour to their famished brethren. She obtained complete success. Probably the Franks had no means of obstructing the passage of the river, so that a convoy of boats could easily penetrate into the town, and at any rate they looked upon Geneviève as something sacred and inspired whom they durst not touch; probably as one of the battle-maids in whom their own myths taught them to believe. One account indeed says that, instead of going alone to obtain help, Geneviève placed herself at the head of a forage party, and that the mere sight of her inspired bearing caused them to be allowed to enter and return in safety; but the boat version seems the more probable, since a single boat on the broad river would more easily elude the enemy than a troop of Gauls pass through their army.

But a city where all the valour resided in one woman could not long hold out, and in another inroad, when Geneviève was absent, Paris was actually seized by the Franks. Their leader, Hilperik, was absolutely afraid of what the mysteriously brave maiden might do to him, and commanded the gates of the city to be carefully guarded lest she should enter; but Geneviève learnt that some of the chief citizens were imprisoned, and that Hilperik intended their death, and nothing could withhold her from making an effort in their behalf. The Franks had made up their minds to settle, and not to destroy. They were not burning and slaying indiscriminately, but while despising the Romans, as they called the Gauls, for their cowardice, they were in awe of their superior civilization and knowledge of arts. The country people had free access to the city, and Geneviève in her homely gown and veil passed by Hilperik's guards without being suspected of being more than any ordinary Gaulish village maid; and thus she fearlessly made her way, even to the old Roman halls, where the long-haired Hilperik was holding his wild carousal. Would that we knew more of that interview—one of the most striking that ever took place! We can only picture to ourselves the Roman tesselated pavement bestrewn with wine, bones, and fragments of the barbarous revelry. There were untamed Franks, their sunburnt hair tied up in a knot at the top of their heads, and falling down like a horse's tail, their faces close shaven, except two huge moustaches, and dressed in tight leather garments, with swords at their wide belts. Some slept, some feasted, some greased their long locks, some shouted out their favourite war songs around the table, which was covered with the spoils of churches, and at their head sat the wild, long-haired chieftain, who was a few years later driven away by his own followers for his excesses—the whole scene was all that was abhorrent to a pure, devout, and faithful nature, most full of terror to a woman. Yet there, in her strength, stood the peasant maiden, her heart full of trust and pity, her looks full of the power that is given by fearlessness of them that can kill the body. What she said we do not know—we only know that the barbarous Hilperik was overawed; he trembled before the expostulations of the brave woman, and granted all she asked—the safety of his prisoners, and mercy to the terrified inhabitants. No wonder that the people of Paris have ever since looked back to Geneviève as their protectress, and that in after ages she has grown to be the patron saint of the city.

She lived to see the son of Hilperik, Chlodweh, or, as he was more commonly called, Clovis, marry a Christian wife, Clotilda, and after a time become a Christian. She saw the foundation of the Cathedral of Nôtre-Dame, and of the two famous Churches of St. Denys and of St. Martin of Tours, and gave her full share to the first efforts for bringing the rude and bloodthirsty conquerors to some knowledge of Christian faith, mercy, and purity. After a life of constant prayer and charity she died, three months after King Clovis, in the year 512, the eighty-ninth of her age.

CHILDE CHARITY

By FRANCES BROWNE

This is one of the unusual stories told in "Granny's Wonderful Chair." Childe Charity was kind to the morose old woman and took care of her ugly-looking dog with the vicious temper, and so she was rewarded by the fairy folk, who, according to all writers of such tales, have good memories and always settle their just debts to mere humans.

ONCE upon a time there lived in the West Country a little girl who had neither father nor mother; they both died when she was very young, and left their daughter to the care of her uncle, who was the richest farmer in all that country. He had houses and lands, flocks and herds, many servants to work about his house and fields, a wife who had brought him a great dowry, and two fair daughters. All their neighbours, being poor, looked up to the family—insomuch that they imagined themselves great people. The father and mother were as proud as peacocks, the daughters thought themselves the greatest beauties in the world, and not one of the family would speak civilly to anybody they thought low.

Now it happened that though she was their near relation, they had this opinion of the orphan girl, partly because she had no fortune, and partly because of her humble, kindly disposition. It was said that the more needy and despised any creature was, the more ready was she to befriend it: on which account the people of the West Country called her Childe Charity, and if she had any other name, I never heard it. Childe Charity was thought very mean in that proud house. Her uncle would not own her for his niece; her cousins would not keep her company; and her aunt sent her to work in the dairy, and to sleep in the back garret, where they kept all sorts of lumber and dry herbs for the winter. All the servants learned the same tune, and Childe Charity had more work than rest among them. All the day she scoured pails, scrubbed dishes, and slept in the back garret as sound as a princess could in her palace chamber.

Her uncle's house was large and white, and stood among green meadows by a river's side. In front it had a porch covered with a vine; behind, it had a farmyard and high granaries. Within, there were two parlours for the rich, and two kitchens for the poor, which the neighbours thought wonderfully grand; and one day in the harvest season, when this rich farmer's corn had been all cut down and housed, he condescended so far as to invite them to a harvest supper. The West Country people came in their holiday clothes and best behaviour. Such heaps of cakes and cheese, such baskets of apples and barrels of ale, had never been at feast before; and they were making merry in kitchen and parlour, when a poor old woman came to the back door, begging for broken victuals and a night's lodging. Her clothes were coarse and ragged; her hair was scanty and grey; her back was bent; her teeth were gone. She had a squinting eye, a clubbed foot, and crooked fingers. In short, she was the poorest and ugliest old woman that ever came begging. The first who saw her was the kitchen-maid, and she ordered her to be gone for an ugly witch. The next was the herd-boy, and he threw her a bone over his shoulder; but Childe Charity, hearing the noise, came out from her seat at the foot of the lowest table, and asked the old woman to take her share of the supper, and sleep that night in her bed in the back garret. The old woman sat down without a word of thanks. All the company laughed at Childe Charity for giving her bed and her supper to a beggar. Her proud cousins said it was just like her mean spirit, but Childe Charity did not mind them. She scraped the pots for her supper that night and slept on a sack among the lumber, while the old woman rested in her warm bed; and next morning, before the little girl awoke, she was up and gone, without so much as saying thank you, or good morning.

That day all the servants were sick after the feast, and mostly cross too—so you may judge how civil they were, when, at supper time, who should come to the back door but the old woman, again asking for broken victuals and a night's lodging. No one would listen to her or give her a morsel, till Childe Charity rose from her seat at the foot of the lowest table and kindly asked her to take her supper, and sleep in her bed in the back garret. Again the old woman sat down without a word. Childe Charity scraped the pots for her supper and slept on the sack. In the morning the old woman was gone; but for six nights after, as sure as the supper was spread, there was she at the back door, and the little girl regularly asked her in.

Childe Charity's aunt said she would let her get enough of beggars. Her cousins made continual game of what they called her genteel visitor. Sometimes the old woman said, "Child, why don't you make this bed softer? And why are your blankets so thin?" but she never gave her a word of thanks nor a civil good morning. At last, on the ninth night from her first coming, when Childe Charity was getting used to scrape the pots and sleep on the sack, her accustomed knock came to the door, and there she stood with an ugly ashy-coloured dog, so stupid-looking and clumsy that no herd-boy would keep him.

"Good evening, my little girl," she said when Childe Charity opened the door. "I will not have your supper and bed to-night—I am going on a long journey to see a friend; but here is a dog of mine, whom nobody in all the West Country will keep for me. He is a little cross, and not very handsome; but I leave him to your care till the shortest day in all the year. Then you and I will count for his keeping."

When the old woman had said the last word she set off with such speed that Childe Charity lost sight of her in a minute. The ugly dog began to fawn upon her, but he snarled at everybody else. The servants said he was a disgrace to the house. The proud cousins wanted him drowned, and it was with great trouble that Childe Charity got leave to keep him in an old ruined cow-house. Ugly and cross as the dog was, he fawned on her, and the old woman had left him to her care. So the little girl gave him part of all her meals, and when the hard frost came took him privately to her own back garret, because the cow-house was damp and cold in the long nights. The dog lay quietly on some straw in a corner. Childe Charity slept soundly, but every morning the servants would say to her:

"What great light and fine talking was that in your back garret?"

"There was no light but the moon shining in through the shutterless window, and no talk that I heard," said Childe Charity, and she thought they must have been dreaming; but night after night, when any of them awoke in the dark and silent hour that comes before the morning, they saw a light brighter and clearer than the Christmas fire, and heard voices like those of lords and ladies in the back garret.

Partly from fear, and partly from laziness, none of the servants would rise to see what might be there; till at length, when the winter nights were at the longest, the little parlour-maid, who did least work and got most favour, because she gathered news for her mistress, crept out of bed when all the rest were sleeping, and set herself to watch at a crevice of the door. She saw the dog lying quietly in the corner, Childe Charity sleeping soundly in her bed, and the moon shining through the shutterless window; but an hour before daybreak there came a glare of lights, and a sound of far-off bugles. The window opened, and in marched a troop of little men clothed in crimson and gold, and bearing every man a torch, till the room looked bright as day. They marched up with great reverence to the dog, where he lay on the straw, and the most richly clothed among them said:

"Royal prince, we have prepared the banquet hall. What will Your Highness please that we do next?"

"Ye have done well," said the dog. "Now prepare the feast, and see that all things be in our first fashion: for the princess and I mean to bring a stranger who never feasted in our halls before."

"Your Highness's commands shall be obeyed," said the little man, making another reverence; and he and his company passed out of the window. By and by there was another glare of lights, and a sound like far-off flutes. The window opened, and there came in a company of little ladies clad in rose-coloured velvet, and carrying each a crystal lamp. They also walked with great reverence up to the dog, and the gayest among them said:

"Royal prince, we have prepared the tapestry. What will Your Highness please that we do next?"

"Ye have done well," said the dog. "Now prepare the robes, and let all things be in our first fashion: for the princess and I will bring with us a stranger who never feasted in our halls before."

"Your Highness's commands shall be obeyed," said the little lady, making a low courtesy; and she and her company passed out through the window, which closed quietly behind them. The dog stretched himself out upon the straw, the little girl turned in her sleep, and the moon shone in on the back garret. The parlour-maid was so much amazed, and so eager to tell this great story to her mistress, that she could not close her eyes that night, and was up before cock-crow; but when she told it her mistress called her a silly wench to have such foolish dreams, and scolded her so that the parlour-maid durst not mention what she had seen to the servants. Nevertheless, Childe Charity's aunt thought there might be something in it worth knowing; so next night, when all the house were asleep, she crept out of bed and set herself to watch at the back garret door. There she saw exactly what the maid told her—the little men with the torches, and the little ladies with the crystal lamps, come in making great reverence to the dog, and the same words passed, only he said to the one, "Now prepare the presents," and to the other, "Prepare the jewels"; and when they were gone the dog stretched himself on the straw, Childe Charity turned in her sleep, and the moon shone in on the back garret.

The mistress could not close her eyes any more than the maid from eagerness to tell the story. She woke up Childe Charity's rich uncle before cock-crow; but when he heard it he laughed at her for a foolish woman, and advised her not to repeat the like before the neighbours, lest they should think she had lost her senses. The mistress could say no more, and the day passed; but that night the master thought he would like to see what went on in the back garret: so when all the house were asleep he slipped out of bed, and set himself to watch at the crevice in the door. The same thing happened again that the maid and the mistress saw: the little men in crimson with their torches, and the little ladies in rose-coloured velvet with their lamps, came in at the window, and made an humble reverence to the ugly dog, the one saying, "Royal prince, we have prepared the presents," and the other, "Royal prince, we have prepared the jewels"; and the dog said to them all, "Ye have done well. To-morrow come and meet me and the princess with horses and chariots, and let all things be in our first fashion: for we will bring a stranger from this house who has never travelled with us, nor feasted in our halls before."

The little men and the little ladies said, "Your Highness's commands shall be obeyed." When they had gone out through the window the ugly dog stretched himself out on the straw, Childe

Charity turned in her sleep, and the moon shone in on the back garret.

The master could not close his eyes any more than the maid or the mistress, for thinking of this strange sight. He remembered to have heard his grandfather say that somewhere near his meadows there lay a path leading to the fairies' country, and the haymakers used to see it shining through the grey summer morning as the fairy bands went home. Nobody had heard or seen the like for many years; but the master concluded that the doings in his back garret must be a fairy business, and the ugly dog a person of great account. His chief wonder was, however, what visitor the fairies intended to take from his house; and after thinking the matter over he was sure it must be one of his daughters—they were so handsome, and had such fine clothes.

Accordingly Childe Charity's rich uncle made it his first business that morning to get ready a breakfast of roast mutton for the ugly dog, and carry it to him in the old cow-house; but not a morsel would the dog taste. On the contrary, he snarled at the master, and would have bitten him if he had not run away with his mutton.

"The fairies have strange ways," said the master to himself; but he called his daughters privately, bidding them dress themselves in their best, for he could not say which of them might be called into great company before nightfall. Childe Charity's proud cousins, hearing this, put on the richest of their silks and laces, and strutted like peacocks from kitchen to parlour all day, waiting for the call their father spoke of, while the little girl scoured and scrubbed in the dairy. They were in very bad humour when night fell, and nobody had come; but just as the family were sitting down to supper the ugly dog began to bark, and the old woman's knock was heard at the back door. Childe Charity opened it, and was going to offer her bed and supper as usual when the old woman said:

"This is the shortest day in all the year, and I am going home to hold a feast after my travels. I see you have taken good care of my dog, and now if you will come with me to my house he and I will do our best to entertain you. Here is our company."

As the old woman spoke there was a sound of far-off flutes and bugles, then a glare of lights; and a great company, clad so grandly that they shone with gold and jewels, came in open chariots, covered with gilding and drawn by snow-white horses. The first and finest of the chariots was empty. The old woman led Childe Charity to it by the hand, and the ugly dog jumped in before her. The proud cousins, in all their finery, had by this time come to the door, but nobody wanted them; and no sooner was the old woman and her dog within the chariot than a marvellous change passed over them, for the ugly old woman turned at once to a beautiful young princess, with long yellow curls and a robe of green and gold, while the ugly dog at her side started up a fair young prince, with nut-brown hair and a robe of purple and silver.

"We are," said they, as the chariots drove on, and the little girl sat astonished, "a prince and princess of Fairyland, and there was a wager between us whether or not there were good people still to be found in these false and greedy times. One said Yes, and the other said No; and I have lost," said the prince, "and must pay the feast and presents."

Childe Charity never heard any more of that story. Some of the farmer's household, who were looking after them through the moonlight night, said the chariots had gone one way across the meadows, some said they had gone another, and till this day they cannot agree upon the direction. But Childe Charity went with that noble company into a country such as she had never seen—for primroses covered all the ground, and the light was always like that of a summer evening. They took her to a royal palace, where there was nothing but feasting and dancing for seven days. She had robes of pale green velvet to wear, and slept in a chamber inlaid with ivory. When the feast was done the prince and princess gave her such heaps of gold and jewels that she could not carry them, but they gave her a chariot to go home in, drawn by six white horses; and on the seventh night, which happened to be Christmas time, when the farmer's family had settled in their own minds that she would never come back, and were sitting down to supper, they heard the sound of her coachman's bugle, and saw her alight with all the jewels and gold at the very back door where she had brought in the ugly old woman. The fairy chariot drove away, and never came back to that farm-house after. But Childe Charity scrubbed and scoured no more, for she grew a great lady, even in the eyes of her proud cousins.

THE OVAL PORTRAIT

By EDGAR ALLAN POE

This story—or, rather, parable—of the beautiful girl-wife whose portrait was painted in a dark turret chamber in an Apennine castle is told in the author's singularly macabre style. The very point of the story is in the last sentence; and, having read it, the reader is left with a strange feeling of pity for the original of the portrait revealed by the lighted candles in the traveller's hand.

THE château into which my valet had ventured to make forcible entrance, rather than permit me, in my desperately wounded condition, to pass a night in the open air, was one of those piles of commingled gloom and grandeur which have so long frowned among the Apennines. To all appearance it had been temporarily and very lately abandoned. We established ourselves in one of the smallest and least sumptuously furnished apartments. It lay in a remote turret of the building. Its decorations were rich, yet tattered and antique. Its walls were hung with tapestry and bedecked with manifold and multiform armorial trophies, together with an unusually great number of very spirited modern paintings in frames of rich golden arabesque. In these paintings, which depended from the walls not only in their main surfaces, but in very many nooks which the bizarre architecture of the château rendered necessary—in these paintings my incipient delirium, perhaps, had caused me to take deep interest; so that I bade Pedro to close the heavy shutters of the room—since it was already night—to light the tongues of a tall candelabrum which stood by the head of my bed, and to throw open far and wide the fringed curtains of black velvet which enveloped the bed itself. I wished all this done that I might resign myself, if not to sleep, at least alternately to the contemplation of these pictures, and the perusal of a small volume which had been found upon the pillow, and which purported to criticize and describe them.

Long, long I read—and devoutly, devoutly I gazed. Rapidly and gloriously the hours flew by and the deep midnight came. The position of the candelabrum displeased me, and outreaching my hand with difficulty, rather than disturb my slumbering valet, I placed it so as to throw its rays more fully upon the book.

But the action produced an effect altogether unanticipated. The rays of the numerous candles (for there were many) now fell within a niche of the room which had hitherto been thrown into deep shade by one of the bedposts. I thus saw in vivid light a picture all unnoticed before. It was the portrait of a young girl just ripening into womanhood. I glanced at the painting hurriedly, and then closed my eyes. Why I did this was not at first apparent even to my own perception. But while my lids remained thus shut, I ran over in my mind my reason for so shutting them. It was an impulsive movement to gain time for thought—to make sure that my vision had not deceived me—to calm and subdue my fancy for a more sober and more certain gaze. In a very few moments I again looked fixedly at the picture.

That I now saw aright I could and would not doubt; for the first flashing of the candles upon that canvas had seemed to dissipate the dreamy stupor which was stealing over my senses, and to startle me at once into waking life.

The portrait, I have already said, was that of a young girl. It was a mere head and shoulders, done in what is technically called a *vignette* manner; much in the style of the favourite heads of Sully. The arms, the bosom, and even the ends of the radiant hair melted imperceptibly into the vague yet deep shadow which formed the background of the whole. The frame was oval, richly gilded and filigreed in *Moresque*. As a thing of art, nothing could be more admirable than the painting itself. But it could have been neither the execution of the work, nor the immortal beauty of the countenance, which had so suddenly and so vehemently moved me. Least of all, could it have been that my fancy, shaken from its half slumber, had mistaken the head for that of a living person. I saw at once that the peculiarities of the design, of the *vignetting*, and of the frame, must have instantly dispelled such idea—must have prevented even its momentary entertainment. Thinking earnestly upon these points, I remained, for an hour perhaps, half sitting, half reclining, with my vision riveted upon the portrait. At length, satisfied with the true secret of its effect, I fell back within the bed. I had found the spell of the picture in an absolute *life-likeliness* of expression, which, at first startling, finally confounded, subdued, and appalled me. With deep and reverent awe I replaced the candelabrum in its former position. The cause of my deep agitation being thus shut from view, I sought eagerly the volume which dis-

cussed the paintings and their histories. Turning to the number which designated the oval portrait, I there read the vague and quaint words which follow:

"She was a maiden of rarest beauty, and not more lovely than full of glee. And evil was the hour when she saw, and loved, and wedded the painter. He, passionate, studious, austere, and having already a bride in his Art: she a maiden of rarest beauty, and not more lovely than full of glee; all light and smiles, and frolicsome as the young fawn; loving and cherishing all things; hating only the Art which was her rival; dreading only the palette and brushes and other untoward instruments which deprived her of the countenance of her lover. It was thus a terrible thing for this lady to hear the painter speak of his desire to portray even his young bride. But she was humble and obedient, and sat meekly for many weeks in the dark high turret-chamber where the light dripped upon the pale canvas only from overhead. But he, the painter, took glory in his work, which went on from hour to hour, and from day to day. And he was a passionate, and wild, and moody man, who became lost in reveries; so that he *would* not see that the light which fell so ghastly in that lone turret withered the health and the spirits of his bride, who pined visibly to all but him. Yet she smiled on and still on, uncomplainingly, because she saw that the painter (who had high renown) took a fervid and burning pleasure in his task, and wrought day and night to depict her who so loved him, yet who grew daily more dispirited and weak. And in sooth some who beheld the portrait spoke of its resemblance in low words, as of a mighty marvel, and a proof not less of the power of the painter than of his deep love for her whom he depicted so surpassingly well. But at length, as the labour drew nearer to its conclusion, there were admitted none into the turret; for the painter had grown wild with the ardour of his work, and turned his eyes from the canvas rarely, even to regard the countenance of his wife. And he *would* not see that the tints which he spread upon the canvas were drawn from the cheeks of her who sat beside him. And when many weeks had passed, and but little remained to do, save one brush upon the mouth and one tint upon the eye, the spirit of the lady again flickered up as the flame within the socket of the lamp. And then the brush was given, and then the tint was placed; and, for one moment, the painter stood entranced before the work which he had wrought; but in the next, while he yet gazed, he grew tremulous and very pallid, and aghast, and crying with a loud voice, 'This is indeed *Life* itself!' turned suddenly to regard his beloved: *She was dead*!"

MEETING ON OLIVET

By LEW WALLACE

Amrah, the old servant of Ben-hur's family, discovers that her mistress and the latter's daughter Tirzah have contracted leprosy and are forced to live in a leper colony outside Jerusalem. Nevertheless, she goes to them with wonderful news, that a Healer is going among the people. She is with them later when the mother and daughter call to Christ for aid and are healed. Ben-Hur himself is in the multitude. In Rome he has prospered, and has now returned to his homeland. The miracle is completed when he recognizes in the leper women his mother and sister—healed. This story is from "Ben-Hur."

THE first person to go out of the city upon the opening of the Sheep's Gate next morning was Amrah, basket on arm. No questions were asked her by the keepers, since the morning itself had not been more regular in coming than she; they knew her somebody's faithful servant, and that was enough for them.

Down the eastern valley she took her way. The side of Olivet, darkly green, was spotted with white tents recently put up by people attending the feasts; the hour, however, was too early for the strangers to be abroad; still, had it not been so, no one would have troubled her. Past Gethsemane; past the tombs at the meeting of the Bethany roads; past the sepulchral village of Siloam she went. Occasionally the decrepit little body staggered; once she sat down to get her breath; rising shortly, she struggled on with renewed haste. The great rocks on either hand, if they had had ears, might have heard her mutter to herself; could they have seen, it would have been to observe how frequently she looked up over the mount, reproving the dawn for its promptness; if it had been possible for them to gossip, not improbably they would have said to each other, "Our friend is in a hurry this morning; the mouths she goes to feed must be very hungry."

When at last she reached the King's garden, she slackened her gait; for then the grim city of the lepers was in view, extending far round the pitted south hill of Hinnom.

She was going to her mistress.

Early as it was, the unhappy woman was up and sitting outside, leaving Tirzah asleep within. The course of the malady had been terribly swift in the three years. Conscious of her appearance, with the refined instincts of her nature, she kept her whole person habitually covered. Seldom as possible she permitted even Tirzah to see her.

This morning she was taking the air with bared head, knowing there was no one to be shocked by the exposure. The light was not full, but enough to show the ravages to which she had been subject.

While she sat there peopling the dusky solitude with thoughts even more cheerless, suddenly a woman came up the hill staggering and spent with exertion.

The widow arose hastily, and covering her head, cried, in a voice unnaturally harsh, "Unclean, unclean!"

In a moment, heedless of the notice, Amrah was at her feet. All the long-pent love of the simple creature burst forth; with tears and passionate exclamations she kissed her mistress's garments, and for a while the latter strove to escape from her; then seeing she could not, she waited till the violence of the paroxysm was over.

"What have you done, Amrah?" she said. "Is it by such disobedience you prove your love for us? Wicked woman! You are lost; and he—your master—you can never, never go back to him."

Amrah grovelled sobbing in the dust.

"The ban of the law is upon you, too; you cannot return to Jerusalem. What will become of us? Who will bring us bread? O wicked, wicked Amrah! We are all, all undone alike!"

"Mercy, mercy!" Amrah answered from the ground.

"You should have been merciful to yourself, and by so doing been most merciful to us. Now where can we fly? There is no one to help us. O false servant! The wrath of the Lord was already too heavy upon us."

Here Tirzah, awakened by the noise, appeared at the door of the tomb. The pen shrinks from the picture she presented.

Amrah rose to her knees, and said, brokenly and with clasped hands, "O good mistress! I am not false—I am not wicked. I bring you good tidings. There is a wonderful man who has power to cure you. He speaks a word, and the sick are made well, and even the dead come to life. I have come to take you to him."

The elder listener was silent again. The skeleton hand shook. We may believe she was struggling to give the story the sanction of faith, and that it was with her as with the men of the day, eye-witnesses of what was done by the Christ, as well as the myriads who have succeeded them. She did not question the performance, but she strove to comprehend the power by which work so astonishing could be done by a man. To Tirzah she said: "This must be the Messiah! Yes," she said to Amrah, "we will go with you. Bring the water which you will find in a jar, and set the food for us. We will eat and be gone."

The breakfast, partaken under excitement, was soon dispatched, and the three women set out on their extraordinary journey. Bethany, Amrah said, was the town the man was coming from.

Tirzah had been walking with great difficulty. Upon reaching the road she fell down exhausted.

"Go on with Amrah, Mother, and leave me here," she said, faintly.

"No, no, Tirzah. What would the gain be to me if I were healed and not you?"

The elder leper arose from bending over the fainting sufferer, and gazed about her with that sensation of hope perishing which is more nearly like annihilation of the soul than anything else. The supremest joy of the thought of cure was inseparable from Tirzah, who was not too old to forget, in the happiness of healthful life to come, the years of misery by which she had been so reduced in body and broken in spirit. Even as the brave woman was about leaving the venture they were engaged in to the determination of God, she saw a man on foot coming rapidly up the road from the east.

"Courage, Tirzah! Be of cheer," she said. "Yonder I know is one to tell us of the Nazarene."

Amrah helped the girl to a sitting posture, and supported her while the man advanced.

"In your goodness, Mother, you forget what we are. The stranger will go around us; his best gift to us will be a curse, if not a stone."

"We will see."

There was no other answer to be given, since the mother was too well and sadly acquainted with the treatment outcasts of the class to which she belonged were accustomed to at the hands of her countrymen. Uncovering her head, a further demand of the law, she shouted shrilly:

"Unclean, unclean!"

To her surprise, the man came steadily on.

"What would you have?" he asked, stopping opposite them not four yards off.

"Thou seest us. Have a care," the mother said, with dignity.

"Woman, I am the courier of Him who speaketh but once to such as thou and they are healed. I am not afraid."

"The Nazarene?"

"The Messiah," he said.

"Is it true that He cometh to the city to-day?"

"He is now at Bethphage."

"On what road, master?"

"This one."

She clasped her hands, and looked up thankfully.

"For whom takest thou Him?" the man asked, with pity.

"The Son of God," she replied.

"Stay thou here then; or, as there is a multitude with Him, take thy stand by the rock yonder, the white one under the tree; and as He goeth by fail not to call to Him; call, and fear not. If thy faith but equal thy knowledge, He will hear thee though all the heavens thunder. I go to tell Israel, assembled in and about the city, that He is at hand, and to make ready to receive Him. Peace to thee and thine, woman."

The stranger moved on.

"Did you hear, Tirzah? Did you hear? The Nazarene is on the road, on this one, and He will hear us. Once more, my child— oh, only once! and let us to the rock. It is but a step."

Thus encouraged Tirzah took Amrah's hand and arose; but as they were going, Amrah said, "Stay, the man is returning." And they waited for him.

"I pray your grace, woman," he said, upon overtaking them. "Remembering that the sun will be hot before the Nazarene arrives, and that the city is near by to give me refreshment should I need it, I thought this water would do thee better than it will me. Take it and be of good cheer. Call to Him as He passes."

He followed the words by offering her a gourd full of water, such as foot-travellers sometimes carried with them in their journeys across the hills; and instead of placing the gift on the ground for her to take up when he was at a safe distance, he gave it into her hand.

"Art thou a Jew?" she asked, surprised.

"I am that, and better; I am a disciple of the Christ who teacheth daily by word and example this thing which I have done unto you. The world hath long known the word charity without understanding it. Again I say peace and good cheer to thee and thine."

He went on, and they went slowly to the rock he had pointed out to them, high as their heads, and scarcely thirty yards from the road on the right. Standing in front of it, the mother satisfied herself they could be seen and heard plainly by passers-by whose notice they desired to attract. There they cast themselves under the tree in its shade, and drank of the gourd, and rested refreshed. Ere long Tirzah slept, and fearing to disturb her, the others held their peace.

During the third hour the road in front of the resting-place of the lepers became gradually more and more frequented by people going in the direction of Bethphage and Bethany; now, however, about the commencement of the fourth hour, a great crowd appeared over the crest of Olivet, and as it defiled down the road thousands in number, the two watchers noticed with wonder that every one in it carried a palm-branch freshly cut. As they sat absorbed by the novelty, the noise of another multitude approaching from the east drew their eyes that way. Then the mother awoke Tirzah.

"What is the meaning of it all?" the latter asked.

"He is coming," answered the mother. "These we see are from the city going to meet Him; those we hear in the east are His friends bearing Him company; and it will not be strange if the processions meet here before us."

Meantime the people in the east came up slowly. When at length the foremost of them were in sight, the gaze of the lepers fixed upon a man riding in the midst of what seemed a chosen company which sang and danced about Him in extravagance of joy. The riden was bareheaded and clad all in white. When He was in distance to be more clearly observed, these, looking anxiously, saw an olive-hued face shaded by long chestnut hair slightly sunburned and parted in the middle. He looked neither to the right nor left. In the noisy abandon of His followers He appeared to have no part; nor did their favour disturb Him in the least, or raise Him out of the profound melancholy into which, as His countenance showed, He was plunged. The sun beat upon the back of His head, and lighting up the floating hair gave it a delicate likeness to a golden nimbus. Behind Him the irregular procession, pouring forward with continuous singing and shouting, extended out of view. There was no need of anyone to tell the lepers that this was He—the wonderful Nazarene!

"He is here, Tirzah," the mother said, "He is here. Come, my child."

As she spoke she glided in front of the white rock and fell upon her knees.

Directly the daughter and servant were by her side. Then at sight of the procession in the west, the thousands from the city halted, and began to wave their green branches, shouting, or rather chanting (for it was all in one voice):

"Blessed is the King of Israel that cometh in the name of the Lord!"

And all the thousands who were of the rider's company, both those near and those afar, replied, so the air shook with the sound, which was as a great wind threshing the side of the hill. Amidst the din the cries of the poor lepers were not more than the twittering of dazed sparrows.

The moment of the meeting of the hosts was come, and with it the opportunity the sufferers were seeking; if not taken, it would be lost for ever, and they would be lost as well.

"Nearer, my child—let us get nearer. He cannot hear us," said the mother.

She arose, and staggered forward. Her ghastly hands were up, and she screamed with horrible shrillness. The people saw her—saw her hideous face, and stopped awe-struck—an effect for which extreme human misery, visible as in this instance, is as potent as majesty in purple and gold. Tirzah, behind her a little way, fell down, too faint and frightened to follow farther.

"The lepers! The lepers!"

"Stone them!"

"The accursed of God! Kill them!"

These, with other yells of like import, broke in upon the hosannas of the part of the multitude too far removed to see and understand the cause of the interruption. Some there were, however, near by, familiar with the nature of the man to whom the unfortunates were appealing—some who, by long intercourse with Him, had caught somewhat of His divine compassion: they gazed at Him, and were silent while, in fair view, He rode up and stopped in front of the woman. She also beheld His face—calm, pitiful, and of exceeding beauty, the large eyes tender with benignant purpose.

And this was the colloquy that ensued:

"O Master, Master! Thou seest our need; Thou canst make us clean. Have mercy upon us—mercy!"

"Believest thou I am able to do this?" He asked.

"Thou art He of whom the prophets spake—Thou art the Messiah!" she replied.

His eyes grew radiant, His manner confident.

"Woman," He said, "great is thy faith; be it unto thee even as thou wilt."

He lingered an instant after, apparently unconscious of the presence of the throng—an instant—then He rode away.

Immediately both the hosts, that from the city and that from Bethphage, closed around Him with their joyous demonstrations, with hosannas and waving of palms, and so He passed from the lepers for ever. Covering her head, the elder hastened to Tirzah, and folded her in her arms, crying, "Daughter, look up! I have His promise; He is indeed the Messiah. We are saved—saved!" And the two remained kneeling while the procession, slowly going, disappeared over the mount. When the noise of its singing afar was a sound scarcely heard the miracle began.

There was first in the hearts of the lepers a freshening of the blood; then it flowed faster and stronger, thrilling their wasted bodies with an infinitely sweet sense of painless healing. Each felt the scourge going from her; their strength revived; they were returning to themselves. Directly, as if to make the purification complete, from body to spirit the quickening ran, exalting them to a very fervour of ecstasy. The power possessing them to this good end was most nearly that of a draught of swift and happy effect; yet it was unlike and superior in that its healing and cleansing were absolute, and not merely a delicious consciousness while in progress, but the planting, growing, and maturing all at once of a recollection so singular and so holy that the simple thought of it should be of itself ever after a formless yet perfect thanksgiving.

To this transformation—for such it may be called quite as properly as a cure—there was a witness other than Amrah. Ben-Hur had followed the Nazarene throughout His wanderings; and the young Jew was present when the leprous woman appeared in the path of the pilgrims. He heard her prayer, and saw her disfigured face; he heard the answer also, and was not so accustomed to incidents of the kind, frequent as they had been, as to have lost interest in them. At the close of the scene, consequently, Ben-Hur had withdrawn from the procession, and crossed the road towards the two women.

As he proceeded, he glanced casually at the figure of the little woman over by the white rock, standing there her face hidden in her hands.

"As the Lord liveth, it is Amrah!" he said to himself.

He hurried on, and passing by the mother and daughter, still without recognizing them, he stopped before the servant.

"Amrah," he said to her, "Amrah, what do you here?"

She rushed forward, and fell upon her knees before him, blinded by her tears, nigh speechless with contending joy and fear.

"O master, master! Thy God and mine, how good He is!"

The knowledge we gain from much sympathy with others passing through trials is but vaguely understood; strangely enough, it enables us, amongst other things, to merge our identity into theirs often so completely that their sorrows and their delights become our own. So poor Amrah, aloof and hiding her face, knew the transformation the lepers were undergoing without a word spoken to her—knew it, and shared all their feeling to the full. Her countenance, her words, her whole manner, betrayed her condition;

and with swift presentiment he connected it with the women he had just passed; he felt her presence there at that time was in some way associated with them, and turned hastily as they arose to their feet. His heart stood still; he became rooted in his tracks—dumb past outcry—awe-struck.

The woman he had seen before the Nazarene was standing with her hands clasped and eyes streaming, looking towards heaven. The mere transformation would have been a sufficient surprise; but it was the least of the causes of his emotion. Could he be mistaken? Never was there in life a stranger so like his mother; and like her as she was the day the Roman snatched her from him. There was but one difference to mar the identity—the hair of this person was a little streaked with grey; yet that was not impossible of reconcilement, since the Intelligence which had directed the miracle might have taken into consideration the natural effect of the passage of years. And who was it by her side, if not Tirzah?—fair, beautiful, perfect, more mature, but in all other respects exactly the same. He had given them over as dead, and time had accustomed him to the bereavement. Scarcely believing his senses, he laid his hand upon the servant's head, and asked tremulously:

"Amrah, Amrah—my mother! Tirzah! tell me if I see aright."

"Speak to them, O master, speak to them!" she said.

He waited no longer, but ran, with outstretched arms, crying, "Mother! mother! Tirzah! Here I am!"

They heard his call, and with a cry as loving started to meet him. Suddenly the mother stopped, drew back, and uttered the old alarm:

"Stay, my son; come not nearer. Unclean, unclean!"

The utterance was not from habit, grown since the dread disease struck her, as much as fear; and the fear was but another form of the ever-thoughtful maternal love. Though they were healed in person, the taint of the scourge might be in their garments ready for communication. He had no such thought. They were before him; he had called them, they had answered. Who or what should keep them from him now? Next moment the three, so long separated, were mingling their tears in each other's arms.

MAGGIE RUNS AWAY

By GEORGE ELIOT

Maggie Tulliver has quarrelled with her brother Tom, and in a mood of unhappy determination has made up her mind to run away and join the first gipsy band she sees. So she sets off across the fields, and after running until her young legs ache at last finds her gipsies. Unfortunately they prove to be very different from what she had imagined, and she is not with them very long before she is wishing to be safely home once more. The story of Maggie and Tom Tulliver is told in "The Mill on the Floss."

MAGGIE'S intentions were on a larger scale than Tom had imagined. She would run away and go to the gipeies, and Tom should never see her any more. That was by no means a new idea to Maggie; she had been so often told she was like a gipsy, and "half wild," that when she was miserable it seemed to her the only way of escaping opprobrium, and being entirely in harmony with circumstances would be to live in a little brown tent on the commons. The gipsies, she considered, would gladly receive her, and pay her much respect on account of her superior knowledge. She had once mentioned her views on this point to Tom, and suggested that he should stain his face brown, and they should run away together; but Tom rejected the scheme with contempt, observing that gipsies were thieves, and hardly got anything to eat, and had nothing to drive but a donkey. To-day, however, Maggie thought her misery had reached a pitch at which gipsydom was her only refuge, and she rose from her seat on the roots of the tree with the sense that this was a great crisis in her life; she would run straight away till she came to Dunlow Common, where there would certainly be gipsies; and cruel Tom should never see her any more. She thought of her father as she ran along, but she reconciled herself to the idea of parting with him by determining that she would secretly send him a letter by a small gipsy, who would run away without telling where she was, and just let him know that she was well and happy, and always loved him very much.

Maggie soon got out of breath with running. She stopped to

pant a little, reflecting that running away was not a pleasant thing until one had got quite to the common where the gipsies were, but she was soon aware, not without trembling, that there were two men coming along the lane in front of her, one of them carrying a bundle on a stick over his shoulder. The man with the bundle stopped, and in a half-whining, half-coaxing tone asked her if she had a copper to give a poor man. Maggie had a sixpence in her pocket which she immediately drew out and gave this poor man with a polite smile, hoping he would feel very kindly towards her as a generous person. "That's the only money I've got," she said apologetically. "Thank you, little miss," said the man in a less respectful and grateful tone than Maggie anticipated, and she even observed that he smiled and winked at his companion. She walked on hurriedly, but was aware that the two men were standing still, probably to look after her, and she presently heard them laughing loudly. Suddenly it occurred to her that they might think she was an idiot. Tom had said that her cropped hair made her look like an idiot, and it was too painful an idea to be readily forgotten. Besides, she had no sleeves on—only a cape and a bonnet. It was clear that she was not likely to make a favourable impression on passengers, and she thought she would turn into the fields. She turned through the first gate that was not locked, and felt a delightful sense of privacy in creeping along by the hedgerows, after her recent humiliating encounter. She was used to wandering about the fields by herself, and was less timid than on the highroad. Sometimes she had to climb over high gates, but that was a small evil; she was getting out of reach very fast, and she should probably soon come within sight of Dunlow Common, or at least of some other common, for she had heard her father say that you couldn't go very far without coming to a common. She hoped so, for she was getting rather tired and hungry and until she reached the gipsies there was no definite prospect of bread and butter. At last, however, the green fields came to an end, and Maggie found herself looking through the bars of a gate into a lane with a wide margin of grass on each side of it. She had never seen such a wide lane before, and, without knowing why, it gave her the impression that the common could not be far off; perhaps it was because she saw a donkey with a log to his foot feeding on the grassy margin, for she had seen a donkey with that pitiable encumbrance on Dunlow Common when she had been across it in her father's gig. She crept through the bars of the gate and walked on with new spirit. It was not without a leaping of the heart that she caught sight of a small pair of bare legs sticking up, feet uppermost, by the side of a hillock; they seemed something hideously preternatural—a diabolical kind of fungus; for she was too much agitated at the first glance to see the ragged clothes and the dark shaggy head attached to them. It was a boy asleep, and Maggie trotted along faster and more lightly, lest she should wake him. It did not occur to her that he was one of her friends the gipsies. But the fact was so, for at the next bend in the lane Maggie actually saw the little semicircular black tent with the blue smoke rising before it. She went on, and thought with some comfort that gipsies most likely knew nothing about idiots, so there was no danger of their falling into the mistake of setting her down at the first glance as an idiot. It was plain she had attracted attention, for a young woman with a baby on her arm walked slowly to meet her. Maggie looked up in the new face rather tremblingly as it approached.

"My little lady, where are you going to?" the gipsy said, in a tone of coaxing deference.

It was delightful, and just what Maggie expected. The gipsies saw at once that she was a little lady, and were prepared to treat her accordingly.

"Not any farther," said Maggie, feeling as if she were saying what she had rehearsed in a dream. "I'm come to stay with *you*, please."

"That's pritty; come, then. Why, what a nice little lady you are, to be sure!" said the gipsy, taking her by the hand. Maggie thought her very agreeable, but wished she had not been so dirty.

There was quite a group round the fire when they reached it. An old gipsy-woman was seated on the ground nursing her knees, and occasionally poking a skewer into the round kettle that sent forth an odorous steam; two small, shock-headed children were lying prone and resting on their elbows, something like small sphinxes; and a placid donkey was bending his head over a tall girl, who, lying on her back, was scratching his nose and indulging him with a bite of excellent stolen hay. The slanting sunlight fell kindly

upon them, and the scene was really very pretty and comfortable, Maggie thought, only she hoped they would soon set out the tea-cups. Everything would be quite charming when she had taught the gipsies to use a washing-basin, and to feel an interest in books. It was a little confusing, though, that the young woman began to speak to the old one in a language which Maggie did not understand, while the tall girl who was feeding the donkey sat up and stared at her without offering any salutation. At last the old woman said:

"What, my pretty lady, are you come to stay with us? Sit ye down, and tell us where you come from."

It was just like a story. Maggie liked to be called pretty lady and treated in this way. She sat down and said:

"I'm come from home because I'm unhappy, and I mean to be a gipsy. I'll live with you, and I can teach you a great many things."

"Such a clever little lady," said the woman with the baby, sitting down by Maggie, and allowing baby to crawl; "and such a pritty bonnet and frock," she added, taking off Maggie's bonnet and looking at it while she made an observation to the old woman in the unknown language. The tall girl snatched the bonnet and put it on her own head hind-foremost with a grin; but Maggie was determined not to show any weakness on this subject, as if she were susceptible about her bonnet.

"I don't want to wear a bonnet," she said; "I'd rather wear a red handkerchief, like yours" (looking at her friend by her side). "My hair was quite long till yesterday, when I cut it off; but I dare say it will grow again very soon."

"Oh, what a nice little lady!—and rich, I'm sure," said the old woman. "Didn't you live in a beautiful house at home?"

"Yes, my home is pretty, and I'm very fond of the river, where we go fishing; but I'm often very unhappy. I should have liked to bring my books with me, but I came away in a hurry, you know. But I can tell you almost everything there is in my books, I've read them so many times, and that will amuse you. And I can tell you something about geography too—that's about the world we live in—very useful and interesting. Did you ever hear about Columbus?"

"Is that where you live, my little lady?" said the old woman.

"Oh, no!" said Maggie, with some pity. "Columbus was a very

wonderful man, who found out half the world; and they put chains on him and treated him very badly, you know—it's in my Catechism of Geography—but perhaps it's rather too long to tell before tea. *I want my tea so.*"

The last words burst from Maggie, in spite of herself, with a sudden drop from patronizing instruction to simple peevishness.

"Why, she's hungry, poor little lady," said the younger woman.

"Here's a bit o' nice victual, then," said the old woman, handing to Maggie a lump of dry bread, which she had taken from a bag of scraps, and a piece of cold bacon.

"Thank you," said Maggie, looking at the food without taking it; "but will you give me some bread and butter and tea instead? I don't like bacon."

"We've got no tea nor butter," said the old woman with something like a scowl, as if she were getting tired of coaxing.

"Oh, a little bread and treacle would do," said Maggie.

"We han't got no treacle," said the old woman crossly; whereupon there followed a sharp dialogue between the two women in their unknown tongue, and one of the small sphinxes snatched at the bread and bacon, and began to eat it. At this moment the tall girl, who had gone a few yards off, came back and said something which produced a strong effect. The old woman, seeming to forget Maggie's hunger, poked the skewer into the pot with new vigour, and the younger crept under the tent, and reached out some platters and spoons. Maggie trembled a little, and was afraid the tears would come into her eyes. Meanwhile the tall girl gave a shrill cry, and presently came running up the boy whom Maggie had passed as he was sleeping—a rough urchin about the age of Tom. He stared at Maggie, and there ensued much incomprehensive chattering. She felt very lonely, and was quite sure she should begin to cry before long. The gipsies didn't seem to mind her at all, and she felt quite weak among them. But the springing tears were checked by a new terror, when two men came up, whose approach had been the cause of the sudden excitement. The elder of the two carried a bag, which he flung down, addressing the women in a loud and scolding tone, which they answered by a shower of treble sauciness; while a black cur ran barking up to Maggie, and threw her into a tremor that only found a new cause in the curses with which the younger man called the dog off, and gave him a rap with a great stick he held in his hand.

At last the younger woman said in her previous deferential, coaxing tone:

"This nice little lady's come to live with us. Aren't you glad?"

"Ay, very glad," said the younger man, who was looking at Maggie's silver thimble and other small matters that had been taken from her pocket. He returned them all except the thimble to the younger woman, with some observation, and she immediately restored them to Maggie's pocket, while the men seated themselves, and began to attack the contents of the kettle—a stew of meat and potatoes—which had been taken off the fire and turned out into a yellow platter.

Maggie began to think that Tom must be right about the gipsies: they must certainly be thieves, unless the man meant to return her thimble by and by. She would willingly have given it to him, for she was not at all attached to her thimble; but the idea that she was among thieves prevented her from feeling any comfort in the revival of deference and attention towards her. All thieves, except Robin Hood, were wicked people. The women saw she was frightened.

"We've got nothing nice for a lady to eat," said the old woman, in her coaxing tone. "And she's so hungry, sweet little lady!"

"Here, my dear, try if you can eat a bit o' this," said the younger woman, handing some of the stew on a brown dish with an iron spoon to Maggie, who, remembering that the old woman had seemed angry with her for not liking the bread and bacon, dared not refuse the stew, though fear had chased away her appetite.

"What! you don't like the smell of it, my dear," said the young woman, observing that Maggie did not even take a spoonful of the stew. "Try a bit—come."

"No, thank you," said Maggie, summoning all her force for a desperate effort, and trying to smile in a friendly way. "I haven't time, I think; it seems getting darker. I think I must go home now, and come again another day, and then I can bring you a basket with some jam-tarts and things."

Maggie rose from her seat as she threw out this illusory prospect; but her hope sank when the old gipsy-woman said, "Stop a bit, stop a bit, little lady; we'll take you home, all safe, when we've done supper. You shall ride home, like a lady."

Maggie sat down again, with little faith in this promise, though she presently saw the tall girl putting a bridle on the donkey, and throwing a couple of bags on his back.

"Now, then, little missis," said the younger man, rising and leading the donkey forward, "tell us where you live; what's the name o' the place?"

"Dorlcote Mill is my home," said Maggie eagerly. "My father is Mr. Tulliver; he lives there."

He lifted Maggie and set her on the donkey.

It now appeared that the man also was to be seated on the donkey, holding Maggie before him, and she was as incapable of remonstrating against this arrangement as the donkey himself, though no nightmare had ever seemed to her more horrible. When the woman had patted her on the back, and said "good-bye," the donkey, at a strong hint from the man's stick, set off at a rapid walk along the lane towards the point Maggie had come from an hour ago, while the tall girl and the rough urchin, also furnished with sticks, obligingly escorted them for the first hundred years, with much screaming and thwacking.

The red light of the setting sun seemed to have a portentous meaning with which the alarming bray of the second donkey with the log on its foot must surely have some connection. Two low thatched cottages—the only houses they passed in this lane—seemed to add to its dreariness. They had no windows to speak of, and the doors were closed. It was probable that they were inhabited by witches, and it was a relief to find that the donkey did not stop there.

At last—oh, sight of joy!—this lane, the longest in the world, was coming to an end, was opening on a broad highroad, where there was actually a coach passing! The gipsy really meant to take her home, then. He was probably a good man after all, and might have been rather hurt at the thought that she didn't like coming with him alone. As they reached a cross-road, Maggie caught sight of some one coming on a white-faced horse.

"Oh, stop, stop!" she cried out. "There's my father—O father, father!"

The sudden joy was almost painful, and before her father reached her she was sobbing. Great was Mr. Tulliver's wonder.

"Why, what's the meaning o' this?" he said, checking his horse, while Maggie slipped from the donkey and ran to her father's stirrup.

"The little miss lost herself, I reckon," said the gipsy. "She'd come to our tent at the far end o' Dunlow Lane, and I was bringing her where she said her home was. It's a good way to come arter being on the tramp all day."

"Oh, yes, father, he's been very good to bring me home," said Maggie—"a very kind, good man!"

"Here, then, my man," said Mr. Tulliver, taking out five shillings. "It's the best day's work *you* ever did. I couldn't afford to lose the little wench. Here, lift her up before me."

"Why, Maggie, how's this, how's this?" he said, as they rode along, while she laid her head against her father and sobbed. "How came you to be rambling about and lose yourself?"

"O father," sobbed Maggie, "I ran away because I was so unhappy; Tom was so angry with me. I couldn't bear it."

"Pooh, pooh!" said Mr. Tulliver soothingly; "you mustn't think o' running away from father. What 'ud father do without his little wench?"

"Oh, no, I never will again, father—never."

Mr. Tulliver spoke his mind very strongly when he reached home that evening, and the effect was seen in the remarkable fact that Maggie never heard one reproach from her mother, or one taunt from Tom, about this foolish business of her running away to the gipsies.

MR. GREAT-HEART LEADS THE WAY

By JOHN BUNYAN

After Christian has started on his pilgrimage to the Celestial City his wife Christiana, with her small sons and accompanied by a neighbour, Mercy, follows. The new pilgrims reach the abode of the Interpreter, who gives them into the charge of Mr. Great-heart, and they continue their way in the wake of Christian. This story, set down as part of the author's dream, is taken from "The Pilgrim's Progress."

THE Interpreter then called for a man-servant of his, one Great-heart, and bid him take sword, and helmet, and shield; and take these, my daughters, said he, conduct them to the house called Beautiful, at which place they will rest next. So he took his weapons and went before them; and the Interpreter said, God speed. So they went on their way.

Now I saw in my dream that they went on, and Great-heart before them. So they went, and came to the place where Christian's burden fell off his back, and tumbled into a sepulchre. Here, then, they made a pause; and here, also, they blessed God.

Now, I saw in my dream that they went on until they were come to the place that Simple, and Sloth, and Presumption lay and slept in when Christian went by on pilgrimage; and, behold, they were hanged up in irons a little way off on the other side.

MERCY. Then said Mercy to him that was their guide and conductor, What are these three men? and for what are they hanged there?

GREAT-HEART. These three men were of very bad qualities: they had no mind to be pilgrims themselves, and whomsoever they could they hindered, they were for sloth and folly themselves, and whomsoever they could persuade they made so too; and, withal, taught them to presume that they should do well at last. They were asleep when Christian went by.

MERCY. But could they persuade any to be of their opinion?

GREAT-HEART. Yes, they turned several out of the way. Besides, they brought up an ill report of your Lord, persuading others that he was a hard taskmaster. They also brought up an evil report of the good land, saying it was not half so good as some pretended it was. They also began to vilify his servants, and to count the very best of them meddlesome, troublesome busy-bodies; further, they would call the bread of God, husks; the comforts of his children, fancies; the travail and labour of pilgrims, things to no purpose.

Nay, said Christiana, if they were such, they never shall be bewailed by me: they have but what they deserve.

Thus they went on till they came at the foot of the hill Difficulty, where again the good Mr. Great-heart took an occasion to tell them what happened there when Christian himself went by. So he had them first to the spring. Lo, said he, this is the spring that Christian drank of before he went up this hill; and then it was clear and good, but now it is dirty with the feet of some that are not desirous that pilgrims here should quench their thirst. Thereat Mercy said, And why so envious, trow? But, said the guide, it will do, if taken up and put into a vessel that is sweet and good; for then the dirt will sink to the bottom, and the water by itself come out more clear. Thus, therefore, Christiana and her companions were compelled to do. They took it up, and put it into an earthen pot, and so let it stand till the dirt was gone to the bottom, and then they drank thereof.

Next he showed them the two byways that were at the foot of the hill, where Formality and Hypocrisy lost themselves. And, said he, these are dangerous paths: two were here cast away when Christian came by. And, although, as you see, these ways are since stopped up with chains, posts, and a ditch, yet there are those that will choose to adventure here rather than take the pains to go up this hill.

CHRISTIANA. "The way of transgressors is hard": it is a wonder that they can get into these ways without danger of breaking their necks.

GREAT-HEART. They will venture; yea, if at any time any of the King's servants doth happen to see them, and do call upon them, and tell them that they are in the wrong way, and do bid them beware of the danger, then they will railingly return them answer, and say, "As for the word that thou hast spoken unto us in the name of the King, we will not hearken unto thee; but we will certainly do whatsoever thing goeth forth out of our own mouth." Nay, if you look a little farther, you will see that these ways are made cautionary enough, not only by these posts, and ditch, and chain, but also by being hedged up; yet they will choose to go there.

CHRISTIANA. They are idle; they love not to take pains; uphill way is unpleasant to them. So it is fulfilled unto them as it is written, "The way of the slothful man is as an hedge of thorns." Yea, they will rather choose to walk upon a snare, than to go up this hill and the rest of this way to the city.

Then they set forward, and began to go up the hill; and up the hill they went; but before they got to the top, Christiana began to pant, and said, I dare say this is a breathing hill; no marvel, if they that love their ease more than their souls, choose to themselves a smoother way. Then said Mercy, I must sit down; also, the least of the children began to cry. Come, come, said Great-heart, sit not down here, for a little above is the Prince's arbour. Then took he the little boy by the hand, and led him up thereto.

When they were come to the arbour, they were very willing to sit down, for they were all in a pelting heat. Then said Mercy, How sweet is rest to them that labour! And how good is the Prince of pilgrims to provide such resting-places for them! Of this arbour I have heard much; but I never saw it before. But here let us beware of sleeping; for, as I have heard, that cost poor Christian dear.

Then said Mr. Great-heart to the little ones, Come, my pretty boys, how do you do? What think you now of going on pilgrimage? Sir, said the least, I was almost beat out of heart; but I thank you for lending me a hand in my need. And I remember now what my mother hath told me, namely, that the way to heaven is as a ladder, and the way to hell is as down a hill. But I had rather go up the ladder to life, than down the hill to death.

Then said Mercy, But the proverb is, "To go down the hill is easy." But James said (for that was his name), The day is coming when, in my opinion, going down the hill will be the hardest of all. 'Tis a good boy, said his master; thou hast given her a right answer. Then Mercy smiled; but the little boy did blush.

Come, said Christiana, will you eat a bit, a little to sweeten your mouths while you sit here to rest your legs? For I have here a piece of pomegranate, which Mr. Interpreter put into my hand just when I came out of his door; he gave me, also, a piece of an honey-comb, and a little bottle of spirits.

I thought he gave you something, said Mercy, because he called you aside.

Yes; so he did, said the other. But, said Christiana, it shall be still as I said it should, when at first we came from home; thou shalt be a sharer in all the good that I have, because thou so willingly didst become my companion.

Then she gave to them, and they did eat, both Mercy and the boys. And said Christiana to Mr. Great-heart, Sir, will you do as we? But he answered, You are going on pilgrimage, and presently I shall return: much good may what you have do to you! At home I eat the same every day.

Now, when they had eaten and drank, and had chatted a little longer, their guide said to them, The day wears away; if you think good, let us prepare to be going. So they got up to go, and the little boys went before; but Christiana forgot to take her bottle of spirits with her, so she sent her little boy back to fetch it. Then said Mercy, I think this is a losing place: here Christian lost his roll; and here Christiana left her bottle behind her. Sir, what is the cause of this? So their guide made answer, and said, The cause is sleep, or forgetfulness: some sleep when they should keep awake, and some forget when they should remember; and this is the very cause why often, at the resting-places, some pilgrims in some things come off losers. Pilgrims should watch, and remember what they have already received under their greatest enjoyments; but for want of doing so, oft-times their rejoicing ends in tears, and their sunshine in a cloud.

When they were come to the place where Mistrust and Timorous met Christian to persuade him to go back for fear of the lions, they perceived, as it were, a stage, and before it, towards the road, a broad plate, with a copy of verses written thereon; and underneath, the reason of raising up of that stage in that place rendered. The verses were these:

Let him that sees this stage take heed
Unto his heart and tongue;
Lest, if he do not, here he speed
As some have long agone.

So they went on, till they came within sight of the lions. Now Mr. Great-heart was a strong man, so he was not afraid of a lion; but yet, when they were come up to the place where the lions were, the boys that went before were now glad to cringe behind, for they were afraid of lions; so they stepped back, and went behind. At this their guide smiled, and said, How now, my boys; do you love to go before when no danger doth approach, and love to come behind so soon as the lions appear?

Now, as they went on, Mr. Great-heart drew his sword, with an intent to make a way for the pilgrims in spite of the lions. Then there appeared one that, it seems, had taken upon him to back the lions; and he said to the pilgrims' guide, What is the cause of your coming hither? Now, the name of that man was Grim, because of his slaying of pilgrims; and he was of the race of the giants.

Then said the pilgrims' guide, These women and children are going on pilgrimage; and this is the way they must go; and go it they shall, in spite of thee and the lions.

GRIM. This is not their way, neither shall they go therein. I am come forth to withstand them, and to that end will back the lions.

Now, to say the truth, by reason of the fierceness of the lions, and of the grim carriage of him that did back them, this way of late had been much unoccupied, and was almost all grown over with grass.

Then said Christiana, Though the highways have been unoccupied heretofore, and though the travellers have been made in times past to walk through bypaths, it must not be so now.

Then he swore by the lions that it should; and therefore bid them turn aside, for they should not have passage there. But Great-heart, their guide, made first his approach unto Grim, and laid so heavily at him with his sword, that he forced him to retreat.

Then said he that attempted to back the lions, Will you slay me upon my own ground?

GREAT-HEART. It is the King's highway that we are in, and in this way it is that thou hast placed the lions; but these women and these children, though weak, shall hold on their way in spite of thy lions. And with that he gave him again a downright blow, and brought him upon his knees. With this blow, also, he broke his helmet, and with the next he cut off an arm. Then did the giant roar so hideously, that his voice frightened the women; and yet they were glad to see him lie sprawling upon the ground. Now the lions were chained, and so of themselves could do nothing. Wherefore, when old Grim, that intended to back them, was dead, Mr. Great-heart said to the pilgrims, Come now, and follow me, and no hurt shall happen to you from the lions. They therefore went on, but the women trembled as they passed by them; the boys, also, looked as if they would die: but they all got by without further hurt.

Now, when they were within sight of the Porter's lodge, they soon came up into it; but they made the more haste after this to go thither, because it is dangerous travelling there in the night. So, when they were come to the gate, the guide knocked, and the Porter cried, Who is there? But as soon as the guide had said, It is I, he knew his voice, and came down; for the guide had oft before that come thither as a conductor of pilgrims. When he was come down he opened the gate, and seeing the guide standing just before it (for he saw not the women, for they were behind him), he said unto him, How now, Mr. Great-heart, what is your business here so late to-night? I have brought, answered he, some pilgrims hither, where, by my Lord's commandment, they must lodge: I had been here some time ago, had I not been opposed by the giant that did use to back the lions. But I, after a long and tedious combat with him, have cut him off, and have brought the pilgrims hither in safety.

THE TWO SISTERS

By MRS. CRAIK

Muriel, the little blind daughter of John Halifax, a prosperous mill-owner, has been knocked down accidentally by a horseman, and day by day her health fails. Phineas Fletcher, her father's life-long friend, who tells this story in "John Halifax, Gentleman," records the coming of Muriel's eleventh birthday. But before that day arrives Muriel holds her new baby sister in her arms and finds fresh joy and happiness. There is that happy Sunday evening, with the whole family laughing and chattering together, and then Muriel's birthday dawns.

WITHOUT any discussion, our plans were tacitly changed—no more was said about going home to dear Longfield. Everyone felt, though no one trusted it to words, that the journey was impossible. For Muriel lay, day after day, on her little bed in an upper chamber, or was carried softly down in the middle of the day by her father, never complaining, but never attempting to move or talk. When we asked her if she felt ill, she always answered, "Oh, no! only so very tired." Nothing more.

"She is dull for want of the others to play with her. The boys should not run out and leave their sister alone," said John, almost sharply, when one bright morning the lads' merry voices came down from the Flat, while he and I were sitting by Muriel's sofa in the still parlour.

"Father, let the boys play without me, please. Indeed, I do not mind. I had rather lie quiet here."

"But it is not good for my little girl always to be quiet, and it grieves father."

"Does it?" She roused herself, sat upright, and began to move her limbs, but wearily.

"That is right, my darling. Now let me see how well you can walk."

Muriel slipped to her feet, and tried to cross the room, catching at table and chairs—now, alas! not only for guidance but actual support. At last she began to stagger, and said, half crying:

"I can't walk, I am so tired. Oh, do take me in your arms, dear father."

Her father took her, looked long in her sightless face, then buried his against her shoulder, saying nothing. But I think in that moment he too saw, glittering and bare, the long-veiled Hand which, for this year past, *I* had seen stretched out of the immutable heavens, claiming that which was its own. Ever after there was discernible in John's countenance a something which all the cares of his anxious yet happy life had never written there—an ineffaceable record, burnt in with fire.

He held her in his arms all day. He invented all sorts of tales and little amusements for her; and when she was tired of these he let her lie in his bosom and sleep. After her bedtime he asked me to go out with him on the Flat.

It was a misty night. The very cows and asses stood up large and spectral as shadows. There was not a single star to be seen.

We took our walk along the terrace and came back again, without exchanging a single word. Then John said hastily:

"I am glad her mother was so busy to-day—too busy to notice."

"Yes," I answered; unconnected as his words were.

"Do you understand me, Phineas? Her mother must not on any account be led to imagine, or to fear—anything. You must not look as you looked this morning. You must not, Phineas."

He spoke almost angrily. I answered in a few quieting words. We were silent, until over the common we caught sight of the light in Muriel's window. Then I felt rather than heard the father's groan.

"Oh, God! my only daughter—my dearest child!"

Yes, she was the dearest. I knew it. Strange mystery, that He should so often take, by death or otherwise, the *dearest*—always the dearest. Strange that He should hear us cry—us writhing in the dust, "O Father! anything, anything but this!" But our Father answers not; and meanwhile the desire of our eyes—be it a life, a love, or a blessing—slowly, slowly goes—is gone. And yet we have to believe in our Father. Perhaps of all trials to human faith this is the sorest. Thanks be to God if He puts into our hearts such love towards Him that even while He slays us we can trust Him still.

This father—this broken-hearted earthly father—could.

When we sat at the supper-table—Ursula, John, and I, the children being all in bed—no one could have told that there was any shadow over us, more than the sadly familiar pain of the darling of the house being "not so strong as she used to be."

"But I think she will be, John. We shall have her quite about again, before——"

The mother stopped, slightly smiling. It was, indeed, an especial mercy of Heaven which put that unaccountable blindness before her eyes, and gave her other duties and other cares to intercept the thought of Muriel. While, from morning till night, it was the incessant secret care of her husband, myself, and good Mrs. Tod, to keep her out of her little daughter's sight, and prevent her mind from catching the danger of one single fear.

Thus, within a week or two, the mother gave another child to the household—a little sister to Muriel.

Muriel was the first to whom the news was told. Her father told it. His natural joy and thankfulness seemed for the moment to efface every other thought.

"She is come, darling! little Maud is come. I am very rich—for I have two daughters now."

"Muriel is glad, father." But she showed her gladness in a strangely quiet, meditative way, unlike a child—unlike even her old self.

"What are you thinking of, my pet?"

"That—though father has another daughter, I hope he will remember the first one sometimes."

"She is jealous!" cried John, in the curious delight with which he always detected in her any weakness, any fault, which brought her down to the safe level of humanity; "see, Uncle Phineas, our Muriel is actually jealous."

But Muriel only smiled.

That smile—so serene—so apart from every feeling or passion appertaining to us who are "of the earth, earthy," smote the father to the heart's core.

He sat down by her, and she crept up into his arms.

"What day is it, father?"

"The first of December."

"I am glad. Little Maud's birthday will be in the same month as mine."

"But you came in the snow, Muriel, and now it is warm and mild."

"There will be snow on my birthday, though. There always is. The snow is fond of me, father. It would like me to lie down and be all covered over, so that you could not find me anywhere."

I heard John try to echo her weak, soft laugh.

"This month it will be eleven years since I was born, will it not, father?"

"Yes, my darling."

"What a long time! Then, when my little sister is as old as I am, I shall be—that is, I should have been—a woman grown. Fancy me twenty years old, as tall as mother, wearing a gown like her, talking and ordering, and busy about the house. How funny!" And she laughed again. "Oh! me, father, I couldn't do it. I had better remain always your little Muriel, weak and small, who liked to creep close to you, and go to sleep in this way."

She ceased talking—very soon she was sound asleep. But—the father!

Muriel faded, though slowly. Sometimes she was so well for an hour or two that the Hand seemed drawn back into the clouds, till of a sudden again we discerned it there.

One Sunday—it was ten days or so after Maud's birth, and the weather had been so bitterly cold that the mother had herself forbidden our bringing Muriel to the other side of the house, where she and the baby lay—Mrs. Tod was laying the dinner, and John stood at the window playing with his three boys.

He turned abruptly, and saw all the chairs placed round the table —all save one.

"Where is Muriel's chair, Mrs. Tod?"

"Sir, she says she feels so tired like, she'd rather not come down to-day," answered Mrs. Tod hesitatingly.

"Not come down?"

"Maybe better not, Mr. Halifax. Look out at the snow. It'll be warmer for the dear child to-morrow."

"You are right. Yes, I had forgotten the snow. She shall come down to-morrow."

I caught Mrs. Tod's eyes; they were running over. She was too wise to speak of it—but she knew the truth as well as we.

This Sunday—I remember it well—was the first day we sat down to dinner with the one place vacant.

For a few days longer her father, every evening when he came in from the mills, persisted in carrying her down, as he had said, holding her on his knee during tea, then amusing her and letting the boys amuse her for half an hour or so before bedtime. But at the week's end even this ceased.

When Mrs. Halifax, quite convalescent, was brought triumphantly to her old place at our happy Sunday dinner-table, and all the boys came pressing about her, vying which should get most kisses from little sister Maud—she looked round, surprised amidst her smiling, and asked:

"Where is Muriel?"

"She seems to feel this bitter weather a good deal," John said; "and I thought it better she should not come down to dinner."

"No," added Guy, wondering and dolefully, "sister has not been down to dinner with us for a great many days."

The mother started; looked first at her husband and then at me.

"Why did nobody tell me this?"

"Love—there was nothing new to be told."

"Has the child had any illness that I do not know of?"

"No."

"Has Dr. Jessop seen her?"

"Several times."

"Mother," said Guy, eager to comfort—for naughty as he was sometimes, he was the most tender-hearted of all the boys, especially to Muriel and to his mother—"sister isn't ill a bit, I know. She was laughing and talking with me just now—saying she knows she could carry baby a great deal better than I could. She is as merry as ever she can be."

The mother kissed him in her quick, eager way—the sole indication of that maternal love which was in her almost a passion. She looked more satisfied.

Nevertheless, when Mrs. Tod came into the parlour, she rose and put little Maud into her arms.

"Take baby, please, while I go up to see Muriel."

"Don't—now don't, please, Mrs. Halifax," cried earnestly the good woman.

Ursula turned very pale. "They ought to have told me," she muttered; "John, *you must* let me go and see my child."

"Presently—presently—Guy, run up and play with Muriel. Phineas, take the others with you. You shall go upstairs in one minute, my darling wife!"

He turned us all out of the room, and shut the door. How he told her that which was necessary she should know—that which Dr. Jessop himself had told us this very morning—how the father and mother had borne this first open revelation of their unutterable grief—for ever remained unknown.

I was sitting by Muriel's bed when they came upstairs. The darling lay listening to her brother, who was squatted on her pillow, making all sorts of funny talk. There was a smile on her face; she looked quite rosy; I hoped Ursula might not notice, just for the time being, the great change the last few weeks had made.

But she did—who could ever blindfold a mother? For a moment I saw her recoil—then turn to her husband with a dumb, piteous, desperate look, as though to say, "Help me—my sorrow is more than I can bear!"

But Muriel, hearing the step, cried with a joyful cry, "Mother! it's my mother!"

The mother folded her to her breast.

Muriel shed a tear or two there—in a satisfied, peaceful way; the mother did not weep at all. Her self-command, so far as speech went, was miraculous. For her look—but then she knew the child was blind.

"Now," she said, "my pet will be good and not cry! It would do her harm. We must be very happy to-day."

"Oh, yes." Then, in a fond whisper, "Please, I do so want to see little Maud?"

"Who?" with an absent gaze.

"My little sister Maud—Maud that is to take my place, and be everybody's darling now."

"Hush, Muriel," said the father hoarsely.

A strangely soft smile broke over her face—and she was silent.

The new baby was carried upstairs proudly, by Mrs. Tod, all the

5

boys following. Quite a levee was held round the bed, where, laid close beside her, her weak hands being guided over the tiny face and form, Muriel first "saw" her little sister. She was greatly pleased. With a grave, elderly-sister air she felt all over the baby limbs, and when Maud set up an indignant cry, began hushing her with so quaint an imitation of motherliness that we were all amused.

"You'll be a capital nurse in a month or two, my pretty!" said Mrs. Tod.

Muriel only smiled. "How fat she is!—and look, how fast her fingers take hold! And her head is so round, and her hair feels so soft—as soft as my doves' necks at Longfield. What colour is it? Like mine?"

It was; nearly the same shade. Maud bore, the mother declared, the strongest likeness to Muriel.

"I am so glad. But these?" touching her eyes anxiously.

"No—my darling. Not like you there," was the low answer.

"I am *very* glad. Please, little Maud, don't cry—it's only sister touching you. How wide open your eyes feel! I wonder"—with a thoughtful pause—"I wonder if you can see me. Little Maud, I should like you to see sister."

"She does see, of course; how she stares!" cried Guy. And then Edwin began to argue to the contrary, protesting that as kittens and puppies could not see at first, he believed little babies did not: which produced a warm altercation among the children gathered round the bed, while Muriel lay back quietly on her pillow, with her little sister fondly hugged to her breast.

The father and mother looked on. It was such a picture—these five darlings, these children which God had given them—a group perfect and complete in itself, like a root of daisies, or a branch of ripening fruit, which not one could be added to, or taken from.

No. I was sure from the parents' smile, that, this once, Mercy had blinded their eyes, so that they saw nothing beyond the present moment.

The children were wildly happy. All the afternoon they kept up their innocent little games by Muriel's bedside; she sometimes sharing, sometimes listening apart. Only once or twice came that wistful, absent look, as if she were listening partly to us, and partly to those we heard not; as if through the wide-open orbs the soul were straining at sights wonderful and new—sights unto which *her* eyes were the clear-seeing, and ours the blank and blind.

It seems strange now, to remember that Sunday afternoon, and how merry we all were; how we drank tea in the queer bedroom at the top of the house; and how afterwards Muriel went to sleep in the twilight, with baby Maud in her arms. Mrs. Halifax sat beside the little bed, a sudden blazing up of the fire showing the intentness of her watch over these two, her eldest and youngest, fast asleep; their breathing so soft, one hardly knew which was frailest, the life slowly fading or the life just begun. Their breaths seemed to mix and mingle, and the two faces, lying close together, to grow into a strange likeness each to each. At least, we all fancied so.

Meanwhile, John kept his boys as still as mice, in the broad window-seat, looking across the white snowy sheet with black bushes peering out here and there, to the feathery beechwood, over the tops of which the new moon was going down. Such a little young moon! and how peacefully—nay, smilingly—she set among the snows!

The children watched her till the very last minute, when Guy startled the deep quiet of the room by exclaiming, "There—she's gone."

"Hush!"

"No, Mother, I am awake," said Muriel. "Who is gone, Guy?"

"The moon—such a pretty little moon."

"Ah, Maud will see the moon some day." She dropped her cheek down again beside the baby sister, and was silent once more.

This is the only incident I remember of that peaceful, heavenly hour.

Maud broke upon its quietude by her waking and wailing; and Muriel very unwillingly let the little sister go.

"I wish she might stay with me—just this one night; and to-morrow is my birthday. Please, Mother, may she stay?"

"We will both stay, my darling. I shall not leave you again."

"I am so glad"; and once more she turned round, as if to go to sleep.

"Are you tired, my pet?" said John, looking intently at her.

"No, Father."

"Shall I take your brothers downstairs?"

"Not yet, dear Father."

"What would you like then?"

"Only to lie here, this Sunday evening, among you all."

He asked her if she would like him to read aloud, as he generally did on Sunday evenings.

"Yes, please; and Guy will come and sit quiet on the bed beside me and listen. That will be pleasant. Guy was always very good to his sister—always."

"I don't know that," said Guy, in a conscience-striken tone. "But I mean to be when I grow a big man—that I do."

No one answered. John opened the large Book—the Book he had taught all his children to long for and to love—and read out of it their favourite history of Joseph and his brethren. The mother sat by him at the fireside, rocking Maud softly on her knees. Edwin and Walter settled themselves on the hearth-rug, with great eyes intently fixed on their father. From behind him the candlelight fell softly down on the motionless figure in the bed, whose hand he held, and whose face he every now and then turned to look at—then, satisfied, continued to read.

For an hour, nearly, we all sat thus—with the wind coming up the valley, howling in the beechwood, and shaking the casement as it passed outside. Within, the only sound was the father's voice. This ceased at last; he shut the Bible, and put it aside. The group—that last perfect household picture—was broken up. It melted away into things of the past, and became only a picture, for evermore.

"Now, boys—it is full time to say good night. There, go and kiss your sister."

"Which?" said Edwin in his funny way. "We've got two now; and I don't know which is the biggest baby."

"I'll thrash you if you say that again," cried Guy. "Which, indeed? Maud is but the baby. Muriel will be always 'sister.'"

'Sister' faintly laughed, as she answered his fond kiss—Guy was often thought to be her favourite brother.

"Now, off with you, boys; and go downstairs quietly—mind, I say quietly."

They obeyed—that is, as literally as boy-nature can obey such an admonition. But an hour after I heard Guy and Edwin arguing vociferously in the dark on the respective merits and future treatment of their two sisters, Muriel and Maud.

John and I sat up late together that night. He could not rest—even though he told me he had left the mother and her two daughters as cosy as a nest of wood-pigeons. We listened to the wild night, till it had almost howled itself away: then our fire went out, and we came and sat over the last faggot in Mrs. Tod's kitchen. We began talking of the long-ago time, and not of this time at all. The vivid present—never out of either mind for an instant—we in our conversation did not touch upon, by at least ten years.

He went upstairs the last thing, and brought down word that mother and children were all sound asleep.

"I think I may leave them until daylight to-morrow. And now, Uncle Phineas, go you to bed, for you look as tired as tired can be."

I went to bed; but all night long I had disturbed dreams. Long before it was light I rose. As I passed the boys' room Guy called out to me:

"Hallo! Uncle Phineas, is it a fine morning? For I want to go down into the wood and get a lot of beech-nuts and fir-cones for sister. It's her birthday to-day, you know."

It *was*, for her. But for us—oh, Muriel, our darling—darling child!

Let me hasten over the story of that morning, for my old heart quails before it still.

John went early to the room upstairs. It was very still. Ursula lay calmly asleep, with baby Maud in her bosom; on her other side, with eyes wide open to the daylight, lay—that which for more than ten years we had been used to call "blind Muriel." She saw, now.

TWO STRANGE PILGRIMS

By CHARLES DICKENS

After losing their home, little Nell and her ageing grandfather set out early one morning from London. Their intention is to wander into the countryside to find a place where they can settle and forget their misfortunes. But they have little money, and their prospects do not seem bright, when they fall in with another strange pair and spend a night in a country inn. The further adventures of little Nell and the old man are told in "The Old Curiosity Shop," from which this story is taken.

OFTEN while they were yet pacing the silent streets of the town on the morning of their departure, the child trembled with a mingled sensation of hope and fear.

The two pilgrims, often pressing each other's hands, or exchanging a smile or cheerful look, pursued their way in silence. Bright and happy as it was, there was something solemn in the long, deserted streets, from which, like bodies without souls, all habitual character and expression had departed, leaving but one dead uniform repose, that made them all alike. All was so still at that early hour, that the few pale people whom they met seemed as much unsuited to the scene as the sickly lamp, which had been here and there left burning, was powerless and faint in the full glory of the sun.

Before they had penetrated very far into the labyrinth of men's abodes which yet lay between them and the outskirts, this aspect began to melt away, and noise and bustle to usurp its place. Some straggling carts and coaches rumbling by first broke the charm, then others came, then others yet more active, then a crowd. The wonder was, at first, to see a tradesman's room window open, but it was a rare thing to see one closed; then smoke rose slowly from the chimneys, and sashes were thrown up to let in air, and doors were opened, and servant girls, looking lazily in all directions but their brooms, scattered brown clouds of dust into the eyes of shrinking passengers, or listened disconsolately to milkmen who spoke of country fairs, and told of wagons in the mews, with awnings and all things complete, and gallant swains to boot, which another hour would see upon their journey.

This quarter passed, they came upon the haunts of commerce and great traffic, where many people were resorting, and business was already rife. The old man looked about him with a startled and bewildered gaze, for these were places that he hoped to shun. He pressed his finger on his lip, and drew the child along by narrow courts and winding ways; nor did he seem at ease until they had left it far behind.

Again this quarter passed, they came upon a straggling neighbourhood, where the mean houses parcelled off in rooms, and windows patched with rags and paper, told of the populous poverty that sheltered there. The shops sold goods that only poverty could buy, and sellers and buyers were pinched and griped alike. Here were poor streets where faded gentility essayed with scanty space and ship-wrecked means to make its last feeble stand, but tax-gatherer and creditor came there as elsewhere, and the poverty that yet faintly struggled was hardly less squalid and manifest than that which had long ago submitted and given up the game.

At length these streets becoming more straggling yet, dwindled and dwindled away, until there were only small garden patches bordering the road, with many a summer-house innocent of paint, and built of old timber or some fragments of a boat, green as the tough cabbage-stalks that grew about it, and grottoed at the seams with toad-stools and tight-sticking snails. Then came a turnpike; then fields again with trees and haystacks; then a hill; and on the top of that the traveller might stop, and—looking back at old Saint Paul's looming through the smoke, its cross peeping above the cloud (if the day were clear), and glittering in the sun; and casting his eyes upon the Babel out of which it grew, until he traced it down to the farthest outposts of the invading army of bricks and mortar whose station lay for the present nearly at his feet—might feel at last that he was clear of London.

Near such a spot as this, and in a pleasant field, the old man and his little guide (if guide she were, who knew not whither they were bound) sat down to rest. She had had the precaution to furnish her basket with some slices of bread and meat, and here they made their frugal breakfast.

The freshness of the day, the singing of the birds, the beauty of the waving grass, the deep green leaves, the wild flowers, and the thousand exquisite scents and sounds that floated in the air—deep joys to most of us, but most of all to those whose life is in a crowd, or who live solitarily in great cities as in the bucket of a human well—sunk into their breasts and made them very glad. The child had repeated her artless prayers once that morning, more earnestly, perhaps, than she had ever done in her life; but as she felt all this, they rose to her lips again. The old man took off his hat—he had no memory for the words—but he said Amen, and that they were very good.

There had been an old copy of the *Pilgrim's Progress*, with strange plates, upon a shelf at home, over which she had often pored whole evenings, wondering whether it was true in every word, and where those distant countries with the curious names might be. As she looked back upon the place they had left, one part of it came strongly on her mind.

"Dear grandfather," she said, "only that this place is prettier and a great deal better than the real one, if that in the book is like it, I feel as if we were both Christian, and laid down on this grass all the cares and troubles we brought with us, never to take them up again."

"No—never to return—never to return," replied the old man, waving his hand towards the city. "Thou and I are free of it now, Nell. They shall never lure us back."

"Are you tired?" said the child; "are you sure you don't feel ill from this long walk?"

"I shall never feel ill again, now that we are once away," was his reply. "Let us be stirring, Nell. We must be further away—a long, long way further. We are too near to stop, and be at rest. Come!"

There was a pool of clear water in the field, in which the child laved her hands and face, and cooled her feet before setting forth to walk again. She would have the old man refresh himself in this way too, and making him sit down upon the grass, cast the water on him with her hands, and dried it with her simple dress.

"I can do nothing for myself, my darling," said the grandfather; "I don't know how it is, I could once, but the time's gone. Don't leave me, Nell; say that thou'lt not leave me. I loved thee all the while, indeed I did. If I lose thee too, my dear, I must die!"

He laid his head upon her shoulder and moaned piteously. The time had been, and a very few days before, when the child could not have restrained her tears and must have wept with him. But now she soothed him with gentle and tender words, smiled at his thinking they could ever part, and rallied him cheerfully upon the jest. He was soon calmed and fell asleep, singing to himself in a low voice, like a little child.

He awoke refreshed, and they continued their journey. The road was pleasant, lying between beautiful pastures and fields of corn, above which, poised high in the clear blue sky, the lark trilled out her happy song. The air came laden with the fragrance it caught upon its way, and the bees, upborne upon its scented breath, hummed forth their drowsy satisfaction as they floated by.

They were now in the open country; the houses were very few and scattered at long intervals, often miles apart. Occasionally they came upon a cluster of poor cottages, some with a chair or low board put across the open door to keep the scrambling children from the road, others shut up close while all the family were working in the fields. These were often the commencement of a little village: and after an interval came a wheelwright's shed, or perhaps a blacksmith's forge; then a thriving farm, with sleepy cows lying about the yard, and horses peering over the low wall and scampering away when harnessed horses passed upon the road, as though in triumph at their freedom. There were dull pigs, too, turning up the ground in search of dainty food, and grunting their monotonous grumblings as they prowled about, or crossed each other in their quest; plump pigeons skimming round the roof or strutting on the eaves; and ducks and geese, far more graceful in their own conceit, waddling awkwardly about the edges of the pond or sailing glibly on its surface. The farm-yard passed, then came the little inn, the humbler beer-shop, and the village tradesman's; then the lawyer's and the parson's, at whose dread names the beer-shop trembled; the church then peeped out modestly from a clump of trees; then there were a few more cottages; then the cage, and pound, and not unfrequently, on a bank by the way-side, a deep old dusty well. Then came the trim-hedged fields on either hand, and the open road again.

They walked all day, and slept that night at a small cottage where beds were let to travellers. Next morning they were afoot again, and though jaded at first, and very tired, recovered before long, and proceeded briskly forward.

They often stopped to rest, but only for a short space at a time, and still kept on, having had but slight refreshment since the morning. It was nearly five o'clock in the afternoon when, drawing near another cluster of labourers' huts, the child looked wistfully in each, doubtful at which to ask for permission to rest awhile, and buy a draught of milk.

At length she stopped at one where the family were seated round the table—chiefly because there was an old man sitting in a cushioned chair beside the hearth, and she thought he was a grandfather, and would feel for hers.

There were, besides, the cottager and his wife, and three young sturdy children, brown as berries. The request was no sooner preferred than granted. The eldest boy ran out to fetch some milk, the second dragged two stools towards the door, and the youngest crept to his mother's gown, and looked at the strangers from beneath his sunburnt hand.

"God save you, master," said the old cottager, in a thin, piping voice; "are you travelling far?"

"Yes, sir, a long way," replied the child; for her grandfather appealed to her.

"From London?" inquired the old man.

The child said yes.

Ah! He had been in London many a time—used to go there often once with wagons. It was nigh two-and-thirty year since he had been there last, and he did hear say there were great changes. Like enough! He had changed himself since then. Two-and-thirty year was a long time, and eighty-four a great age, though there was some he had known that had lived to very hard upon a hundred, and not so hearty as he, neither—no, nothing like it.

"Sit thee down, master, in the elbow chair," said the old man, knocking his stick upon the brick floor, and trying to do so sharply. "Take a pinch out o' that box; I don't take much myself, for it comes dear, but I find it wakes me up sometimes."

The milk arrived, and the child, producing her little basket, and selecting its best fragments for her grandfather, they made a hearty meal. The furniture of the room was very homely, of course—a few rough chairs and a table, a corner cupboard, with their little stock of crockery and delf, a gaudy tea-tray, representing a lady in bright red walking out with a very blue parasol, a few common-coloured Scripture subjects in frames upon the wall and chimney, an old dwarf clothes-press, and an eight-day clock, with a few bright saucepans and a kettle, comprised the whole. But everything was clean and neat; and as the child glanced round, she felt a tranquil air of comfort and content to which she had long been unaccustomed.

"How far is it to any town or village?" she asked of the husband.

"A matter of good five mile, my dear," was the reply; "but you're not going on to-night?"

"Yes, yes, Nell," said the old man hastily, urging her, too, by signs. "Further on, further on, darling—further away, if we walk till midnight."

"There's a good barn hard by, master," said the man, "or there's travellers' lodging, I know, at the Plow an' Harrer. Excuse me, but you do seem a little tired, and unless you're very anxious to get on——"

"Yes, yes, we are," returned the old man fretfully. "Further away, dear Nell—pray further away."

"We must go on, indeed," said the child, yielding to his restless wish. "We thank you very much, but we cannot stop so soon. I'm quite ready grandfather."

But the woman had observed, from the young wanderer's gait, that one of her little feet was blistered and sore, and being a woman and a mother too, she would not suffer her to go until she had washed the place and applied some simple remedy, which she did so carefully and with such a gentle hand—rough-grained and hard though it was, with work—that the child's heart was too full to admit of her saying more than a fervent "God bless you!" nor could she look back nor trust herself to speak, until they had left the cottage some distance behind. When she turned her head, she saw that the whole family, even the old grandfather, were standing in the road watching them as they went, and so, with many waves of the hand, and cheering nods, and on one side at least not without tears, they parted company.

They trudged forward, more slowly and painfully than they had done yet, for another mile or thereabouts, when they heard the sound of wheels behind them, and looking round observed an empty cart approaching pretty briskly. The driver on coming up to them stopped his horse and looked earnestly at Nell.

"Didn't you stop to rest at a cottage yonder?" he said.

"Yes, sir," replied the child.

"Ah! they asked me to look out for you," said the man. "I'm going your way. Give me your hand—jump up, master."

This was a great relief, for they were very much fatigued and could scarcely crawl along. To them the jolting cart was a luxurious carriage, and the ride the most delicious in the world. Nell had scarcely settled herself on a little heap of straw in one corner, when she fell fast asleep, for the first time that day.

She was awakened by the stopping of the cart, which was about to turn up a by-lane. The driver kindly got down to help her out, and pointing to some trees at a very short distance before them, said that the town lay there, and that they had better take the path which they would see leading through the churchyard. Accordingly, towards this spot they directed their weary steps.

The sun was setting when they reached the wicket-gate at which the path began, and as the rain falls upon the just and unjust alike, it shed its warm tint even upon the resting-places of the dead, and bade them be of good hope for its rising on the morrow. The church was old and grey, with ivy clinging to the walls and round the porch. Shunning the tombs, it crept about the mounds, beneath which slept poor humble men, twining for them the first wreaths they had ever won, but wreaths less liable to wither, and far more lasting in their kind, than some which were graven deep in stone and marble.

The old man and the child quitted the gravel path, and strayed among the tombs, for there the ground was soft and easy to their tired feet. As they passed behind the church they heard voices near at hand, and presently came on those who had spoken.

They were two men who were seated in easy attitudes upon the grass, and so busily engaged as to be at first unconscious of intruders. It was not difficult to divine that they were of a class of itinerant showmen—exhibitors of the freaks of Punch, for perched

cross-legged upon a tombstone behind them was a figure of that hero himself, his nose and chin as hooked and his face as beaming as usual. Perhaps his imperturbable character was never more strikingly developed, for he preserved his usual equable smile notwithstanding that his body was dangling in a most uncomfortable position, all loose and limp and shapeless, while his long peaked cap, unequally balanced against his exceedingly slight legs, threatened every instant to bring him toppling down.

In part scattered upon the ground at the feet of the two men, and in part jumbled together in a long flat box, were the other persons of the drama. Their owners had evidently come to that spot to make some needful repairs in the stage arrangements.

They raised their eyes when the old man and his young companion were close upon them, and pausing in their work, returned their looks of curiosity. One of them, the actual exhibitor no doubt, was a little merry-faced man with a twinkling eye and a red nose, who seemed to have unconsciously imbibed something of his hero's character. The other—that was he who took the money—had rather a careful and cautious look, which was perhaps inseparable from his occupation also.

The merry man was the first to greet the strangers with a nod; and following the old man's eyes, he observed that perhaps that was the first time he had ever seen a Punch off the stage.

"Why do you come here to do this?" said the old man, sitting down beside them, and looking at the figures with extreme delight.

"Why, you see," rejoined the little man, "we're putting up for to-night at the public-house yonder, and it wouldn't do to let 'em see the present company undergoing repair."

"No!" cried the old man, making signs to Nell to listen; "why not, eh? why not?"

"Because it would destroy all the delusion, and take away all the interest, wouldn't it?" replied the little man. "Would you care a ha'penny for the Lord Chancellor if you know'd him in private and without his wig?—certainly not."

"Good!" said the old man, venturing to touch one of the puppets and drawing his hand away with a shrill laugh. "Are you going to show 'em to-night—are you?"

"That is the intention, governor," replied the other; "and unless

I'm much mistaken, Tommy Codlin is a-calculating at this minute what we've lost through your coming upon us. Cheer up, Tommy, it can't be much."

The little man accompanied these latter words with a wink, expressive of the estimate he had formed of the travellers' finances.

To this Mr. Codlin, who had a surly, grumbling manner, replied, as he twitched Punch off the tombstone and flung him into the box:

"I don't care if we haven't lost a farden, but you're too free. If you stood in front of the curtain and see the public's faces, as I do, you'd know human natur' better."

"Ah! it's been the spoiling of you, Tommy, your taking to that branch," rejoined his companion. "When you played the ghost in the reg'lar drama in the fairs, you believed in everything—except ghosts. But now you're a universal mistruster. *I* never see a man so changed."

"Never mind," said Mr. Codlin, with the air of a discontented philosopher. "I know better now, and p'raps I'm sorry for it."

Turning over the figures in the box like one who knew and despised them, Mr. Codlin drew one forth, and held it up for the inspection of his friend.

"Look here; here's all this Judy's clothes falling to pieces again. "You haven't got a needle and thread, I suppose?"

The little man shook his head, and scratched it ruefully as he contemplated this severe indisposition of a principal performer. Seeing that they were at a loss, the child said timidly:

"I have a needle, sir, in my basket, and thread too. Will you let me try to mend it for you? I think I could do it neater than you could."

Even Mr. Codlin had nothing to urge against a proposal so seasonable. Nelly, kneeling down beside the box, was soon busily engaged in her task, and accomplishing it to a miracle.

While she was thus engaged, the merry little man looked at her with an interest which did not appear to be diminished when he glanced at her helpless companion. When she had finished her work he thanked her, and inquired whither they were travelling.

"N—no further to-night, I think," said the child, looking towards her grandfather.

"If you're wanting a place to stop at," the man remarked, "I should advise you to take up at the same house with us. That's it. The long, low, white house there. It's very cheap."

The old man, notwithstanding his fatigue, would have remained in the churchyard all night if his new acquaintances had stayed there too. As he yielded to this suggestion a ready and rapturous assent, they all rose and walked away together; he keeping close to the box of puppets in which he was quite absorbed, the merry little man carrying it slung over his arm by a strap attached to it for the purpose, Nelly having hold of her grandfather's hand, and Mr. Codlin sauntering slowly behind, casting up at the church tower and neighbouring trees such looks as he was accustomed in town-practice to direct to drawing-room and nursery windows, when seeking for a profitable spot on which to plant the show.

The public-house was kept by a fat old landlord and landlady, who made no objection to receiving their new guests, but praised Nelly's beauty, and were at once prepossessed in her behalf. The landlady was very much astonished to learn that they had come all the way from London.

"These two gentlemen have ordered supper in an hour's time," she said, taking her into the bar, "and your best plan will be to sup with them. Meanwhile you shall have a little taste of something that'll do you good, for I'm sure you must want it after all you've gone through to-day. Now, don't look after the old gentleman, because when you've drunk that he shall have some too."

As nothing could induce the child to leave him alone, however, or to touch anything in which he was not the first and greatest sharer, the old lady was obliged to help him first. When they had been thus refreshed, the whole house hurried away into an empty stable where the show stood, and where, by the light of a few flaring candles stuck round a hoop which hung by a line from the ceiling, it was to be forthwith exhibited.

The whole performance was applauded to the echo, and voluntary contributions were showered in with a liberality which testified yet more strongly to the general delight. Among the laughter none was more loud and frequent than the old man's. Nell's was unheard, for she, poor child, with her head drooping on his shoulder, had fallen asleep, and slept too soundly to be roused by any of his efforts to awaken her to a participation in his glee.

The supper was very good, but she was too tired to eat, and yet would not leave the old man until she had kissed him in his bed. He, happily, insensible to every care and anxiety, sat listening with a vacant smile and admiring face to all that his new friends said; and it was not until they retired yawning to their room that he followed the child upstairs.

It was but a loft partitioned into two compartments where they were to rest, but they were well pleased with their lodging, and had hoped for none so good. The old man was uneasy when he had lain down, and begged that Nell would come and sit at his bedside as she had done for so many nights. She hastened to him, and sat there till he slept.

There was a little window, hardly more than a chink in the wall, in her room, and when she left him she opened it, quite wondering at the silence. The sight of the old church and the graves about it in the moonlight, and the dark trees whispering among themselves, made her more thoughtful than before. She closed the window again, and sitting down upon the bed, thought of the life that was before them.

She had a little money, but it was very little, and when that was gone, they must begin to beg. There was one piece of gold among it, and an emergency might come when its worth to them would be increased a hundredfold. It would be best to hide this coin, and never produce it unless their case was absolutely desperate, and no other resource was left them.

Her resolution taken, she sewed the piece of gold into her dress, and going to bed with a lighter heart, sunk into a deep slumber.

WOUNDED PRIDE

By MARK TWAIN

After running away from his Aunt Polly to be a pirate, Tom Sawyer returns home just in time to interrupt his own funeral service, and as a result becomes something of a hero with the other children. Even Becky Thatcher, with whom he had quarrelled, is anxious to be friends again. But Tom stands on his dignity until Becky finds herself in trouble, and then he discovers that he has to help her—and he does, with painful consequences. This story is taken from "The Adventures of Tom Sawyer."

WHAT a hero Tom was become now! He did not go skipping and prancing, but moved with a dignified swagger, as became a pirate who felt that the public eye was on him. And indeed it was: he tried not to seem to see the looks or hear the remarks as he passed along, but they were food and drink to him.

Tom decided that he could be independent of Becky Thatcher now. Glory was sufficient. He would live for glory. Now that he was distinguished, maybe she would be wanting to "make up." Well, let her—she should see that he could be as indifferent as some other people. Presently she arrived. Tom pretended not to see her. He moved away and joined a group of boys and girls, and began to talk. Soon he observed that she was tripping gaily back and forth with flushed face and dancing eyes, pretending to be busy chasing schoolmates, and screaming with laughter when she made a capture, but he noticed that she always made her captures in his vicinity, and that she seemed to cast a conscious eye in his direction at such times, too. Presently she gave over skylarking, and moved irresolutely about, sighing once or twice and glancing furtively and wistfully towards Tom. Then she observed that now Tom was talking more particularly to Amy Lawrence than to anyone else. She felt a sharp pang and grew disturbed and uneasy at once. She tried to go away, but her feet were treacherous, and carried her to the group instead. She said to a girl almost at Tom's elbow—with sham vivacity:

"Why, Mary Austin! you bad girl, why didn't you come to Sunday school?"

"I did come—didn't you see me?"

"Why, no! Did you? Where did you sit?"

"I was in Miss Peters's class, where I always go. I saw you."

"Did you? Why, it's funny I didn't see you. I wanted to tell you about the picnic."

"Oh, that's jolly. Who's going to give it?"

"My ma's going to let me have one."

"Oh, goody; I hope she'll let me come."

"Well, she will. The picnic's for me. She'll let anybody come that I want, and I want you."

"That's ever so nice. When is it going to be?"

"By and by. Maybe about vacation."

"Oh, won't it be fun! You going to have all the girls and boys?"

"Yes, every one that's friends to me—or wants to be," and she glanced ever so furtively at Tom, but he talked right along to Amy Lawrence about the terrible storm on the island, and how the lightning tore the great sycamore-tree "all to flinders" while he was "standing within three feet of it."

"Oh, may I come?" said Gracie Miller.

"Yes."

"And me?" said Sally Rogers.

"Yes."

"And me too?" said Susy Harper. "And Joe?"

"Yes."

And so on, with clapping of joyful hands, till all the group had begged for invitations but Tom and Amy. Then Tom turned coolly away, still talking, and took Amy with him. Becky's lips trembled and the tears came to her eyes; she hid these signs with a forced gaiety and went on chattering, but the life had gone out of the picnic now, and out of everything else; she got away as soon as she could and hid herself, and had what her sex call "a good cry." Then she sat moody, with wounded pride, till the bell rang. She roused up now, with a vindictive cast in her eye, and gave her plaited tails a shake, and said she knew what she'd do.

At recess Tom continued his flirtation with Amy with jubilant self-satisfaction. And he kept drifting about to find Becky and lacerate her with the performance. At last he spied her, but there was a sudden falling of his mercury. She was sitting cosily on a little bench behind the schoolhouse, looking at a picture-book with Alfred Temple; and so absorbed were they, and their heads so close together over the book, that they did not seem to be conscious of anything in the world beside. Jealousy ran red-hot through Tom's veins. He began to hate himself for throwing away the chance Becky had offered for a reconciliation. He called himself a fool, and all the other hard names he could think of. He wanted to cry with vexation. Amy chatted happily along, as they walked, for her heart was singing, but Tom's tongue had lost its function. He did not hear what Amy was saying, and whenever she paused expectantly, he could only stammer an awkward assent, which was as often misplaced as otherwise. He kept drifting to the rear of the schoolhouse again and again, to sear his eyeballs with the hateful spectacle there. He could not help it. And it maddened him to see, as he thought he saw, that Becky Thatcher never once suspected that he was even in the land of the living. But she did see, nevertheless; and she knew she was winning her fight, too, and was glad to see him suffer as she had suffered.

Tom fled home at noon. His conscience could not endure any more of Amy's grateful happiness, and his jealousy could bear no more of the other distress. Becky resumed her picture inspections with Alfred, but as the minutes dragged along and no Tom came to suffer, her triumph began to cloud, and she lost interest; gravity and absent-mindedness followed, and then melancholy; two or three times she pricked up her ear at a footstep, but it was a false hope; no Tom came. At last she grew entirely miserable, and wished she hadn't carried it so far. When poor Alfred, seeing that he was losing her he did not know how, and kept exclaiming: "Oh, here's a jolly one! look at this!" she lost patience at last and said, "Oh, don't bother me! I don't care for them!" and burst into tears, and got up and walked away.

Alfred dropped alongside and was going to try and comfort her, but she said:

"Go away and leave me alone, can't you? I hate you!"

So the boy halted, wondering what he could have done, and she walked on, crying. Then Alfred went musing into the deserted schoolhouse. He was humiliated and angry. He easily guessed his way to the truth—the girl had simply made a convenience of him to vent her spite upon Tom Sawyer. He was far from hating Tom the less when this thought occurred to him. He wished there was some way to get that boy into trouble without much risk to himself. Tom's spelling-book fell under his eye. Here was his opportunity. He gratefully opened to the lesson for the afternoon, and poured ink upon the page. Becky, glancing in at a window behind him at the moment, saw the act and moved on without discovering herself. She started homeward now, intending to find Tom and tell him: Tom would be thankful, and their troubles would be healed. Before she was half-way home, however, she had changed her mind. The thought of Tom's treatment of her when she was talking about her picnic came scorching back, and filled her with shame. She resolved to let him get whipped on the damaged spelling-book's account, and to hate him for ever into the bargain.

There was something about Aunt Polly's manner, when she kissed Tom, that swept away his low spirits and made him light-hearted and happy again. He started to school, and had the luck of coming upon Becky Thatcher at the head of Meadow Lane. His mood always determined his manner. Without a moment's hesitation he ran to her and said:

"I acted mighty mean to-day, Becky, and I'm so sorry. I won't ever, ever do that way again as long as ever I live—please make up, won't you?"

The girl stopped and looked him scornfully in the face:

"I'll thank you to keep yourself *to* yourself, Mr. Thomas Sawyer. I'll never speak to you again."

She tossed her head and passed on. Tom was so stunned that he had not even the presence of mind enough to say "Who cares, Miss Smarty?" until the right time to say it had gone by. So he said nothing. But he was in a fine rage, nevertheless. He moped into the school-yard wishing she were a boy, and imagining how he would trounce her if she were. He presently encountered her and delivered a stinging remark as he passed. She hurled one in return, and the angry breach was complete. It seemed to Becky, in her hot resentment, that she could hardly wait for school to "take in," she was so impatient to see Tom flogged for the injured spelling-book. If she had had any lingering notion of exposing Alfred Temple, Tom's offensive fling had driven it entirely away.

Poor girl, she did not know how fast she was nearing trouble herself. The master, Mr. Dobbins, had reached middle age with an unsatisfied ambition. The darling of his desires was to be a doctor, but poverty had decreed that he should be nothing higher than a village schoolmaster. Every day he took a mysterious book out of his desk, and absorbed himself in it at times when no classes were reciting. He kept that book under lock and key. There was not an urchin in school but was perishing to have a glimpse of it, but the chance never came. Every boy and girl had a theory about the nature of that book; but no two theories were alike, and there was no way of getting at the facts in the case. Now as Becky was passing by the desk, which stood near the door, she noticed that the key was in the lock! It was a precious moment. She glanced around; found herself alone, and the next instant she had the book in her hands. The title-page—Professor somebody's *Anatomy*—carried no information to her mind; so she began to turn the leaves. She came at once upon a handsomely engraved and coloured frontispiece—a human figure. At that moment a shadow fell on the page, and Tom Sawyer stepped in at the door and caught a glimpse of the picture. Becky snatched at the book to close it, and had the hard luck to tear the pictured page half down the middle. She thrust the volume into the desk, turned the key, and burst out crying with shame and vexation:

"Tom Sawyer, you are just as mean as you can be, to sneak up on a person and look at what they're looking at."

"How could *I* know you was looking at anything?"

"You ought to be ashamed of yourself, Tom Sawyer; you know you're going to tell on me; and, oh, what shall I do, what shall I do! I'll be whipped, and I never was whipped in school."

Then she stamped her little foot and said:

"*Be* so mean if you want to! *I* know something that's going to happen. You just wait, and you'll see! Hateful, hateful, hateful!" and she flung out of the house with a new explosion of crying.

Tom joined the mob of skylarking fellows outside. In a few moments the master arrived and school "took in." Tom did not feel a strong interest in his studies. Every time he stole a glance at the girls' side of the room Becky's face troubled him. Considering all things, he did not want to pity her, and yet it was all he could do to help it. He could get up no exultation that was really worth the name. Presently the spelling-book discovery was made, and Tom's mind was entirely full of his own matters for a while after that. Becky roused up from her lethargy of distress, and showed good interest in the proceedings. She did not expect Tom could get out of his trouble by denying that he spilt the ink on the book himself; and she was right. The denial only seemed to make the thing worse for Tom. Becky supposed she would be glad of that, and she tried to believe she was glad of it, but she found she was not certain. When the worst came to the worst, she had an impulse to get up and tell on Alfred Temple, but she made an effort and forced herself to keep still, because, said she to herself, "He'll tell about me tearing the picture, sure. I wouldn't say a word, not to save his life!"

Tom took his whipping and went back to his seat not at all broken-hearted, for he thought it was possible that he had unknowingly upset the ink on the spelling-book himself, in some skylarking bout—he had denied it for form's sake and because it was custom, and had stuck to the denial from principle.

A whole hour drifted by; the master sat nodding in his throne, the air was drowsy with the hum of study. By and by Mr. Dobbins straightened himself up, yawned, then unlocked his desk, and reached for his book, but seemed undecided whether to take it out or leave it. Most of the pupils glanced up languidly, but there were two among them that watched his movements with intent eyes. Mr. Dobbins fingered his book absently for a while, then took it out, and settled himself in his chair to read.

Tom shot a glance at Becky. He had seen a hunted and helpless rabbit look as she did, with a gun levelled at its head. Instantly he forgot his quarrel with her. The next moment the master faced the school. Every eye sank under his gaze; there was that in it which smote even the innocent with fear. There was silence while one might count ten; the master was gathering his wrath. Then he spoke:

"Who tore this book?"

There was not a sound. One could have heard a pin drop. The stillness continued; the master searched face after face for signs of guilt.

"Benjamin Rogers, did you tear this book?"

A denial. Another pause.

"Joseph Harper, did you?"

Another denial. Tom's uneasiness grew more and more intense under the slow torture of these proceedings. The master scanned the ranks of boys, considered a while, then turned to the girls:

"Amy Lawrence?"

A shake of the head.

"Gracie Miller?"

The same sign.

"Susan Harper, did you do this?"

Another negative. The next girl was Becky Thatcher. Tom was trembling from head to foot with excitement, and a sense of the hopelessness of the situation.

"Rebecca Thatcher"—(Tom glanced at her face; it was white with terror)—"did you tear—no, look me in the face"—(her hands rose in appeal)—"did you tear this book?"

A thought shot like lightning through Tom's brain. He sprang to his feet and shouted:

"*I* done it!"

The school stared in perplexity at this incredible folly. Tom stood a moment to gather his dismembered faculties; and when he stepped forward to go to his punishment, the surprise, the gratitude, the adoration that shone upon him out of poor Becky's eyes seemed pay enough for a hundred floggings. Inspired by the splendour of his own act, he took without an outcry the most merciless flogging that even Mr. Dobbins had ever administered; and also received with indifference the added cruelty of a command to remain two hours after school should be dismissed—for he knew who would wait for him outside till his captivity was done, and not count the tedious time as loss either.

Tom went to bed that night planning vengeance against Alfred Temple; for with shame and repentance Becky had told him all, not forgetting her own treachery; but even the longing for vengeance had to give way soon to pleasanter musings, and he fell asleep at last with Becky's latest words lingering dreamily in his ear:

"Tom, how *could* you be so noble!"

INTO EXILE

By JANE PORTER

Sir William Wallace, a Scottish chieftain who does not stand idly by while English soldiers garrison the towns of his beloved Scotland, becomes involved in a fight in the streets of Lanark, and as a result has to flee from his wife and home. The fortitude of his wife, Marion, the quick wit of his faithful retainer, Halbert, and some luck save him when the English invade his home and a flight of arrows is loosed into the branches of an oak-tree. This story is taken from "The Scottish Chiefs."

THE darkness was almost impenetrable. Wallace rode on till, crossing the bridge of Lanark, he saw the rising moon silver the tops of the distant hills. This was the time he had promised Marion he should be returned, and he had yet five long miles to go, before he could reach the glen of Elderslie; he thought of her being alone —of watching, with an anxious heart, the minutes of his delay. Scotland and its wrongs he now forgot, in the idea of her whose happiness was dearer to him than life. He could not achieve the deliverance of the one, but it was his bliss to preserve the peace of the other; and putting spurs to his horse, under the now bright beams of the moon, he hastened through the town.

Abruptly turning an angle leading to the Mouse river, a cry of murder arrested his ear. He checked his horse and listened. The clashing of arms told him the sound had issued from an alley to the left. He alighted in an instant, and drawing his sword, threw away the scabbard (prophetic omen!); then, leaving his horse with one of his servants, hastened, with the other three, to the spot whence the noise proceeded.

On arriving, he discovered two men in tartans, with their backs to the opposite wall, furiously assaulted by a throng of Edward's soldiers. At this sight, the Scots who accompanied Wallace were so enraged that, blowing their bugles to encourage the assailed, they joined hand to hand with their gallant leader, and attacking the banditti, each man cut his opponent to the ground.

Such unexpected assistance reanimated the drooping strength of one of the two, from whom the cry had issued. He sprang from the wall with the vigour of a tiger, but at the moment received a wound in his back, which would have thrown him at the feet of his enemies, had not Wallace caught him in his left arm, and with his right cleared the way, while he cried to his men who were fighting near him—"To the Glen!" As he spoke, he threw the now insensible stranger into their arms. The other man, whose voice had first attracted Wallace, at that instant sunk, covered with blood, on the pavement.

Two of the servants, obeying their master, carried their senseless burden towards the horses; but the third, being hemmed in by the furious soldiers, could not move. Wallace made a passage to his rescue, and effected it; but one base wretch, while the now wounded Scot was retreating, made a stroke which would have severed his head from his body, had not the trusty claymore of Wallace struck down the pending weapon of the coward, and received his rushing body upon its point. He fell with bitter imprecations, calling aloud for vengeance.

A dreadful cry was now raised by the whole band of assassins——"Murder! treason! Arthur Heselrigge is slain!" The uproar became general. The windows of the adjoining houses were thrown open; people armed and unarmed issued from their doors, and pressed forward to inquire the cause of the alarm. Wallace was nearly overpowered; a hundred swords flashed in the torch-light; but at the moment he expected they would be sheathed in his heart, the earth gave way under his feet, and he sunk into utter darkness.

He fell upon a quantity of gathered broom; and concluding that the weight of the thronging multitude had burst his way through the arch of a cellar, he sprung on his feet: and though he heard the curses of several wretches who had fallen with him and fared worse, he made but one step to a half-opened door, pointed out to him by a gleam from an inner passage. The men uttered a shout as they saw him darken the light which glimmered through it; but they were incapable of pursuit; and Wallace, aware of his danger, darting across the adjoining apartment, burst open a window, and leaped out at the foot of the Lanark hills.

The oaths of the soldiers, enraged at his escape, echoed in his ears till distance sunk them into hoarse murmurs. He pursued his way over the craigs, through the valley, and across the river, to the cliffs which embattled the garden of Elderslie. Springing on the projecting point of the nearest, he leaped into a thicket of honeysuckles. This was the favourite bower of his Marion! The soft perfume, as it saluted the senses, seemed to breathe peace and safety; and as he emerged from its fragrant embrace, he walked with a calmer step towards the house. He approached a door which led into the garden. It was open. He beheld his beloved leaning over a couch, on which was laid the person he had rescued. Halbert was dressing his wounds.

Wallace paused for a moment to contemplate his lovely wife in this more lovely act of charity. Her beautiful hands held a cup to the lips of the stranger; while her long hair, escaped from its band, fell in jetty ringlets, and mingled with his silver locks.

"Marion!"

She looked up at the well-known sound, and with a cry of joy, rushing forward, threw herself into his arms; her tears flowed, she sobbed, she clung to his breast. It was the first time Wallace had been from her; she had feared it would have been the last. The hour—the conflict—the bleeding stranger! But now he was returned—he was safe!

"Art thou indeed here!" exclaimed she. Blood fell from his forehead upon her face and bosom. "Oh, my Wallace!" cried she in agony.

"Fear not, my love! all is well, since our wounded countryman is safe."

"But you bleed!" returned she. No tears now impeded her voice. Terror had checked their joyful currents; and she felt as if she expected his life-blood to issue from the wound on which she gazed.

"Save, save yourself, my master!" cried a man, rushing in from the garden; "you are pursued; save, save——"

While he spoke he fell insensible at Wallace's feet. The chief perceived that it was Dugald—he whom he had rescued from the blow of Heselrigge, and who, from the bleeding of his wounds and consequent debility, had been all this while reaching Elderslie.

Wallace had hardly time to give him to the care of Halbert, when the voice of war assailed his ears. The tumult of men demanding admittance, and the terrific sound of spears rattling against the shields of their owners, told the astonished group within that the house was beset by armed foes.

"Blood for blood!" cried a horrid voice, which penetrated the almost palsied senses of Lady Marion. "Vengeance on Wallace for the murder of Heselrigge!"

"Fly, fly!" cried she, looking wildly at her husband.

As she spoke, there was a violent crash, and a tremendous burst of imprecations. Three of Wallace's men ran panting into the room. Two of the assailants had climbed to the hall window; and had just been thrown back upon the cliffs, where one was killed. "Conceal yourself," said the Scots to Wallace; "for in a few minutes more your men will not be able to maintain the gates."

"Yes, my dear lord," cried Halbert, "there is the dry well at the end of the garden; at the bottom of that you will be safe."

"I shall be safe," whispered Marion; "only fly; while you are here, their shouts kill me."

A party of the English, having come round the heights, had leaped the wall of the garden, and were within a few yards of the well. For Wallace to descend now was impossible. "That tree!" whispered Marion, pointing to an oak. As she spoke, she slid from his arms, and along with the venerable Halbert, who had seized her hand, disappeared.

Wallace, finding himself alone, the next instant, like one of his native eagles, was looking down from the towering top of the wood, upon his enemies. They passed beneath him, denouncing vengeance upon the *assassin of Arthur Heselrigge*! One, who by the brightness of his armour seemed to be their leader, stopped under the tree, and complained he had so sprained his ankle in leaping the wall he must wait a few minutes to recover himself. Several soldiers drew towards him; but he ordered them to pursue their duty, search the house, and bring Wallace, dead or alive, before him.

They obeyed; but others, who had gained admittance to the tower through the now forced gates, soon ran to him with information that the murderer could nowhere be found.

"But here is a gay lady," cried one; "perhaps she can tell of his hiding-place." And at that moment, Marion, with Halbert, appeared amongst a band of men. The lighted torches which the soldiers held, shone full on her face. Though pale as monumental marble, the exquisite beauty of her features, and the calm dignity which commanded from her eyes, awed the officer into respect and admiration.

"Soldiers, stand back!" cried he, advancing to Lady Wallace.

"Fear not, madam." As the words passed his lips, a flight of arrows flew into the bosom of the tree. A piercing shriek from Marion was her only answer.

"Ha! my lady's falcon!" cried Halbert, alarmed doubly for the fate of his master. Halbert's ready excuse, both for the disturbance in the tree and his lady's shriek, was prompted and warranted true by the appearance of a large bird, which the rushing of the arrows had frighted from her nest: she rose suddenly from amongst the branches, and soared away, far to the east, with loud screams.

All being again still, Marion hoped that her husband had escaped any serious injury from the arrows; and turning with recovered composure to the officer, heard him, with a glow of comfort, reprimand his men for daring to draw their bows without his orders.

The officer paused for a moment, and then ordering his soldiers to fall farther back, when they were at a sufficient distance, he offered to take Lady Wallace's hand. She withstood his motion with a reserved air, and said, "Speak, sir, what you would say, or allow me to retire."

"I meant not to offend you, noble lady," continued he; "had I a wife lovely as yourself, and I in like circumstances, I hope in the like manner she would defend my life and honour. I knew not the particulars of the affair in which Arthur Heselrigge fell, till I heard them from your lips. I can easily credit them, for I know his unmanly character. Wallace is a Scot, and acted in Scotland as Gilbert Hambledon would have done in England, were it possible for any vile foreigner to there put his foot upon the neck of a countryman of his. Wherever you have concealed your husband, let it be a distant asylum. At present no track within the jurisdiction of Lanark will be left unsearched by the governor's indefatigable revenge."

Lady Wallace, overcome with gratitude at this generous speech of the English officer, uttered some inarticulate words, expressive more in sound than clearness, of her grateful feelings.

"Sweet lady," answered Hambledon, "God is indeed the benefactor of a true soldier; and though I serve my king, and obey my commanders, yet it is only to the Lord of battles that I look for a sure reward. And whether he pay me here with victories and honours, or take my soul through a rent in my breast, to receive my laurel in paradise, it is all one to Gilbert Hambledon. But the night is cold; I must see you safe within your own doors; and then, lady, farewell!"

Lady Wallace yielded to the impulse of his hand, and with redoubled haste, as she heard another rustling in the tree above her head. Hambledon did not notice it; but desiring Halbert to follow, in a few minutes disappeared with the agitated Marion into the house.

Wallace, whose spirit could ill brook the sight of his domains filled with hostile troops, and the wife of his bosom brought a prisoner before their commander, would instantly have braved all dangers, and have leaped down amongst them; but at the instant he placed his foot on a lower bough to make a spring, the courteous address of Hambledon to his wife made him hesitate.

"Sir William! my master!" cried a well-known voice, in a suppressed tone, as if still fearful of being overheard. It was Halbert's. "Speak, my dear lord; are you safe?"

"In heart and body!" returned Wallace, sliding from the tree, and leaping on the ground. "One only of the arrows touched me; and that merely striking my bugle, fell back amongst the leaves. I must now hasten to the dearest, the noblest of women!"

Halbert begged him to stay till they should hear the retreat from the English trumpets. "Till their troops are out of sight," added he, "I cannot believe you safe."

"Hark!" cried Wallace, "the horses are now descending the craig. That must satisfy you, honest Halbert." With these words he flew across the grass, and entering the house, met the returning Marion, who had just bade farewell to Hambledon. She rushed into his arms, and, with the excess of a disturbed and uncertain joy, fainted on his neck. Her gentle spirit had been too powerfully excited by the preceding scenes. Unaccustomed to tumult of any kind, and nursed in the bosom of fondness till now, no blast had blown on her tender form, no harshness had ever ruffled the blissful serenity of her mind. What, then, was the shock of this evening's violence! Her husband pursued as a murderer; herself exposed to the midnight air, and dragged by the hands of merciless soldiers to betray the man she loved! All these scenes were new to her; and though a kind of preternatural strength had supported her through them, yet when the cause of immediate exertion was over, when she fell once more into her husband's extended arms, she seemed there to have found again her shelter, and the pillow whereon her harassed soul might repose.

"My life! my best treasure! preserver of thy Wallace! look on him!" exclaimed he; "bless him with a smile from those dear eyes."

His voice, his caresses, soon restored her to sensibility and recollection. She wept on his breast, and with love's own eloquence, thanked Heaven, that he had escaped the search and the arrows of his enemies.

"But, my dear lady," interrupted Halbert, "remember my master must not stay here. You know the English commander said he must fly far away. Nay, spies may even now be lurking to betray him."

"You are right," cried she. "My Wallace, you must depart. Should the guard arrive soon, your flight may be prevented. You must go now—but, oh! whither?"

"Not very distant, my love. In going from thee, I leave behind all that makes life precious to me; how then can I go far away! No! there are recesses among the Cartlane craigs, I discovered while hunting, and which I believe have been visited by no mortal foot but my own. There will I be, my Marion, before sunrise; and before it sets, thither must you send Halbert, to tell me how you fare. Three notes from thine own sweet strains of *Thusa ha measg na reultan mor*, blown by his pipe, shall be a sign to me that he is there; and I will come forth to hear tidings of thee."

"Ah, my Wallace, let me go with thee!"

"What, dearest!" returned he, "to live amidst rocks and streams! To expose thy tender self to all the accidents of such a lodging!"

"But are not you going to so rough, so dangerous a lodging?" asked she: "Oh! would not rocks and streams be heaven's paradise to me, when blessed with the presence of my husband? Ah! let me go!"

"Impossible, my lady," cried Halbert, afraid that the melting heart of his master would consent; "you are safe here; and your flight would awaken suspicion in the English, that he had gone far. Your ease and safety are dearer to him than his own life; and most likely by his cares to preserve them, he would be traced, and so fall a ready sacrifice to the enemy."

"It is true, my Marion; I could not preserve you in the places to which I go."

"But the hardships you will endure!" cried she; "to sleep on the cold stones, with no covering but the sky, or the dripping vault of some dreary cave! I have not courage to abandon you alone to such cruel rigours."

"Cease, my beloved!" interrupted he, "cease these groundless alarms. Neither rocks nor storms have any threats to me. It is only tender woman's cares that make man's body delicate. Before I was thine, my Marion, I have lain whole nights upon the mountain's brow, counting the wintry stars, as I impatiently awaited the hunter's horn that was to recall me to the chase in Glenfinlass. Alike to Wallace is the couch of down or the bed of heather; so, best-beloved of my heart, grieve not at hardships which were once my sport, and will now be my safety."

"Then, farewell! May good angels guard thee!" Her voice failed; she put his hand to her lips.

"Courage, my Marion," said he. "Revive, be happy, for my sake; and, God who putteth down the oppressor, will restore me to thine arms." She spoke not, but rising from his breast, clasped her hands together, and looked up with an expression of fervent prayer; then smiling through a shower of tears, she waved her hand to him to depart, and instantly disappeared into her own chamber.

Wallace gazed at the closed door, with his soul in his eyes. To leave his Marion thus—to quit her who was the best part of his being, who seemed the very spring of the life now throbbing in his heart, was a contention with his fond, fond love, almost too powerful with his resolution. Here indeed his brave spirit gave way; and he would have followed her, and perhaps have determined to await his fate at her side, had not Halbert, reading his mind in his countenance, taken him by the arm, and drawn him towards the portal.

Wallace, girding on his sword, and taking his hunting-spear, he pressed the faithful hand that presented it, and again enjoining him to be watchful of the tranquillity of his lady, and to send him tidings of her in the evening, to the cave near the Corie Lynn, he climbed the wall, and was out of sight in an instant.

THE FOREST SECRETARY

By CAPTAIN MARRYAT

Living in a cottage in the New Forest are Edward, Humphrey, Alice, and Edith, the orphan children of Colonel Beverley of Arnwood, a stout Royalist who was killed at the battle of Naseby. The children are thought to have perished when a fire destroyed Arnwood. To save themselves from Roundhead troops they pretend to be relatives of one of their father's retainers, who has since died. Then Edward, the eldest, is offered the post of secretary to the forest Intendant, Mr. Heatherstone, a Roundhead, and on the advice of Oswald Partridge, a forester who knows his secret, he accepts. This story is taken from "The Children of the New Forest."

EDWARD remained at the cottage, expecting to hear some message from the Intendant. He was right in his conjecture, for on the third day Oswald Partridge came over to say that the Intendant would be happy to see him, if he could make it convenient to go over, which Edward assented to do on the following day. Oswald had ridden over on a pony. Edward arranged to take Billy and return with him. They started early the next morning, and Edward asked Oswald if he knew why the Intendant had sent for him.

"Not exactly," replied Oswald; "but I think, from what I heard Miss Patience say, it is to offer you some situation, if you could be prevailed upon to accept it."

"Very true," replied Edward; "he offers me the post of secretary. What do you think?"

"Why, sir, I think I would accept it: at all events, I would take it on trial—there can be no harm done. If you do not like it you can only go back to the cottage again. One thing I am sure of, which is that Master Heatherstone will make it as pleasant to you as he can, for he is most anxious to serve you."

"That I really believe," replied Edward; "and I have pretty well made up my mind to accept the office. It is a post of confidence, and I shall know all that is going on, which I cannot do while I am secluded in the forest; and, depend upon it, we shall have stirring news."

The conversation then changed, and after a ride of eight hours, they arrived at the Intendant's house. Edward gave Billy into Oswald's charge, and knocked at the door. Phœbe let him in, and asked him into the sitting-room, where he found the Intendant alone.

"Edward Armitage, I am glad to see you; and shall be still more so if I find that you have made up your mind to accept my proposition. What is your reply?"

"I am very thankful to you for the offer, sir," replied Edward, "and will accept it if you think that I am fitting for it, and if I find that I am equal to it: I can but give it a trial, and leave if I find it too arduous or too irksome."

"Too arduous it shall not be—that shall be my concern; and too irksome I hope you will not find it. My letters are not so many but that I could answer them myself, were it not that my eyes are getting weak, and I wish to save them as much as possible. You will therefore have to write chiefly what I shall dictate. But it is not only for that I require a person that I can confide in: I very often shall send you to London instead of going myself, and to that, I presume, you will have no objection?"

"Certainly none, sir."

"Well, then, it is no use saying any more just now. You will have a chamber in this house, and you will live with me, and at my table altogether. Neither shall I say anything just now about remuneration, as I am convinced that you will be satisfied. All that I require now is to know the day that you will come, that everything may be ready."

"I suppose, sir, I must change my attire!" replied Edward, looking at his forester's dress; "that will hardly accord with the office of secretary."

"I agree with you that it will be better to keep that dress for your forest excursions, as I presume you will not altogether abandon them," replied the Intendant. "You can provide yourself with a suit at Lymington. Well, then, that is settled; and I suppose you would like to see your accommodation. Patience and Clara are in the next room. You can join them, and you will make my daughter very happy by telling her that you are to become a resident with us. You will, of course, dine with us to-day, and sleep here to-night."

Mr. Heatherstone then opened the door, and saying to his daughter Patience, "My dear, I leave you to entertain Edward Armitage till dinner-time," he ushered Edward in, and closed the door again. Clara ran up to Edward as soon as he went in; and having kissed him, Edward then took Patience's offered hand.

"Then you have consented?" said Patience inquiringly.

"Yes, I could not refuse such kindness," replied Edward.

"And when do you come?"

"On Monday night, if I can be ready by that time."

"Why, what have you to get ready?" said Clara.

"I must not appear in a forester's dress, my little Clara. I can wear that with a gun in my hand, but not with a pen; so I must go to Lymington and see what a tailor can do for me."

"You will feel as strange in a secretary's dress as I did in boys' clothes," said Clara.

"Perhaps I may," said Edward, although he felt that such would not be the case, having been accustomed to much better clothes when at Arnwood than what were usually worn by secretaries; and this remembrance brought back Arnwood in its train, and Edward became silent and pensive.

Patience observed it, and after a time said:

"You will be able to watch over your sisters, Mr. Armitage, as well here almost as if you were at the cottage. You do not return till to-morrow? How did you come over?"

"I rode the pony Billy, Mistress Patience."

"Why do you call her Mistress Patience, Edward?" said Clara. "You call me Clara; why not call her Patience?"

"You forget that I am only a forester, Clara," replied Edward with a grave smile.

"No, you are a secretary now," replied Clara.

"Mistress Patience is older than you by several years. I call you Clara because you are but a little girl; but I must not take that liberty with Mistress Heatherstone."

"Do you think so, Patience?" said Clara.

"I certainly do not think that it would be a liberty in a person, after being well acquainted with me, to call me Patience," replied she, "especially when that person lives in the house with us, eats and associates with us as one of the family, and is received on an equality; but I dare say, Clara, that Master Armitage will be guided by his own feelings, and act as he considers to be proper."

"But you give him leave, and then it is proper," replied Clara.

"Yes, if he gave himself leave, Clara," said Patience. "But we will now show him his own room, Clara," continued Patience, wishing to change the subject of conversation.—"Will you follow us, sir?" said Patience, with a little mock ceremony.

Edward did so without replying, and was ushered into a large airy room, very neatly furnished.

"This is your future lodging," said Patience. "I hope you will like it."

"Why, he never saw anything like it before," said Clara.

"Yes, I have, Clara," replied Edward.

"Where did you?"

"At Arnwood; the apartments were on a much larger scale."

"Arnwood! Oh yes, I have heard my father speak of it," said Clara, with the tears starting in her eyes at his memory. "Yes, it was burnt down, and all the children burnt to death."

"So they say, Clara; but I was not there when it was burnt."

"Where were you, then?"

"I was at the cottage where I now live." Edward turned round to Patience, and perceived that her eyes were fixed upon him, as if she would have read his thoughts. Edward smiled, and said:

"Do you doubt what I say?"

"No, indeed!" said she—"I have no doubt that you were at the cottage at the time; but I was thinking that if the apartments at Arnwood were more splendid, those at your cottage are less comfortable. You have been used to better and to worse, and therefore will, I trust, be content with these."

"I trust I have shown no signs of discontent. I should indeed be difficult to please if an apartment like this did not suit me. Besides, allow me to observe that, although I stated that the apartments at Arnwood were on a grander scale, I never said that I had ever been a possessor of one of them."

Patience smiled and made no reply.

"Now that you know your way to your apartment, Master Armitage, we will, if you please, go back to the sitting-room," said she. As they were going back into the sitting-room she said, "When you come over, you will, I presume, bring your clothes in a cart? I ask it because I promised some flowers and other things to your sisters, which I can send back by the cart."

"You are very kind to think of them, Mistress Patience," replied Edward; "they are fond of flowers, and will be much pleased with possessing any."

"You sleep here to-night, I think my father said?" inquired Patience.

"He did make the proposal, and I shall gladly avail myself of it," said Edward.

"I hope you are hungry, Edward," said Clara. "Dinner is almost ready."

"I dare say I shall eat more than you do, Clara."

"So you ought, a great big man like you. How old are you, Edward?" said Clara. "I am thirteen; Patience is past sixteen; now how old are you?"

"I am not yet eighteen, Clara; so that I can hardly be called a man."

"Why, you are as tall as Mr. Heatherstone."

"Yes, I believe I am."

"And can't you do everything that a man can do?"

"I really don't know; but I certainly shall always try so to do."

"Well, then, you must be a man."

"Well, Clara, if it pleases you, I will be a man."

"Here comes Mr. Heatherstone, so I know dinner is ready.—Is it not, sir?"

"Yes, my child, it is," replied Mr. Heatherstone, kissing Clara; "so let us all go in."

Mr. Heatherstone, as was usual at that time with the people to whose party he ostensibly belonged, said a grace before meat, of considerable length, and then they sat down to table. As soon as the repast was over, Mr. Heatherstone returned to his study, and Edward went out to find Oswald Partridge, with whom he remained the larger portion of the afternoon, going to the kennel, and examining the dogs, and talking of the chase.

"I have not two men that can stalk a deer," observed Oswald. "The men appointed here as verderers and keepers have not one of them been brought up to the business. Most of them are men who have been in the army, and I believe have been appointed to these situations to get rid of them, because they were troublesome; and they are anything but good characters. The consequence is that we kill but few deer, for I have so much to attend to here, as none of them know their duties, that I can seldom take my own gun out. I stated so to the Intendant, and he said that if you accepted an offer he had made you, and came over here, we should not want venison; so it is clear that he does not expect you to have your pen always in your hand."

"I am glad to hear that," replied Edward. "Depend upon it, his own table, at all events, shall be well supplied."

Edward did not sleep much that night. The novelty of his situation—the novelty of his prospects, and his speculations thereon—kept him awake till near morning. He was, however, up in good time, and having assisted at the morning prayers, and afterwards eaten a most substantial breakfast, he took his leave of the Intendant and the two girls, and set off on his return to the cottage, having renewed his promise of coming to take up his abode with them. Billy was fresh, and cantered gaily along, so that Edward was back early in the afternoon, and once more welcomed by his household. He stated to Humphrey all that had occurred, and Humphrey was much pleased at Edward having accepted the offer of the Intendant. Alice and Edith did not quite so much approve of it, and a few tears were shed at the idea of Edward leaving the cottage. The next day Edward and Humphrey set off for Lymington, with Billy in the cart.

On their arrival at Lymington they went straight to the hostelrie, and found the landlord at home. He recommended a tailor to Edward, who sent for him to the inn, and was measured by him for a plain suit of dark cloth. Edward and Humphrey then went out, as Edward had to procure boots and many other articles of dress, to correspond with the one which he was about to assume.

"I am most puzzled about a hat, Humphrey," said Edward. "I hate those steeple-crowned hats worn by the Roundheads; yet the hat and feather is not proper for a secretary."

"I would advise you to submit to wear the steeple-crowned hats, nevertheless," said Humphrey. "Your dress, as I consider, is a sort of disgrace to a Cavalier born, and the heir of Arnwood; why not, therefore, take its hat as well? As secretary to the Intendant, you should dress like him; if not, you may occasion remarks, especially when you travel on his concerns."

"You are right, Humphrey; I must not do things by halves; and unless I wear the hat, I might be suspected."

"I doubt if the Intendant wears it for any other reason," said Humphrey.

"At all events I will not go to the height of the fashion," replied Edward, laughing. "Some of the hats are not quite so tall as the others."

"Here is the shop for the hat and for the sword-belt."

Edward chose a hat and a plain sword-belt, paid for them, and desired the man to carry them to the hostelrie.

"We have dipped somewhat into the bag to-day, Edward," said Humphrey; "but the money is well spent."

"I think so, Humphrey; but I have no doubt that I shall be able to replace the money very soon, as the Intendant will pay me for my services. However, I shall be close at hand if you want me, and Oswald will always call and see how you get on."

"I hope you will manage that he calls once a week."

"I will if I can, Humphrey, for I shall be just as anxious as you are to know if all goes on well. Indeed, I shall insist upon coming over to you once a fortnight; and I hardly think the Intendant will refuse me—indeed I am sure that he will not."

"So am I," replied Humphrey. "I am certain that he wishes us all well, and has, in a measure, taken us under his protection; but, Edward, recollect I shall never kill any venison after this, and so you may tell the Intendant."

"I will, and that will be an excuse for him to send some over, if he pleases. Indeed, as I know I shall be permitted to go out with Oswald, it will be hard if a stray buck does not find its way to the cottage."

SNATCHED FROM DEATH

By VICTOR HUGO

In Paris a great concourse of people is assembled to witness the execution of La Esmeralda, a young gipsy girl who has been tried and found guilty of witchcraft. Before the executioners can complete their grim task there is a dramatic intervention. Quasimodo, the hunchback bell-ringer of Nôtre-Dame Cathedral, has remembered how once the gipsy girl was kind to him when he stood in the pillory, and in his own fashion he repays the debt. This story is taken from "Nôtre-Dame de Paris."

THE clock of Nôtre-Dame slowly struck twelve. A murmur of satisfaction burst from the crowd. The last vibration of the twelfth stroke had hardly expired on the air, when the heads of the multitude were all set in motion like the waves before a sudden gale, and an immense shout rose at once, from the ground, from the windows, and from the roofs, of "Here she comes!"

A tumbrel drawn by a strong Norman dray-horse, and quite surrounded by horsemen in violet uniforms with white crosses, had just entered the Place from the Rue Saint-Pierre-aux-Bœufs. The sergeants of the watch made way for it through the multitude by a vigorous use of their white leather *boullayes*. By the side of the tumbrel rode some officers of justice and of police, distinguishable by their black costume and their awkwardness on horseback. In the fatal cart a young girl was seated, with her hands tied behind her, and without any priest at her side. She was in her shift; her long black hair (for it was the custom not to cut it until reaching the foot of the gibbet) fell unbound upon her neck and over her half-uncovered shoulders.

Across those dishevelled and undulating locks, more shining than a raven's plumage, was seen, twisted and knotted, a thick brown cord, which roughly chafed the poor girl's pretty fragile neck, encircling it like an earthworm twined about a flower. Beneath that rope glittered a small amulet, ornamented with green glass, which, no doubt, she had been allowed to keep merely because it was thought not worth while to refuse it to one just going to die. The spectators up at the windows could discern at the bottom of the tumbrel her naked legs, which she strove to conceal under her as if through a last remaining instinct of her sex. At her feet was a little she-goat, with its limbs also bound. The condemned was holding together with her teeth her ill-tied chemise. It seemed as if she still suffered in her misery from being thus exposed almost naked before all eyes. Alas! it was not for shudderings like this that feminine modesty was designed.

The condemned kept her eyes fixed upon the bottom of the tumbrel. It was but too truly La Esmeralda. In this last stage of ignominy and misfortune, she was still beautiful—her large black eyes looked larger for the sinking of her cheeks, and her livid profile was pure and sublime.

They untied her hands, and made her descend from the vehicle accompanied by her goat, which they also unbound, and which bleated with joy to feel itself at liberty. They then made her walk barefoot over the pavement, to the bottom of the great steps of entrance; the rope that was passed round her neck trailing behind her, and looking like a serpent closely pursuing her.

The halberds of the motley dressed yeomen of the bishop were heard to clang upon the floor; and in a few minutes a long procession, of priests in their chasubles and deacons in their dalmatics, coming, psalm-singing, slowly along, developed itself to the view of the condemned and to that of the multitude. But her eye fixed itself upon the one who walked at their head, immediately after the cross-bearer.

It was the archdeacon. At the moment that he appeared in the broad daylight, under the high-pointed doorway, wrapped in an ample silver cope, marked with a black cross, he was so pale that some among the crowd actually thought that one of the marble bishops kneeling on the tombstones in the choir had risen upon his feet, and was come to receive on the threshold of the grave her who was going to die.

She herself, no less pale and statue-like, had scarcely perceived that they had put into her hand a heavy lighted taper of yellow wax. She had not hearkened to the clamorous voice of the registrar reading over the fatal tenor of the *amende honorable*: only, when they had told her to answer amen she had answered "Amen!"

She was not brought back to some slight consciousness of life and strength until she saw the priest make a sign to her guards to retire, and himself advanced towards her. But now she felt her blood boiling in her head, and a remaining spark of indignation was kindled in that spirit already benumbed and cold.

The archdeacon approached her slowly.

Lifting his hand over the gipsy girl, he exclaimed in a sepulchral voice, *"I nunc anima anceps, et sit tibi Deus misericors."* (Go thy way now, lingering soul, and may God have mercy upon thee.)

This was the awful formula with which it was the custom to close that gloomy ceremonial. It was the preconcerted signal given by the priest to the executioner.

Hereupon the people knelt down.

"*Kyrie Eleison!*" said the priests, remaining under the great arched doorway.

"*Kyrie Eleison!*" repeated the multitude, with that murmuring noise which runs over a sea of heads, like the plashing of the waves of the sea itself when in agitation.

"Amen!" said the archdeacon.

He turned his back upon the condemned; his head fell upon his breast; his hands crossed themselves; he returned to his train of priests, and in a minute he was seen to disappear with the cross, the tapers, and the copes, under the dim arches of the cathedral.

The unfortunate girl at the moment of re-ascending the fatal cart, and moving on towards her final scene, was seized, perhaps, by some last overwhelming clinging to life. She lifted her dry reddened eyes to heaven, to the sky, to the sun, to the silvery clouds, intermingled with patches of brilliant blue; then she cast them around her upon the ground, the people, the houses. All at once, while the man in yellow was pinioning her, she uttered a terrible cry. She fell senseless upon the ground.

No one had yet remarked, in the gallery of royal statues carved immediately above the arches of the portal, a strange-looking spectator, who, until then, had been observing all that passed with such absolute passiveness, a neck so intently stretched, a visage so deformed, that, but for his habiliments, half red and half violet, he might have been taken for one of the stone monsters through whose mouths the long gutters of the cathedral have disgorged themselves for six hundred years. No visible circumstance of all that had been transacted before the entrance of Nôtre-Dame since the hour of twelve had escaped this spectator. And at the very commencement, without anyone's noticing the action, he had fastened firmly to one of the small columns of the gallery a strong knotted rope, the other end of which fell down below upon the top of the steps of the entrance. This being done, he had set himself to look quietly on, only whistling from time to time when some blackbird flew by him. All at once he strided over the balustrade of the gallery, gripped the cord with his feet, his knees, and his hands; then he was seen to slide down over that part of the façade, like a drop of rain gliding down a pane of glass, run up to the two sub-executioners with the speed of a cat just dropped from a housetop, knock them both down with a pair of enormous fists, carry off the gipsy girl with one hand, as a child does a doll, and leap, at one bound, into the church, lifting the girl above his head and crying out with a formidable voice, "Sanctuary!"

This was done with such rapidity that, had it been night, the whole might have been seen by the glare of a single flash of lightning.

"Sanctuary! sanctuary!" repeated the crowd; and the clapping of ten thousand hands made Quasimodo's only eye sparkle with joy and pride.

This shock brought the condemned to her senses. She lifted her eyelids, looked at Quasimodo, then suddenly dropped them again, as if terrified at her deliverer.

The executioners and the whole escort were confounded. The fact that within the walls of Nôtre-Dame the condemned was inviolable. The cathedral was a recognized place of refuge; all temporal jurisdiction expired upon its theshold.

Quasimodo had stopped under the grand doorway. His broad feet seemed to rest as solidly upon the floor of the church as the heavy Roman pillars themselves. His great dishevelled head looked compressed between his shoulders, like that of a lion, which animal in like manner, has a mane but no neck. He held the young girl, all palpitating, suspended in his horny hands, like a piece of white drapery, but he bore her so cautiously that he seemed to be afraid of breaking or withering her. It was as if he felt that she was something delicate, exquisite, precious, made for other hands than his.

At some moments he looked as if not daring to touch her, even with his breath. Then, all at once, he would strain her closely in his arms to his angular breast, as if she were his only good, his treasure, as the mother of that child would have done. His gnome's eye, bent down upon her, poured over her a flood of tenderness, grief, and pity, and then again it was lifted up all flashing. Then the women laughed and wept, the crowd stamped their feet with enthusiasm, for at that moment Quasimodo had really a beauty of his own. Yes, that orphan, that foundling, that outcast was fair to look upon. He felt himself august in his strength. He stood erect, looking full in the face that society from which he was banished, yet in which he was displaying so powerful an intervention; that human justice from which he had snatched its prey; all those tigers whose longing jaws he forced to remain empty; all those police agents, those judges, those executioners; all that force of the King which he, poor and helpless as he was, had broken with the force of God.

And then there was something affecting in that protection falling from a being so deformed upon one so unfortunate; in the circumstance of a poor girl condemned to death being saved by Quasimodo. It was the extremity of natural and that of social wretchedness, meeting and assisting each other.

Meanwhile, after a few minutes' triumph, Quasimodo had suddenly plunged, with his burden, into the darksome interior of the church. The people, fond of any display of prowess, sought him with their eyes under the gloomy nave, regretting that he had so quickly withdrawn himself from their acclamations. All at once he was seen to reappear at one extremity of the gallery of the royal statues. He passed along it, running like a madman, lifting up his conquest in his arms, and shouting "Sanctuary!" Fresh plaudits burst from the multitude. Having traversed the gallery, he plunged again into the interior of the church. A minute afterwards he appeared upon the upper platform, still bearing the gipsy in his arms, still running wildly along, still shouting "Sanctuary!" and the crowd still applauding. At last he made a third appearance on the summit of the tower of the great bell: from thence he seemed to show exultingly to the whole city the fair creature he had saved; and his thundering voice, that voice which was heard so seldom, and which he never heard at all, thrice repeated with frantic vehemence, even in the very clouds, "Sanctuary! Sanctuary! Sanctuary!"

"*Noel! Noel!*" cried the people in their turn; and that multitudinous acclamation resounded upon the opposite shore of the Seine.

The next morning the poor gipsy girl perceived, on waking, that she had slept—a thing which astonished her—she had been so long unaccustomed to sleep! Some cheerful rays of the rising sun streamed through her window, and fell upon her face. At the same time with the sun, she saw at the window the unfortunate face of Quasimodo. Involuntarily her eyes closed again, but in vain—she still thought she saw, through her roseate eyelids, that gnome's visage, one-eyed and gap-toothed. Then, still keeping her eyes shut, she heard a rough voice saying, very gently, "Don't be afraid, I'm your friend. I was come to look at you sleeping. That doesn't hurt you, does it—that I should come and see you asleep? What does it signify to you my being here when you have your eyes shut? Now I'm going away. There. I've put myself behind the wall—now you may open your eyes again."

There was something yet more plaintive than these words; it was the tone in which they were uttered. The gipsy girl, affected at them, opened her eyes. He had, in fact, gone away from the window. She went up to it, and saw the poor hunchback crouching in an angle of the wall, in a posture of sorrow and resignation. She made an effort to overcome the repugnance which she felt at the sight of him. "Come hither," said she softly. From the movement of her lips Quasimodo thought that she was bidding him go away; then he rose up and retreated, limping, slow, hanging his head, not venturing to lift up to the young girl his despairing countenance. "Come hither, I say," cried she but he continued to move away. Then she hurried out of the cell, ran after him, and laid hold of his arm. On feeling the pressure, Quasimodo trembled in every limb. He lifted a suppliant eye; and finding that she was trying to draw him toward her, his whole face beamed with joy and tenderness. She tried to make him enter her cell; but he persisted in remaining on the threshold. "No, no," said he, "the owl goes not into the nest of the lark."

Then she gracefully squatted down upon her couch, with her

goat asleep at her feet. Both parties remained motionless for a few minutes, absorbed in the contemplation—he, of so much grace—she, of so much ugliness. Every moment she discovered in Quasimodo some additional deformity. Her eye wandered over him, from his bow legs to his hump back, from his hump back to his one eye. She could not understand how a being so awkwardly fashioned could be in existence. Yet over the whole there was diffused an air of so much sadness and gentleness that she was beginning to be reconciled to it.

He was the first to break silence. "So you were telling me to come back"

She nodded affirmatively, and said, "Yes."

He understood the motion of her head. "Alas!" said he, as if hesitating to finish the sentence, "you see, I'm deaf."

"Poor man!" exclaimed the gipsy girl, with an expression of benevolent pity.

He smiled sorrowfully. "You thought that was all I wanted—didn't you? Yes, I'm deaf. That's the way I'm made. It's horrible isn't it? You now, you're so beautiful."

In the poor creature's tone there was so deep a feeling of his wretchedness that she had not resolution to say a word. Besides, he would not have heard it. He continued:

"Never did I see my ugliness as I do now. When I compare myself to you, I do indeed pity myself, poor unhappy monster that I am. You must think I look like a beast. Tell me, now. You are a sunbeam—a dewdrop—a bird's song. But me—I'm something frightful—neither man nor brute—a sort of a thing that's harder, and more trod upon, and more unshapely than a flint-stone."

Then he laughed—a heart-rending laugh. He went on:

"Yes, I'm deaf—but you'll speak to me by gestures and signs. I've a master that talks to me that way. And then, I shall know your will very quickly, by seeing how your lips move, and how you look."

"Well, then," said she, smiling, "tell me why you saved me."

He looked at her intently while she was speaking.

"Oh, I understand," he replied, "you ask me why it was I saved you. You've forgotten a poor wretch that you brought relief to on their shameful pillory—a drop of water and a little pity. There was more than I can pay you back with all my life. You've forgotten that poor wretch—but he remembers."

She listened to him with deep emotion. A tear stood in the poor ringer's eye—but it did not fall—he seemed to make it, as it were, a point of honour to retain it. "Just hear me," said he, when he was no longer afraid that this tear would escape him, "we've very high towers here—if a man was to fall from one, he'd be dead before he got to the ground: when you like me to fall in that way, you'll not so much as have to say a word—a glance of your eye will be enough."

Then he rose up from his leaning posture. This odd being, unhappy as the gipsy girl herself was, yet awakened some compassion in her breast. She motioned to him to remain.

"No, no," said he, "I mustn't stay too long—I'm not at my ease. It's all for pity that you don't turn away your eyes. I'm going somewhere whence I shall see you and you won't see me—that will be better."

He drew from his pocket a small metal whistle. "There," said he; "when you want me—when you wish me to come—when you'll not be too much horrified at the sight of me—you'll whistle with that. I can hear that noise."

He laid the whistle on the ground and went his way.

REUNION AND CALAMITY

By OLIVER GOLDSMITH

Dr. Primrose, a gentle and lovable country clergyman, leaves his family and sets out to find his daughter Olivia, who has been deceived by a plausible rogue, and is afraid to return home. He finds her by happy chance, and, overjoyed, returns home to prepare a welcome, only for further misfortune to overtake his sorely tried family. The family's adventures and misadventures are related by Dr. Primrose in "The Vicar of Wakefield," from which this story is taken.

THE next morning I took leave of the good family that had been kind enough to entertain me so long. I left them in the enjoyment of all that happiness which affluence and good breeding procure, and returned towards home, despairing of ever finding my daughter more, but sending a sigh to Heaven to spare and forgive her. I was now come within about twenty miles of home, having hired a horse to carry me, as I was yet but weak, and comforted myself with the hopes of soon seeing all I held dearest upon earth. But the night coming on, I put up at a little public-house by the roadside, and asked for the landlord's company over a pint of wine. We sat beside his kitchen fire, which was the best room in the house, and chatted on politics and the news of the country.

As we continued our discourse, his wife, who had been out to get change, returned, and perceiving that her husband was enjoying a pleasure in which she was not a sharer, she asked him, in an angry tone, what he did there; to which he only replied in an ironical way, by drinking her health. "Mr. Symonds," cried she, "you use me very ill, and I'll bear it no longer. Here three parts of the business is left for me to do, and the fourth left unfinished; while you do nothing but soak with the guests all day long; whereas if a spoonful of liquor were to cure me of a fever, I never touch a drop." I now found what she would be at, and immediately poured her out a glass, which she received with a courtesy, and drinking towards my good health, "Sir," resumed she, "it is not so much for the value of the liquor I am angry, but one cannot help it when the house is going out of the windows. If the customers or guests are to be dunned, all the burden lies upon my back; he'd as lief eat that glass as budge after them himself. There now, above-stairs, we have a young woman who has come to take up her lodgings here, and I don't believe she has got any money, by her over-civility. I am certain she is very slow of payment, and I wish she were put in mind of it."—"What signifies minding her?" cried the host; "if she be slow she is sure." "I don't know that," replied the wife; "but I know that I am sure she has been here for a fortnight, and we have not yet seen the cross of her money."—"I suppose, my dear," cried he, "we shall have it all in a lump."—"In a lump!" cried the other. "I hope we may get it any way; and that I am resolved this very night, or out she tramps, bag and baggage." —"Consider, my dear," cried the husband, "she is a gentlewoman, and deserves more respect."—"As for the matter of that," returned the hostess, "gentle or simple, out she shall pack. Gentry may be good things where they take; but for my part I never saw much good of them at the sign of the Harrow."

Thus saying, she ran up a narrow flight of stairs that went from the kitchen to a room overhead, and I soon perceived, by the loudness of her voice and the bitterness of her reproaches, that no money was to be had from her lodger. I could hear her remonstrances very distinctly: "Out, I say: pack out this moment, or I'll give thee a mark you won't be the better for this three months. What! to come and take up an honest house without cross or coin to bless yourself with; come along, I say!"—"Oh, dear madam," cried the stranger, "pity me, pity a poor creature for one night, and death will soon do the rest!" I instantly knew the voice of my poor child Olivia. I flew to her rescue, while the woman was dragging her along by the hair, and I caught the dear forlorn wretch in my arms. "Welcome, any way welcome, my dearest lost one, my treasure, to your poor old father's bosom! Though the vicious forsake thee, there is yet one in the world that will never forsake thee; though thou hadst ten thousand crimes to answer for, he will forget them all,"—"Oh, my own dear"—for minutes she could say no more—"my own dearest, good papa! Could angels be kinder! How do I deserve so much. You can't forgive me. I know you cannot."—"Yes, my child, from my heart I do forgive thee! We shall see many pleasant days yet, my Olivia!"—"Ah, never, sir, never. But alas! papa, you look much paler than you used to do. Could such a thing as I am give so much uneasiness? Surely you have too much wisdom to take the miseries of my guilt upon yourself."—"Our wisdom, young woman——" replied I. "Ah, why so cold a name, papa?" cried she. "This is the first time you ever called me by so cold a name."—"I ask pardon, my darling," returned I; "but I was going to observe that wisdom makes but a slow defence against trouble, though at last a sure one."

The landlady now returned to know if we did not choose a more genteel apartment; to which assenting, we were shown a room where we could converse more freely. After we had talked ourselves into some degree of tranquillity, I could not avoid desiring some account of the graduations that led to her present wretched situation.

"Have patience, my child," cried I, "and I hope things will yet be better. Take some repose to-night, and to-morrow I'll carry you home to your mother and the rest of the family, from whom you'll receive a kind reception. Poor woman! this has gone to her heart, but she loves you still, Olivia, and will forget it."

The next morning I took my daughter behind me, and set out on my return home. As we travelled along, I strove by every persuasion to calm her sorrows and fears, and to arm her with resolution to bear the presence of her offended mother. I took every opportunity, from the prospect of a fine country, through which we passed, to observe how much kinder Heaven was to us than we were to each other, and that the misfortunes of nature's making were very few. I assured her that she should never perceive any change in my affections, and that during my life, which yet might be long, she might depend upon a guardian and an instructor. I armed her against the censures of the world; showed her that books were sweet, unreproaching companions to the miserable, and that if they could not bring us to enjoy life, they would at least teach us to endure it.

The hired horse that we rode was to be put up that night at an inn by the way, within about five miles from my house; and as I was willing to prepare my family for my daughter's reception, I determined to leave her that night at the inn, and to return for her, accompanied by my daughter Sophia, early the next morning. It was night before we reached our appointed stage; however, after seeing her provided with a decent apartment, and having ordered the hostess to prepare proper refreshments, I kissed her, and proceeded onwards home. And now my heart caught new sensations of pleasure the nearer I approached that peaceful mansion. As a bird that had been frightened from its nest, my affections outwent my haste, and hovered round my little fireside with all the rapture of expectation. I called up the many fond things I had to say, and anticipated the welcome I was to receive. I already felt my wife's tender embrace, and smiled at the joy of my little ones. As I walked but slowly, the night waned apace. The labourers of the day were all retired to rest; the lights were out in every cottage; no sounds were heard but the shrilling cock, and the deep-mouthed watch-dog at the hollow distance. I approached my little abode of pleasure, and before I was within a furlong of the place, our honest mastiff came running to welcome me.

It was now near midnight that I came to knock at my door; all was still and silent; my heart dilated with unutterable happiness; when to my amazement, I saw the house bursting out in a blaze of fire, and every aperture red with conflagration! I gave a loud convulsive outcry, and fell upon the pavement insensible. This alarmed my son, who had till this been asleep, and he perceiving the flames instantly waked my wife and daughter, and all running out naked and wild with apprehension, recalled me to life with their anguish. But it was only to objects of new terror; for the flames had by this time caught the roof of our dwelling, part after part continuing to fall in, while the family stood with silent agony looking on as if they enjoyed the blaze. I gazed upon them and upon it by turns, and then looked round for my two little ones: but they were not to be seen. O misery! "Where," cried I, "where are my little ones?"—"They are burnt to death in the flames," said my wife calmly, "and I will die with them." That moment I heard the cry of the babes within, who were just awaked by the fire, and nothing could have stopped me. "Where, where are my children?" cried I, rushing through the flames, and bursting the door of the chamber in which they were confined. "Where are my little ones?" —"Here, dear papa, here we are," cried they together, while the flames were just catching the bed where they lay. I caught them both in my arms, and snatched them through the fire as fast as possible, while just as I was got out, the roof sunk in. "Now," cried I, holding up my children, "now let the flames burn on, and all my possessions perish. Here they are; I have saved my treasure. Here, my dearest, here are our treasures, and we shall yet be happy." We kissed our little darlings a thousand times, they clasped us round the neck, and seemed to share our transports, while their mother laughed and wept by turns.

I now stood a calm spectator of the flames, and after some time began to perceive that my arm to the shoulder was scorched in a terrible manner. It was, therefore, out of my power to give my son any assistance, either in attempting to save our goods, or preventing the flames spreading to our corn. By this time the neighbours were alarmed, and came running to our assistance; but all they could do was to stand, like us, spectators of the calamity. My goods, among which were the notes I had reserved for my daughters' fortunes, were entirely consumed, except a box with some papers that stood in the kitchen, and two or three things more of little consequence, which my son brought away in the beginning. The neighbours contributed, however, what they could to lighten our distress. They brought us clothes, and furnished one of our outhouses with kitchen utensils; so that by daylight we had another, though a wretched dwelling, to retire to. My honest next neighbour and his children were not the least assiduous in providing us with everything necessary, and offering whatever consolation untutored benevolence could suggest.

When the fears of my family had subsided, curiosity to know the cause of my long stay began to take place; having, therefore, informed them of every particular, I proceeded to prepare them for the reception of our lost one, and though we had nothing but wretchedness now to impart, I was willing to procure her a welcome to what we had. This task would have been more difficult but for our recent calamity, which had humbled my wife's pride and blunted it by more poignant afflictions. Being unable to go for my poor child myself, as my arm grew very painful, I sent my son and daughter, who soon returned, supporting the wretched delinquent, who had not the courage to look up at her mother, whom no instructions of mine could persuade to a perfect reconciliation; for women have a much stronger sense of female error than men. "Ah, madam," cried her mother, "this is but a poor place you have come to after so much finery. My daughter Sophy and I can afford but little entertainment to persons who have kept company only with people of distinction. Yes, Miss Livy, your poor father and I have suffered very much of late, but I hope Heaven will forgive you." During this reception the unhappy victim stood pale and trembling, unable to weep or to reply; but I could not continue a silent spectator of her distress; wherefore assuming a degree of severity in my voice and manner, which was ever followed with instant submission: "I entreat, woman, that my words may be now marked once for all; I have here brought you back a poor deluded wanderer: her return to duty demands the revival of our tenderness. The real hardships of life are now coming fast upon us; let us not, therefore, increase them by dissension among each other. If we live harmoniously together we may yet be contented, as there are enough of us to shut out the censuring world and keep each other in countenance. The kindness of Heaven is promised to the penitent, and let ours be directed by the example. Heaven, we are assured, is much more pleased to view a repentant sinner, than ninety-nine persons who have supported a course of undeviating rectitude. And this is right; for that single effort by which we stop short in the downhill path to perdition, is itself a greater exertion of virtue than a hundred acts of justice."

DOUBLE ENCOUNTER

By EVELYN EVERETT-GREEN

When Dorothy Ewing returned from India and joined the girls at Greyshott Manor, an exclusive finishing school, she did not know that there were many encounters and surprises awaiting her. However, she quickly took a dislike to Laura Vacher, just as she warmed to the friendliness of Margot James, otherwise Magpie. This story is taken from "Miss Greyshott's Girls," in which life at Greyshott Manor is related.

DOROTHY EWING looked up from the letter she was writing. "A walk, Madge? Yes, I should like a walk with you very much. But I think, if Laura is going, I had better not come."

Margot twisted herself about to get her hat straighter by the aid of Dorothy's toilet glass, and, shooting a queer little look across at the quiet figure by the table, asked:

"Why don't you like Laura?"

"Isn't that rather an odd way of putting it? It is Laura who has shown from the first that she does not like me!"

"Oh, well, that is rather Laura's way; but it doesn't mean so very much. You were sprung upon us rather suddenly; but I've got over it. You're a queer little quiet soul; but you've got some spunk in you for all that. I like you, and I don't care what Laura says. I'll be friends with you if you'll let me; but you're a bit *difficile*, you know, my child!"

Dorothy was smiling in that odd little way of hers which none of her companions quite understood. She sat a great deal up here in her pleasant little room. She was not fond of the company of the rest of the girls. Miss Greyshott did not interfere. The girls were left to their own devices to a great extent, and all this tended to keep Dorothy apart from the rest.

"Laura's got a temper; but she's not bad when you know her, especially if you give her her own way. Tell me why you don't like her, Dolly; I'm sure you don't."

"If you wish to know, Laura Vacher seems to me rather a vulgar girl."

Madge stared with all her eyes.

"Vulgar! But don't you know her father is an earl?"

"Oh, yes, I think we all know that. Lady Laura is not reticent upon that subject. I did not say she was not an earl's daughter. I only said she was rather vulgar."

This was quite a new idea to Margot, and her face said as much. Dorothy's small head was held a little high; the lines of the sensative mouth expressed a certain amount of quiet disdain.

"It may be a prejudice on my part, but I prefer to mix with well-born and well-mannered persons myself. Mushroom peerages bestowed on wealthy tradesmen do not confer either of these qualifications."

"Oh, Dorothy, you do talk like a book!"

Then Dorothy's face relaxed. A merry little smile woke in her eyes first, and then curved her lips, whilst the colour stole most becomingly into her pale cheeks.

"Magpie, I'm afraid I do. I'm sometimes afraid I'm rather a prig! I've always lived with old people. I believe I think old, and I know I talk old. I know I must be a bore to you all. Run off and walk with Laura. I want to finish my letter, and then I'll go out myself."

"Dolly, you've got it in you to be jolly, I know you have. I'm going to rout you out of your demure ways; but perhaps we'll not take Laura into our confidence. So I'll be off with her to-day; but you'll not escape me another time!"

Laura was waiting rather impatiently. This going out together along the quiet country roads was a pleasure which was something of a novelty. Before this summer, Miss Selina or the French governess used to accompany the girls when they went beyond the limits of the grounds.

"What a time you've been! I hate kicking my heels!"

"I've scarcely been a minute; I just looked in to see if Dorothy wanted to come; but she didn't."

"Dorothy! What do you want bothering with her? I hope you're not going to take up with a little——"

"Oh, bother, Laura, don't nag! Dorothy's a queer little cuss, as boys would say; but I don't think she's a bad sort——"

"She's no business to be here, anyhow, a little low-born chit like that!"

"How do you know she is low-born?" asked Margot, mirth

beginning to sparkle from her eyes. "I thought Colonel Ewing was a rather distinguished soldier."

"So she pretends, perhaps; but only Indian army—Hyderabad contingent, I think she said; so's the brother. Shows they're poor, you know—good pay, but no prestige. And her mother—do you notice one can never get a word out of her about her mother's family? I expect she was—well, perhaps a half-caste or something disreputable——"

"Laura, why do you have such horrid ideas about people? No wonder Dorothy thinks you vulgar!"

The word escaped her unawares; the moment after she would have recalled it if she could; but it was too late. Laura's face was a study of astonishment, anger, and mortification. She was scarlet with passion, and held her teeth tightly clenched.

"She said that—Dorothy Ewing—the Guttersnipe!"

Madge looked round for some way of escape. Laura in a rage was no pleasant companion. They had been walking rapidly along a path across a meadow, which led by a stile into the highway, and were now near enough to see a stretch of the road. With a sense of relief Madge was able to avoid a direct reply by uttering an eager exclamation—

"Oh, Laura, look! What a dear little boy, and what a sweet pony! That must be little Sir Hugh from Winborough Manor—Lady Keith's little boy. And, oh, look, who can that be with him? Did you ever see anybody quite so handsome?"

Laura looked, and instantly became so absorbingly interested that she forgot her rising gust of passion, though the memory of that intolerable criticism would be certain to remain and to rankle later. It was most interesting this sudden glimpse of the newcomers at Winborough Manor. They had heard the news of an arrival, but had not expected to encounter any of the party so soon. Yet here was a delightful boy in khaki and leather gaiters, bestriding a frolicsome small pony, whilst at his side strode a very tall man with fair hair and extraordinarily handsome face. When a thrush in a tree overhead suddenly broke into song, the young man threw up his head and whistled back in such marvellous imitation that the bird was completely deceived, whilst the little boy on the pony shouted aloud for glee.

"Oh, Uncle Arnold, Uncle Arnold, you do do it so well! All the birds think you belong to them!"

"Perhaps they are not far wrong, young shaver. I'm rather on the bird tack myself—enjoying the sunshine of life, and letting the future take care of itself. Now, I wonder whether I can find the nearest path down to the old water-mill, as I promised. I know my bearings, but things have changed a bit since I was here. There used to be a copse over yonder which is all cut down now; but the river must be there all right enough. Ah, here are some ladies; I'll condescend to ask my way. I want my sketch, and you want your mill."

"The old water-mill?" repeated Laura, when the question was put. "Oh, yes, we were just going there ourselves. The paths are rather overgrown and intricate; but it is not far. Shall we show you the way?"

"That is more than kind. Hughie, we are in luck's way! These ladies will take us where we want to go. I wonder if the pony can make his way along too!"

Margot was at the pony's head, stroking, kissing, and caressing him in a rapture of admiration. She loved all animals, and was eager to hear the history of this particular one. Laura walked on with the tall young man, who talked in the easiest and most interesting way.

"I've known the Miss Greyshotts all my life. They always stand in my mind for the type of the perfect gentlewoman of last century. We do not get such types now. Women keep their youth most marvellously; but they lose that delicate aroma of old-world spinsterhood that is so restful and refreshing. But you are too young to understand that yet," he added, turning his clear, sunny gaze upon his companion; "though you have had privileges, if you have grown up at Greyshott Manor. I always said when I heard what those two brave women meant to do, 'They will deserve the thanks of a good many husbands in the days to come. When I go wife-hunting, I shall seek first amongst Miss Greyshott's girls!'"

His laugh rang out like a silver bell. Laura felt little thrills of delight and excitement course through her veins. She looked up in the speaker's face, and said with arch frankness:

"I think you must be one of Lady Keith's brothers from Winborough Manor. People are all talking about you."

"Are they? Ah, yes, of course! Winborough is our old home, though we have been exiles for some time. Yes, I am the idle brother, the scapegrace and ne'er-do-well. Arnold Musgave was a by-word once for laziness and general incompetence——"

"Oh, but you have done things. You have written songs—poems—all sorts of things. I've heard of you——"

He bowed laughingly, genuinely amused at her tone. Admiration was so readily accorded to him that he accepted it almost as a matter of course; but a girl's admiration is never unwelcome to a man, and Laura's was genuine enough.

She looked very handsome to-day, a damask colour in her rather sunburnt face—a regular brunette type, he remarked to himself, with fine eyes just a trifle too near together, and a gipsy-like style of face which appealed to him as being in its right place down here amongst these woodlands, beside the meandering stream, where the old and half-ruined water-mill was so picturesquely set.

"If you would only sit for me as the genius of the place!" he said, as he unstrapped his paraphernalia from the pony, and set up his easel. "I always want a figure for my foregrounds. A bit of scarlet over your head—ah, that scarf is the very thing! *The Haunt of the Gipsy*—that is the sort of name to catch on! Sitting and gazing into the water, and just looking up—so—with eyes full of mystery! Ah, I see you have the dramatic instinct! We shall understand each other!"

Laura sat entranced; Margot played awhile with the child, and then she too was drawn by the fascination of watching the picture grow; and little Hughie, seeing them all absorbed in matters too grown up for his taste, climbed upon his pony cleverly enough, and set off to explore on his own account.

Meantime Dorothy finished her letter for the Indian mail, and then sallied forth to post it herself, and to walk as far as Miss Drury's to pay her a little visit.

She took the paths through the copses and fields to the village, and then, tempted by the beauty and brightness of the day, she wandered on dreamily, not heeding her direction very much, till she was awakened from the reverie by the sound of a gay child's voice, uttering whoops and cries, to the accompaniment of the thudding sound of horse-hoofs over the soft earth.

Suddenly she got clear of the woodland, and found herself upon a stretch of open common, where a small boy upon a small pony was careering about in great enjoyment, putting the pony at little jumps—over ditches or across furze bushes—exciting him by his shouts and digs of the heels, and sharp switches across his neck, till, just as Dorothy appeared, the little fellow suddenly jerked down his head, took the bit between his teeth, flourished up his heels, and made off at a gallop for the woods. Dorothy saw the danger and shouted to the child:

"Slip off, slip off behind, if you can; don't let him carry you into the copse!"

But either the warning came too late, or was not heard, for the next instant the pony dashed into the underwood, and the small rider was literally swept to the ground by the low-hanging branches, and lay there full length, whilst the pony tore away, snorting and riderless, with clashing stirrups and trailing reins.

With a face as white as her collar, Dorothy ran up to the prostrate child. To her great relief his eyes were opened, and he greeted her approach with a smile.

"I'm all right—not hurt a bit—but I can't just—breathe yet!" he panted, and Dorothy bent over him, and lifted him half up; and the next minute he was on his feet, breathless still, and with clothes all awry, but unhurt in limbs and all agog with eagerness to avoid frightening his mother.

"If Wagtail runs home without me she'll be awful scared! I say, do you know the way home? If I could get there first——"

"To Winborough Manor?"

"Yes—that's it. I don't want mummy scared. It was only play. I didn't think of those trees. Come along! Take me home. Mummy will be so much obliged to you for helping me. Do you know the way?"

"Yes, dear. The Manor is quite near, just across the wood and through a field. I expect the pony thought it was dinner-time, and made off. Let me just set your collar straight, and wipe the moss off your jacket. There, I don't think anybody would guess you had had a fall. And if we are quick on our feet, perhaps Wagtail will not be home first. Ponies often stop to feed when they are free."

"Yes, and Wagtail hasn't been there long—only just a few days.

Uncle Gordon had him sent on trial. He's a jolly little beggar. Uncle Arnold calls him so. I want to keep him; so I don't want mummy to be frightened."

The little boy appeared not to know the meaning of shyness. Dorothy had no need to ask questions; she was hearing all about Winborough Manor and its inmates as fast as the child's tongue could wag. As they neared the inner ring fence, they saw the pony careering round in search of the gate to his stable-yard. Hugh laughed gleefully as he climbed the fence and made believe to help Dorothy over.

"We shall be home first—mother won't be frightened! Oh, but you must come—indeed, you must. I want to tell her how kind you've been to me!"

Lady Keith espied her little boy from afar, and came walking over the park-like sweep of meadow to meet them.

"Mummy, darling, I've had a lovely time. Uncle Arnold got some ladies and is drawing them and the mill, and I and Wagtail had steeplechases over the common. And Wagtail ran into the wood, and I slipped off him; and this lady came and brushed me and showed me the way home; and I've had a lovely time!"

Lady Keith's hand was extended towards Dorothy; her kind, sweet eyes seemed to go straight to the girl's heart.

"I am so much obliged to you. Hughie is rather too rash and venturesome with his ponies. Did he get a fall?"

"He was not thrown; he rides splendidly; but the brushwood was too thick. I was so glad he was able to fall safely as the pony galloped under the trees. He is not hurt, but he did not quite know where he was. So he asked me to show him."

"I am so much obliged. We are strangers here just at present; but that will soon be changed. Perhaps I may know your—your—parents—or friends—though you would have been a child when I left."

"I do not belong here," answered Dorothy, with a quick upward glance into the kind, questioning face; "I have no real home anywhere. I am one of Miss Greyshott's girls."

let me go, and may all knights-errant be as erring to themselves as they have been with me."

Sancho took out of his bag a piece of bread and cheese, and, giving it to the lad, said: "Take it, brother Andrew, for each of us has a share in your misfortune."

"What share have you in it?" asked Andrew.

"This piece of bread and cheese which I give thee," said Sancho, "for no one knows whether I shall have need of it again or not. For you must know, my friend, that we squires to knights-errant suffer great hunger and ill-luck, and many things which are better felt than told."

Andrew laid hold of his bread and cheese, and, seeing that no one gave him anything else, bowed his head and went on his way.

When they had finished their dinner they saddled and went to horse once more, and travelled all that day and the next without any adventure of note, until they arrived at the inn, which was the dread and terror of Sancho Panza, and though he would rather not have entered it, yet he could not avoid doing so. The innkeeper, the hostess, and her daughter, seeing Don Quixote and Sancho return, went out to meet them with tokens of great love and joy. The knight returned their compliments with grave courtesy, and bade them prepare a better bed than they gave him the last time.

"Sir," said the hostess, "if you would pay us better than the last time, we would give you one fit for a prince."

Don Quixote answered that he would, and they prepared a reasonable good bed for him in the same room where he lay before. Then he went off to bed at once, because he was tired and weary, both in body and mind.

Don Quixote was still asleep when the dinner was served, and during dinner—the innkeeper, his wife and his daughter being there, as well as all the travellers—they talked of Don Quixote's strange craze, and of the state in which they had found him.

The curate explained it was the books of knighthood that Don Quixote had read that had turned his head.

"I know not how that can be," said the innkeeper, "for to my thinking there is no finer reading in the world; and when it is harvest-time the reapers here often collect during the midday heat, and one who can read takes one of these books in hand, while some thirty of us get round him, and sit listening with so much delight that I could find it in my heart to be hearing such stories day and night."

"And I think well of them, too," said the hostess, "for when the reading is going on you are so full of it that you forget to scold me, and I have a good time of it."

"Ah," said her daughter, "I too listen, and though I like not the fights which please my father, yet the lamentations which the knights make when they are away from their ladies make me weep for pity, and I enjoy that."

"We have need here," said the curate, "of our friends. Beware, my good host, of these books, and take care that they carry you not on the road they have taken Don Quixote."

"Not so," said the innkeeper. "I shall not be such a fool as to turn knight-errant; for I see well enough that it is not the fashion now to do as they used to do in the times when these famous knights roamed about the world. All that is of no use nowadays."

Sancho came in in the midst of this, and was amazed to hear them say that knights-errant now were of no use, and that books of knighthood were full of follies and lies, and he made up his mind to see the end of this journey of his master, and if that did not turn out as happily as he expected, to return home to his wife and children and to his former labours.

At this moment a noise came from the room where Don Quixote was lying, and Sancho went hastily to see if his master wanted anything.

In a few moments he returned, rushing wildly back, and shouting at the top of his voice: "Come, good sirs, quickly, and help my master, who is engaged in one of the most terrible battles my eyes have ever seen. I swear he has given the giant such a cut that he has sliced his head clean off like a turnip."

"What sayest thou, friend?" said the curate. "Art thou in thy wits, Sancho? How can it be as you say?"

By this time they heard a marvellous great noise within the chamber, and Don Quixote shouting out: "Hold, thief, scoundrel, rogue! Now I have thee, and thy scimitar shall not avail thee!"

And it seemed as if he were striking a number of mighty blows on the walls.

"Do not stand there listening," cried Sancho, "but go in and part the fray, or aid my master. Though I think it will not be necessary, for doubtless the giant is dead by now, and giving an account of the ill life he led; for I saw his blood was all about the house and his head cut off, which is as big as a great wine-bag."

"May I be hewed in pieces," cried the innkeeper on hearing this, "if Don Quixote has not been slashing at one of the skins of red wine that are standing filled at his bed head, and the wine that is spilt must be what this fellow takes for blood."

So saying he ran into the room, and the rest followed him, and found Don Quixote in the strangest guise imaginable. He was in his shirt, which did not reach to his knees. His legs were very long and lean, covered with hair, and not overclean. On his head he wore a greasy red nightcap which belonged to the innkeeper. Round his left arm he had folded the blanket from off his bed. In his right hand he gripped his naked sword, with which he laid round about him with many a thwack, shouting out as if indeed he was at battle with some terrible giant. The best sport of all was that his eyes were not open, for he was indeed asleep and dreaming that he was fighting a giant. He had given so many blows to the wine-bags, supposing them to be the giant, that the whole chamber flowed with wine.

When the innkeeper saw this he flew into such a rage that he set upon Don Quixote with his clenched fist, and began to pummel him, so that if the curate had not pulled him off he would have finished the battle of the giant altogether. In spite of this the poor knight did not awake until a great kettleful of cold water from the well was thrown right over him, when Don Quixote woke up, but even then did not understand where he was.

As for Sancho, he went up and down the floor, searching for the giant's head, and seeing he could not find it, said: "Now I know that everything I see in this house is enchanted, for his head is not to be seen here, though I myself saw it cut off with my own eyes, and the blood running from the body as from a fountain."

"What blood or what fountain dost thou cackle of here?" cried the innkeeper. "Thou thief! Dost thou not see that the blood and the fountain is no other thing but the wine-bags which are ripped open, and the red wine which swims up and down the room?"

"I know nothing but this," replied Sancho, "that if I cannot find the giant's head my earldom will dissolve like salt cast into water." For indeed Sancho awake was worse than his master asleep, so greatly had his master's promises turned his brain.

The innkeeper was at his wits' end at seeing the stupidity of the squire and the mischief done by his master, but he determined that they should not as before go away without paying; that knighthood should be no excuse for this, and he would make them pay for the very patches in the wine-skins that had been ruined.

All this time the curate was holding Don Quixote's hands, who, believing that he had finished the adventure and was in the presence of the Princess Micomicona, fell on his knees before the curate and said: "Your highness, exalted and beautiful lady, may live from henceforth secure from any danger that this wretched giant might have done to you; and I am also freed this day from the promise I made to you, seeing that I have, with the assistance of her through whose favour I live and breathe, so happily completed my labour."

"Did I not say so?" cried Sancho, hearing his master. "I was not drunk. My master has salted the giant down this time, and my earldom is secure."

Who could help laughing at the follies of the two, master and man? All of them laughed except the innkeeper, who burst out into fits of anger ten times worse than before.

At length the curate quelled the storm, promising to satisfy him for the wine and the skins.

ROSE VISITS THE WHITE WITCH

By CHARLES KINGSLEY

Rose Salterne, a pretty Devon lass with no parents to help her, goes to visit Lucy Passmore, known locally as the White Witch, to discover if the supposed sorceress can provide her with a means of peering into the future. Lucy provides her, instead, with a strange adventure on the shore at midnight. Rose is one of the many interesting characters presented in "Westward Ho!" a tale of stirring deeds in the days of Good Queen Bess.

ROSE SALTERNE was a thorough specimen of a West-coast maiden, full of passionate, impulsive affections, and wild, dreamy imaginations, a fit subject, as the North Devon women are still, for all romantic and gentle superstitions. Left early without a mother's care, she had fed her fancy upon the legends and ballads of her native land, till she believed—what did she not believe?—of mermaids and pixies, charms and witches, dreams and omens, and all that world of magic in which most of the countrywomen, and countrymen too, believed firmly enough.

Rose did not break her heart for any of her admirers, and why should they break theirs for her? They were all very charming, each in his way; but one of them was not so very much better than the other.

Poor little Rose! Had she but had a mother! But she was to learn her lesson, such as it was, in another school. She would go and see Lucy Passmore, the White Witch; Lucy knew everything; Lucy would tell her what to do; perhaps even whom to marry.

Lucy was a fat, jolly woman of fifty, with little pig-eyes, which twinkled like sparks of fire, and eyebrows which sloped upwards and outwards, like those of a satyr, as if she had been (as indeed she had) all her life looking out of the corners of her eyes. Her qualifications as White Witch were boundless cunning, equally boundless good nature, considerable knowledge of human weaknesses, some mesmeric power, some skill in "yarbs," as she called her simples, a firm faith in the virtue of her own incantations, and the faculty of holding her tongue. By dint of these she contrived to gain a fair share of money, and also (which she liked even better) of power, among the simple folk for many miles round. If a child was scalded, a tooth ached, a piece of silver was stolen, a heifer shrew-struck, a pig bewitched, a young damsel crost in love, Lucy was called in, and Lucy found a remedy, especially for the latter complaint. Now and then she found herself on ticklish ground, for the kind-heartedness which compelled her to help all distressed damsels out of a scrape, sometimes compelled her also to help them into one; whereon enraged fathers called Lucy ugly names, and threatened to send her into Exeter gaol for a witch, and she smiled quietly, and hinted that if she were "like some that were ready to return evil for evil, such talk as that would bring no blessing on them that spoke it."

The Prophetess, when Rose approached her oracular cave, was seated on a tripod in front of the fire, distilling strong waters out of penny royal. "Bless my dear soul alive, who ever would have thought to see the Rose of Torridge to my poor little place!"

Rose sat down: and then? How to begin was more than she knew, and she stayed silent a full five minutes, looking earnestly at the point of her shoe, till Lucy, who was an adept in such cases, thought it best to proceed to business at once, and save Rose the delicate operation of opening the ball herself; and so, in her own way, half fawning, half familiar:

"Well, my dear young lady, and what is it I can do for ye? For I guess you want a bit of old Lucy's help, eh? Though I'm most mazed to see ye here, surely. I should have supposed that pretty face could manage they sort of matters for itself. Eh?"

Rose, thus bluntly charged, confessed at once, and with many blushes and hesitations, made her soon understand that what she wanted was "To have her fortune told."

"Eh? Oh! I see. The pretty face has managed it a bit too well already, eh?"

Rose shook her head.

"Well, well," said Lucy, who took nothing by her move, simply because there was nothing to take; "think over it—think over it, my dear life; and if you did set your mind on any one—why, then —then maybe I might help you to a sight of him."

"A sight of him?"

"Oh, I can show ye that, tu, I can. Ben there's a way to't, a sure way; but 'tis mortal cold for the time o' year, you zee."

"But what is it, then?" said Rose, who had in her heart been longing for something of that very kind, and had half made up her mind to ask for a charm.

"Why, you'm not afraid to goo into the say by night for a minute, are you? And to-morrow night would serve, too; 'twill be just low tide to midnight."

"If you would come with me perhaps——"

"I'll come, I'll come, and stand within call, to be sure. Only do ye mind this, dear soul alive, not to goo telling a crumb about mun, noo, not for the world, or yu'll see nought at all, indeed, now. And beside, there's a noxious business grow'd up against me; and I hear tell how I shall to Exeter gaol for a witch—did ye ever hear the likes? They be mortal feared of witches, they Papists, and mortal hard on 'em, even on a pure body like me, that doth a bit in the white way; 'case why you see, dear life," said she, with one of her humorous twinkles, "tu to a trade do never agree. Do ye try my bit of a charm, now; do ye!"

Rose could not resist the temptation; and between them both the charm was agreed on, and the next night was fixed for its trial, on the payment of certain current coins of the realm (for Lucy, of course, must live by her trade).

Rose, fevered with curiosity and superstition, and allured by the very wildness and possible danger of the spell, kept her appointment; and, a few minutes before midnight, stood on the grey shingle beach with her counsellor.

"You be safe enough here to-night, Miss. My old man is snoring sound abed, and there's no other soul ever sets foot here o' nights, except it be the mermaids now and then. Goodness, Father, where's our boat? It ought to be up here on the pebbles."

Rose pointed to a strip of sand some forty yards nearer the sea, where the boat lay.

"Oh, the lazy old villain! He's been round the rocks after pollock this evening, and never taken the trouble to hale the boat up. I'll trounce him for it when I get home. I only hope he's made her fast where she is, that's all! He's more plague to me than ever my money will be. O deary me!"

And the goodwife bustled down toward the boat, with Rose behind her.

"Iss, 'tis fast, sure enough: and the oars aboard too! Well, I never! Oh, the lazy thief, to leave they here to be stole! I'll just sit in the boat, dear, and watch mun, while you go down to the say; for you must be all alone to yourself you know, or you'll see nothing. There's the looking-glass; now go, and dip your head three times, and mind you don't look to land or sea before you've said the words, and looked upon the glass. Now, be quick, it's just upon midnight."

And she coiled herself up in the boat, while Rose went faltering down the strip of sand, some twenty yards farther, and there slipping off her clothes, stood shivering and trembling for a moment before she entered the sea.

She was between two walls of rock; that on her left hand, some twenty feet high, hid her in deepest shade; that on her right, though much lower, took the whole blaze of the midnight moon. Great festoons of live and purple seaweed hung from it, shading dark cracks and crevices, fit haunts for all the goblins of the sea. On her left hand, the peaks of the rock frowned down ghastly black; on her right hand, far aloft, the downs slept bright and cold.

The breeze had died away; not even a roller broke the perfect stillness of the cove. The gulls were all asleep upon the ledges. Over all was a true autumn silence; a silence which may be heard. She stood awed, and listened in hope of a sound which might tell her that any living thing beside herself existed.

There was a faint bleat, as of a new-born lamb, high above her head; she started and looked up. Then a wail from the cliffs, as of a child in pain, answered by another from the opposite rocks. They were but the passing snipe, and the otter calling to her brood; but to her they were mysterious, supernatural goblins, come to answer to her call. Nevertheless, they only quickened her expectation; and the witch had told her not to fear them. If she performed the rite duly, nothing would harm her: but she could hear the beating of her own heart, as she stepped, mirror in hand, into the cold water, waded hastily, as far as she dare, and then stopped aghast.

A ring of flame was round her waist; every limb was bathed in lambent light; all the multitudinous life of the autumn sea, stirred by her approach, had flashed suddenly into glory. She could see every shell which crawled on the white sand at her feet, every rock-fish which played in and out of the crannies, and stared at her with its broad, bright eyes; while the great palmate oarweeds which waved along the chasm, half-seen in the glimmering water, seemed to beckon her down with long brown hands to a grave amid their chilly bowers. She turned to flee, but she had gone too far now to retreat; hasily dipping her head three times, she hurried out to the sea-marge, and looking through her dripping locks at the magic mirror, pronounced the incantation.

"A maiden pure, here I stand,
Neither on sea, nor yet on land;
Angels watch me on either hand.
If you be landsman, come down the strand;
If you be sailor, come up the sand;
If you be angel, come from the sky,
Look in my glass, and pass me by.
Look in my glass, and go from the shore;
Leave me, but love me for evermore."

The incantation was hardly finished; her eyes were straining into the mirror, where, as may be supposed, nothing appeared but the sparkle of the drops from her own tresses, when she heard rattling down the pebbles the hasty feet of men and horses.

She darted into a cavern of the high rock, and hastily dressed herself; the steps held on right to the boat. Peeping out, half-dead with terror, she saw there four men, two of whom had just leaped from their horses, and turning them adrift, began to help the other two in running the boat down.

Whereon, out of the stern sheets, arose, like an angry ghost, the portly figure of Lucy Passmore, and shrieked in shrillest treble:

"Eh! ye villains, ye roogs, what do ye want staling poor folks' boats by night like this?"

The whole party recoiled in terror, and one turned to run up the beach, shouting at the top of his voice, "'Tis a marmaiden—a marmaiden asleep in Willy Passmore's boat!"

"I wish it were any sich good luck," she could hear Will say; "'tis my wife, oh dear!" and he cowered down, expecting the hearty cuff which he received duly, as the White Witch, leaping out of the boat, dared any man to touch it, and thundered to her husband to go home to bed.

"Lucy, Lucy!" shrieked her husband, in shrillest Devon falsetto, "be you mazed? Be you mazed, lass? They promised me two gold nobles before I'd lend them the boot!"

"Tu?" shrieked the matron, with a tone of ineffable scorn. "And do ye call yourself a man?"

"Tu nobles! tu nobles!" shrieked he again, hopping about at oar's length.

"Tu? And would you sell your soul under ten? Ten nobles, or I'll kep ye here till morning!" And the ten nobles were paid into her hand.

And now the boat, its dragon guardian being pacified, was run down to the sea, and close past the nook where poor little Rose was squeezing herself into the farthest and darkest corner, among wet seaweed and rough barnacles, holding her breath as they approached.

They passed her, and the boat's keel was already in the water; Lucy had followed them close, for reasons of her own, and perceiving close to the water's edge a dark cavern, cunningly surmised that it contained Rose, and planted her ample person right across its mouth, while she grumbled at her husband.

But the night's adventures were not ended yet; for just as the boat was launched, a faint halloo was heard upon the beach, and a minute after, a horseman plunged down the pebbles, and along the sand, and pulling his horse up on its haunches close to the terrified group, dropped, rather than leaped, from the saddle.

As he passed Rose, she saw his ghastly bleeding face, half bound up with a handkerchief, which could not conceal the convulsions of rage, shame, and despair, which twisted it from all its usual beauty. His eyes glared wildly round—and once, right into the cavern. They met hers, so full, and keen, and dreadful, that forgetting she was utterly invisible, the terrified girl was on the point of shrieking aloud.

"He has overlooked me!" said she, shuddering to herself.

The boat was thrust into the sea, faster than ever it went before, it was round the rocks, and out of sight, when the rattle of horse-hoofs was heard above.

Said Lucy Passmore aloud, "You lie still there, dear life, and settle your sperrits; you'm so safe as ever was rabbit to burrow. I'll see what happens, if I die for it!" And so saying, she squeezed herself up through a cleft to a higher ledge, from whence she could see what passed in the valley.

Down she came again.

"And now then, my dear life, us be better to goo hoom and get you sommat warm. You'm mortal cold, I rackon, by now. I was cruel fear'd for ye: but I kept mun off clever, didn't I now? Goodness, Father! And all this while us have forgot the very thing us come about! Who did you see?"

"Only that face!" said Rose, shuddering.

"Not in the glass, maid? Say then, not in the glass?"

"Would to heaven it had been! Lucy, what if he were the man I was fated to——"

"He's a pretty wooer!" said Lucy at last contemptuously. "Be a brave maid, then, be a brave maid, and never terrify yourself with his unlucky face. It's because there was none here worthy of ye, that ye seed none in glass. Maybe he's to be a foreigner, from over seas, and that's why his sperrit was so long a coming. A duke, or a prince to the least, I'll warrant, he'll be, that carries off the Rose of Bideford."

But in spite of all the good dame's flattery, Rose could not wipe that fierce face away from her eyeballs. She reached home safely, and crept to bed undiscovered: and when the next morning, as was to be expected, found her laid up with something very like a fever, from excitement, terror, and cold, the phantom grew stronger and stronger before her, and it required all her tact and self-restraint to avoid betraying by her exclamations what had happened on that fantastic night.

MIDAS AND MARYGOLD

By NATHANIEL HAWTHORNE

King Midas, whose love of gold drove wisdom from his mind, was given his heart's desire by a smiling stranger. Only then did the greedy king learn that what he had desired so earnestly and above all else was no boon, but rather a curse. His daughter Marygold, whom he loved dearly, was lost to him because of his insane greed. But because Midas was wise enough to realize his folly the smiling stranger withdrew the magic gift, and Marygold was restored to her despairing father. This story is taken from "A Wonder Book."

ONCE upon a time, there lived a very rich man, and a king besides, whose name was Midas; and he had a little daughter, whom nobody but myself ever heard of, and whose name I either never knew, or have entirely forgotten. So, because I love odd names for little girls, I choose to call her Marygold.

This King Midas was fonder of gold than of anything else in the world. He valued his royal crown chiefly because it was composed of that precious metal. If he loved anything better, or half so well, it was the one little maiden who played so merrily around her father's footstool. But the more Midas loved his daughter, the more did he desire and seek for wealth. He thought, foolish man! that the best thing he could possibly do for this dear child would be to bequeath her the immensest pile of yellow glistening coin that had ever been heaped together since the world was made. Thus, he gave all his thoughts and all his time to this one purpose. If ever he happened to gaze for an instant at the gold-tinted clouds of sunset, he wished that they were real gold, and that they could be squeezed safely into his strong box. When little Marygold ran to meet him, with a bunch of buttercups and dandelions, he used to say, "Poh, poh, child! If these flowers were as golden as they look, they would be worth plucking!"

And yet, in his earlier days, before he was so entirely possessed of this insane desire for riches, King Midas had shown a great taste for flowers. He had planted a garden, in which grew the biggest and beautifullest and sweetest roses that any mortal ever saw or smelt. These roses were still growing in the garden, as large, as lovely, and as fragrant, as when Midas used to pass whole hours in gazing at them, and inhaling their perfume. But now, if he looked at them at all, it was only to calculate how much the garden would be worth if each of the innumerable rose-petals were a thin plate of gold. And though he once was fond of music (in spite of an idle story about his ears, which were said to resemble those of an ass), the only music for poor Midas, now, was the chink of one coin against another.

At length (as people always grow more and more foolish, unless they take care to grow wiser and wiser), Midas had got to be so exceedingly unreasonable that he could scarcely bear to see or touch any object that was not gold. He made it his custom, therefore, to pass a large portion of every day in a dark and dreary apartment, under ground, at the basement of his palace. It was here that he kept his wealth. To this dismal hole—for it was little better than a dungeon—Midas betook himself whenever he wanted to be particularly happy.

Midas was enjoying himself in his treasure-room one day, as usual, when he perceived a shadow fall over the heaps of gold; and, looking suddenly up, what should he behold but the figure of a stranger, standing in the bright and narrow sunbeam! It was a young man, with a cheerful and ruddy face.

The stranger gazed about the room; and when his lustrous smile had glistened up all the golden objects there, he turned to Midas.

"You are a wealthy man, friend Midas!" he observed. "I doubt whether any other four walls on earth contain so much gold as you have contrived to pile up in this room."

"I have done pretty well—pretty well," answered Midas, in a discontented tone. "But, after all, it is but a trifle, when you consider that it has taken me my whole life to get it together. If one could live a thousand years, he might have time to grow rich!"

"What!" exclaimed the stranger. "Then you are not satisfied?"

Midas shook his head.

"And pray what would satisfy you?" asked the stranger. "Merely for the curiosity of the thing I should be glad to know."

Midas paused and meditated. Raising his head, he looked the lustrous stranger in the face.

"Well, Midas," observed his visitor, "I see that you have at length hit upon something that will satisfy you. Tell me your wish."

"It is only this," replied Midas. "I am weary of collecting my

treasures with so much trouble, and beholding the heap so diminutive after I have done my best. I wish everything that I touch to be changed to gold!"

The stranger's smile grew so very broad that it seemed to fill the room.

"The Golden Touch!" exclaimed he. "You certainly deserve

credit, friend Midas, for striking out so brilliant a conception. But are you quite sure that this will satisfy you?"

"How could it fail?" said Midas.

"And will you never regret the possession of it?"

"What could induce me?" asked Midas. "I ask nothing else to render me perfectly happy."

"Be it as you wish, then," replied the stranger, waving his hand in token of farewell. "To-morrow, at sunrise, you will find yourself gifted with the Golden Touch."

The figure of the stranger then became exceedingly bright, and Midas involuntarily closed his eyes. On opening them again, he beheld only one yellow sunbeam in the room, and, all around him, the glistening of the precious metal which he had spent his life in hoarding up.

Whether Midas slept as usual that night, the story does not say. Asleep or awake, however, his mind was probably in the state of a child's to whom a beautiful new plaything has been promised in the morning. At any rate, day had hardly peeped over the hills when King Midas was broad awake, and, stretching his arms out of bed, began to touch the objects that were within reach. He was anxious to prove whether the Golden Touch had really come according to the stranger's promise. So he laid his finger on a chair by the bed-side, and on various other things, but was grievously disappointed to perceive that they remained of exactly the same substance as before.

All this while, it was only the grey of the morning, with but a streak of brightness along the edge of the sky, where Midas could not see it. He lay in a very disconsolate mood, regretting the downfall of his hopes, and kept growing sadder and sadder, until the earliest sunbeam shone through the window and gilded the ceiling over his head. It seemed to Midas that this bright yellow sunbeam was reflected in rather a singular way on the white covering of the bed. Looking more closely, what was his astonishment and delight, when he found that this linen fabric had been transmuted to what seemed a woven texture of the purest and brightest gold! The Golden Touch had come to him, with the first sunbeam!

Midas started up in joyful frenzy, and ran about the room grasping at everything that happened to be in his way. He hurriedly put on his clothes, and was enraptured to see himself in a magnificent suit of gold cloth, which retained its flexibility and softness, although it burdened him a little with its weight. He drew out his handkerchief, which little Marygold had hemmed for him. That was likewise gold, with the dear child's neat and pretty stitches running all along the border in gold thread!

Somehow or other, this last transformation did not quite please King Midas. He would rather that his little daughter's handiwork should have remained just the same as when she climbed his knee and put it into his hand.

But it was not worth while to vex himself about a trifle. Midas now took his spectacles from his pocket, and put them on his nose, in order that he might see more distinctly what he was about. In those days spectacles for common people had not been invented, but were already worn by kings; else, how could Midas have had any? To his great perplexity, however, excellent as the glasses were, he discovered that he could not possibly see through them. But this was the most natural thing in the world; for, on taking them off, the transparent crystals turned out to be plates of yellow metal, and, of course, were worthless as spectacles, though valuable as gold. It struck Midas as rather inconvenient, that with all his wealth, he could never again be rich enough to own a pair of serviceable spectacles.

"It is no great matter, nevertheless," said he to himself, very philosophically. "We cannot expect any great good without its being accompanied with some small inconvenience. The Golden Touch is worth the sacrifice of a pair of spectacles, at least, if not of one's very eyesight. My own eyes will serve for ordinary purposes, and little Marygold will soon be old enough to read to me."

What was usually a king's breakfast, in the days of Midas, I really do not know, and cannot stop now to investigate. To the best of my belief, however, on this particular morning, the breakfast consisted of hot cakes, some nice little brook-trout, roasted potatoes, fresh boiled eggs, and coffee, for King Midas himself, and a bowl of bread and milk for his daughter Marygold. At all events, this is a breakfast fit to be set before a king; and whether he had it or not, King Midas could not have had a better.

Little Marygold had not yet made her appearance. Her father ordered her to be called, and, seating himself at table, awaited the child's coming, in order to begin his own breakfast. To do Midas justice, he really loved his daughter, and loved her so much the more this morning on account of the good fortune which had befallen him. It was not a great while before he heard her coming along the passage crying bitterly. The circumstance surprised him, because Marygold was one of the cheerfullest little people whom you would see in a summer's day, and hardly shed a thimbleful of tears in a twelvemonth. When Midas heard her sobs, he determined to put little Marygold into better spirits by an agreeable surprise; so, leaning across the table, he touched his daughter's bowl (which was a china one, with pretty figures all around it), and transmuted it to gleaming gold.

Meanwhile, Marygold slowly and disconsolately opened the door, and showed herself with her apron at her eyes, still sobbing as if her heart would break.

"How now, my little lady!" cried Midas. "Pray what is the matter with you, this bright morning?"

Marygold, without taking the apron from her eyes, held out her hand, in which was one of the roses which Midas had so recently transmuted.

"Beautiful!" exclaimed her father. "And what is there in this magnificent golden rose to make you cry?"

"Ah, dear father!" answered the child, as well as her sobs would let her; "it is not beautiful, but the ugliest flower that ever grew! As soon as I was dressed, I ran into the garden to gather some roses for you; because I know you like them, and like them better when gathered by your little daughter. But, oh dear, dear me! What do you think has happened? Such a misfortune! All the beautiful roses, that smelled so sweetly and had so many lovely blushes, are blighted and spoilt! They are grown quite yellow, as you see this one, and have no longer any fragrance! What can have been the matter with them?"

"Poh, my dear little girl—pray don't cry about it!" said Midas, who was ashamed to confess that he himself had wrought the change which so greatly afflicted her. "Sit down and eat your bread and milk! You will find it easy enough to exchange a golden rose like that (which will last hundreds of years) for an ordinary one, which would wither in a day."

"I don't care for such roses as this!" cried Marygold, tossing it contemptuously away. "It has no smell, and the hard petals prick my nose!"

The child now sat down to the table, but was so occupied with her grief for the blighted roses that she did not even notice the wonderful transmutation of her china bowl. Perhaps this was all the better; for Marygold was accustomed to take pleasure in looking at the queer figures and strange trees and houses that were painted on the circumference of the bowl; and those ornaments were now entirely lost in the yellow hue of the metal.

Midas, meanwhile, had poured out a cup of coffee; and, as a matter of course, the coffee-pot, whatever metal it may have been when he took it up, was gold when he set it down. He thought to himself, that it was rather an extravagant style of splendour, in a king of his simple habits, to breakfast off a service of gold, and began to be puzzled with the difficulty of keeping his treasures safe. The cupboard and the kitchen would no longer be a secure place of deposit for articles so valuable as golden bowls and coffee-pots.

Amid these thoughts, he lifted a spoonful of coffee to his lips, and, sipping it, was astonished to perceive that, the instant his lips touched the liquid, it became molten gold, and, the next moment, hardened into a lump!

"Ha!" exclaimed Midas, rather aghast.

"What is the matter, father?" asked little Marygold, gazing at him, with the tears still standing in her eyes.

"Nothing, child, nothing!" said Midas. "Eat your milk, before it gets quite cold."

He took one of the nice little trout on his plate, and, by way of experiment, touched its tail with his finger. To his horror, it was immediately transmuted from an admirably-fried brook-trout into a gold fish, though not one of those gold-fishes which people often keep in glass globes, as ornaments for the parlour. No; but it was really a metallic fish, and looked as if it had been very cunningly made by the nicest goldsmith in the world. Its little bones were now golden wires; its fins and tail were thin plates of gold; and there were the marks of the fork in it, and all the delicate, frothy appearance of a nicely fried fish, exactly imitated in metal. A very pretty piece of work, as you may suppose; only King Midas, just at that moment, would much rather have had a real trout in his dish than this elaborate and valuable imitation of one.

"Well, this is a quandary!" thought he, leaning back in his chair, and looking quite enviously at little Marygold, who was now eating her bread and milk with great satisfaction. "Such a costly breakfast before me, and nothing that can be eaten!"

Hoping that, by dint of great dispatch, he might avoid what he now felt to be a considerable inconvenience, King Midas next snatched a hot potato, and attempted to cram it into his mouth, and swallow it in a hurry. But the Golden Touch was too nimble for him. He found his mouth full, not of mealy potato, but of solid metal, which so burnt his tongue that he roared aloud, and, jumping up from the table, began to dance and stamp about the room, both with pain and affright.

"Father, dear father!" cried little Marygold, who was a very affectionate child, "pray what is the matter? Have you burnt your mouth?"

"Ah, dear child," groaned Midas, dolefully, "I don't know what is to become of your poor father!"

So great was his hunger and the perplexity of his situation, that he again groaned aloud, and very grievously too. Our pretty Marygold could endure it no longer. She sat a moment gazing at her father, and trying, with all the might of her little wits, to find out what was the matter with him. Then, with a sweet and sorrowful impulse to comfort him, she started from her chair, and running to Midas, threw her arms affectionately about his knees. He bent down and kissed her. He felt that his little daughter's love was worth a thousand times more than he had gained by the Golden Touch.

"My precious, precious Marygold!" cried he.

But Marygold made no answer.

Alas, what had he done? How fatal was the gift which the stranger bestowed! The moment the lips of Midas touched Marygold's forehead, a change had taken place. Her sweet, rosy face, so full of affection as it had been, assumed a glittering yellow colour, with yellow tear-drops congealing on her cheeks. Her beautiful brown ringlets took the same tint. Her soft and tender little form grew hard and inflexible within her father's encircling arms. O, terrible misfortune! The victim of his insatiable desire for wealth, little Marygold was a human child no longer, but a golden statue!

It would be too sad a story if I were to tell you how Midas, in the fullness of all his gratified desires, began to wring his hands and bemoan himself.

While he was in this tumult of despair, he suddenly beheld a stranger standing near the door. Midas bent down his head, without speaking; for he recognized the same figure which had appeared to him the day before in the treasure-room, and had bestowed on him this disastrous faculty of the Golden Touch.

"Well, friend Midas," said the stranger, "pray how do you succeed with the Golden Touch?"

Midas shook his head.

"Gold is not everything," answered Midas. "And I have lost all that my heart really cared for."

"Ah! So you have made a discovery since yesterday?" observed the stranger. "Let us see, then. Which of these two things do you think is really worth the most—the gift of the Golden Touch, or one cup of clear cold water?"

"O, blessed water!" exclaimed Midas. "It will never moisten my parched throat again!"

"The Golden Touch," continued the stranger, "or a crust of bread?"

"A piece of bread," answered Midas, "is worth all the gold on earth!"

"The Golden Touch," asked the stranger, "or your own little Marygold, warm, soft, and loving, as she was an hour ago?"

"O, my child, my dear child!" cried poor Midas, wringing his hands. "I would not have given that one small dimple on her chin for the power of changing this whole big earth into a solid lump of gold!"

"You are wiser than you were, King Midas!" said the stranger, looking seriously at him. "Your own heart, I perceive, has not been entirely changed from flesh to gold. Were it so, your case would indeed be desperate. Tell me, now, do you sincerely desire to rid yourself of this Golden Touch?"

"It is hateful to me!" replied Midas.

A fly settled on his nose, but immediately fell to the floor; for it, too, had become gold. Midas shuddered.

"Go, then," said the stranger, "and plunge into the river that glides past the bottom of your garden. Take likewise a vase of the same water, and sprinkle it over any object that you may desire to change back again from gold into its former substance. If you do this in earnestness and sincerity, it may possibly repair the mischief which your avarice has occasioned."

King Midas bowed low; and when he lifted his head, the lustrous stranger had vanished.

You will easily believe that Midas lost no time in snatching up a great earthen pitcher (but, alas! it was no longer earthen after he touched it), and hastening to the river-side. On reaching the river's brink, he plunged headlong in, without waiting so much as to pull off his shoes.

"Poof! poof! poof!" snorted King Midas, as his head emerged out of the water. "Well; this is really a refreshing bath, and I think it must have washed away the Golden Touch. And now for filling my pitcher!"

As he dipped the pitcher into the water, it gladdened his very heart to see it change from gold into the same good, honest earthen vessel which it had been before he touched it. The curse of the Golden Touch had really been removed from him.

King Midas hastened back to the palace. The first thing he did, as you need hardly be told, was to sprinkle it by handfuls over the golden figure of little Marygold.

No sooner did it fall on her than you would have laughed to see how the rosy colour came back to the dear child's cheek!—and how she began to sneeze and splutter!—and how astonished she was to find herself dripping wet, and her father still throwing more water over her!

"Pray do not, dear father!" she cried. "See how you have wet my nice frock, which I put on only this morning!"

For Marygold did not know that she had been a little golden statue; nor could she remember anything that had happened since the moment when she ran, with outstretched arms, to comfort poor King Midas.

NEWS FROM QUEEN'S CRAWLEY

By WILLIAM MAKEPEACE THACKERAY

Rebecca Sharp—more familiarly known as Becky—has taken the post of governess to Sir Pitt Crawley's two daughters. As soon as she is settled in at her new home, Queen's Crawley, after a tiring journey from London, she writes to her friend Amelia Sedley, in Russell Square, London, with whom she has stayed after the two girls left school together. Amelia has been both kind and helpful to Becky, who, without money or influential relatives, has to consider making her own way in the world and fending for herself. This story in letter form is taken from "Vanity Fair."

MY dearest, sweetest Amelia,—With what mingled joy and sorrow do I take up the pen to write to my dearest friend! Oh, what a change between to-day and yesterday! *Now* I am friendless and alone; yesterday I was at home, in the sweet company of a sister, whom I shall ever, *ever* cherish!

I will not tell you in what tears and sadness I passed the fatal night in which I separated from you. I was brought by the groom in the old carriage to Sir Pitt Crawley's town house, where I was given over to Sir P.'s care, and made to pass the night in an old, gloomy bed, and by the side of a horrid, gloomy old charwoman, who keeps the house. I did not sleep one single wink the whole night.

Sir Pitt is not what we silly girls imagined a baronet must have been. Anything, indeed, less like Lord Orville cannot be imagined. Fancy an old, stumpy, short, vulgar, and very dirty man, in old clothes and shabby old gaiters, who smokes a horrid pipe, and cooks his own horrid supper in a saucepan. He speaks with a country accent, and swore a great deal at the old charwoman, at the hackney coachman who drove us to the inn where the coach went from, and on which I made the journey *outside for the greater part of the way.*

I was awakened at daybreak by the charwoman, and having

arrived at the inn, was at first placed inside the coach. But when we got to a place called Leakington, where the rain began to fall very heavily—will you believe it?—I was forced to come outside; for Sir Pitt is a proprietor of the coach, and as a passenger came at Mudbury, who wanted an inside place, I was obliged to go outside in the rain, where, however, a young gentleman from Cambridge College sheltered me very kindly in one of his *several* greatcoats.

This gentleman and the guard seemed to know Sir Pitt very well, and laughed at him a great deal. They both agreed in calling him an *old screw*, which means a very stingy, avaricious person. He never gives any money to anybody, they said (and this meanness I hate); and the young gentleman made me remark that we drove very slow for the last two stages on the road, because Sir Pitt was on the box, and because he is proprietor of the horses for this part of the journey. "But won't I flog 'em on to Squashmore, when I take the ribbons?" said the young *Cantab*. "And sarve 'em right, Master Jack," said the guard. When I comprehended the meaning of this phrase, and that Master Jack intended to drive the rest of the way, and revenge himself on Sir Pitt's horses, of course I laughed too.

A carriage and four splendid horses, covered with armorial bearings, however, awaited me at Mudbury, four miles from Queen's Crawley, and we made our entrance to the baronet's park in state. There is a fine avenue of a mile long leading to the house, and the woman at the lodge-gate (over the pillars of which are a serpent and a dove, the supporters of the Crawley arms) made us a number of curtsies as she flung open the old iron carved doors.

"There's an avenue," said Sir Pitt, "a mile long. There's six thousand pound of timber in them there trees. Do you call that nothing?" He pronounced avenue—*evenue*, and nothing—*nothink*, so droll; and he had a Mr. Hodson, his hind from Mudbury, into the carriage with him, and they talked about distraining, and selling up, and draining and subsoiling, and a great deal about tenants and farming—much more than I could understand. Sam Miles had been caught poaching, and Peter Bailey had gone to the workhouse at last. "Serve him right," said Sir Pitt; "him and his family has been cheating me on that farm these hundred and fifty years."

Some old tenant, I suppose, who could not pay his rent. Sir Pitt might have said "*he* and his family," to be sure; but rich baronets do not need to be careful about grammar, as poor governesses must be.

As we passed, I remarked a beautiful church spire rising above some old elms in the park; and before them, in the midst of a lawn, and some outhouses, an old red house with tall chimneys covered with ivy, and the windows shining in the sun. "Is that your church, sir?" I said.

"Yes, hang it" (said Sir Pitt, only he used, dear, *a much wickeder word*); "how's Buty, Hodson? Buty's my brother Bute, my dear—my brother the parson. Buty and the Beast, I call him, ha, ha!"

Hodson laughed too, and then looking more grave and nodding his head, said, "I'm afraid he's better, Sir Pitt. He was out on his pony yesterday, looking at our corn."

"Looking after his tithes, hang 'un" (only he used the same wicked word). "Will brandy and water never kill him? He's as tough as old whatdyecallum—old Methusalem."

Mr. Hodson laughed again. "The young men is home from college. They've whopped John Scroggins till he's well-nigh dead."

"Whop my second keeper!" roared out Sir Pitt.

"He was on the parson's ground, sir," replied Mr. Hodson; and Sir Pitt in a fury swore that if ever he caught 'em poaching on his ground, he'd transport 'em, by the Lord he would.

Presently, seeing two little boys gathering sticks in the wood, Mr. Hodson jumped out of the carriage, at Sir Pitt's order, and rushed upon them with his whip. "Pitch into 'em, Hodson," roared the Baronet; "flog their little souls out, and bring 'em up to the house, the vagabonds; I'll commit 'em as sure as my name's Pitt." And presently we heard Mr. Hodson's whip cracking on the shoulders of the poor little blubbering wretches, and Sir Pitt seeing that the malefactors were in custody, drove on to the hall.

All the servants were ready to meet us, and

. . . . . .

Here, my dear, I was interrupted last night by a dreadful thumping at my door; and who do you think it was? Sir Pitt Crawley in his night-cap and dressing-gown, such a figure! As I shrank away from such a visitor, he came forward and seized my candle. "No candles after eleven o'clock, Miss Becky," said he. "Go to bed in the dark, you pretty little hussey" (that is what he called me), "and unless you wish me to come for the candle every night, mind and be in bed at eleven." And with this, he and Mr. Horrocks the butler went off laughing. You may be sure I shall not encourage any more of their visits. They let loose two immense bloodhounds at night, which all last night were yelling and howling at the moon. "I call the dog Gorer," said Sir Pitt; "he's killed a man that dog has, and is master of a bull, and the mother I used to call Flora; but now I calls her Aroarer, for she's too old to bite. Haw, haw!"

Before the house of Queen's Crawley, which is an odious old-fashioned red brick mansion, with tall chimneys and gables of the style of Queen Bess, there is a terrace flanked by the family dove and serpent, and on which the great hall-door opens. The great hall has a large fireplace, and the grate is big enough to roast an ox at the very least. Round the room hang I don't know how many generations of Crawleys, some with beards and ruffs, some with huge wigs and toes turned out, some dressed in long straight stays and gowns that look as stiff as towers, and some with long ringlets, and oh, my dear! scarcely any stays at all. At one end of the hall is the great staircase all in black oak, as dismal as may be, and on either side are tall doors with stags' heads over them, leading to the billiard-room and the library, and the great yellow saloon and the morning rooms. I think there are at least twenty bedrooms on the first floor; and one of them has the bed in which Queen Elizabeth slept; and I have been taken by my new pupils through all these fine apartments this morning. They are not rendered less gloomy, I promise you, by having the shutters always shut; and there is scarce one of the apartments but, when the light was let into it, I expected to see a ghost in the room. We have a schoolroom on the second floor, with my bedroom leading into it on one side, and that of the young ladies on the other. Then there are Mr. Pitt's apartments—Mr. Crawley, he is called—the eldest son, and Mr. Rawdon Crawley's rooms—he is an officer, and away with his regiment. There is no want of room, I assure you. You might lodge all the people in Russell Square in the house, I think, and have space to spare.

Half an hour after our arrival the great dinner-bell was rung, and I came down with my two pupils (they are very thin, insignificant little chits of ten and eight years old). I came down in your *dear* muslin gown; for I am to be treated as one of the family, except on company days, when the young ladies and I are to dine upstairs.

Well, the great dinner-bell rang, and we all assembled in the little drawing-room where my Lady Crawley sits. She is the second Lady Crawley, and mother of the young ladies. She was an ironmonger's daughter, and her marriage was thought a great match. She looks as if she had been handsome once, and her eyes are always weeping for the loss of her beauty. She is pale and meagre and high-shouldered, and has not a word to say for herself, evidently. Her stepson, Mr. Crawley, was likewise in the room. He was in full dress, as pompous as an undertaker. He is pale, thin, ugly, silent; he has thin legs, no chest, hay-coloured whiskers, and straw-coloured hair. He is the very picture of his sainted mother over the mantelpiece—Griselda of the noble house of Binkie.

"This is the new governess, Mr. Crawley," said Lady Crawley, coming forward and taking my hand. "Miss Sharp."

"Oh!" said Mr. Crawley, and pushed his head once forward, and began again to read a great pamphlet with which he was busy.

"I hope you will be kind to my girls," said Lady Crawley, with her pink eyes always full of tears.

"Law, Ma, of course she will," said the eldest; and I saw at a glance that I need not be afraid of *that* woman.

"My lady is served," says the butler in black, in an immense white shirt-frill, that looked as if it had been one of the Queen Elizabeth's ruffs depicted in the hall; and so, taking Mr. Crawley's arm, she led the way to the dining-room, whither I followed with my little pupils in each hand.

Sir Pitt was already in the room with a silver jug. He had just been to the cellar, and was in full dress too—that is, he had taken his gaiters off, and showed his little dumpy legs in black worsted stockings. The sideboard was covered with glistening old plate—old cups, both gold and silver; old salvers and cruet-stands. Everything on the table was in silver too, and two footmen, with red hair and canary-coloured liveries, stood on either side of the sideboard.

Mr. Crawley said a long grace, and Sir Pitt said Amen, and the great silver dish-covers were removed.

"What have we for dinner, Betsy?" said the baronet.

"Mutton broth, I believe, Sir Pitt," answered Lady Crawley.

"*Mouton aux navets,*" added the butler gravely (pronounced, if you please, mountongonavvy); "and the soup is *potage de mouton à l'Ecossaise.* The side-dishes contain *pommes de terre au naturel* and *choufleur à l'eau.*"

"Mutton's mutton," said the baronet, "and a devilish good thing. What *ship* was it, Horrocks, and when did you kill?"

"One of the black-faced Scotch, Sir Pitt; we killed on Thursday."

"Who took any?"

"Steel, of Mudbury, took the saddle and two legs, Sir Pitt; but he says the last was too young and confounded woolly, Sir Pitt."

"Will you take some *potage,* Miss ah—Miss Blunt?" said Mr. Crawley.

"Capital Scotch broth, my dear," said Sir Pitt, "though they call it by a French name."

"I believe it is the custom, sir, in decent society," said Mr. Crawley haughtily, "to call the dish as I have called it"; and it was served to us on silver soup-plates by the footmen in the canary coats, with the *mouton aux navets.* Then "ale and water" were brought, and served to us young ladies in wine-glasses. I am not a judge of ale, but I can say with a clear conscience I prefer water.

While we were enjoying our repast, Sir Pitt took occasion to ask what had become of the shoulders of the mutton.

"I believe they were eaten in the servants' hall," said my lady humbly.

"They was, my lady," said Horrocks; "and precious little else we get there neither."

Sir Pitt burst into a horse-laugh, and continued his conversation with Mr. Horrocks. "That there little black pig of the Kent sow's breed must be uncommon fat now."

"It's not quite busting, Sir Pitt," said the butler with the gravest air, at which Sir Pitt, and with him the young ladies this time, began to laugh violently.

"Miss Crawley, Miss Rose Crawley," said Mr. Crawley, "your laughter strikes me as being exceedingly out of place."

"Never mind, my lord," said the baronet, "we'll try the porker on Saturday. Kill un on Saturday morning, John Horrocks. Miss Sharp adores pork, don't you, Miss Sharp?"

And I think this is all the conversation that I remember at dinner. When the repast was concluded, a jug of hot water was placed before Sir Pitt, with a case-bottle containing, I believe, rum. Mr. Horrocks served myself and my pupils with three little glasses of wine, and a bumper was poured out for my lady. When we retired, she took from her work-drawer an enormous interminable piece of knitting; the young ladies began to play at cribbage with a dirty pack of cards. We had but one candle lighted, but it was in a magnificent old silver candlestick; and after a very few questions from my lady, I had my choice of amusement between a volume of sermons, and a pamphlet on the corn-laws, which Mr. Crawley had been reading before dinner.

So we sat for an hour until steps were heard.

"Put away the cards, girls," cried my lady, in a great tremor; "put down Mr. Crawley's books, Miss Sharp"; and these orders had been scarcely obeyed, when Mr. Crawley entered the room.

"We will resume yesterday's discourse, young ladies," said he, "and you shall each read a page by turns; so that Miss a—Miss Short may have an opportunity of hearing you"; and the poor girls began to spell a long dismal sermon delivered at Bethesda Chapel, Liverpool, on behalf of the mission for the Chickasaw Indians. Was it not a charming evening?

At ten the servants were told to call Sir Pitt and the household to prayers. Sir Pitt came in first, very much flushed, and rather unsteady in his gait; and after him the butler, the canaries, Mr. Crawley's man, three other men, smelling very much of the stable, and four women, one of whom, I remarked, was very much overdressed, and who flung me a look of great scorn as she plumped down on her knees.

After Mr. Crawley had done haranguing and expounding, we received our candles, and then we went to bed; and then I was disturbed in my writing, as I have described to my dearest sweetest Amelia.

Good night. A thousand, thousand, thousand kisses!

Saturday.—This morning, at five, I heard the shrieking of the little black pig. Rose and Violet introduced me to it yesterday; and to the stables, and to the kennel, and to the gardener, who was picking fruit to send to market, and from whom they begged hard a bunch of hothouse grapes; but he said that Sir Pitt had numbered every "Man Jack" of them, and it would be as much as his place was worth to give any away. The darling girls caught a colt in a paddock, and asked me if I would ride, and began to ride themselves, when the groom, coming with horrid oaths, drove them away.

Lady Crawley is always knitting the worsted. Sir Pitt is always tipsy, every night; and, I believe, sits with Horrocks, the butler. Mr. Crawley always reads sermons in the evening, and in the morning is locked up in his study, or else rides to Mudbury, on county business, or to Squashmore, where he preaches, on Wednesdays and Fridays, to the tenants there.

A hundred thousand grateful loves to your dear papa and mamma. Is your poor brother recovered of his rack punch? O dear! O dear! How men should beware of wicked punch!

Ever and ever thine own

REBECCA

THE STORY OF REBEKAH

Rebekah, the wife of Isaac, had twin sons, and one she loved more than the other. Because of this great love she was prepared to help her favourite gain that which was not rightfully his to inherit. This story of the young girl at the well who was kind to the traveller, and who later conspired against her elder son, is taken from the Book of Genesis in the Bible.

AND Abraham was old, and well stricken in age: and the Lord had blessed Abraham in all things. And Abraham said unto his eldest servant of his house, that ruled over all that he had, Swear by the Lord, the God of heaven, and the God of the earth, that thou shalt not take a wife unto my son of the daughters of the Canaanites, among whom I dwell: but thou shalt go unto my country, and to my kindred, and take a wife unto my son Isaac.

And the servant said unto him, Peradventure the woman will not be willing to follow me unto this land: must I needs bring thy son again unto the land from whence thou camest? And Abraham said unto him, Beware thou that thou bring not my son thither again. The Lord God of heaven, which took me from my father's house, and from the land of my kindred, and which spake unto me, and that sware unto me, saying, Unto thy seed will I give this land; he shall send his angel before thee, and thou shalt take a wife unto my son from thence. And if the woman will not be willing to follow thee, then thou shalt be clear from this my oath: only bring not my son thither again. And the servant sware to him concerning that matter.

And the servant took ten camels of the camels of his master, and departed; for all the goods of his master were in his hand: and he went to Mesopotamia, unto the city of Nahor. And he made his camels to kneel down without the city by a well of water at the time of the evening, even the time that women go out to draw water.

And he said, O Lord God of my master Abraham, I pray Thee, send me good speed this day, and shew kindness unto my master Abraham. Behold, I stand here by the well of water; and the daughters of the men of the city come out to draw water: and let it come to pass, that the damsel to whom I shall say, Let down thy pitcher, I pray thee, that I may drink; and she shall say, Drink, and I will give thy camels drink also: let the same be she that thou hast appointed for thy servant Isaac; and thereby shall I know that thou hast shewed kindness unto my master.

And it came to pass, before he had done speaking, that, behold, Rebekah came out, who was born to Bethuel, son of Milcah, the wife of Nahor, Abraham's brother, with her pitcher upon her shoulder. And the damsel was very fair to look upon: and she went down to the well, and filled her pitcher, and came up.

And the servant ran to meet her, and said, Let me, I pray thee, drink a little water of thy pitcher. And she said, Drink, my lord: and she hasted, and let down her pitcher upon her hand, and gave him drink. And when she had done giving him drink, she said, I will draw water for thy camels also, until they have done drinking. And she hasted, and emptied her pitcher into the trough, and ran again unto the well to draw water, and drew for all his camels. And the man wondering at her held his peace, to wit whether the Lord had made his journey prosperous or not.

And it came to pass, as the camels had done drinking, that the man took a golden earring of half a shekel weight, and two bracelets for her hands of ten shekels weight of gold; and said, Whose daughter art thou, tell me, I pray thee: is there room in thy father's house for us to lodge in? And she said unto him, I am the daughter of Bethuel the son of Milcah, which she bare unto Nahor. She said moreover unto him, We have both straw and provender enough, and room to lodge in. And the man bowed down his head and worshipped the Lord. And he said, Blessed be the Lord God of my master Abraham, who hath not left destitute my master of his mercy and his truth: I being in the way, the Lord led me to the house of my master's brethren. And the damsel ran, and told them of her mother's house these things.

And Rebekah had a brother, and his name was Laban: and Laban ran out unto the man, unto the well. And it came to pass, when he saw the earring and bracelets upon his sister's hands, and when he heard the words of Rebekah his sister, saying, Thus spake the man unto me; that he came unto the man; and, behold, he stood by the camels at the well. And he said, Come in, thou blessed of the Lord; wherefore standest thou without; for I have prepared the house, and room for the camels.

And the man came into the house: and he ungirded his camels, and gave straw and provender for the camels, and water to wash his feet, and the men's feet that were with him. And there was set meat before him to eat: but he said, I will not eat, until I have told mine errand. And he said, Speak on.

Then Laban and Bethuel answered and said, The thing proceedeth from the Lord: we cannot speak unto thee bad or good. Behold, Rebekah is before thee, take her, and go, and let her be thy master's son's wife, as the Lord hath spoken.

And it came to pass, that, when Abraham's servant heard their words, he worshipped the Lord, bowing himself to the earth. And the servant brought forth jewels of silver, and jewels of gold, and raiment, and gave them to Rebekah: he gave also to her brother and to her mother precious things. And they did eat and drink, he and the men that were with him, and tarried all night; and they rose up in the morning, and he said, Send me away unto my master.

And her brother and her mother said, Let the damsel abide with us a few days, at the least ten; after that she shall go. And he said unto them, Hinder me not, seeing the Lord hath prospered my way; send me away that I may go to my master. And they said, We will call the damsel and enquire at her mouth.

And they called Rebekah, and said unto her, Wilt thou go with this man? And she said, I will go. And they sent away Rebekah their sister, and her nurse, and Abraham's servant, and his men. And they blessed Rebekah, and said unto her, Thou art our sister, be thou the mother of thousands of millions, and let thy seed possess the gate of those which hate them.

And Rebekah arose, and her damels, and they rode upon the camels, and followed the man: and the servant took Rebekah, and went his way.

And Isaac came from the way of the well Lahai-roi; for he dwelt in the south country. And Isaac went out to meditate in the field at the eventide: and he lifted up his eyes, and saw, and, behold, the camels were coming. And Rebekah lifted up her eyes, and when she saw Isaac, she lighted off the camel. For she had said unto the servant, What man is this that walketh in the field to meet us? And the servant had said, It is my master: therefore she took a vail, and covered herself. And the servant told Isaac all things that he had done. And Isaac brought her into his mother Sarah's tent, and took Rebekah, and she became his wife; and he loved her: and Isaac was comforted after his mother's death.

And Isaac was forty years old when he took Rebekah to wife. And in due time, behold, twins were born to her, and the elder was named Esau, and the younger Jacob.

And the boys grew: and Esau was a cunning hunter, a man of the field; and Jacob was a plain man, dwelling in tents. And Isaac loved Esau, because he did eat of his venison: but Rebekah loved Jacob.

And it came to pass, that when Isaac was old, and his eyes were dim, so that he could not see, he called Esau his eldest son, and said unto him, My son: and he said unto him, Behold, here am I. And he said, Behold now, I am old, I know not the day of my death: now therefore take, I pray thee, thy weapons, thy quiver and thy bow, and go out to the field, and take me some venison; and make me savoury meat, such as I love, and bring it to me, that I may eat; that my soul may bless thee before I die. And Rebekah heard when Isaac spake to Esau his son. And Esau went to the field to hunt for venison, and to bring it.

And Rebekah spake unto Jacob her son, saying, Behold, I heard thy father speak unto Esau thy brother, saying, Bring me venison, and make me savoury meat, that I may eat, and bless thee before the Lord before my death. Now therefore, my son, obey my voice according to that which I command thee. Go now to the flock, and fetch me from thence two good kids of the goats; and I will make them savoury meat for thy father, such as he loveth: and thou shalt bring it to thy father, that he may eat, and that he may bless thee before his death.

And Jacob said to Rebekah his mother, Behold, Esau my brother is a hairy man, and I am a smooth man: my father peradventure will feel me, and I shall seem to him as a deceiver; and I shall bring a curse upon me, and not a blessing. And his mother said unto him, Upon me be thy curse, my son: only obey my voice, and go fetch me them.

And he went, and fetched, and brought them to his mother: and his mother made savoury meat, such as his father loved. And Rebekah took goodly raiment of her eldest son Esau, which were with her in the house, and put them upon Jacob her youngest son: and she put the skins of the kids of the goats upon his hands, and upon the smooth of his neck: and she gave the savoury meat and

the bread, which she had prepared, into the hand of her son Jacob.

And he came unto his father, and said, My father: and he said, Here am I; who art thou, my son? And Jacob said unto his father, I am Esau thy firstborn; I have done according as thou badest me: arise, I pray thee, sit and eat of my venison, that thy soul may bless me. And Isaac said unto his son, How is it that thou hast found it so quickly, my son? And he said, Because the Lord thy God brought it to me.

And Isaac said unto Jacob, Come near, I pray thee, that I may feel thee, my son, whether thou be my very son Esau or not. And

Jacob went near unto Isaac his father; and he felt him, and said, The voice is Jacob's voice, but the hands are the hands of Esau. And he discerned him not, because his hands were hairy, as his brother Esau's hands: so he blessed him. And he said, Art thou my very son Esau? And he said, I am. And he said, Bring it near to me, and I will eat of my son's venison, that my soul may bless thee. And he brought it near to him, and he did eat: and he brought him wine, and he drank.

And his father Isaac said unto him, Come near now and kiss me, my son. And he came near, and kissed him: and he smelled the smell of his raiment, and blessed him, and said, See, the smell of my son is as the smell of a field which the Lord hath blessed: therefore God give thee of the dew of heaven, and the fatness of the earth, and plenty of corn and wine: let people serve thee, and nations bow down to thee: be lord over thy brethren, and let thy mother's sons bow down to thee: cursed be every one that curseth thee, and blessed be he that blesseth thee.

And it came to pass, as soon as Isaac had made an end of blessing Jacob, and Jacob was yet scarce gone out from the presence of Isaac his father, that Esau his brother came in from his hunting. And he also had made savoury meat, and brought it unto his father, and said unto his father, Let my father arise, and eat of his son's venison, that thy soul may bless me.

And Isaac his father said unto him, Who art thou? And he said, I am thy son, thy firstborn Esau. And Isaac trembled exceedingly, and said, Who? where is he that hath taken venison, and brought it me, and I have eaten of all before thou camest, and have blessed him? yea, and he shall be blessed. And when Esau heard the words of his father, he cried with a great and exceeding bitter cry, and said unto his father, Bless me, even me also, O my father.

And he said, Thy brother came with subtilty, and hath taken away thy blessing. And he said, Is not he rightly named Jacob? for he hath taken away my blessing. And he said, Hast thou not reserved a blessing for me?

And Isaac answered and said unto Esau, Behold, I have made him thy lord, and all his brethren have I given to him for servants; and with corn and wine have I sustained him: and what shall I do now unto thee, my son? And Esau said unto his father, Hast thou but one blessing, my father? bless me, even me also, O my father. And Esau lifted up his voice, and wept.

And Isaac his father answered and said unto him, Behold, thy dwelling shall be the fatness of the earth, and of the dew of heaven from above; and by thy sword shalt thou live, and shalt serve thy brother; and it shall come to pass when thou shalt have the dominion, that thou shalt break his yoke from off thy neck.

And Esau hated Jacob because of the blessing wherewith his father blessed him: and Esau said in his heart, The days of mourning for my father are at hand; then will I slay my brother Jacob. And these words of Esau her elder son were told to Rebekah: and she sent and called Jacob her younger son, and said unto him, Behold, thy brother Esau, as touching thee, doth comfort himself, purposing to kill thee. Now therefore, my son, obey my voice; and arise, flee thou to Laban my brother to Haran; and tarry with him a few days, until thy brother's fury turn away; until thy brother's anger turn away from thee, and he forget that which thou hast done to him: then I will send, and fetch thee from thence: why should I be deprived also of you both in one day?

And Rebekah said to Isaac, I am weary of my life because of the daughters of Heth: if Jacob take a wife of the daughters of Heth, such as these which are of the daughters of the land, what good shall my life do me?

And Isaac called Jacob, and blessed him, and charged him, and said unto him, Thou shalt not take a wife of the daughters of Canaan. Arise, go to Padan-aram, to the house of Bethuel thy mother's father; and take thee a wife from thence of the daughters of Laban thy mother's brother. And God Almighty bless thee, and make thee fruitful, and multiply thee, that thou mayest be a multitude of people; and give thee the blessing of Abraham, to thee, and to thy seed with thee; that thou mayest inherit the land wherein thou art a stranger, which God gave unto Abraham. And Isaac sent away Jacob: and he went to Padan-aram unto Laban, son of Bethuel the Syrian, the brother of Rebekah, Jacob's and Esau's mother.

SLAVE GIRL OF POMPEII

By LORD LYTTON

Burbo, an ex-gladiator who now keeps a wine-shop in Pompeii frequented by gladiators, and his hag-like wife, Stratonice, are making money by the artistic accomplishments of their blind slave girl Nydia. But when the girl rebels the treatment she receives from her mistress is harsh. However, three young blades of the Roman city enter, one of them Glaucus, a rich Greek who always buys his flowers from the blind slave girl, and when he hears her cries he recognizes her voice. Before he leaves the wine-shop Nydia is assured that her days of terror and fear are over. This story is taken from "The Last Days of Pompeii."

IN the earlier times of Rome the priesthood was a profession, not of lucre, but of honour. It was embraced by the noblest citizens —it was forbidden to the plebeians. Afterwards, and long previous to the present date, it was equally open to all ranks, at least that part of the profession which embraced the flamens, or priests, not of religion generally, but of peculiar gods. Even the priest of Jupiter (the Flamen Dialis), proceeded by a lictor, and entitled by his office to the entrance of the Senate, at first the especial dignitary of the patricians, was subsequently the choice of the people. The less national and less honoured deities were usually served by plebeian ministers, and many embraced the profession less from the impulse of devotion than the suggestions of a calculating poverty. Thus Calenus, the priest of Isis, was of the lowest origin. His relations, though not his parents, were freedmen. He had received from them a liberal education, and from his father a small patrimony, which he had soon exhausted. He embraced the priesthood as a last resource from distress. Whatever the state emoluments of the sacred profession, which at that time were probably small, the officers of a popular temple could never complain of the profits of their calling. There is no profession so lucrative as that which practises on the superstition of the multitude.

Calenus had but one surviving relative at Pompeii, and that was Burbo. Various dark and disreputable ties, stronger than those of blood, united together their hearts and interest; and often the minister of Isis stole disguised and furtively from the supposed austerity of his devotions; and gliding through the back-door of the retired gladiator, a man infamous alike by vices and by profession, rejoiced to throw off the last rag of an hypocrisy which, but for the dictates of avarice, his ruling passion, would at all times have sat clumsily upon a nature too brutal for even the mimicry of virtue.

Wrapped in one of those large mantles which came in use among the Romans in proportion as they dismissed the toga, whose ample folds well concealed the form, and in which a sort of hood, attached to it, afforded no less a security to the features, Calenus now sat in the small and private chamber of the wine-seller, from which a small faux, or passage, ran at once to that back entrance with which nearly all the houses of Pompeii were furnished.

Opposite to him sat the sturdy Burbo, carefully counting, on a table between them, a little pile of coins which the priest had just poured from his purse; for purses were as common then as now, with this difference, they were usually better furnished!

"You see," said Calenus, "that we pay you handsomely, and you ought to thank me for recommending you to so advantageous a market."

"I do, my cousin, I do," replied Burbo affectionately, as he swept the coins into a leathern receptacle which he then deposited in his girdle, drawing the buckle round his capacious waist more closely than he was wont to do in the lax hours of his domestic avocations. "And by Isis, Pisis, and Nisis, or whatever other gods there may be in Egypt, my little Nydia is a very Hesperides, a garden of gold to me."

"She sings well, and plays like a muse," returned Calenus; "those are virtues that he who employs me always pays liberally."

"He is a god," cried Burbo enthusiastically; "every rich man who is generous deserves to be worshipped. But come, a cup of wine, old friend: tell me more about it. What does she do? She is frightened."

At this moment they heard a slight noise at the door, as of one feeling the handle. The priest lowered the cowl over his head.

"Tush!" whispered the host, "it is but the blind girl," as Nydia opened the door and entered the apartment.

"Ho! girl, and how dost thou? Thou lookest pale, thou hast kept late revels? No matter, the young must be always the young," said Burbo encouragingly.

The girl made no answer, but she dropped on one of the seats with an air of lassitude. Her colour went and came rapidly; she beat the floor impatiently with her small feet, then she suddenly raised her face, and said with a determined voice:

"Master, you may starve me if you will, you may beat me, you may threaten me with death, but I will go no more to that unholy place!"

"How, fool!" said Burbo in a savage voice, and his heavy brows met darkly over his fierce and bloodshot eyes. "How, rebellious! take care."

"I have said it," said the poor girl, crossing her hands on her breast.

"What! my modest one, sweet vestal, thou wilt go no more? Very well, thou shalt be carried."

"I will raise the city with my cries," said she passionately, and the colour mounted to her brow.

"We will take care of that, too; thou shalt go gagged."

"Then may the gods help me!" said Nydia, rising: "I will appeal to the magistrates."

A trembling shook the frame of the unfortunate girl; she clasped her hands imploringly, and burst violently into sobs.

Whether or not it was the sound of that vehement sorrow which brought the gentle Stratonice to the spot, her grisly form at this moment appeared in the chamber.

"How now? What hast thou been doing with my slave, brute?" said she angrily to Burbo.

"Be quiet, wife," said he, in a tone half sullen, half timid; "you want new girdles and fine clothes, do you? Well, then, take care of your slave, or you may want them long. *Væ capitituo*—vengeance on thy head, wretched one!"

"What is this?" said the hag, looking from one to the other.

Nydia started as by a sudden impulse from the wall, against which she had leant; she threw herself at the feet of Stratonice; she embraced her knees, and looking up at her with those sightless but touching eyes: "O my mistress!" sobbed she, "you are a woman, you have had sisters, you have been young like me; feel for me, save me! I will go to those horrible feasts no more."

"Stuff!" said the hag, dragging her up rudely by one of those delicate hands, fit for no harsher labour than that of weaving the flowers which made her pleasure or her trade. "Stuff! these fine scruples are not for slaves."

"Hark ye," said Burbo, drawing forth his purse, and chinkling its contents; "you hear this music, wife. By Pollux! if you do not break in yon colt with a tight rein, you will hear it no more."

"The girl is tired," said Stratonice, nodding to Calenus; "she will be more docile when you next want her."

"*You! you!* Who is here?" cried Nydia, casting her eyes round the apartment with so fearful and straining a survey that Calenus rose in alarm from his seat.

"She *must* see with those eyes!" muttered he.

"Who is here? Speak in heaven's name! Ah! if you were blind like me, you would be less cruel," said she. And she again burst into tears.

"Take her away," said Burbo impatiently. "I hate these whimperings."

"Come," said Stratonice, pushing the poor child by the shoulders.

Nydia drew herself aside with an air to which resolution gave dignity.

"Hear me," she said. "I have served you faithfully, I who was brought up—— Ah! my mother, my poor mother! Didst thou dream I should come to this?" She dashed the tear from her eyes, and proceeded: "Command me in aught else, and I will obey; but I tell you now, hard, stern, and inexorable as you are—I tell you that I will go there no more; or, if I am forced there, that I will implore the mercy of the prætor himself. I have said it. Hear me, ye gods, I swear!"

The hag's eyes glowed with fire. She seized the child by the hair with one hand, and raised on high the other; that formidable right hand, the least blow of which seemed capable to crush the frail and delicate form that trembled in her grasp. That thought itself appeared to strike her, for she suspended the blow, changed her purpose, and, dragging Nydia to the wall, seized from a hook a rope, often, alas! applied to a similar purpose; and the next moment the shrill, the agonized shrieks of the blind girl rang piercingly through the house.

"Hollo, my brave fellows!" said Lepidus, stooping his head, as he entered the low doorway of the house of Burbo. "We have come to see which of you most honours your lanista." The gladiators rose from the table, in respect to three gallants, known to be among the gayest and richest youths of Pompeii, and whose voices were therefore the dispensers of amphitheatrical reputation.

"What fine animals!" said Clodius to Glaucus; "worthy to be gladiators!"

"It is a pity they are not warriors," returned Glaucus.

A singular thing it was to see the dainty and fastidious Lepidus, whom in a banquet a ray of daylight seemed to blind, whom in a bath a breeze of air seemed to blast, in whom Nature seemed twisted and perverted from every natural impulse, and curdled into one dubious thing of effeminacy and art; a singular thing was it to see this Lepidus, now all eagerness, and energy, and life, patting the vast shoulders of the gladiators with a blanched and girlish hand, feeling with a mincing gripe their great brawn and iron muscles, all lost in calculating admiration at that manhood which he had spent his life in carefully banishing from himself.

"But I don't see Burbo; where is Burbo? I must talk with Burbo," cried Clodius.

"And Stratonice, the brave old lass, where is she?" quoth Lepidus.

At this moment a loud cry of pain and terror startled the group.

"Oh, spare me! spare me! I am but a child, I am blind. Is not *that* punishment enough?"

"O Pallas! I know that voice; it is my poor flower-girl!" exclaimed Glaucus, and he darted at once into the quarter whence the cry rose.

He burst the door; he beheld Nydia writhing in the grasp of the infuriate hag; the cord, already dabbled with blood, was raised in the air; it was suddenly arrested.

"Fury!" said Glaucus, and with his left hand he caught Nydia from her grasp; "how dare ye use thus a girl—one of your own sex—a child? My Nydia, my poor infant!"

"Oh! is that you—is that Glaucus?" exclaimed the flower-girl;

the tears stood arrested on her cheek; she smiled, she clung to his breast, she kissed his robe as she clung.

"And how dare you, pert stranger, interfere between a free woman

and her slave! By the gods! despite your fine tunic and your filthy perfumes, I doubt whether you are even a Roman citizen, my mannikin."

"Fair words, mistress, fair words!" said Clodius, now entering with Lepidus. "This is my friend and sworn brother; he must be put under shelter of your tongue, sweet one; it rains stones!"

"Give me my slave!" shrieked the virago, placing her mighty grasp on the breast of the Greek.

"Not if all your sister Furies could help you." answered Glaucus. "Fear not, sweet Nydia; an Athenian never forsook distress!"

"Hollo!" said Burbo, rising reluctantly, "what turmoil is all this about a slave? Let go the young gentleman—wife, let him go; for his sake the pert thing shall be spared this once." So saying, he drew, or rather dragged off, his ferocious helpmate.

"Methought when we entered," said Clodius, "there was another man present."

"He is gone."

For the priest of Isis had indeed thought it high time to vanish.

"Oh, a friend of mine! a brother cupman, a quiet dog who does not love these snarlings," said Burbo carelessly. "But go, child; you will tear the gentleman's tunic if you cling to him so tight; go, you are pardoned."

"Oh, do not, do not forsake me!" cried Nydia, clinging yet closer to the Athenian.

Moved by her forlorn situation, her appeal to him, her own innumerable and touching graces, the Greek seated himself on one of the rude chairs. He held her on his knees, he wiped the blood from her shoulders with his long hair, he kissed the tears from her cheeks, he whispered to her a thousand of those soothing words with which we calm the grief of a child; and so beautiful did he seem in his gentle and consoling task that even the fierce heart of Stratonice was touched. His presence seemed to shed light over that base haunt; young, beautiful, glorious, he was the emblem of all that earth made most happy, comforting one that earth had abandoned!

"Well, who would have thought our blind Nydia had been so honoured?" said the virago, wiping her heated brow.

Glaucus looked up at Burbo.

"My good man," said he, "this is your slave; she sings well, she is accustomed to the care of flowers; I wish to make a present of such a slave to a lady. Will you sell her to me?" As he spoke he felt the whole frame of the poor girl tremble with delight; she started up, she put her dishevelled hair from her eyes, she looked round, as if, alas! she had the power to *see*!

"Sell our Nydia! no, indeed," said Stratonice gruffly.

Nydia sank back with a long sigh, and again clasped the robe of her protector.

"Nonsense!" said Clodius imperiously. "You must oblige me. What, man! what, old dame! offend me, and your trade is ruined. Is not Burbo my kinsman Pansa's client? Am I not the oracle of the amphitheatre and its heroes? If I say the word, break up your wine-jars, you sell no more. Glaucus, the slave is yours."

Burbo scratched his huge head in evident embarrassment.

"The girl is worth her weight in gold to me."

"Name your price; I am rich," said Glaucus.

The ancient Italians were like the modern, there was nothing they would not sell, much less a poor blind girl.

"I paid six sestertia for her, she is worth twelve now," muttered Stratonice.

"You shall have twenty; come to the magistrate's at once, and then to my house for your money."

"I would not have sold the dear girl for a hundred, but to oblige noble Clodius," said Burbo whiningly. "And you will speak to Pansa about the place of *designator* at the amphitheatre, noble Clodius? It would just suit me."

"Thou shalt have it," said Clodius; adding in a whisper to Burbo, "Yon Greek can make your fortune; money runs through him like a sieve; mark to-day with white chalk, my Priam."

"*An Dabis?*" said Glaucus, in the formal question of sale and barter.

"*Dabitur,*" answered Burbo.

"Then, then, I am to go with you—with you? O happiness!" murmured Nydia.

"Pretty one, yes; and thy hardest task henceforth shall be to sing thy Grecian hymns to the loveliest lady in Pompeii."

ERICA AND THE PIRATE

By HARRIET MARTINEAU

Erica, a young Norwegian girl who works for the wife of Erlingsen, a prosperous farmer, wanders up the mountain-side to tell her master news brought by a man named Hund, who is suspected of being in league with the pirates infesting the inlets and fiords of that part of the coast. She is a girl whose mind is filled with all the superstitions about demons and evil spirits common to Norwegian peasants in the eighteenth century. When she is suddenly confronted by a stranger she has to decide whether he is a demon or a pirate. This story is taken from "Feats on the Fiord."

HERE was Erica on the free mountain-side, where all was silent except the occasional rattle of a brook over the stones, and the hum of a cloud of summer flies.

The sun was hot, and her path occasionally lay under rocks which reflected the heat. Then she had to pass through a swamp, whence issued a host of mosquitoes, to annoy any who intruded upon their domain, but she did not heed them. When somewhat higher up, she saw in the lofty distance a sunny slope of long grass undulating in the wind, like the surface of a lake.

She looked behind her at the entrance of a ravine which would hide from her the fiord and the dwelling she had left. Thor Islet lay like a fragment of the leafy forest cast into the blue waters, but Vogel Islet could not be seen. It was not too far down to be seen from an elevation like this, but it was hidden behind the promontories by which the fiord was contracted. Erica could see what she next looked for, knowing, as she did, precisely where to look. She could see the two graves belonging to the household—the two hillocks which were railed in behind the house. She looked behind her no more, but made her way rapidly through the ravine, the more rapidly because she had seen a man ascending by the same path at no great distance, and she had little inclination to be joined by a party of wandering Laplanders seeking a fresh pasture for their reindeer, still less by any neighbour from the fiord who might think civility required that he should escort her. This wayfarer was walking at a pace so much faster than hers that he would soon pass, and she would hide among the rocks beside the tarn at the head of the ravine till he had gone by.

It was refreshing to come out of the hot steep ravine upon the grass at the upper end of it. Such grass! A line of pathway was trodden in it straight upwards by those who had before ascended the mountain, but Erica left this path and turned to the right to seek the tarn which there lay hidden among the rocks. The herbage was knee-deep and gay with flowers—with wild geranium, pansies, and especially with the yellow blossoms which give its peculiar hue and flavour to the Gammel cheese, and to the butter made in the mountain dairies of Norway. Through this rich pasture Erica waded till she reached the tarn which fed the stream that gambolled down the ravine. The death-cold unfathomed waters lay calm and still under the shelter of the rocks which nearly surrounded them. Even where crags did not rise abruptly from the water huge blocks were scattered—masses which seemed to have lain so long as to have seen the springing herbage of a thousand summers.

In the shadow of one of these blocks Erica sank down into the grass. There she and her bundle were half buried; and this, at last, felt something like rest. Here she would remain long enough to let the other wayfarer have a good start up the mountain, and by that time she should be cool and tranquillized—yes, tranquillized—for here she could seek that peace which never failed when she sought it as Christians may. She hid her face in the fragrant grass, and did not look up again till the grief of her soul was stilled. Then her eye and her heart were open to the beauty of the place which she had made her temple of worship, and she gazed around till she saw something that surprised her. A reindeer stood on the ridge, his whole form, from his branching head to his slender legs, being clearly marked against the bright sky. He was not alone. He was the sentinel set to watch on behalf of several companions, two or three being perched on ledges of the rock browsing, one standing half buried in the herbage of the pasture, and one on the margin of the water, drinking, as he would not have dreamed of doing if the wind had not been in the wrong quarter for letting him know how near the hidden Erica was.

This pretty sight was soon over. In a few moments the whole

company appeared to take flight all at once without her having stirred a muscle. Away they went, with such speed and noiselessness that they appeared not to touch the ground. From point to point of the rock they sprang, and the last branchy head disappeared over the ridge almost before Erica could stand upright to see all she could of them.

She soon discovered the cause of their alarm. She thought it could not have been herself, and it was not. The traveller, who she had hoped was now some way up the mountain, was standing on the margin of the tarn, immediately opposite to her, so that the wind had carried the scent to the herd. The traveller saw her at the same moment that she percieved him, but Erica did not discover this, and sank down again into the grass, hoping so to remain undisturbed. She could not thus observe what his proceedings were but her ear soon informed her that he was close by. His feet were rustling in the grass.

She sat up and took her bundle, believing now that she must accept the unwelcome civility of an escort, and thinking that she might as well make haste and get it over. The man, however, seemed in no hurry. Before she could rise he took his seat on the huge stone beside her, crossed his arms, made no greeting, but looked her full in the face.

She did not know the face, nor was it like any that she had ever seen. There was such long hair and so much beard that the eyes seemed the only feature which made any distinct impression. Erica's heart now began to beat violently. Though wishing to be alone, she had not dreamed of being afraid till now; but now it occurred to her that she was seeing the rarest of sights—one not seen twice in a century—no other than the mountain-demon. Sulitelma, as the highest mountain in Norway, was thought to be his favourite haunt, and, considering his strange appearance and his silence, it could hardly be other than himself.

The test would be whether he would speak first, a test which she resolved to try, though it was rather difficult to meet and return the stare of such a neighbour without speaking. She could not keep this up for more than a minute, so she sprang to her feet, took her bundle in her hand, and began to wade back through the high grass to the pathway, almost expecting to be seized by a strong hand

and cast into the unfathomable tarn, whose waters were said to well up from the centre of the earth. Her companion, however, merely walked by her side. As he did not offer to carry her bundle he could be no countryman of hers. There was not a peasant in Nordland who would not have had more courtesy.

They walked quietly on till the tarn was left some way behind. Erica found she was not to die that way. Presently after she came in sight of a settlement of Lapps, a cluster of low and dirty tents, round which some tame reindeer were feeding. Erica was not sorry to see these, though no one knew better than she the helpless cowardice of these people; and it was not easy to say what assistance they could afford against the mountain-demon. Yet they were human beings, and would appear in answer to a cry. The stranger stopped to look at the distant tents, and Erica went on at the same pace. He presently overtook her, and pointed towards the Lapps with an inquiring look. Erica only nodded.

"Why you no speak?" growled the stranger, in broken language.

"Because I have nothing to say," declared Frica, in the sudden vivacity inspired by the discovery that this was probably no demon.

Her doubts were renewed, however, by the next question.

"Is the bishop coming?"

Now, none were supposed to have a deeper interest in the holy bishop's travels than the evil spirits of any region through which he was to pass.

"Yes, he is coming," replied Erica. "Are you afraid of him?"

The stranger burst into a loud laugh at her question: and very like a mocking fiend he looked, as his thick beard parted to show his wide mouth with its two ranges of teeth. When he finished laughing he said, "No, no; we fear no bishop."

"We!" repeated Erica to herself. "He speaks for his tribe, as well as himself."

"We no fear bishop," said the stranger, still laughing. "You no fear——" and he pointed to the long stretch of path—the prodigious ascent before them.

Erica said there was nothing to fear on the mountain for those who did their duty to the powers, as it was her intention to do. Her first Gammel cheese was to be for him whose due it was, and it should be the best she could make.

This speech, she thought, would suit, whatever might be the nature of her companion. If it was the demon, she could do no more to please him than promise him his cheese.

Her companion seemed not to understand or attend to what she said. He again asked if she was not afraid to travel alone in so dreary a place, adding that if his country-women were to be overtaken by a stranger like him, on the wilds of a mountain, they would scream and fly—all which he acted very vividly, by way of making out his imperfect speech, and trying her courage at the same time.

When Erica saw that she had no demon for a companion, but only a foreigner, she was so much relieved as not to be afraid at all. She said that nobody thought of being frightened in summer-time in her country. Winter was the time for that. When the days were long, so that travellers knew their way, and when everybody was abroad, so that you could not go far without meeting a friend, there was nothing to fear.

"You go abroad to meet friends, and leave your enemy behind."

He turned to look back. Erica could not now help watching him, and she cast a glance homewards too. They were so high up the mountain that the fiord and its shores were in full view; and more, for the river was seen in its windings from the very skirts of the mountain to the fiord, and the town of Saltdalen standing on its banks. In short, the whole landscape to the west lay before them, from Sulitelma to the point of the horizon where the islands and rocks melted into the sea.

The stranger had picked up an eagle's feather in his walk, and he now pointed with it to the tiny cove in which Erlingsen's farm might be seen, looking no bigger than an infant's toy, and said, "Do you leave an enemy there, or is Hund now your friend?"

"Hund is nobody's friend, unless he happens to be yours," Erica replied, perceiving at once that her companion belonged to the pirates. "Hund is everybody's enemy; and, above all, he is an enemy to himself. He is a wretched man."

"The bishop will cure that," said the stranger. "He is coward enough to call in the bishop to cure all. When comes the bishop?"

"Next week."

"What day, and what hour?"

Erica did not choose to gratify so close a curiosity as this. She did not reply; and while silent, was not sorry to hear the distant sound of cattle-bells—and Erlingsen's cattle-bells too. The stranger did not seem to notice the sound, even though quickening his pace to suit Erica's, who pressed on faster when she believed protection was at hand. And yet the next thing the stranger said brought her to a full stop. He said he thought a part of Hund's business with the bishop would be to get him to disenchant the fiord, so that boats might not be spirited away almost before men's eyes; and that a rower and his skiff might not sink like lead one day, and the man maybe heard the second day, and seen the third, so that there was no satisfactory knowledge as to whether he was really dead. Erica stopped, and her eager looks made the inquiry which her lips could not speak. Her eagerness put her companion on his guard, and he would explain no further than by saying that the fiord was certainly enchanted, and that strange tales were circulating all round its shores, very striking to a stranger; a stranger had nothing more to do with the wonders of a country than to listen to them. He wanted to turn the conversation back to Hund. Having found out that he was at Erlingsen's, he next tried to discover what he had said and done since his arrival. Erica told the little there was to tell—that he seemed full of sorrow and remorse. She told this in hope of a further explanation about drowned men being seen alive; but the stranger stopped when the bells were heard again, and a woman's voice singing, nearer still. He complimented Erica on her courage, and turned to go back the way he came.

"Stay," said Erica. "Do come to the dairy, now you are so near."

The man walked away rapidly.

"My master is here close at hand, he will be glad to see a stranger," she said, following him. The stranger did not turn, but only walked on faster, and with longer strides, down the slope.

The only thing now to be done was to run forwards, and send a messenger after him. Erica forgot heat, weariness, and the safety of her property, and ran on towards the singing voice. In five minutes she found the singer, Frolich, lying along the ground and picking cloudberries, with which she was filling her basket for supper.

"Where is Erlingsen? Quick—quick!" cried Erica.

"My father? You may just see him with your good eyes—up there."

And Frølich pointed to a patch of verdue on the slope high up the mountain, where the gazer might just discern that there were haycocks standing, and two or three moving figures beside them.

"Stiorna is there to-day, besides Jan. They hope to finish this evening," said Frolich; "and so here I am, all alone; and I am glad you have come, to help me to have a good supper ready for them. Their hunger will beat all my berry-gathering."

"You are alone?" said Erica, discovering that it was well that the pirate had turned back when he did. "You alone, and gathering berries, instead of having an eye on the cattle! Who has an eye on the cattle?"

"Why, no one," answered Frolich. "Come, now, do not tease me with bidding me remember the Bishop of Tronyem's cattle. The underground people have something to do elsewhere to-day; they give no heed to us."

"We must give heed to them, however," said Erica. "Show me where the cattle are, and I will collect them, and have an eye on them till supper is ready."

"You shall do no such thing, Erica. You shall lie down here and pick berries with me, and tell me the news. That will rest you and me at the same time, for I am as tired of being alone as you can be of climbing the mountain."

Erica told her she could not answer to Erlingsen for letting one of his children follow the steps of a pirate who might return at any moment.

Frolich started off towards the sleeping-shed, and never stopped till she had entered it and driven a provision-chest against the door, leaving Erica far behind.

Erica, indeed, was in no hurry to follow. She returned for her bundle and then, uneasy about the cattle being left without an eye upon them, and thus confided to the negligence of the underground people, she proceeded to an eminence where two or three of her cows were grazing, and there sounded her lure. She put her whole strength to it, in hope that others besides the cattle might appear in answer, for she was really anxious to see her master.

The peculiar and far from musical sounds did spread wide over the pastures and up the slopes, and through the distant woods, so that the cattle stood to listen, and her own cows began to move, leaving the sweetest tufts of grass, and rising up from their couches in the richest herbage, to converge towards the point whence she called. The far-off herdsman observed to his fellow that there was a new call among the pastures; and Erlingsen, on the upland, began his descent to learn whether Erica had brought any news from home.

Long before he could appear, Frolich stole out trembling, and looking round her at every step. When she saw Erica, she flew over the grass, and threw herself down in it at Erica's feet.

"Where is he?" she whispered. "Has he come back?"

"I have not seen him. I dare say he is far off by this time, at the Black Tarn, where I met with him."

"The Black Tarn! And do you mean that? No, you cannot mean that you came all the way together from the Black Tarn hither. Did you run? Did you fly? Did you shriek? Oh, what did you do, with a pirate at your heels?"

"By my side," said Erica. "We walked and talked."

"With a pirate! But how did you know it was a pirate? Did he tell you so?"

"No; and at first I thought"—and she sank her voice into a reverential whisper—"I thought for some time it was the demon of this place. When I found it was only a pirate I did not mind."

"Only a pirate—did not mind!" exclaimed Frolich. "You are the strangest girl; you are the most perverse creature! You think nothing of a pirate walking at your elbow for miles; and you would make a slave of yourself and me about these underground people that my father laughs at, and that nobody ever saw. Ah! you say nothing aloud, but I know you are saying in your own mind, 'Remember the Bishop of Tronyem's cattle.'"

"You want news," said Erica, avoiding as usual all conversation about her superstitions. "How will it please you that the bishop is coming?"

"Very much, if we had any chance of seeing him."

Erica then inquired whether any Gammel cheese was made yet.

"No," said Frolich, inwardly sighing for news. "We have the

whey, but not sweet cream enough till after this evening's milking. So you are just in time."

Erica was glad, as she could not otherwise have been sure of the demon having his due.

"There is your father," said Erica. "Now do go and gather more berries, Frolich. There are not half enough; and you cannot be afraid of the pirate, with your father within call. Now, do go."

"You want me not to hear what you have to tell my father," said Frolich, unwilling to depart.

"That is very true. I shall tell him nothing till you are out of hearing. He can repeat to you what he pleases afterwards; and he will indulge you all the more for your giving him a good supper."

"So he will; and I will fill his cup myself," observed Frolich. "He says the corn-brandy is uncommonly good; and I will fill his cup till it will not hold another drop."

"You will not reach his heart that way, Frolich. He knows to a drop what his quantity is; and there he stops."

"I know where there are some manyberries ripe," said Frolich; and he likes them above all berries. They lie this way, at the edge of the swamp, where the pirate will never think of coming."

And off she went, as Erica rose from the grass to curtsy to Erlingsen on his approach.

PRAIRIE GIPSY

By BRET HARTE

Melissa Smith—"Mliss" to every one in the Western settlement of Smith's Pocket, in the Red Mountain country—was a wild little gipsy of the prairie whose father was a dissolute miner seeking gold in the hills. But one day she had an idea, and went to the schoolmaster. However, she found that her idea was not easy to live up to, and it was not until the understanding schoolmaster had shown her the true meaning of forgiveness that Mliss began to solve her own difficulties. This story is taken from "Mliss."

"THE Master," as he was known to his little flock, sat alone one night in the schoolhouse, with some open copy-books before him, carefully making those bold and full characters which are supposed to combine the extremes of chirographical and moral excellence, and had got as far as "Riches are deceitful," and was elaborating the noun with an insincerity of flourish that was quite in the spirit of his text, when he heard a gentle tapping. The woodpeckers had been busy about the roof during the day, and the noise did not disturb his work. But the opening of the door, and the tapping continuing from the inside, caused him to look up. He was slightly startled by the figure of a young girl, dirty and shabbily clad. Still, her great black eyes, her coarse, uncombed, lustreless black hair falling over the sunburnt face, her red arms and feet streaked with the red soil, were all familiar to him. It was Melissa Smith.

"What can she want here?" thought the master. Everybody knew "Mliss," as she was called, throughout the length and height of Red Mountain. Everybody knew her as an incorrigible girl. Her fierce, ungovernable disposition, her mad freaks and lawless character, were, in their way, as proverbial as the story of her father's weaknesses, and as philosophically accepted by the townsfolk. She wrangled with and fought the schoolboys with keener invective and quite as powerful arm. She followed the trails with a woodman's craft, and the master had met her before, miles away, shoeless, stockingless, and bareheaded on the mountain road. Such were the antecedents, and such the character of Mliss, as she stood before the master. It was shown in the ragged dress, the unkempt hair, and bleeding feet, and asked his pity. It flashed from her black, fearless eyes, and commanded his respect.

"I come here to-night," she said rapidly and boldly, keeping her hard glance on his, "because I knew you was alone. I wouldn't come here when them gals was here. I hate 'em and they hates me. That's why. You keep school, don't you? I want to be teached!"

If to the shabbiness of her apparel and uncomeliness of her tangled hair and dirty face she had added the humility of tears, the master would have extended to her the usual moiety of pity, and nothing more. But with the natural, though illogical instincts of his species, her boldness awakened in him something of that respect which all original natures pay unconsciously to one another in any grade. And he gazed at her the more fixedly as she went on still rapidly, her hand on that door-latch and her eyes on his:

"My name's Mliss—Mliss Smith! You can bet your life on that. Mliss Smith—and I'm coming to school."

"Well?" said the master.

Accustomed to be thwarted and opposed, often wantonly and cruelly, for no other purpose than to excite the violent impulses of her nature, the master's phlegm evidently took her by surprise. She stopped; she began to twist a lock of her hair between her fingers; and the rigid line of upper lip, drawn over the wicked little teeth, relaxed and quivered slightly. Then her eyes dropped, and something like a blush struggled up to her cheek, and tried to assert itself through the splashes of redder soil, and the sunburn of years. Suddenly she threw herself forward, calling on God to strike her dead, and fell quite weak and helpless, with her face on the master's desk, crying and sobbing as if her heart would break.

The master lifted her gently and waited for the paroxysm to pass. Then, raising her to her feet, he wrapped his shawl around her, and, bidding her come early in the morning, he walked with her down the road. There he bade her good-night. The moon shone brightly on the narrow path before them. He stood and watched the bent little figure as it staggered down the road, and waited until it had passed the little graveyard and reached the curve of the hill, where it turned and stood for a moment, a mere atom of suffering outlined against the far-off patient stars. Then he went back to his work. But the lines of the copy-book thereafter faded into long parallels of never-ending road, over which childish figures seemed to pass sobbing and crying into the night. Then, the little schoolhouse seeming lonelier than before, he shut the door and went home.

The next morning Mliss came to school. Her face had been washed, and her coarse black hair bore evidence of recent struggles with the comb, in which both had evidently suffered. The old defiant look shone occasionally in her eyes, but her manner was tamer and more subdued. Then began a series of little trials and self-sacrifices, in which master and pupil bore an equal part, and which increased the confidence and sympathy between them. Although obedient under the master's eye, at times during the recess, if thwarted or stung by a fancied slight, Mliss would rage in ungovernable fury, and many a palpitating young savage, finding himself matched with his own weapons of torment, would seek the master with torn jacket and scratched face, and complaints of the dreadful Mliss. There was a serious division among the townspeople on the subject; some threatening to withdraw their children from such evil companionship, and others as warmly upholding the course of the master in his work of reclamation. Meanwhile, with a steady persistence that seemed quite astonishing to him on looking back afterward, the master drew Mliss gradually out of the shadow of her past life, as though it were but her natural progress down the narrow path on which he had set her feet the moonlit night of their first meeting. A few of the plainer people had made up a little sum by which the ragged Mliss was enabled to assume the garments of respect and civilization; and often a rough shake of the hand, and words of homely commendation from a red-shirted and burly figure, sent a glow to the cheek of the young master, and set him to thinking if it was altogether deserved.

Three months had passed from the time of their first meeting, and the master was sitting late one evening over the moral and sententious copies, when there came a tap at the door, and again Mliss stood before him. She was neatly clad, and clean-faced, and there was nothing, perhaps, but the long black hair and bright black eyes to remind him of his former apparition. "Are you busy?"

she asked; "can you come with me?" And on his signifying his readiness, in her old wilful way she said, "Come, then, quick."

They passed out of the door together, and into the dark road. As they entered the town the master asked her whither she was going. She replied, "To see my father."

It was the first time he had heard her call him by that filial title, or indeed anything more than "Old Smith," or the "Old Man." It was the first time in three months that she had spoken of him at all, and the master knew she had kept resolutely aloof from him since her great change. Satisfied from her manner that it was fruitless to question her purpose, he passively followed. The child whispered in his ear that there was a cabin on the other side of the creek, crossed by the long flume, where she thought he might be. Thither they crossed—a toilsome half-hour's walk, but in vain. They were returning by the ditch at the abutment of the flume, gazing at the lights of the town on the opposite bank, when suddenly, sharply, a quick report rang out on the clear night air. The echoes caught it, and carried it round and round Red Mountain, and set the dogs to barking all along the streams. Lights seemed to dance and move quickly on the outskirts of the town for a few moments, the stream rippled quite audibly beside them, a few stones loosened themselves from the hill-side, and splashed into the stream, a heavy wind seemed to surge the branches of the funeral pines, and then the silence seemed to fall thicker, heavier, and deadlier. The master turned towards Mliss with an unconscious gesture of protection, but the child had gone. Oppressed by a strange fear, he ran quickly down the trail to the river's bed, and, jumping from boulder to boulder, reached the base of Red Mountain and the outskirts of the village. Midway of the crossing he looked up and held his breath in awe. For high above him, on the narrow flume, he saw the fluttering little figure of his late companion crossing swiftly in the darkness.

He climbed the bank, and, guided by a few lights moving about a central point on the mountain, soon found himself breathless among a crowd of awe-stricken and sorrowful men. Out from among them the child appeared, and, taking the master's hand, led him silently before what seemed a ragged hole in the mountain. Her face was quite white, but her excited manner gone, and her look that of one to whom some long-expected event had at last happened—an expression that, to the master in his bewilderment, seemed almost like relief. The walls of the cavern were partly propped by decaying timbers. The child pointed to what appeared to be some ragged cast-off clothes left in the hole by the late occupant. The master approached nearer with his flaming dip, and bent over them. It was Smith, already cold, with a pistol in his hand, and a bullet in his heart, lying beside his empty pocket.

The long dry summer came. As each fierce day burned itself out in little whiffs of pearl-grey smoke on the mountain summits, and the upspringing breeze scattered its red embers over the landscape, the green wave which in early spring upheaved above Smith's grave grew sere, and dry, and hard. In those days the master, strolling in the little churchyard of a Sabbath afternoon, was sometimes surprised to find a few wild flowers plucked from the damp pine forest scattered there, and oftener rude wreaths hung upon the little pine cross. Most of these wreaths were formed of a sweet-scented grass, which the children loved to keep in their desks, intertwined with the plumes of the buckeye, the syringa, and the wood anemone; and here and there the master noticed the dark blue cowl of the monk's-hood or deadly aconite. There was something in the odd association of this noxious plant with these memorials which occasioned a painful sensation to the master deeper than his esthetic sense. One day, during a long walk, in crossing a wooded ridge, he came upon Mliss in the heart of the forest, perched upon a prostrate pine, on a fantastic throne formed by the hanging plumes of lifeless branches, her lap full of grasses and pine-burrs, and crooning to herself one of the negro melodies of her younger life. Recognizing him at a distance, she made room for him on her elevated throne, and with a grave assumption of hospitality and patronage that would have been ridiculous had it not been so terribly earnest, she fed him with pine nuts and crab-apples. The master took that opportunity to point out to her the noxious and deadly qualities of the monk's-hood, whose dark blossoms he saw in her lap, and extorted from her a promise not to meddle with it as long as she remained his pupil. This done—as the master had tested her integrity before—he rested satisfied, and the strange feeling which had overcome him on seeing them died away.

Of the homes that were offered Mliss when her conversion became known, the master preferred that of Mrs. Morpher, a womanly and kind-hearted specimen of south-western efflorescence, known in her maidenhood as the "Per-rarie Rose." Being one of those who contend resolutely against their own natures, Mrs. Morpher, by a long series of self-sacrifices and struggles, had at last subjugated her naturally careless disposition to principles of "order." Again her old nature asserted itself in her children. Lycurgus dipped into the cupboard "between meals," and Aristides came home from school without shoes, leaving those important articles on the threshold, for the delight of a barefooted walk down the ditches. Octavia and Cassandra were "keerless" of their clothes. So with but one exception, however much the "Prairie Rose" might have trimmed and pruned and trained her own natural luxuriance, the little shoots came up defiantly wild and straggling. That one exception was Clytemnestra Morpher, aged fifteen. She was the realization of her mother's immaculate conception—neat, orderly, and dull.

It was an amiable weakness of Mrs. Morpher to imagine that Clytie was a consolation and model for Mliss. Following this fallacy Mrs. Morpher threw Clytie at the head of Mliss when she was "bad," and set her up before the child for adoration in her penitential moments. It was not, therefore, surprising to the master to hear that Clytie was coming to school, obviously as a favour to the master and as an example for Mliss and others. For Clytie was quite a young lady. The youth of "Smith's Pocket," to whom this kind of flower was rare, sighed for her in April and languished in May. Enamoured swains haunted the schoolhouse at the hour of dismissal. A few were jealous of the master.

Perhaps it was this latter circumstance that opened the master's eyes to another. He could not help noticing that Clytie was romantic; that in school she required a great deal of attention; that her pens were uniformly bad and wanted fixing; that she usually accompanied the request with a certain expectation in her eye that was somewhat disproportionate to the quality of service she verbally required; that she sometimes allowed the curves of a round, plump white arm to rest on his when he was writing her copies; that she always blushed and flung back her blond curls when she did so. I don't remember whether I have stated that the master was a young man—it's of little consequence, however; he had been severely educated in the school in which Clytie was taking her first lesson, and, on the whole, withstood the flexible curves and factitious glance like the fine young Spartan that he was. Perhaps an insufficient quality of food may have tended to this ascetism. He generally avoided Clytie; but one evening when she returned to the schoolhouse after something she had forgotten, and did not find it until the master walked home with her, I hear that he endeavoured to make himself particularly agreeable—partly from the fact, I imagine, that his conduct was adding gall and bitterness to the already overcharged hearts of Clytemnestra's admirers.

The morning after this affecting episode Mliss did not come to school. Noon came, but not Mliss. Questioning Clytie on the subject, it appeared that they had left for school together, but the wilful Mliss had taken another road. The afternoon brought her not. In the evening he called on Mrs. Morpher, whose motherly heart was really alarmed. Mr. Morpher had spent all day in search of her, without discovering a trace that might lead to her discovery. Aristides was summoned as a probable accomplice, but that equitable infant succeeded in impressing the household with his innocence. Mrs. Morpher entertained a vivid impression that the child would yet be found drowned in a ditch. Sick at heart, the master returned to the schoolhouse. As he lit his lamp and seated himself at his desk, he found a note lying before him addressed to himself, in Mliss's handwriting. It seemed to be written on a leaf torn from some old memorandum book and, to prevent sacrilegious trifling, had been sealed with six broken wafers. Opening it almost tenderly, the master read as follows:

> RESPECTED SIR,—When you read this, I am run away. Never to come back. *Never*, NEVER, NEVER. You can give my beeds to Mary Jennings, and my Amerika's Pride [a highly coloured lithograph from a tobacco-box] to Sally Flanders. But don't you give anything to Clytie Morpher. Don't you dare to. Do you know what my opinion is of her, it is this, she is perfekly disgustin. That is all and no more at present from
>
> Yours respectfully,
>
> MELISSA SMITH

The master sat pondering on this strange epistle till the moon lifted its bright face above the distant hills, and illuminated the trail that led to the schoolhouse, beaten quite hard with the coming and going of little feet. Then, more satisfied in mind, he tore the missive into fragments and scattered them along the road.

At sunrise the next morning he was picking his way through the palm-like fern and thick underbrush of the pine-forest, starting the hare from its form, and awakening a querulous protest from a few dissipated crows, who had evidently been making a night of it, and so came to the wooded ridge where he had once found Mliss. There he found the prostrate pine and tasselled branches, but the throne was vacant. As he drew nearer, what might have been some frightened animal started through the crackling limbs. It ran up the tossed arms of the fallen monarch, and sheltered itself in some friendly foliage. The master, reaching the old seat, found the nest still warm; looking up in the intertwining branches, he met the black eyes of the errant Mliss. They gazed at each other without speaking. She was the first to break the silence.

"What do you want?" she asked curtly.

The master had decided on a course of action. "I want some crab-apples," he said humbly.

"Shan't have 'em; go away. Why don't you get 'em of Clytemnerestera?" (It seemed to be a relief to Mliss to express her contempt in additional syllables to that classical young woman's already long-drawn title.) "O you wicked thing!"

"I am hungry, Lissy. I have eaten nothing since dinner yesterday. I am famished!" and the young man, in a state of remarkable exhaustion, leaned against the tree.

Melissa's heart was touched. In the bitter days of her gipsy life she had known the sensation he so artfully simulated. Overcome by his heart-broken tone, but not entirely divested of suspicion, she said:

"Dig under the tree near the roots, and you'll find lots; but mind you don't tell," for Mliss had *her* hoards as well as the rats and squirrels.

But the master, of course, was unable to find them; the effects of hunger probably blinding his senses. Mliss grew uneasy. At length she peered at him through the leaves in an elfish way, and questioned:

"If I come down and give you some, you'll promise you won't touch me?"

The master promised.

"Hope you'll die if you do!"

The master accepted instant dissolution as a forfeit. Mliss slid down the tree. For a few moments nothing transpired but the munching of the pine-nuts. "Do you feel better?" she asked, with some solicitude. The master confessed to a recuperated feeling, and then, gravely thanking her, proceeded to retrace his steps. As he expected, he had not gone far before she called him. He turned. She was standing there quite white, with tears in her widely opened orbs. The master felt that the right moment had come. Going up to her, he took both her hands, and, looking in her tearful eyes, said, gravely, "Lissy, do you remember the first evening you came to see me?"

Lissy remembered.

"You asked me if you might come to school, for you wanted to learn something and be better, and I said——"

"Come," responded the child promptly.

"What would *you* say if the master now came to you and said that he was lonely without his little scholar, and that he wanted her to come and teach him to be better?"

The child hung her head for a few moments in silence. The master waited patiently. Tempted by the quiet, a hare ran close to the couple, and raising her bright eyes and velvet forepaws, sat and gazed at them. A squirrel ran half-way down the furrowed bark of the fallen tree, and there stopped.

"We are waiting, Lissy," said the master, in a whisper, and the child smiled. Stirred by a passing breeze, the tree-tops rocked, and a long pencil of light stole through their interlaced boughs full on the doubting face and irresolute little figure. Suddenly she took the master's hand in her quick way. What she said was scarcely audible, but the master, putting the black hair from her forehead, kissed her; and so, hand in hand, they passed out of the damp aisles and forest odours into the open sunlit road.

THE RED SHOES

By HANS ANDERSEN

This fairy story is of a little girl whose vanity led her to much trouble and suffering. Karen's one thought was for her beautiful shiny red shoes that had been made for the daughter of a count, and which, when she wore them, made her feet tingle so that she had to dance and go whither the shoes took her. And they took her very far astray.

THERE was once a little girl, very pretty and delicate, but so poor that in summer-time she went barefoot, and in winter wore large wooden shoes, so that her little ankles grew quite red and sore.

In the village dwelt the shoemaker's mother; she sat down one day, and made out of some old pieces of red cloth a pair of little shoes. They were clumsy enough certainly, but they fitted the little girl, and she gave them to her. The little girl's name was Karen.

It was the day of her mother's funeral when the red shoes were given to Karen. They were not at all suitable for mourning, but she had no others, and in them she walked with bare legs behind the bier.

Just then a large old carriage rolled by; in it sat a large old lady. She looked at the little girl and pitied her, and she said to the priest, "Give me the little girl, and I will take care of her."

And Karen thought it was all for the sake of the red shoes that old lady had taken this fancy to her; but the old lady said they were frightful, and they were burnt. And Karen was dressed very neatly; she was taught to read and to work; and people told her she was pretty, but the Mirror said, "Thou are more than pretty, thou are beautiful!"

It happened one day that the Queen travelled through that part of the country, with her little daughter, the Princess; and all the people, Karen amongst them, crowded in front of the palace, whilst the little Princess stood, dressed in white, at a window, for every one to see her. She wore neither train nor gold crown; but on her feet were pretty red morocco shoes, much prettier ones, indeed, than those the shoemaker's mother had made for little Karen. Nothing in the world could be compared to these red shoes!

Karen was now old enough to be confirmed; she was to have both new frock and new shoes. The rich shoemaker in the town took the measure of her little foot. Large glass cases, full of neat shoes and shining boots, were fixed round the room; but the old lady's sight was not very good, and, naturally enough, she had not so much pleasure in looking at them as Karen had. Amongst the shoes was a pair of red ones, just like those worn by the Princess. How gay they were! and the shoemaker said, they had been made for a count's daughter, but had not quite fitted her.

"They are of polished leather," said the old lady; "see how they shine!"

"Yes, they shine beautifully!" exclaimed Karen. And as the shoes fitted her, they were bought, but the old lady did not know that they were red, for she would never have suffered Karen to go to confirmation in red shoes. But Karen did so.

Everybody looked at her feet, and as she walked up the nave to the chancel, it seemed to her that even the antique sculptured figures on the monuments, with their stiff ruffs and long black robes, fixed their eyes on her red shoes. And all through the solemn service, Karen could think of nothing but her red shoes.

That afternoon, when the old lady was told that Karen had worn red shoes at her confirmation, she was much vexed, and told Karen that they were quite unsuitable, and that henceforward, whenever she went to church, she must wear black shoes, were they ever so old.

Next Sunday was the Communion day; Karen looked first at the red shoes, then at the black ones, then at the red again, and—put them on.

It was beautiful, sunshiny weather. Karen and the old lady walked to church through the cornfields, and the path was very dusty.

At the church door stood an old soldier; he was leaning on crutches, and had a marvellously long beard, not white, but reddish-hued, and he bowed almost to the earth, and asked the old lady if he might wipe the dust off her shoes. And Karen put out her little foot also. "Oh, what pretty dancing shoes!" quoth the old soldier; "take care, and mind you do not let them slip off when you dance;" and he passed his hands over them.

The old lady gave the soldier a halfpenny, and then went with Karen into church.

And every one looked at Karen's red shoes; and all the carved figures, too, bent their gaze upon them; and when Karen knelt before the altar, the red shoes still floated before her eyes. She thought of them, and of them only, and she forgot to join in the hymn of praise—she forgot to repeat "Our Father."

At last all the people came out of church, and the old lady got into her carriage. Karen was just lifting her foot to follow her, when the old soldier standing in the porch exclaimed, "Only look, what pretty dancing-shoes!" And Karen could not help it, she felt she must make a few of her dancing-steps; and after she had begun, her feet continued to move, just as though the shoes had received power over them. She danced round the churchyard—she could not stop—the coachman was obliged to run after her—he took hold of her and lifted her into the carriage, but the feet still continued to dance, so as to kick the good old lady all the way home. At last the shoes were taken off, and the feet had rest.

And now the shoes were put away in a press, but Karen could not help going to look at them every now and then.

The old lady now lay ill in bed. The doctor said she could not live much longer; she certainly needed careful nursing, and who should be her nurse and constant attendant but Karen? But there was to be a grand ball in the town; Karen was invited; she looked at the old lady, who was almost dying, she looked at the red shoes—she put them on; there could be no harm in doing that, at least; she went to the ball, and began to dance.

But when she wanted to move to the right, the shoes bore her to the left; and when she would dance up the room, the shoes danced down the room, danced down the stairs, through the streets, and through the gates of the town. Dance she did, and dance she must, straight out into the dark wood.

Something all at once shone through the trees! She thought at first it must be the moon's bright face, shining through the night mists; but no, it was the old soldier with the red beard—he sat there, nodding at her, and repeating, "Only look, what pretty dancing-shoes!"

She was very much frightened, and tried to throw off her red shoes, but could not unclasp them. She hastily tore off her stockings; but the shoes she could not get rid of—they had, it seemed, grown on to her feet. Away she danced, over field and meadow, in rain and in sunshine, by night and by day—by night! that was most unpleasant! She danced into the lonely churchyard, but the dead there danced not—they were at rest: she would fain have sat down on the poor man's grave, where the bitter tansy grew, but for her there was neither rest nor respite. She danced past the open church-door; and there she saw an Angel, clad in long white robes, and with wings that reached from his shoulders to the earth. His countenance was grave and stern, and in his hand he held a broad glittering sword.

"Thou shalt dance," said he; "dance on, in thy red shoes, till thou art pale and cold, and thy body becomes bent and shrunken! Thou shalt dance still, from door to door; and wherever proud, vain children live, thou shalt knock, so that they may hear thee and fear! Thou shalt dance on——"

"Mercy!" cried Karen; but she heard not the Angel's answer, for the shoes carried her through the gate, into the fields, along highways and by-ways, and still she must dance.

One morning she danced past a door she knew well. She heard psalm-singing from within, and presently a coffin, strewn with flowers, was borne out. Then Karen knew that the good old lady was dead, and she felt herself a thing forsaken by all mankind.

Dance she did, and dance she must, even through the dark night. The shoes bore her continually over thorns and briers, till her limbs were torn and bleeding. Away she danced over the heath to a little solitary house; she knew that the headsman dwelt there, and she tapped with her fingers against the panes, crying:

"Come out! come out! I cannot come in to you, I am dancing."

And the headsman replied, "Surely thou knowest not who I am. I cut off the heads of wicked men, and my axe is very sharp and keen."

"Cut not off my head!" said Karen; "for then I could not live to repent of my sin; but cut off my feet with the red shoes."

And then she confessed to him all her sin, and the headsman cut off her feet with the red shoes on them; but even after this the shoes still danced away with those little feet over the fields, and into the deep forests.

And the headsman made her a pair of wooden feet, and hewed down some boughs to serve her as crutches. And he taught her the psalm which is always repeated by criminals, and she kissed the hand that had guided the axe, and went her way over the heath.

"Now I have certainly suffered quite enough through the red shoes," thought Karen; "I will go to church and let people see me once more!" and she went as fast as she could to the church-porch. But as she approached it, the red shoes danced before her, and she was frightened and turned back.

All that week through she endured the keenest anguish and shed many bitter tears; but when Sunday came, she said to herself, "Well, I must have suffered and striven enough by this time; I dare say I am quite as good as many of those who are holding their heads so high in church." So she took courage and went there, but she had not passed the churchyard-gate before she saw the red shoes again dancing before her, and in great terror she again turned back, and more deeply than ever bewailed her sin.

She then went to the pastor's house, and begged that some employment might be given her, promising to work diligently and do all she could. She did not wish for any wages, she said, she only wanted a roof to shelter her, and to dwell with good people. And the pastor's wife had pity on her, and took her into her service. And Karen was grateful and industrious. Every evening she sat silently listening to the pastor, while he read the Holy Scriptures aloud. All the children loved her, but when she heard them talk about dress and finery, and about being as beautiful as a queen, she would sorrowfully shake her head.

Again Sunday came; all the pastor's household went to church, and they asked her if she would not go too, but she sighed and looked with tears in her eyes upon her crutches.

When they were all gone, she went into her own little lowly chamber—it was but just large enough to contain a bed and a chair—and there she sat down with her psalm-book in her hand; and whilst she was meekly and devoutly reading it, the wind wafted the tones of the organ from the church into her room, and she lifted up her face to heaven and prayed, with tears, "Oh, God, help me!"

Then the sun shone brightly, so brightly!—and behold! close before her stood the white-robed Angel of God, the same whom she had seen on that night of horror at the church-porch; but his hand wielded not now, as then, a sharp, threatening sword—he held a lovely green bough, full of roses. With this he touched the ceiling, which immediately rose to a great height, a bright gold star sparkling in the spot where the Angel's green bough had touched it. And he touched the walls, whereupon the room widened, and Karen saw the organ, the old monuments, and the congregation all sitting in their richly-carved seats and singing from their psalm-books.

For the church had come home to the poor girl in her little narrow chamber, or rather the chamber had grown, as it were, into the church. She sat with the rest of the pastor's household, and when the psalm was ended, they looked up and nodded to her, saying, "Thou didst well to come, Karen!"

"This is mercy!" said she.

And the organ played again, and the children's voices in the choir mingled so sweetly and plaintively with it! The bright sunbeams streamed warmly through the windows upon Karen's seat; her heart was so full of sunshine, of peace and gladness, that it broke. Her soul flew upon a sunbeam to her Father in heaven, where not a look of reproach awaited her—not a word was breathed of the Red Shoes.

LOST IN THE SNOW

By R. M. BALLANTYNE

Roy and Nelly were the children of Robin Gore, a backwoodsman in North America in the days when the continent was still largely peopled by roving bands of redskins and settlers carried flint and tinder instead of boxes of matches. One day in winter the two children left their home at Fort Enterprise and wandered off into the falling snow. They then found reason to be grateful that they had learned how to fend for themselves in that wild country. This story is taken from "Silver Lake," in which the further adventures of the two children are narrated.

WHEN Roy and Nelly set out for a ramble they had at first no intention of going beyond their usual haunts in the woods around the Fort; but Roy had been inspirited by his successful march that day with his father, and felt inclined to show Nelly some new scenes to which they had not, up to that time, dared to penetrate together.

The snowstorm had commenced gradually. When the children set forth on their ramble only a few flakes were falling, but they had not been away half an hour when snow fell so thickly that they could not see distinctly more than a few yards ahead of them. There was no wind, however, so they continued to advance, rather pleased than otherwise with the state of things.

"Oh, I *do* like to see falling snow," cried Nelly, with a burst of animation.

"So do I," said Roy, looking back at his sister with a bright smile, "and I like it best when it comes down thick and heavy, in big flakes, on a *very* calm day, don't you?"

"Yes. Oh, it's so nice," responded Nelly sympathetically.

They paused for a few minutes to shake some of the snow from their garments, and beat their hands together, for their fingers were cold, and to laugh boisterously, for their hearts were merry. Then they resumed their march, Roy beating the track manfully and Nelly following in his footsteps.

In passing a tall fir-tree Roy chanced to touch a twig. The result was literally overwhelming, for in a moment he was almost buried in snow, to the unutterable delight of his sister, who stood screaming with laughter as the unfortunate boy struggled to disentomb himself.

In those Northern wilds, where snow falls frequently and in great abundance, masses are constantly accumulating on the branches of trees, particularly on the pines, on the broad flat branches of which these masses attain to considerable size. A slight touch is generally sufficient to bring these down, but, being soft, they never do any injury worth mentioning.

When Roy had fairly emerged from the snow he joined his sister in the laugh, but suddenly he stopped, and his face became very grave.

"What's the matter?" asked Nelly, with an anxious look.

"My snowshoe's broken," said Roy.

There was greater cause for anxiety on account of this accident than the reader is perhaps aware of. It may be easily understood that in a country where the snow averages four feet in depth no one can walk half a mile without snowshoes without being thoroughly exhausted; on the other hand, a man can walk thirty or forty miles a day by means of snowshoes.

"Can't you mend it?" asked Nelly.

Roy, who had been carefully examining the damaged shoe, shook his head.

"I've nothing here to do it with; besides, it's an awful smash. I must just try to scramble home the best way I can. Come, it's not very far. We'll only be a bit late for dinner."

The snowshoe having been bandaged, after a fashion, with a pocket handkerchief, the little wanderers began to retrace their steps; but this was now a matter of extreme difficulty, owing to the quantity of snow which had fallen and almost obliterated the tracks. The broken shoe, also, was constantly giving way, so that ere long the children became bewildered as well as anxious, and soon lost the track of their outward march altogether. To make matters worse, the wind began to blow clouds of snowdrift into their faces, compelling them to seek the denser parts of the forest for shelter.

They wandered on, however, in the belief that they were drawing nearer home every step, and Roy, whose heart was stout and brave, cheered up his sister's spirit so much that she began to feel confident their troubles would soon be over.

Presently all their hopes were dashed to the ground by their suddenly emerging upon an open space, close to the very spot where the snow-mass had fallen on Roy's head. After the first feeling of alarm and disappointment had subsided Roy plucked up heart and encouraged Nelly by pointing out to her that they had at all events recovered their old track, which they would be very careful not to lose sight of again.

Poor Nelly whimpered a little, partly from cold and hunger as well as from disappointment, as she listened to her brother's words; then she dried her eyes and said she was ready to begin again. So they set off once more. But the difficulty of discerning the track, if great at first, was greater now, because the falling and drifting snow had well-nigh covered it up completely. In a very few minutes Roy stopped, and, confessing that he had lost it again, proposed to return once more to their starting-point to try to recover it. Nelly agreed, for she was by this time too much fatigued and alarmed to have any will of her own, and was quite ready to do whatever she was told without question.

After wandering about for nearly an hour in this state of uncertainty Roy at last stopped, and, putting his arm round his sister's waist, said that he had lost himself altogether! Poor Nelly, whose heart had been gradually sinking, fairly broke down; she hid her face in her brother's bosom, and wept.

"Come now, don't do that, dear Nell," said Roy tenderly. "I'll tell you what we shall do—we'll camp in the snow! We have often done it close to the house, you know, for fun, so we'll do it now in earnest."

"But it's so dark and cold," sobbed Nelly, looking round with a shudder into the dark recesses of the forest, which were by that time enshrouded by the gathering shades of night; "and I'm *so* hungry too! Oh, me! what shall we do?"

"Now don't get so despairing," urged Roy, whose courage rose in proportion as his sister's sank; "it's not such an awful business after all, for father is sure to scour the woods in search of us, an' if we only get a comfortable encampment made, an' a roarin' fire kindled, why, we'll sit beside it an' tell stories till they find us. They'll be sure to see the fire, you know, so come—let's to work."

Roy said this so cheerfully that the child felt a little comforted, dried her eyes, and said she would "help to make the camp."

This matter of making an encampment in the snow, although laborious work, was by no means a novelty to these children of the backwoods. They had often been taught how to do it and had made "playing at camps" their chief amusement on fine winter days. When therefore they found themselves compelled to "camp

out" from necessity, neither of them was at a loss how to proceed. Roy drew a circle in the snow about three yards in diameter, at the foot of a large tree, and then both set to work to dig a hole in this space, using their snow-shoes as shovels. It took an hour's hard work to reach the ground, and when they did so the piled-up snow all round raised the walls of this hole to the height of about six feet.

"Now for bedding," cried Roy, scrambling over the walls of their camp and going into the woods in search of a young pine-tree, while Nelly sat down on the ground to rest after her toil.

It was a dark night, and the woods were so profoundly obscured that Roy had to grope about for some time before he found a suitable tree. Cutting it down with the axe which always hung at his girdle, he returned to camp with it on his shoulder, and cut off the small soft branches, which Nelly spread over the ground to a depth of nearly half a foot. This "pine-brush," as it is called, formed a soft elastic couch.

The fire was the next business. Again Roy went into the bush and gathered a large bundle of dry branches.

"Now, Nelly, do you break a lot of the small twigs," said Roy, "and I'll strike a light."

He pulled his firebag from his belt as he spoke, and drew from it flint, steel, and tinder. No one ever travels in the wilds of which we write without such means of procuring fire. Roy followed the example of his elder companions in carrying a firebag, although he did not, like them, carry tobacco and pipe in it.

Soon the bright sparks that flew from the flint caught on the tinder. This was placed in a handful of dry grass, and whirled rapidly round until it was fanned into a flame. Nelly had prepared another handful of dry grass with small twigs above it. The light was applied, the fire leaped up, more sticks were piled on, and at last the fire roared upward, sending bright showers of sparks into the branches overhead, lighting the white walls of the camp with a glow that caused them to sparkle as with millions of gems, and filling the hearts of the children with a sensation of comfort and gladness while they stood before the blaze and warmed themselves, rubbing their hands and laughing with glee.

No one, save those who have experienced it, can form any conception of the cheering effect of a fire in the heart of a dark wood at night. Roy and Nelly quite forgot their lost condition for a short time in the enjoyment of the comforting heat and the bright gladsome blaze. The brother cut firewood until he was rendered almost breathless, the sister heaped on the wood until the fire roared and leaped high above their heads. Strange though it may appear to some, the snow did not melt. The weather was too cold for that; only a little of that which was nearest the fire melted—the snow walls remained hard frozen all round.

Roy soon sat down to rest, as close to the fire as he could without getting scorched; then Nelly seated herself by his side and nestled her head in his breast. There they sat, telling stories and gazing at the fire, and waiting for "father to come."

ELLEN MAKES A DISCOVERY

By ELIZABETH WETHERELL

When, after her mother's death, Ellen goes to stay on a farm with Miss Fortune, her aunt, she finds the life strange and the people even stranger. She feels alone and shy, until she meets Nancy and goes off on a ramble with the girl who has lived in the country all her life. That is when Ellen discovers the real beauty of the countryside, and life is suddenly filled with good things for her. This story is taken from "The Wide, Wide World."

ON the evening of that day, as Miss Fortune was setting her table for tea, and Ellen sitting before the fire weary of everything, the kitchen door opened, and a girl somewhat larger and older than herself came in. She had a pitcher in her hand, and, marching straight up to the tea-table, she said:

"Will you let granny have a little milk to-night, Miss Fortune? I can't find the cow. I'll bring it back to-morrow."

"You han't lost her, Nancy?"

"Have, though," said the other; "she's been away these two days."

"Why didn't you go somewhere nearer for milk?"

"Oh, I don't know—I guess your'n is the sweetest," said the girl, with a look Ellen did not understand.

Miss Fortune took the pitcher and went into the pantry. While she was gone the two children improved the time in looking very hard at each other. Ellen's gaze was modest enough, though it showed a great deal of interest in the new object; but the broad, searching stare of the other seemed intended to take in all there was of Ellen from her head to her feet, and keep it, and find out what sort of a creature she was at once. Ellen almost shrank from the bold black eyes, but they never wavered, till Miss Fortune's voice broke the spell.

"How's your grandmother, Nancy?"

"She's tolerable, ma'am, thank you."

"Now, if you don't bring it back to-morrow, you won't get any more in a hurry," said Miss Fortune, as she handed the pitcher back to the girl.

The next morning was calm and fine, and Ellen spent nearly the whole of it out of doors. Towards noon she was standing by the little gate at the back of the house, unwilling to go in, but not knowing what more to do, when Mr. Van Brunt came from the lane with a load of wood. Ellen watched the oxen toiling up the ascent, and thought it looked like very hard work; she was sorry for them.

"Isn't that a very heavy load?" she asked of their driver, as he was throwing it down under the apple-tree.

"Heavy? Not a bit of it. It ain't nothing at all to 'em. They'd take twice as much any day with pleasure."

"I shouldn't think so," said Ellen: "they don't look as if there was much pleasure about it. What makes them lean over so against each other when they are coming uphill?"

"Oh, that's just a way they've got. They're so fond of each other, I suppose. Perhaps they've something particular to say, and want to put their heads together for the purpose."

"No," said Ellen, half laughing, "it can't be that: they wouldn't take the very hardest time for that; they would wait till they got to the top of the hill. But there they stand just as if they were asleep, only their eyes are open. Poor things!"

"They're not very poor, anyhow," said Mr. Van Brunt; "there ain't a finer yoke of oxen to be seen than them are, nor in better condition."

He went on throwing the wood out of the cart, and Ellen stood looking at him.

"What'll you give me if I'll make you a scup one of these days?" said Mr. Van Brunt.

"I don't know what it is," said Ellen.

"A scup! Maybe you don't know it by that name; some folks call it a swing."

"A swing! Oh, yes," said Ellen. "Oh, I like it very much."

"Would you like to have one?"

"Yes, indeed I should, very much."

"Well, what'll you give me if I fix you out?"

"I don't know," said Ellen; "I have nothing to give. I'll be very much obliged to you indeed."

"Well now, come, I'll make a bargain with you: I'll engage to fix up a scup for you if you'll give me a kiss."

Poor Ellen was struck dumb. The good-natured Dutchman had taken a fancy to the little pale-faced, sad-looking stranger, and really felt very kindly disposed towards her, but she neither knew, nor at the moment cared about that. She stood motionless, utterly astounded at his unheard-of proposal, and not a little indignant; but when, with a good-natured smile upon his round face, he came near to claim the kiss he no doubt thought himself sure of, Ellen shot from him like an arrow from a bow. She rushed to the house, and, bursting open the door, stood with flushed face and sparkling eyes in the presence of her astonished aunt.

"What in the world is the matter?" exclaimed that lady.

"He wanted to kiss me!" said Ellen, scarce knowing whom she was talking to, and crimsoning more and more.

"Who wanted to kiss you?"

"That man out there."

"What man?"

"The man that drives the oxen."

"What! Mr. Van Brunt?" And Ellen never forgot the loud "Ha! ha!" which burst from Miss Fortune's wide-open mouth. "Well, why didn't you let him kiss you?"

The laugh, the look, the tone, stung Ellen to the very quick. She dashed away out of the kitchen, and up to her own room. And there, for a while, anger drove over her with such violence that conscience had hardly time to whisper. Sorrow came in again as passion faded, and gentler but very bitter weeping took the place of convulsive sobs of rage and mortification, and then the whispers of conscience began to be heard a little.

"O mamma! mamma!" cried poor Ellen in her heart, "how miserable I am without you! I never can like Aunt Fortune—it's of no use—I never can like her. I hope I shan't get to hate her; and that isn't right. I am forgetting all that is good, and there's nobody to put me in mind. O mamma, if I could lay my head in your lap for a minute!"

It was long after midday when Ellen rose. Her passion was all gone—she felt more gentle and pleasant than she had done for days; but at the bottom of her heart resentment was not all gone. She still thought she had cause to be angry, and she could not think of her aunt's look and tone without a thrill of painful feeling. In a very different mood, however, from that in which she had flown upstairs two or three hours before, she now came softly down, and went out by the front door, to avoid meeting her aunt. She had visited that morning a little brook which ran through the meadow on the other side of the road. It had great charms for her; and now, crossing the lane and creeping under the fence, she made her way again to its banks. At a particular spot, where the brook made one of its sudden turns, Ellen sat down upon the grass, and watched the dark water, whirling, brawling over the stones, hurrying past her, with ever the same soft pleasant sound, and she was never tired of it. She did not hear footsteps drawing near, and it was not till someone was close beside her, and a voice spoke almost in her ears, that she raised her startled eyes and saw the little girl who had come the evening before for a pitcher of milk.

"What are you doing?" asked the latter.

"I'm watching for fish," said Ellen.

"Watching for fish!" said the other, rather disdainfully.

"Yes," said Ellen; "there, in that little quiet place, they come sometimes. I've seen two."

"You can look for fish another time. Come now and take a walk with me."

"Where?" said Ellen.

"Oh, you shall see. Come; I'll take you all about and show you. You han't been anywhere yet, have you?"

"No," said Ellen, "and I should like dearly to go, but——"

"Well, what are you thinking about?" said the girl. "What's the matter? Won't you come?"

"Yes," said Ellen; "I'm ready. Which way shall we go?"

With the assurance from the other that she would show her plenty of ways, they set off down the lane. The afternoon was fair and mild, the footing pleasant, and Ellen felt like a bird out of a cage. She was ready to be delighted with every trifle; her companion could not by any means understand or enter into her bursts of pleasure at many a little thing which she of the black eyes thought not worthy of notice. She tried to bring Ellen back to higher subjects of conversation.

"How long have you been here?" she asked.

"Oh, a good while," said Ellen. "I don't know exactly; it's a week, I believe."

"Why, do you call that a good while?" said the other.

"Well, it seems a good while to me," said Ellen, sighing; "it seems as long as four, I am sure."

"Then you don't like to live here much, do you?"

"I had rather be at home, of course."

"How do you like your Aunt Fortune?"

"How do I like her?" said Ellen, hesitating. "I think she's good-looking and very smart."

"Yes, you needn't tell me she's smart—everybody knows that; that ain't what I ask you. How do you *like* her?"

"How do I like her?" said Ellen again. "How can I tell how I shall like her? I haven't lived with her but a week yet."

"You might just as well ha' spoke out," said the other, somewhat scornfully. "Do you think I don't know you half hate her already? And it'll be whole hating in another week more. When I first heard you'd come, I guessed you'd have a sweet time with her."

"Why?" said Ellen.

"Oh, don't ask me why," said the other impatiently, "when you know as well as I do. Every soul that speaks of you says 'Poor child!' and 'I'm glad I ain't her.' You needn't try to come cunning over me. I shall be too much for you, I tell you."

"I don't know what you mean," said Ellen.

"Oh, no, I suppose you don't," said the other in the same tone—"of course you don't. I suppose you don't know whether your tongue is your own or somebody's else. You think Miss Fortune is an angel, and so do I; to be sure she is!"

Not very well pleased with this kind of talk, Ellen walked on for a while in grave silence. Her companion meantime recollected herself; when she spoke again it was with an altered tone.

"How do you like Mr. Van Brunt?"

"I don't like him at all," said Ellen, reddening.

"Don't you!" said the other, surprised. "Why, everybody likes him. What don't you like him for?"

"I don't like him," repeated Ellen.

"Ain't Miss Fortune queer to live in the way she does?"

"What way?" asked Ellen.

"Why, without any help—doing all her own work, and living all alone, when she's so rich as she is."

"Is she rich?" asked Ellen.

"Rich! I guess she is. She's one of the very best farms in the country, and money enough to have a dozen helps, if she wanted 'em. Van Brunt takes care of the farm, you know."

"Does he?"

"Why, yes, of course he does: didn't you know that? What did you think he was at your house all the time for?"

"I am sure I don't know," said Ellen. "And are those Aunt Fortune's oxen that he drives?"

"To be sure they are. Well, I do think you *are* green, to have been there all this time and not found that out. Mr. Van Brunt does just what he pleases over the whole farm, though—hires what help he wants, manages everything; and then he has his share of all that comes off it. I tell you what: you'd better make friends with Van Brunt, for if anybody can help you when your aunt gets one of her ugly fits, it's him; she don't care to meddle with him much."

Leaving the lane, the two girls took a footpath leading across the fields. The stranger was greatly amused here with Ellen's awkwardness in climbing fences. As they went along, she pointed out to Ellen two or three houses in the distance, and gave her not a little gossip about the people who lived in them; but all this Ellen scarcely heard, and cared nothing at all about. She had paused by the side of a large rock standing alone by the wayside, and was looking very closely at its surface.

"What is this curious brown stuff," said Ellen, "growing all over the rock, like shrivelled and dried-up leaves? Isn't it curious? Part of it stands out like a leaf, and part of it sticks fast. I wonder if it grows here, or what it is?"

"Oh, never mind," said the other; "it always grows on the rocks everywhere. I don't know what it is, and what's more I don't care. 'Tain't worth looking at. Come!"

Ellen followed her. But presently the path entered an open woodland, and now her delight broke forth beyond bounds.

"Oh, how pleasant this is! How lovely this is. Isn't it beautiful?" she exclaimed.

"Isn't *what* beautiful? I do think you are the queerest girl, Ellen."

"Why, everything," said Ellen, not minding the latter part of the sentence: "the ground is beautiful, and those tall trees, and that beautiful blue sky—only look at it."

"The ground is all covered with stones and rocks—is that what you call beautiful? And the trees are as homely as they can be, with their great brown stems and no leaves. Come! What *are* you staring at?"

Ellen's eyes were fixed on a string of dark spots which were rapidly passing overhead.

"Hark!" said she; "Do you hear that noise? What is that?"

"It's only a flock of ducks," said the other contemptuously. "Come! Do come!"

But Ellen was rooted to the ground, and her eyes followed the airy travellers till the last one had quitted the piece of blue sky which the surrounding woods left to be seen. And scarcely were these gone when a second flight came in view, following exactly in the track of the first.

"Where are they going?" said Ellen.

"I am sure I don't know where they are going; they never told me. I know where *I* am going; I should like to know whether you are going along with me."

Ellen, however, was in no hurry. The ducks had disappeared, but her eye had caught something else that charmed it.

"What is this?" said Ellen.

"Nothing but moss."

"Is that moss? How beautiful! How green and soft it is! I declare it's as soft as a carpet."

"As soft as a carpet," reflected the other; "I should like to see a carpet as soft as that! *You* never did, I guess."

"Indeed I have, though," said Ellen, who was gently jumping up and down on the green moss to try its softness, with a face of great satisfaction. "Come; I'll go with you now. I do think this is the loveliest place I ever did see. Are there any flowers here in the spring?"

"I don't know—yes, lots of 'em."

"Pretty ones?" said Ellen.

"*You'd* think so, I suppose; I never look at 'em."

"Oh, how lovely that will be!" said Ellen, clasping her hands; "how pleasant it must be to live in the country!"

"Pleasant indeed!" said the other; "I think it's hateful. You'd think so, too, if you lived where I do. It makes me mad at granny every day because she won't go to Thirlwall."

Shocked a little at her companion's language, Ellen again walked on in sober silence. Gradually the ground became more broken, sinking rapidly from the side of the path, and rising again in a steep bank on the other side of a narrow dell; both sides were thickly wooded, but stripped of green now, except where here and there a hemlock flung its graceful branches abroad, and stood in lonely beauty among its leafless companions. Now the gurgling of waters was heard.

"Where is that?" said Ellen, stopping short.

"Way down at the bottom there. It's the brook."

"What brook? Not the same that goes by Aunt Fortune's?"

"Yes, it's the very same. It's the crookedest thing you ever saw. It runs over there," said the speaker, pointing with her arm, "and then it takes a turn and goes that way, and then it comes round so, and then it shoots off in that way again and passes by your house; and after that the dear knows where it goes, for I don't. But I don't suppose it could run straight if it was to try."

"Can't we get down to it?" asked Ellen.

"To be sure we can, unless you're afraid of steep banks."

Very steep indeed it was, and strewn with loose stones; but Ellen did not falter, and though once or twice in imminent danger of exchanging her cautious stepping for one long roll to the bottom, she got there safely on her two feet. When there, everything was forgotten in delight. It was a wild little place. The high close sides of the dell left only a little strip of sky overhead; and at their feet ran the brook, much more noisy and lively here than where Ellen had before made its acquaintance—leaping from rock to rock, eddying round large stones, and boiling over the small ones, and now and then pouring quietly over some great trunk of a tree that had fallen across its bed and dammed up the whole stream. Ellen could scarcely contain herself at the magnificence of many of the waterfalls, the beauty of the little quiet pools where the water lay still behind some large stone, and the variety of graceful tiny cascades.

"Look here, Nancy!" cried Ellen: "that's the Falls of Niagara—do you see?—that large one. Oh, that is splendid! And this will do for Trenton Falls. What a fine foam it makes! Isn't it a beauty? And what shall we call this? I don't know what to call it; I wish we could name them all. But there's no end to them. Oh, just look at that one! That's too pretty not to have a name; what shall it be?"

"Black Falls," suggested the other.

"Black!" said Ellen dubiously; "why, I don't like that."

"Why, the water's all dark and black, don't you see?"

"Well," said Ellen, "let it be Black, then; but I don't like it. Now, remember: this is Niagara, that is Black, and this is Trenton; and what is this?"

"If you are a-going to name them all," said Nancy, "we shan't get home to-night; you might as well name all the trees; there's a hundred of 'em and more. I say, Ellen! suppos'n we follow the brook instead of climbing up yonder again; it will take us out to the open fields by and by."

"Oh, do let's!" said Ellen; "that will be lovely."

It proved a rough way; but Ellen still thought and called it "lovely." Often by the side of the stream there was no footing at all, and the girls picked their way over the stones, large and small, wet and dry, which strewed its bed; against which the water foamed, and fumed, and fretted, as if in great impatience. It was ticklish work getting along over these stones, now tottering on an unsteady one, now slipping on a wet one, and every now and then making huge leaps from rock to rock, which there was no other method of reaching, at the imminent hazard of falling in. But they laughed at the danger; sprang on in great glee, delighted with the exercise and the fun; didn't stay long enough anywhere to lose their balance, and enjoyed themselves amazingly. There was many a hair-breadth escape, many an *almost* sousing; but that made it all the more lively. In due time, though with no little difficulty, they reached the spot where the brook came forth from the wood into the open day, and thence making a sharp turn to the right, skirted along by the edge of the trees, as if unwilling to part company with them.

"I guess we'd better get back now," said Miss Nancy; "we're a pretty good way from home."

HART ROYAL

By HARRISON AINSWORTH

In Windsor Forest, King Henry the Eighth, a great lover of all kinds of sports and pastimes, holds a royal hunt in the company of Anne Boleyn, soon to be England's new Queen. To mark the occasion the forest verderers and keepers have caught a hart royal, and it is waiting to be loosed for the hunt. It is this animal which brings the day's sport to a sudden close in a strange manner, as related in "Windsor Castle," from which this story is taken.

IN consequence of the announcement that a grand hunting-party would be held in the forest, all the verderers, rangers, and keepers, assembled at an early hour on the fourth day after the King's arrival at Windsor, in an open space on the west side of the great avenue, where a wooden stand was erected, canopied over with green boughs and festooned with garlands of flowers, for the accommodation of the Lady Anne Boleyn and her dames, who, it was understood, would be present at the chase.

At a little distance from the stand, an extensive cover was fenced round with stout poles to which nets were attached, so as to form a haye, or preserve, where the game intended for the royal sport was confined; and though many of the animals thus brought together were of hostile natures, they were all so terrified, and seemingly so conscious of the danger impending over them, that they did not molest each other. The foxes and martins, of which there were abundance, slunk into the brush-wood with the hares and rabbits, but left their prey untouched. The harts made violent efforts to break forth, and, entangling their horns in the nets, were with difficulty extricated and driven back; while the timid does, not daring to follow them, stood warily watching the result of the struggle.

Amongst the antlered captives was a fine buck, which, having been once before hunted by the King, was styled a "hart royal," and this noble animal would certainly have effected his escape, if he had not been attacked and driven back by Morgan Fenwolf, who throughout the morning's proceedings displayed great energy and skill.

The party then sat down to breakfast beneath the trees, and the talk fell upon Herne the hunter, and his frequent appearance of late in the forest (for most of the keepers had heard of, or encountered, the spectral huntsman); and while they were discussing this topic, and a plentiful allowance of cold meat, bread, ale, and mead, at the same time, two persons were seen approaching along a vista on the right, who specially attracted their attention.

The newcomers were an old man, and a comely young damsel. The former, though nearer seventy than sixty, was still hale and athletic; with fresh complexion, somewhat tanned by the sun, and a keen grey eye, which had lost nothing of its fire. He was habited in a stout leathern doublet, hose of the same material, and boots rudely fashioned out of untanned ox-hide, and drawn above the knee. In his girdle was thrust a large hunting-knife; a horn with a silver mouth-piece, depended from his shoulder; and he wore a long bow, and a quiver full of arrows at his back. A flat bonnet, made of fox-skin, and ornamented with a raven's wing covered his hair, which was as white as silver.

But it was not upon this old forester, for such his attire proclaimed him, that the attention of the beholders was fixed—but upon his companion. Amongst the many lovely and high-born dames, who had so recently graced the procession of the castle, were few, if any, comparable to this lowly damsel. Her dress—probably owing to the pride felt in her by her old relative—was somewhat superior to her station. A tightly-laced green kirtle displayed to perfection her slight but exquisitely formed figure. A gown of orange-coloured cloth, sufficiently short to display her small ankles, and a pair of green buskins, embroidered with silver, together with a collar of the whitest and finest linen, though shamed by the neck it concealed, and fastened by a small clasp, completed her attire. Her girdle was embroidered with silver, and her sleeves were fastened by aiglets of the same metal.

"How proud old Tristram Lyndwood seems of his granddaughter!" remarked one of the keepers.

"And with reason," replied another. "Mabel Lyndwood is the comeliest lass in Berkshire."

"Ay, marry is she," rejoined the first speaker; "and to my thinking, she is a fairer and sweeter flower than any that blooms in yon stately castle—the flower that finds so much favour in the eyes of our royal Hal not excepted."

"Have a care, Gabriel Lapp," observed another keeper. "Recollect that Mark Fytton, the butcher, was hanged for speaking slightingly of the Lady Anne Boleyn; and you may share his fate, if you disparage her beauty."

"Nay, I mean not to disparage the Lady Anne," replied Gabriel. "Hal may marry her when he will for aught I care. If he marries fifty wives, I shall like him all the better. The more the merrier, say I."

"Tush, Gabriel!" said Morgan Fenwolf, darting an angry look at him.

"You are jealous, Morgan Fenwolf," rejoined Gabriel, with a malignant grin. "We all know you are in love with Mabel yourself."

"And we all know, likewise, that Mabel will have nothing to say to you!" cried another keeper, while the others laughed in chorus. "Come and sit down beside us, Morgan, and finish your breakfast."

But the keeper turned moodily away, and hied towards Tristram Lyndwood and his grand-daughter. The old forester shook him cordially by the hand, and after questioning him as to what had taken place, and hearing how he had managed to drive the hart royal into the haye, clapped him on the shoulder, and said: "Thou art a brave huntsman, Morgan. I wish Mab could only think as well of thee as I do."

To this speech, Mabel not only paid no attention, but looked studiously another way.

"I am glad your grandfather has brought you out to see the chase to-day, Mabel," observed Morgan Fenwolf.

"I came not to see the chase, but the King," she replied, somewhat petulantly.

"It is not every fair maid who would confess so much," observed Fenwolf, frowning.

"Then I am franker than some of my sex," replied Mabel. "But who is the strange man looking at us from behind that tree, grandfather?"

"I see no one," replied the old forester.

"Neither do I," added Morgan Fenwolf, with a shudder.

"You are wilfully blind," rejoined Mabel. "But see, the person

I mentioned stalks forth. Now, perhaps, he is visible to you both."

And as she spoke, a tall, wild-looking figure armed with a hunting spear, emerged from the trees, and advanced towards them. The garb of the newcomer somewhat resembled that of a forester; but his arms and lower limbs were destitute of covering, and appeared singularly muscular, while his skin was swarthy as that of a gipsy. His jet black hair hung in elflocks over his savage-looking features.

In another moment, he was beside them, and fixed his dark, piercing eyes on Mabel, in such a manner as to compel her to avert her gaze.

"What brings you here this morning, Tristram Lyndwood?" he demanded, in a hoarse, imperious tone.

"The same motive that brought you, Valentine Hagthorne," replied the old forester, "to see the royal chase."

"This, I suppose, is your grand-daughter?" pursued Hagthorne.

"Ay," replied Tristram, bluntly.

"Strange I should never have seen her before," rejoined the other. "She is very fair. Be ruled by me, friend Tristram—take her home again. If she sees the King, ill will come of it."

"Hagthorne advises well," interposed Fenwolf. "Mabel will be better at home."

"But she has no intention of returning at present," replied Mabel. "You brought me here for pastime, dear grandfather, and will not take me back at the recommendation of this strange man?"

"Content you, child—content you," replied Tristram kindly. "You shall remain where you are."

"You will repent it!" cried Hagthorne.

And hastily darting among the trees, he disappeared from view.

Affecting to laugh at the occurrence, though evidently annoyed by it, the old forester led his grand-daughter towards the stand, where he was cordially greeted by the keepers, most of whom, while expressing their pleasure at seeing him, strove to render themselves agreeable in the eyes of Mabel.

An hour or two after this, when the sun was higher in the heavens, and the dew dried upon the greensward, the King, and a large company of lords and ladies, rode forth from the upper gate of the castle, and taking their way along the great avenue, struck off on the right, when about half-way up it, and shaped their course towards the haye.

A goodly sight it was to see this gallant company riding beneath the trees; and pleasant was it, also, to listen to the blithe sound of their voices, amid which Anne Boleyn's musical laugh could be

plainly distinguished. Henry was attended by his customary band of archers and yeomen of the guard; and by the Duke of Shoreditch and his followers. On reaching the haye, the King dismounted, and, assisting the Lady Anne from her steed, ascended the stand with her.

He then took a small and beautifully fashioned bow from an attendant, and, stringing it, presented it to her.

"I trust this will not prove too strong for your fair hands," he said.

"I will make shift to draw it," replied Anne, raising the bow, and gracefully pulling the string. "Would I could wound Your Majesty as surely as I shall hit the first roe that passes."

"That were a needless labour," rejoined Henry, "seeing that you have already stricken me to the heart. You should cure the wound you have already made, sweetheart—not inflict a new one."

At this juncture, the chief verderer, mounted on a powerful steed, and followed by two keepers, each holding a couple of staghounds in leash, rode up to the royal stand, and, placing his horn to his lips, blew three long mootes from it. At the same moment, part of the network of the haye was lifted up, and a roebuck set free.

By the management of the keepers, the animal was driven past the royal stand; and Anne Boleyn, who had drawn an arrow nearly to the head, let it fly with such good aim that she pierced the buck to the heart. A loud shout from the spectators rewarded the prowess of the fair huntress; and Henry was so enchanted that he bent the knee to her, and pressed her hand to his lips. Satisfied, however, with the achievement, Anne prudently declined another shot. Henry then took a bow from one of the archers, and, other roes being turned out, he approved upon them his unerring skill as a marksman.

Meanwhile the hounds, being held in leash, kept up a loud and incessant baying; and Henry, wearying of his slaughterous sport, turned to Anne, and asked her whether she was disposed for the chase. She answered in the affirmative, and the King motioned his henchmen to bring forward the steeds.

In doing this, he caught sight of Mabel, who was standing with her grandsire among the keepers, at a little distance from the stand, and, struck with her extraordinary beauty, he regarded her for a moment intently, and then called to Gabriel Lapp, who chanced to be near him, and demanded her name.

"It is Mabel Lyndwood, an' please Your Majesty," replied Gabriel. "She is grand-daughter to old Tristram Lyndwood, who dwells at Black Nest, near the lake, at the further extremity of Windsor Forest, and who was forester to your royal father, King Henry the Seventh, of blessed memory."

"Ha! is it so?" cried Henry.

But he was prevented from further remark by Anne Boleyn, who, perceiving how his attention was attracted, suddenly interposed.

"Your Majesty spoke of the chase," she said, impatiently. "But perhaps you have found other pastime more diverting?"

"Not so—not so, sweetheart," he replied hastily.

"There is a hart royal in the haye," said Gabriel Lapp. "Is it Your Majesty's pleasure that I set him free?"

"It is, good fellow—it is," replied the King.

And as Gabriel hastened to the netted fencework, and prepared to drive forth the hart, Henry assisted Anne Boleyn, who could not help exhibiting some slight jealous pique, to mount her steed, and, having sprung into his own saddle, they waited the liberation of the buck, which was accomplished in a somewhat unexpected manner.

Separated from the rest of the herd, the noble animal made a sudden dart towards Gabriel, and, upsetting him in his wild career, darted past the King, and made towards the upper part of the forest. In another instant the hounds were uncoupled, and at his heels, while Henry and Anne urged their steeds after him, the King shouting at the top of his lusty voice. The rest of the royal party followed as they might, and the woods resounded with their cries.

The hart royal proved himself worthy of his designation. Dashing forward with extraordinary swiftness, he rapidly gained upon his pursuers—for though Henry, by putting his courser to his utmost speed, could have kept near him, he did not choose to quit his fair companion.

In this way, they scoured the forest, until the King, seeing they should be speedily distanced, commanded Sir Thomas Wyat, who, with the Dukes of Suffolk and Norfolk, was riding close behind him, to cross by the lower ground on the left, and turn the stag. Wyat instantly obeyed, and, plunging his spurs deeply into his horse's sides, started off at a furious pace, and was soon after seen shaping his rapid course through a devious glade.

Meanwhile Henry and his fair companion rode on without relaxing their pace, until they reached the summit of a knoll, crowned by an old oak and beech-tree, and commanding a superb view of the castle, where they drew in the rein.

From this eminence they could witness the progress of the chase as it continued in the valley beyond. An ardent lover of hunting, the King watched it with the deepest interest, rose in his saddle, and, uttering various exclamations, shewed, from his impatience, that he was only restrained by the stronger passion of love from joining it.

Ere long stag, hounds, and huntsmen were lost amid a thicket, and nothing could be distinguished but a distant baying and shouts. At last even these sounds died away.

Henry, who had ill brooked the previous restraint, now grew so impatient that Anne begged him to set off after them, when suddenly the cry of hounds burst upon their ear, and the hart was seen issuing from the dell, closely followed by his pursuers.

The affrighted animal, to the King's great satisfaction, made his way directly towards the spot where he was stationed; but on reaching the side of the knoll, and seeing his new foes, he darted off on the right, and tried to regain the thicket below. But he was turned by another band of keepers, and again driven towards the knoll.

Scarcely had Sir Thomas Wyat reined in his steed by the side of the King than the hart again appeared bounding up the hill. Anne Boleyn, who had turned her horse's head to obtain a better view of the hunt, alarmed by the animal's menacing appearance, tried to get out of his way. But it was too late. Hemmed in on all sides, and driven to desperation by the cries of hounds and huntsmen in front, the hart lowered his horns, and made a furious push at her.

Dreadfully alarmed, Anne drew in the rein so suddenly and sharply that she almost pulled her steed back upon his haunches; and, in trying to avoid the stag's attack, caught hold of Sir Thomas Wyat, who was close beside her.

In all probability she would have received some serious injury from the infuriated animal, who was just about to repeat his assault, and more successfully, when a bolt from a crossbow, discharged by Morgan Fenwolf, who suddenly made his appearance from behind the beech-tree, brought him to the ground.

But Anne Boleyn escaped one danger only to encounter another equally serious. On seeing her fling herself into the arms of Sir Thomas Wyat, Henry regarded her in stern displeasure for a moment, and then, calling angrily to his train, without so much as deigning to inquire whether she had sustained any damage from the accident, or making the slightest remark upon her conduct, rode sullenly towards the castle.

HER LAST HALF-CROWN

By JOHN BROWN

This is a story set in one of the poorer districts of Edinburgh, where the unfortunates of days gone by lived in squalor and eked out a miserable existence. But even in such unlikely surroundings the lessons learned in a happier childhood survived, as Hugh Miller discovered one wet, cold day when he attended the funeral of poor Mary Duff. This story is taken from "Rab and His Friends and Other Papers."

HUGH Miller, the geologist, journalist, and man of genius, was sitting in his newspaper office late one dreary winter night. The clerks had all left, and he was preparing to go, when a quick rap came to the door. He said "Come in," and, looking towards the entrance, saw a little ragged child all wet with sleet.

"Are ye Hugh Miller?"

"Yes."

"Mary Duff wants ye."

"What does she want?"

"She's deein."

Some misty recollection of the name made him at once set out, and, with his well-known plaid and stick, he was soon striding after the child, who trotted through the now deserted High Street, into the Canongate. By the time he got to the Old Playhouse Close, Hugh had revived his memory of Mary Duff; a lively girl who had been bred up beside him in Cromarty. The last time he had seen her was at a brother mason's marriage, where Mary was "best maid," and he "best man." He seemed still to see her bright young careless face, her tidy shortgown, and her dark eyes, and to hear her bantering, merry tongue.

Down the close went the ragged little woman, and up an outside stair, Hugh keeping near her with difficulty; in the passage she held out her hand and touched him; taking it in his great palm, he felt that she wanted a thumb. Finding her way like a cat through the darkness, she opened a door, and saying "That's her!" vanished.

By the light of a dying fire he saw lying in the corner of the large empty room something like a woman's clothes, and on drawing nearer became aware of a thin pale face and two dark eyes

looking keenly but helplessly up at him. The ey
Mary Duff's, though he could recognize no other fe
silently, gazing steadily at him.

"Are you Mary Duff?"

"It's a' that's o' me, Hugh."

She then tried to speak to him, something p
urgency, but she couldn't, and seeing that she was
making herself worse, he put half a crown into he
and said he would call again in the morning. He
formation about her from the neighbours: they
asleep.

When he returned next morning the little girl
stair-head, and said, "She's deid." He went in, a
was true; there she lay, the fire out, her face plac
ness to her maiden self restored. Hugh thought
known her now, even with those bright black eye
were, *in æternum.*

Seeking out a neighbour, he said he would lik
Duff, and arranged for the funeral with an undert
Little seemed to be known of the poor outcast.

On the day of the funeral one or two reside
accompanied him to the Canongate Churchyard.
decent-looking little old woman watching them, an
distance, though the day was wet and bitter. Aft
filled, and he had taken off his hat, as the men fir
ness by putting on and slapping the sod, he saw
remaining.

She came up and, courtesying, said, "Ye wad ke

"Yes; I knew her when she was young."

The woman then burst into tears, and told
"keepit a bit shop at the Closemooth, and Mary
aye paid reglar, and I was feared she was dead, fo
month awin' me half a crown": and then with a l
awe, she told him how on the night he was sent
ately after he had left, she had been awakened by
room; and by her bright fire—for she was a *bein*
—she had seen the wasted dying creature, who c
said, "Wasn't it half a crown?"

"Yes."

"There it is," and putting it under the bolster, vanished!

Alas for Mary Duff! her career had been a sad one since the day when she had stood side by side with Hugh at the wedding of their friends. Her father died not long after, and her mother supplanted her in the affections of the man to whom she had given

her heart. The shock was overwhelming, and made home intolerable. Mary fled from it blighted and embittered, and after a life of sorrow crept into the corner of her wretched garret, to die deserted and alone; giving evidence in her latest act that honesty had survived.

"My thoughts are not your thoughts, neither are your ways my ways, saith the Lord. For as the heavens are higher than the earth, so are my ways higher than your ways, and my thoughts than your thoughts."

THE STORY OF GRACE DARLING

By ANDREW LANG

Many a lifeboat launched into stormy seas around Britain's coasts has had the proud name "Grace Darling" painted on its tossing bows. The brave-hearted girl whose courage inspired the formation of the British lifeboat service, with its wonderful record of lives saved from wave-battered wrecks, little thought that her action one grey September morning more than a hundred years ago would live in story and that her name would be remembered as long as men put out from shore to rescue their fellows in peril at sea. This story is taken from "The True Story Book."

A CAREFUL reader of *The Times* on the morning of Tuesday, September 11, 1838, might have found, if he cared to look, a certain paragraph in an obscure corner headed "The Wreck of the *Forfarshire*." It is printed in the small type of that period; the story is four days old, for in those days news was not flashed from one end of the country to the other; and, moreover, the story is very incomplete.

On the evening of Wednesday, September 5, the steamship *Forfarshire* left Hull for Dundee, carrying a cargo of iron, and having some forty passengers on board. The ship was only eight years old; the master, John Humble, was an experienced seaman; and the crew, including firemen and engineers, was complete. But even before the vessel left the dock one passenger at least had felt uneasily that something was wrong—that there was an unusual commotion among officials and sailors. Still, no alarm was given, and at dusk the vessel steamed prosperously down the Humber.

The next day (Thursday, the 6th) the weather changed, the wind blowing N.N.W., and increasing towards midnight to a perfect gale. On the morning of Friday, the 7th, a sloop from Montrose, making for South Shields, saw a small boat labouring hard in the trough of the sea. The Montrose vessel bore down on it, and in spite of the state of the weather managed to get the boat's crew on board.

They were the sole survivors, as they believed themselves to be, of the crew and passengers of the *Forfarshire*, which was then lying a total wreck on Longstone, one of the outermost of the Farne Islands.

It was a wretched story they had to tell of lives thrown away through carelessness and negligence, unredeemed, as far as their story went, by any heroism or unselfish courage.

While still in the Humber, and not twenty miles from Hull, it was found that one of the boilers leaked, but the captain refused to put about. The pumps were set to work to fill the boiler, and the vessel kept on her way, though slowly, not passing between the Farne Islands and the mainland till Thursday evening. It was eight o'clock when they entered Berwick Bay; the wind freshened and was soon blowing hard from the N.N.W. The motion of the vessel increased the leakage, and it was now found that there were holes in all the three boilers. Two men were set to work the pumps, one or two of the passengers also assisting, but as fast as the water was pumped into the boilers it poured out again. The bilge was so full of steam and boiling water that the firemen could not get to the fires. Still the steamer struggled on, labouring heavily, for the sea was running very high. At midnight they were off St. Abb's Head, when the engineers reported that the case was hopeless; the engines had entirely ceased to work. The ship rolled helplessly in the waves, and the rocky coast was at no great distance. They ran up the sails fore and aft to try and keep her off the rocks, and put her round so that she might run before the wind, and as the tide was setting southward she drifted fast with wind and tide. Torrents of rain were falling, and in spite of the wind there was a thick fog. Some of the passengers were below, others were on deck with crew and captain, knowing well their danger.

About three the noise of breakers was distinctly heard a little way ahead, and at the same time a light was seen away to the left, glimmering faintly through the darkness. It came home to the anxious crew with sickening certainty that they were being driven on the Farne Islands. These islands form a group of desolate whinstone rocks lying off the Northumbrian coast. They are twenty in number, some only uncovered at low tide, and all offering a rugged iron wall to any ill-fated boat that may be driven upon them. Even in calm weather and by daylight seamen are glad to give them a wide berth.

The master of the *Forfarshire* in this desperate strait attempted to make for the channel which runs between the islands and the mainland. It was at best a forlorn chance; it was hopeless here; the vessel refused to answer her helm! On she drove in the darkness, nearer and nearer came the sound of the breakers; the fear and agitation on board the boat grew frantic. Women wailed and shrieked; the captain's wife clung to him, weeping; the crew lost all instinct of discipline, and thought of nothing but saving their skins.

Between three and four the shock came—a hideous grinding noise, a strain and shiver of the whole ship, and she struck violently against a great rock. In the awful moment which followed five of the crew succeeded in lowering the larboard quarter-boat and pushed off in her. The mate swung himself over the side, and also reached her; and a passenger rushing at this moment up from the cabin and seeing the boat already three yards from the ship, cleared the space with a bound and landed safely in her, though nearly upsetting her by his weight. She righted, and the crew pulled off with the desperate energy of men rowing for their lives. The sight of agonised faces, the shrieks of the drowning, were lost in the darkness and in the howling winds, and the boat with the seven men on board was swept by the rapidly flowing tide.

Such was the story the exhausted boat's crew told next morning to their rescuers on board the Montrose sloop. And the rest of the ship's company—what of them? Had they all gone down by the island crag with never a hand stretched out to help them?

Hardly had the boat escaped from the stranded vessel when a great wave struck her on the quarter, lifted her up bodily, and dashed her back on the rock. She struck midships on the sharp edge and broke at once into two pieces. The after part was washed clean away with about twenty passengers clinging to it, the captain and his wife being among them. A group of people, about nine in number, were huddled together near the bow; they, with the whole fore part of the ship, were lifted right on to the rock. In the fore cabin was a poor woman, Mrs. Dawson, with a child on each arm. When the vessel was stranded on the rock the waves rushed into the exposed cabin, but she managed to keep her position, cowering in a corner. First one and then the other child died from cold and exhaustion, and falling from the fainting mother were swept from her sight by the waves, but the poor soul herself survived all the horrors of the night.

It was now four o'clock; the storm was raging with unabated violence, and it was still two hours to daybreak. About a mile from Longstone, the island on which the vessel struck, lies Brownsman, the outermost of the Farne Islands, on which stands the lighthouse. At this time the keeper of the lighthouse was a man of the name of William Darling. He was elderly, almost an old man, and the only other inmates of the lighthouse were his wife and daughter Grace, a girl of twenty-two. On this Friday night she was awake, and throught the raging of the storm heard shrieks more persistent and despairing than those of the wildest sea-birds. In great trouble she rose and awakened her father. The cries continued, but in the darkness they could do nothing. Even after day broke it was difficult to make out distant objects, for a mist was still hanging over the sea. At length, with a glass they could discern the wreck on Longstone, and figures moving about on it. Between the two islands lay a mile of yeasty sea, and the tide was running hard between them. The only boat on the lighthouse was a clumsily built jolly-boat, heavy enough to tax the strength of two strong men in ordinary weather, and here there was but an old man and a young girl to face a raging sea and tide running dead against them. Darling hesitated to undertake anything so dangerous, but his daughter would hear of no delay. On the other side of that rough mile of sea men were perishing, and she could not stay where she was and see them die.

So off they set in the heavy coble, the old man with one oar, the girl with the other, rowing with straining breath and beating hearts. Any moment they might be whelmed in the sea or dashed against the rocks. Even if they got the crew off it would be doubtful if they could row them to the lighthouse; the tide was about to turn, and would be against them on their homeward journey; death seemed to face them on every side.

When close to the rock there was imminent danger of their being dashed to pieces against it. Steadying the boat an instant, Darling managed to jump on to the rock, while Grace rapidly rowed out a little and kept the boat from going on the rocks by rowing continually. It is difficult to imagine how the nine shipwrecked people, exhausted and wearied as they were, were got into the boat in such a sea, especially as the poor woman, Mrs. Dawson, was in an almost fainting condition; but finally got on board they all were. Fortunately, one or two of the rescued crew were able to assist in the heavy task of rowing the boat back to Brownsman.

The storm continued to rage for several days after, and the whole party had to remain in the lighthouse. Moreover, a boat-load which had come to their rescue from North Shields was also storm-stayed, twenty guests in all, so that the housewifely powers of Grace and her mother were taxed to the utmost.

It is told of this admirable girl that she was the tenderest and gentlest of nurses and hostesses, as she was certainly one of the most singularly courageous of women.

She could never be brought to look upon her exploit as in any way remarkable, and when by and by honours and distinctions were showered upon her, and people came from long distances to see her, she kept through it all the dignity of perfect simplicity and modesty.

Close to Bamborough, on a windy hill, lie a little grey church and a quiet churchyard. At all seasons high winds from the North Sea blow over the graves and fret and eat away the soft grey sandstone of which the plain headstones are made. So great is the wear and tear of these winds that comparatively recent monuments look like those which have stood for centuries. On one of these stones lies a recumbent figure, with what looks not unlike a lance clasped in the hand and laid across the breast. Involuntarily one thinks of the stone Crusaders, who lie in their armour, clasping their half-drawn swords, awaiting the Resurrection morning. It is the monument of Grace Darling, who here lies at rest with her oar still clasped in her strong right hand.

A LETTER FULL OF NEWS

By SIR WALTER SCOTT

Julia Mannering, in this letter to her friend Matilda Marchmont, describes an attack by smugglers upon her father's home, Woodbourne House. Lucy Bertram and Dominie Sampson, staying with the Mannerings, and Charles Hazlewood, a friend, are also present during the attack. This letter is taken from "Guy Mannering."

I RISE from a sick bed, my dearest Matilda, to communicate the strange and frightful scenes which have just passed. Alas, how little we ought to jest with futurity! I closed my letter to you in high spirits, with some flippant remarks on your taste for the romantic and extraordinary in fictitious narrative. How little I expected to have had such events to record in the course of a few days! And to witness scenes of terror, or to contemplate them in description, is as different, my dearest Matilda, as to bend over the brink of a precipice holding by the frail tenure of a half-rooted shrub, or to admire the same precipice as represented in the landscape of Salvator. But I will not anticipate my narrative.

The first part of my story is frightful enough, though it had nothing to interest my feelings. You must know that this country is particularly favourable to the commerce of a set of desperate men from the Isle of Man, which is nearly opposite. These smugglers are numerous, resolute, and formidable, and have at different times become the dread of the neighbourhood when any one has interfered with their contraband trade. The local magistrates, from timidity or worse motives, have become shy of acting against them, and impunity has rendered them equally daring and desperate. With all this, my father, a stranger in the land, and invested with no official authority, had, one would think, nothing to do. But it must be owned that, as he himself expresses it, he was born when Mars was lord of his ascendant, and that strife and bloodshed find him out in circumstances and situations the most retired and pacific.

About eleven o'clock on last Tuesday morning, while Hazlewood and my father were proposing to walk to a little lake about three miles distance, for the purpose of shooting wild ducks, and while

Lucy and I were busied with arranging our plan of work and study for the day, we were alarmed by the sound of horses' feet, advancing very fast up the avenue. The ground was hardened by a severe frost, which made the clatter of the hoofs sound yet louder and sharper. In a moment, two or three men, armed, mounted, and each leading a spare horse loaded with packages, appeared on the lawn, and without keeping upon the road, which makes a small sweep, pushed right across for the door of the house. Their appearance was in the utmost degree hurried and disordered, and they frequently looked back like men who apprehended a close and deadly pursuit. My father and Hazlewood hurried to the front door to demand who they were, and what was their business. They were revenue officers, they stated, who had seized these horses, loaded with contraband articles, at a place about three miles off. But the smugglers had been reinforced, and were now pursuing them with the avowed purpose of recovering the goods and putting to death the officers who had presumed to do their duty. The men said that, their horses being loaded, and the pursuers gaining ground upon them, they had fled to Woodbourne, conceiving that as my father had served the king, he would not refuse to protect the servants of government when threatened to be murdered in the discharge of their duty.

My father, to whom in his enthusiastic feelings of military loyalty, even a dog would be of importance if he came in the king's name, gave prompt orders for securing the goods in the hall, arming the servants, and defending the house in case it should be necessary. Hazlewood seconded him with great spirit, and even the strange animal they call Sampson stalked out of his den, and seized upon a fowling-piece, which my father had laid aside, to take what they call a rifle-gun, with which they shoot tigers, etc., in the East. The piece went off in the awkward hands of the poor parson, and very nearly shot one of the excise men. At this unexpected and involuntary explosion of his weapon, the Dominie (such is his nickname) exclaimed, "Prodigious!" which is his usual ejaculation when astonished. But no power could force the man to part with his discharged piece, so they were content to let him retain it, with the precaution of trusting him with no ammunition. This (excepting the alarm occasioned by the report) escaped my notice at the time, you may easily believe; but in talking over the scene afterwards, Hazlewood made us very merry with the Dominie's ignorant but zealous valour.

When my father had got everything into proper order for defence, and his people stationed at the windows with their firearms, he wanted to order us out of danger—into the cellar, I believe—but we could not be prevailed upon to stir. Though terrified to death, I have so much of his own spirit that I would look upon the peril which threatens us rather than hear it rage around me without knowing its nature or its purpose. Lucy, looking as pale as a marble statue, and keeping her eyes fixed on Hazlewood, seemed not even to hear the prayers with which he conjured her to leave the front of the house. But, in truth unless the hall-door should be forced, we were in little danger; the windows being almost blocked up with cushions and pillows, and, what the Dominie most lamented, with folio volumes brought hastily from the library, leaving only spaces through which the defenders might fire upon the assailants.

My father had now made his dispositions, and we sat in breathless expectation in the darkened apartment, the men remaining all silent upon their posts, in anxious contemplation probably of the approaching danger. My father, who was quite at home in such a scene, walked from one to another, and reiterated his orders that no one should presume to fire until he gave the word. Hazlewood, who seemed to catch courage from his eye, acted as his aide-de-camp, and displayed the utmost alertness in bearing his directions from one place to another, and seeing them properly carried into execution. Our force, with the strangers included, might amount to about twelve men.

At length the silence of this awful period of expectation was broken by a sound which, at a distance, was like the rushing of a stream of water; but as it approached, we distinguished the thick-beating clang of a number of horses advancing very fast. I had arranged a loop-hole for myself, from which I could see the approach of the enemy. The noise increased and came nearer, and at length thirty horsemen and more rushed at once upon the lawn. You never saw such horrid wretches! Notwithstanding the severity of the season, they were most of them stripped to their shirts and trousers, with silk handkerchiefs knotted about their heads, and all well armed with carbines, pistols, and cutlasses. I, who am a soldier's daughter, and accustomed to see war from my infancy, was never so terrified in my life as by the savage appearance of these ruffians, their horses reeking with the speed at which they had ridden, and their furious exclamations of rage and disappointment when they saw themselves balked of their prey. They paused, however, when they saw the preparations made to receive them, and appeared to hold a moment's consultation among themselves. At length one of the party, his face blackened with gunpowder by way of disguise, came forward with a white handkerchief on the end of his carbine, and asked to speak with Colonel Mannering. My father, to my infinite terror, threw open a window near which he was posted, and demanded what he wanted. "We want our goods, which we have been robbed of by these sharks," said the fellow; "and our lieutenant bids me say that if they are delivered, we'll go off for this bout without clearing scores with the rascals who took them; but if not, we'll burn the house, and have the heart's blood of every one in it"—a threat which he repeated more than once, graced by a fresh variety of implications and the most horrid denunciations that cruelty could suggest.

"And which is your lieutenant?" said my father in reply.

"That gentleman on the gray horse," said the miscreant, "with the red handkerchief bound about his brow."

"Then be pleased to tell that gentleman that if he and the scoundrels who are with him do not ride off the lawn this instant, I will fire upon them without ceremony." So saying, my father shut the window and broke short the conference.

The fellow no sooner regained his troop than, with a loud hurrah, or rather a savage yell, they fired a volley against our garrison. The glass of the windows was shattered in every direction; but the precautions already noticed saved the party within from suffering. Three such volleys were fired without a shot being returned from within. My father then observed them getting hatchets and crows, probably to assail the hall-door, and called aloud, "Let none fire but Hazlewood and me: Hazlewood, mark the ambassador." He himself aimed at the man on the gray horse, who fell on receiving his shot. Hazlewood was equally successful.

He shot the spokesman, who had dismounted, and was advancing with an axe in his hand. Their fall discouraged the rest, who began to turn round their horses; and a few shots fired at them

soon sent them off, bearing along with them their slain or wounded companions. We could not observe that they suffered any further loss. Shortly after their retreat a party of soldiers made, their appearance, to my infinite relief. These men were quartered at a village some miles distant, and had marched on the first rumour of the skirmish. A part of them escorted the terrified revenue officers and their seizure to a neighbouring seaport as a place of safety, and at my earnest request two or three files remained with us for that and the following day, for the security of the house from the vengeance of these banditti.

Such, dearest Matilda, was my first alarm. I must not forget to add that the ruffians left, at a cottage on the roadside, the man whose face was blackened with powder, apparently because he was unable to bear transportation. He died in about half an hour after. On examining the corpse, it proved to be that of a profligate boor in the neighbourhood, a person notorious as a poacher and smuggler. We received many messages of congratulation from the neighbouring families; and it was generally allowed that a few such instances of spirited resistance would greatly check the presumption of these lawless men. My father distributed rewards among his servants, and praised Hazlewood's courage and coolness to the skies. Lucy and I came in for a share of his applause because we had stood fire with firmness, and had not disturbed him with screams or expostulations. As for the Dominie, my father took an opportunity of begging to exchange snuff-boxes with him. The honest gentleman was much flattered with the proposal, and extolled the beauty of his new snuff-box excessively. "It looked," he said, "as well as if it were real gold from Ophir"—indeed it would be odd if it should not, being formed in fact of that very metal; but, to do this honest creature justice, I believe the knowledge of its real value would not enhance his sense of my father's kindness, supposing it, as he does, to be pinchbeck gilded. He has had a hard task replacing the folios which were used in the barricade, smoothing out the creases and dog's-ears, and repairing the other disasters they have sustained during their service in the fortification. He brought us some pieces of lead and bullets which these ponderous tomes had intercepted during the action, and which he had extracted with great care. I feel, however, so much fatigued with my present exertion that I cannot resume the pen till to-morrow. I will detain this letter, notwithstanding, that you may not feel any anxiety upon account of your own.

JULIA MANNERING.

MIRACLE IN ROME

By HENRYK SIENKIEWICZ

Lygia, a young Christian maiden loved by the youthful tribune Marcus Vinicius, is condemned to death in the terrible circus at Rome. It is thought that nothing can save the beautiful Christian girl from being destroyed, for Nero is hunting down and persecuting members of the strange peace-loving sect to which she belongs. However, in the crowded amphitheatre, under the stars, a miracle is wrought by a simple man of great strength, who believes in his God, and the awestruck mob break their silence to demand a pardon from a reluctant Cæsar.

This story is taken from "Quo Vadis."

IT was in Nero's day that Rome first conceived a taste for evening performances in circuses and amphitheatres. The news that the end of the games was approaching, and that the last of the Christians were to die at an evening spectacle, brought a vast crowd to witness the entertainment. Those who, in former days, had seen Lygia at Plautius' house had marvellous tales to relate concerning her beauty; while some there were whose exclusive preoccupation it was to wager whether or no she would actually appear in the arena. Some persons even alleged that Nero would restore her, and cited as their reason that she was a hostage, and therefore possessed, under the law of nations, of a right to worship what diety she pleased, and in no case to be punished for so doing.

Indeed, upon the spectators also had this uncertainty, this curiosity, this expectation taken a hold. Cæsar arrived later than had been his wont. The Prætorians were present in greater numbers than usual, and were commanded not by a centurion, but by the tribune Subrius Flavus, who was known to all for his blind attachment to the Imperial person.

Petronius, still uncertain as to what was about to happen, had done no more than ask his nephew if he was ready for the ordeal, and if he intended to be present at the spectacle. To both questions Vinicius had returned an answer in the affirmative, but a shudder had shaken him from head to foot, since he suspected that Petronius had reason for his inquiries. For a long time past the young man had been half-alive. Already he had entered the portals of death, as well as accepted the fact that Lygia was about to do the same, since for both the act of death would mean at once deliverance and reunion. This alone had enabled him to contemplate the fatal moment with calmness. But now the blow had fallen—now, under his very eyes, there was to take place the martyrdom of the being who was dearer to him than life itself! Once more the despair which he had conquered began to rage in his soul; once more the desire to rescue Lygia at all costs took possession of him. Since dawn he had been trying to obtain admittance to the arena dungeons, in order to ascertain if she were really there; but Prætorians had been on guard at every entrance, and they had been armed with such strict orders that even those of their number who knew him had not dared to yield either to his prayers or to his gold. Indeed, he felt as though the uncertainty would kill him even before he came to behold the spectacle itself. Yet still at the bottom of his heart there lurked a last remnant of hope. "Thou, and only Thou, canst save her!" he kept repeating as he twisted his hands convulsively. "Thou, and only Thou, has the power!" Never had he foreseen how unspeakably terrible the moment would be. He felt that, should he be forced to witness Lygia's agony, his love for Christ would turn to hatred, and his faith to despair. Yet still he dreaded to offend the Christ whom he was imploring; wherefore he did not pray that Lygia might be spared, but only that she might die before she had been dragged into the arena. At length, like a man who, rolling towards the edge of a precipice, clutches at anything which may break his fall, Vinicius fastened upon the idea that by faith he still could save her. Faith was all that remained to him: and had not Peter said that faith could shake the world to its foundations?

Absorbed in this hope, he put away all doubt from his mind, and threw his whole being into the words, "I have faith." Surely a miracle would come of them.

Yet, even as excessive tension bursts a cord, so the efforts put forth by Vinicius broke his spirit. A deathlike pallor overspread his countenance; gradually a cold torpor crept through his body. Under the belief that his prayer had been granted, he imagined himself to be at the point of death. Also it seemed to him that Lygia must be already dead, and that Christ was taking them to Himself. Suddenly the arena, the gleam of the countless white togas, the light of thousands upon thousands of lanterns and torches alike vanished from before his eyes.

Yet the fainting fit was of short duration, for soon the impatient shouts of the crowd recalled him to himself.

"You are ill," whispered Petronius in his ear. "Have yourself taken home." And, without paying further attention to what Cæsar was saying, he rose to support the young tribune towards the entrance. Pity was surging in his heart, and he felt infuriated to see Nero, with his emerald at his eye, calmly watching Vinicius' agony —doubtless in order, at some future date, to describe it in mock-pathetic stanzas, and so to win applause from the mob!

Vinicius shook his head. He might die in that amphitheatre, but he would never leave it.

Just at that moment the Prefect threw down upon the sand a red scarf; and as he did so the gate facing the Imperial balcony grated upon its hinges, and from the dark opening behind it there emerged into the brilliantly lighted arena the figure of the Lygian, Ursus. At first he blinked his eyelids, as though dazzled; then he advanced to the centre of the circle, and looked around him to discern what it was he had to meet. From tier to tier the murmurs rose. Gladiators of exceptional physique were not lacking in Rome, but never had the eyes of the citizens seen a giant like this.

He remained perfectly motionless in the centre of the arena—looking, as he stood there, like a colossus of granite which had in its barbaric countenance a tinge of sadness mingled with vigilance. At length, perceiving the arena to be empty, he turned his blue, childlike eyes in turn upon the spectators, upon Cæsar, and upon the gratings whence he expected executioners to issue.

At the moment of entering the arena his heart had for a second quivered with the hope that he was about to die upon the cross; but, on perceiving neither cross nor socket-hole, he conceived that he had been adjudged unworthy of such a favour, and was to meet his end in some other fashion—probably under the fangs of wild beasts. He was unarmed, and had resolved to die patiently, even as the Lamb would have had him do; but since he wished to address one more prayer to the Redeemer, he knelt down, joined his hands together, and raised his eyes to the stars.

The mob had not long to wait. Suddenly there resounded a deafening clatter of iron bars, and from out of the grating opposite to the Imperial balcony there rushed, amid the yells of the beast-keepers, one of the monstrous aurochs of Germany, with, bound upon its head, a woman.

"Lygia, Lygia!" shouted Vinicius. Again and again he gasped in a hoarse, inhuman voice:

"I have faith! I have faith! O Christ work a miracle!"

Indeed, he did not feel Petronius throw a toga over his head as he uttered the words. He only felt that either death or agony had darkened all before his eyes. He could look at nothing, he could see nothing when he did so. The sensation of this wrapped him in a sort of horrible darkness, with no idea left to him but to keep his lips deliriously repeating:

"I have faith! I have faith! I have faith!"

The amphitheatre had suddenly become absolutely still. In the arena there was passing an unprecedented scene. At the sight of his princess bound upon the horns of the savage bull, the Lygian, hitherto humble and prepared for death, had sprung forward like a man scorched with living fire, and, with back bent, was creeping, zigzag fashion, towards the maddened beast.

Then from every throat there issued a short, a tremulous cry of amazement, followed by a profound silence. For with a single bound the Lygian had reached the beast and gripped its horns!

"Look!" cried Petronius as he snatched away the toga from Vinicius' head. The other rose, lifted a face of a deadly whiteness and stared with wild, fixed eyes at the arena. Not a man present could breathe. A fly might have been heard winging its way through the arena. Never since Rome had been Rome had such a sight been seen.

The man was holding the beast by the horns. Up to the ankles his feet were planted in the sand; his back was bent like the arch of a drawn bow; his head had disappeared between his shoulders; the muscles of his arms had emerged in such relief that the skin seemed as though it must crack under the strain of their enlargement. Yet he had stopped the bull full in its career, and now was fixed with it in such absolute immobility, that the spectators saw before them, as it were, a statuesque representation of the feats of Theseus or of Hercules. Nevertheless this apparent immobility was the result of the unseen tension of two furious forces. The

aurochs also had its feet planted in the sand, while the dark, shaggy bulk of its body had curled together like a gigantic ball. Which of the two adversaries would first become exhausted, which of the two adversaries would first fall—that, for the entranced spectators of the struggle, meant, at that moment, more than their own fortunes, more than the fate of Rome, more than the world-wide dominion of the Roman Empire. This Lygian had suddenly become a demigod. Cæsar himself had risen to his feet to view the spectacle.

And now everyone was contemplating with stupefaction the picture presented—incapable of believing that it was real. Some people had raised their arms, and were standing fixed in that posture; others had their foreheads running with sweat, as though it was they themselves who were struggling with the bull. In all that vast circle there was to be heard only the singing sound of the lantern flames and the crackling of brackets under their weight of torches. Speech had died on every lip, and hearts were beating as though they would burst the breasts which contained them. For every spectator the struggle seemed to be lasting for centuries.

And all this while the man and the beast remained fixed in their frightful effort—remained chained, as it were, to the ground.

Suddenly a deep, groaning bellow mounted from the arena. Every throat let forth a shout. Then again there was absolute silence. Men believed themselves to be dreaming. *For under the iron arms of the barbarian the monstrous head of the aurochs was slowly turning round!*

The Lygian's face, neck, and arms had become purple, and the arch of his back had bent yet more. It was clear that he was rallying the remainder of his superhuman strength, and that soon the latter would be exhausted.

Always growing more and more stifled and hoarse and painful, the aurochs' bellowing mingled with the strident breathing of the Lygian. Gradually the animal's head was turning more and more to one side; until suddenly there escaped from its gullet a huge slobbering tongue. An instant later the ears of the spectators who were nearest to the arena caught the dull sound of bones breaking. Then, with its withers twisted under it, the beast collapsed in a heap—dead!

In a twinkling the giant had released the horns, and taken the girl into his arms. Then he fell to panting vehemently. His face was pale, his hair was plastered with sweat, and his shoulders and arms were dripping. For a moment or two he stood motionless, as though dazed; then he raised his eyes, and looked at the spectators.

The audience had gone mad. The walls of the immense building were quivering with the clamour of tens of thousands of throats. The spectators on the upper tiers had left their places, flowed downwards towards the arena, and crammed themselves into the passage-ways, the better to view the Hercules. From every quarter came voices demanding his pardon—passionate, insistent voices which soon combined into an immense outcry. To a mob which, above all things, admired physical strength, the giant had become an idol—he had become the first personage of Rome.

For his own part, he understood that the people were demanding for him his life and liberty; but it was not of those boons that he was thinking. For a moment or two he cast his eyes around him; then he approached the Imperial balcony—balancing the form of the young girl in his outstretched arms as he raised suppliant eyes which said: "It is *her* pardon that I ask for; it is *she* who must be saved; it is for *her* that I have done this."

At once the spectators divined his desire. At the sight of the unconscious maiden, who, beside the huge body of the Lygian, looked like a tiny child, emotion seized upon knights, Senators, and the mob alike. Her frail figure, her unconscious condition, the frightful danger from which the giant had just rescued her, and, finally, her beauty and the devotion of the Lygian all combined to touch the popular heart. Some even thought that it was a father demanding pardon for his daughter, and pity flamed up in them the more. With voices strangled with sobs they demanded that Lygia and Ursus should be forgiven.

Meanwhile Ursus continued to parade the arena with the young girl balanced in his arms, and to implore both with eyes and gesture that Lygia's life should be preserved to her. Suddenly Vinicius leapt from his seat, crossed the partition wall of the tier, and, rushing up to Lygia, covered with his toga the body of his betrothed. Then he tore open his tunic at the breast, and, exposing to view the scars which he had received in Armenia, extended his arms towards the people.

Upon that the popular frenzy surpassed anything that the amphitheatre had ever witnessed. The entire populace fell to stamping its feet and shouting. Voices which had hitherto been suppliant now became menacing, and thousands of spectators turned towards Cæsar, and shook their fists at him, with the light of fury gleaming in their eyes.

Nero prevaricated. Fury showed itself on his fat-disfigured features, since, apart from anything else, his conceit forbade him to submit to the popular will, even though his native cowardice urged him also not to oppose it.

So he set himself to scan those around him, in the hope that at least among the Augustans he would see a thumb pointing downwards, in token of death. But Petronius extended his hand with thumb upwards, and, with a slight nod of defiance, looked Cæsar straight in the eyes. Thereafter the same thing was done by many others; on seeing which Cæsar removed the emerald from his eye with an expression of anger and contempt.

Nero turned towards the spot where, at the head of his guard, there was standing the ferocious Subrius Flavus—a man who hitherto had been devoted to him, body and soul. And as Nero looked he saw an unwonted sight. The forbidding face of the old tribune was bathed in tears, and with his raised hand he was making the sign of the cross!

Meanwhile rage had taken complete possession of the multitude. Under the incessant stamping of feet a cloud of dust wrapped the amphitheatre in an obscurity whence came shouts and imprecations. Nero took alarm at this. In the Circus the people were absolute masters. True, his predecessors, more especially Caligula, had more than once taken it upon themselves to oppose the popular will, and so to risk certain disorder and probable rioting; but Nero was less favourably situated. In the first place, as a comedian and a vocalist, he had need of the favour of the people; in the second place, he wished, in his struggle with the Senate and the patricians, to have the people on his side; and, finally, since the burning of Rome he had been forced to conciliate the mob by every means in his power, and to divert its anger in the direction of the Christians. Consequently he knew that it would be dangerous to show further resistance, since sedition born in the Circus might soon involve the whole city, and produce incalculable consequences.

So, after glancing at Subrius Flavus, and at the soldiers in general, and seeing everywhere only frowns, agitated features, and angry looks at himself, he gave the sign of pardon.

From top to bottom of the amphitheatre there arose a storm of applause. The people assured the lives of the condemned, and from that moment onwards the latter were under the people's protection, and no one, not even Cæsar, might dare to persecute them further.

FOR THE WANT OF A NAIL

By SUSAN COOLIDGE

High-spirited Katy Carr learned a very important lesson when one day she got into a number of scrapes at school. Previously she had thought trivial everyday things unimportant simply because they were small when compared with the more exciting things that were to be done. But after invading a rival school's playground, and inventing a new game which almost wrecked the schoolroom, the adventurous American schoolgirl came to see the truth of these things. Her further scrapes and adventures can be read in "What Katy Did," from which this story is taken.

MRS. KNIGHT'S school, to which Katy and Clover and Cecy went, stood quite at the other end of the town from Dr. Carr's. It was a low, one-story building, and had a yard behind it, in which the girls played at recess. Unfortunately, next door to it was Miss Miller's school, equally large and popular, and with a yard behind it also. Only a high board fence separated the two playgrounds.

Mrs. Knight was a stout, gentle woman, who moved slowly, and had a face which made you think of an amiable and well-disposed cow. Miss Miller, on the contrary, had black eyes, with black corkscrew curls waving about them, and was generally brisk and snappy. A constant feud raged between the two schools as to the respective merits of the teachers and the instruction. The Knight girls, for some unknown reason, considered themselves genteel and the Miller girls vulgar, and took no pains to conceal this opinion; while the Miller girls, on the other hand, retaliated by being as aggravating as they knew how. They spent their recesses and intermissions mostly in making faces through the knot-holes in the fence, and over the top of it when they could get there, which wasn't an easy thing to do, as the fence was pretty high. The Knight girls could make faces, too, for all their gentility. Their yard had one great advantage over the other; it possessed a woodshed, with a climbable roof, which commanded Miss Miller's premises, and upon this the girls used to sit in rows, turning up their noses at the next yard, and irritating the foe by jeering remarks. "Knights" and "Millerites" the two schools called each other; and the feud raged so high that sometimes it was hardly safe for a Knight to meet a Millerite in the street; all of which, as may be imagined, was exceedingly improving both to the manners and morals of the young ladies concerned.

One morning Katy was late. She could not find her things. Her algebra, as she expressed it, "had gone and lost itself," her slate was missing, and the string was off her sunbonnet. She ran about, searching for these articles, and banging doors, till Aunt Izzie was out of patience.

"As for your algebra," she said, "if it is that very dirty book with only one cover, and scribbled all over the leaves, you will find it under the kitchen table. How you do manage to spoil your school-books in this manner, Katy, I cannot imagine. It is less than a month since your father got you a new algebra, and look at it now —not fit to be carried about.

"About your slate," she went on, "I know nothing; but here is the bonnet string"; taking it out of her pocket.

"Oh, thank you!" said Katy, hastily sticking it on with a pin.

"Katy Carr!" almost screamed Miss Izzie, "what *are* you about? Pinning on your bonnet-string! Mercy on me, what shiftless thing will you do next? Now stand still, and don't fidget. You shan't stir till I have sewed it on properly."

It wasn't easy to "stand still and not fidget," with Aunt Izzie fussing away and lecturing, and now and then, in a moment of forgetfulness, sticking her needle into one's chin. Katy bore it as well as she could, only shifting perpetually from one foot to the other like an impatient horse. The minute she was released she flew into the kitchen, seized the algebra, and rushing like a whirlwind to the gate, where good little Clover stood patiently waiting, though all ready herself, and terribly afraid she would be late.

"We shall have to run," gasped Katy, quite out of breath. "Aunt Izzie kept me. She has been so horrid!"

They did run as fast as they could, but time ran faster, and before they were half-way to school the town clock struck nine, and all hope was over. This vexed Katy very much; for, though often late, she was always eager to be early.

"There," she said, stopping short, "I shall just tell Aunt Izzie that it was her fault. It is *too* bad." And she marched into school in a very cross mood.

A day begun in this manner is pretty sure to end badly, as most of us know. All the morning through things seemed to go wrong. Katy missed twice in her grammar lesson, and lost her place in the class. Her hand shook so when she copied her composition that the writing, not good at best, turned out almost illegible, so that Mrs. Knight said it must all be done over again. This made Katy crosser than ever; and almost before she thought she had whispered to Clover, "How hateful!" The tears came into her eyes from vexation! and, for fear the other girls would notice them, she made a bolt for the yard as soon as the bell rang, and mounted up all alone to the wood-house roof, where she sat with her back to the school, fighting with her eyes, and trying to get her face in order before the rest should come.

Miss Miller's clock was about four minutes slower than Mrs. Knight's, so the next playground was empty. It was a warm, breezy day, and as Katy sat there suddenly a gust of wind came, and seizing her sunbonnet, which was only half tied on, whirled it across the roof. She clutched after it as it flew, but too late. Once, twice, thrice, it flapped, then it disappeared over the edge, and Katy, flying after, saw it lying a crumpled lilac heap in the very middle of the enemy's yard.

This was horrible! Not merely losing the bonnet, for Katy was comfortably indifferent as to what became of her clothes, but to lose it *so*. In another minute the Miller girls would be out. Already she seemed to see them dancing war-dances round the unfortunate bonnet, pinning it on a pole, using it as a football, waving it over the fence, and otherwise treating it as Indians treat a captive taken in war. Was it to be endured? Never! Better die first! And with very much the feeling of a person who faces destruction rather than forfeit honour Katy set her teeth, and, sliding rapidly down the roof, seized the fence, and vaulted into Miss Miller's yard.

Just then the recess bell tinkled; and a little Millerite who sat by the window, and who, for two seconds, had been dying to give the exciting information, squeaked out to the others: "There's Katy Carr in our back-yard!"

Out poured the Millerites big and little. Their wrath and indignation at this daring invasion cannot be described. With a howl of fury they precipitated themselves upon Katy, but she was as quick as they, and, holding the rescued bonnet in her hand, was already half-way up the fence.

There are moments when it is a fine thing to be tall. On this occasion Katy's long legs and arms served her an excellent turn. Nothing but a daddy long-legs ever climbed so fast or so wildly as she did now. In one second she had gained the top of the fence. Just as she went over a Millerite seized her by the last foot, and almost dragged her boot off.

Almost, not quite, thanks to the stout thread with which Aunt Izzie had sewed on the buttons. With a frantic kick Katy released herself, and had the satisfaction of seeing her assailant go head over heels backwards, while, with a shriek of triumph and fright, she plunged headlong into the midst of a group of Knights. They were listening with open mouths to the uproar, and now stood transfixed at the astonishing spectacle of one of their number absolutely returning alive from the camp of the enemy.

I cannot tell you what a commotion ensued. The Knights were beside themselves with pride and triumph. Katy was kissed and hugged, and made to tell her story over and over again, while rows of exulting girls sat on the wood-house roof to crow over the discomfited Millerites; and when, later, the foe rallied and began to retort over the fence, Clover, armed with a tack-hammer, was lifted up in the arms of one of the tall girls to rap the intruding knuckles as they appeared on the top. This she did with such good-will that the Millerites were glad to drop down again, and mutter vengeance at a safe distance. Altogether it was a great day for the school, a day to be remembered. As time went on Katy, what with the excitement of her adventure, and of being praised and petted by the big girls, grew perfectly reckless, and hardly knew what she said or did.

A good many of the scholars lived too far from school to go home at noon, and were in the habit of bringing their lunches in baskets, and staying all day. Katy and Clover were of this number. This noon, after the dinners were eaten, it was proposed that they should play something in the schoolroom, and Katy's unlucky star put it into her head to invent a new game, which she called the Game of Rivers.

It was played in the following manner: each girl took the name of a river, and laid out for herself an appointed path through the room, winding among the desks and benches, and making a low, roaring sound, to imitate the noise of water. Cecy was the Platte, Marianne Brooks, a tall girl, the Mississippi, Alice Blair the Ohio, Clover the Penobscot, and so on. They were instructed to run into each other once in a while, because, as Katy said, "rivers do." As for Katy herself, she was "Father Ocean," and, growling horribly, raged up and down the platform where Mrs. Knight usually sat. Every now and then, when the others were at the far end of the room, she would suddenly cry out, "Now for a meeting of the waters!" whereupon all the rivers, bouncing, bounding, scrambling, screaming, would turn and run towards Father Ocean; while she roared up and down to represent the movement of waves.

Such a noise as this beautiful game made was never heard in the town of Burnet before or since. It was like the bellowing of the bulls of Bashan, the squeaking of pigs, the cackle of turkey-cocks, and the laugh of wild hyenas all at once; and, in addition, there was a great banging of furniture and scraping of many feet on an uncarpeted floor. People going by stopped and stared, children cried, an old lady asked why someone didn't run for a policeman; while the Miller girls listened to the proceedings with malicious pleasure, and told everybody that it was the noise that Mrs. Knight's scholars "usually made in play-hours."

Mrs. Knight, coming back from dinner, was much amazed to see a crowd of people collected in front of her school. As she drew near the sounds reached her, and then she became really frightened, for she thought that somebody was being murdered on her premises. Hurrying in, she threw open the door, and there, to her dismay, was the whole room in a frightful state of confusion and uproar; chairs flung down, desks upset, ink streaming on the floor; while in the midst of the ruin the frantic rivers raced and screamed, and Old Father Ocean, with a face as red as fire, capered like a lunatic on the platform.

"What *does* this mean?" gasped poor Mrs. Knight, almost unable to speak for horror.

At the sound of her voice the Rivers stood still; Father Ocean brought his prances to an abrupt close, and slunk down from the platform. All of a sudden each girl seemed to realize what a condition the room was in, and what a horrible thing she had done. The timid ones cowered behind their desks, the bold ones tried to look unconscious, and, to make matters worse, the scholars who had gone home to dinner began to return, staring at the scene of disaster, and asking, in whispers, what had been going on?

Mrs. Knight rang the bell. When the school had come to order she had the desks and chairs picked up, while she herself brought wet cloths to sop the ink from the floor. This was done in profound silence; and the expression of Mrs. Knight's face was so direful and solemn that a fresh damp fell upon the spirits of the guilty Rivers, and Father Ocean wished himself thousands of miles away.

When all was in order again, and the girls had taken their seats, Mrs. Knight made a short speech. She said she never was so shocked in her life before; she had supposed that she could trust them to behave like ladies when her back was turned. The idea that they could act so disgracefully, make such an uproar, and alarm people going by, had never occurred to her, and she was deeply pained. It was setting a bad example to all the neighbourhood—by which Mrs. Knight meant the rival school, Miss Miller having just sent over a little girl, with her compliments, to ask if anyone was hurt, and could *she* do anything? Which was naturally aggravating! Mrs. Knight hoped they were sorry; she thought they must be—sorry and ashamed. Of course, some punishment would be inflicted for the offence, but she should have to reflect before deciding what it ought to be. Meantime she wanted them to think it over seriously; and if anyone felt she was more to blame than the others now was the moment to rise and confess it.

Katy's heart gave a great thump, but she rose bravely. "I made up the game, and I was Father Ocean," she said to the astonished Mrs. Knight, who glared at her for a minute, and then replied solemnly, "Very well, Katy—sit down"; which Katy did, feeling more ashamed than ever, but somehow relieved in her mind. There is a saving grace in truth which helps truth-tellers through the worst of their troubles, and Katy found this out now.

The afternoon was long and hard. Mrs. Knight did not smile

once; the lessons dragged; and Katy, after the heat and excitement of the forenoon, began to feel miserable. She had received more than one hard blow during the meetings of the waters, and had bruised herself, almost without knowing it, against the desks and chairs. All the places now began to ache; her head throbbed so that she could hardly see, and a lump of something heavy seemed to be lying on her heart.

When school was over Mrs. Knight rose and said, "The young ladies who took part in the game this afternoon are requested to remain." All the others went away, and shut the door behind them. It was a horrible moment: the girls never forgot it, or the hopeless sound of the door as the last departing scholar clapped it after her as she left.

I can't begin to tell you what it was that Mrs. Knight said to them: it was very affecting and before long most of the girls began to cry. The penalty of their offence was announced to be the loss of holidays—recess she called them—for three weeks; but that wasn't half so bad as seeing Mrs. Knight so "afflicted," as Cecy told her mother afterward. One by one the sobbing sinners departed from the schoolroom. When most of them were gone Mrs. Knight called Katy up to the platform and said a few words to her specially. She was not really severe, but Katy was too penitent and worn out to bear much, and before long was weeping like a water-spout, or like the ocean she had pretended to be.

At this, tender-hearted Mrs. Knight was so much affected that she let her off at once, and even kissed her in token of forgiveness, which made poor Ocean sob harder than ever. All the way home she sobbed; faithful little Clover, running along by her side in great distress, begging her to stop crying, and trying in vain to hold up the fragments of her dress, which was torn in at least a dozen places. Katy could not stop crying, and it was fortunate that Aunt Izzie happened to be out, and that the only person who saw her in this piteous plight was Mary, the nurse, who doted on the children, and was always ready to help them out of their troubles.

On this occasion she petted and cosseted Katy exactly as if it had been Johnny or little Phil. She took her on her lap, bathed the hot head, brushed the hair, put arnica on the bruises, and produced a clean frock so that by tea-time the poor child, except for her red eyes, looked like herself again, and Aunt Izzie didn't notice anything unusual.

For a wonder Dr. Carr was at home that evening. It was always a great treat to the children when this happened, and Katy thought herself happy when, after the little ones had gone to bed, she got papa to herself, and told him the whole story.

"Papa," she said, sitting on his knee, which, big girl as she was, she liked very much to do, "what is the reason that makes some days so lucky and other days so unlucky? Now, to-day began all wrong, and everything that happened in it was wrong, and on other days I begin right, and all goes right, straight through. If Aunt Izzie hadn't kept me in the morning, I shouldn't have lost my mark, and then I shouldn't have been cross, and then *perhaps* I shouldn't have got in my other scrapes."

"But what made Aunt Izzie keep you, Katy?"

"To sew on the string of my bonnet, Papa."

"But how did it happen that the string was off?"

"Well," said Katy reluctantly, "I am afraid that was *my* fault, for it came off on Tuesday, and I didn't fasten it on."

"So you see we must go further back than Aunt Izzie for the beginning of this unlucky day of yours, Childie. Did you ever hear the old saying about 'For the want of a nail the shoe was lost'?"

"No, never—tell it to me!" cried Katy, who loved stories as well as when she was three years old.

So Dr. Carr repeated:

"For the want of a nail the shoe was lost,
For the want of a shoe the horse was lost,
For the want of a horse the rider was lost,
For the want of a rider the battle was lost,
For the want of the battle the kingdom was lost,
And all for the want of a horse-shoe nail."

"Oh, Papa!" exclaimed Katy, giving him a great hug as she got off his knee. "I see what you mean! Who would have thought such a little speck of a thing as not sewing on my string could make a difference! But I don't believe I shall get in any more scrapes, for I shan't forget—

For the want of a nail the shoe was lost."

A MIDSUMMER NIGHT'S DREAM

By CHARLES and MARY LAMB

This story of the distress that came to true hearts through an excusable mistake made by Puck, the fairy king's spritely attendant, is taken from the authors' "Tales from Shakespeare." However, in such a fairy world of charms and potent philtres mistakes are not difficult to put right, and it is therefore not at all surprising that all ends very happily.

THERE was a law in the city of Athens which gave to its citizens the power of compelling their daughters to marry whomsoever they pleased; for upon a daughter's refusing to marry the man her father had chosen to be her husband, the father was empowered by this law to cause her to be put to death; but as fathers do not often desire the death of their own daughters, even though they do happen to prove a little refractory, this law was seldom or never put in execution, though perhaps the young ladies of that city were not unfrequently threatened by their parents with the terrors of it.

There was one instance, however, of an old man, whose name was Egeus, who actually did come before Theseus (at that time the reigning Duke of Athens) to complain that his daughter Hermia, whom he had commanded to marry Demetrius, a young man of a noble Athenian family, refused to obey him, because she loved another young Athenian, named Lysander. Egeus demanded justice of Theseus, and desired that this cruel law might be put in force against his daughter.

Hermia pleaded in excuse for her disobedience, that Demetrius had formerly professed love for her dear friend Helena, and that Helena loved Demetrius to distraction; but this honourable reason which Hermia gave for not obeying her father's command moved not the stern Egeus.

Theseus, though a great and merciful prince, had no power to alter the laws of his country; therefore he could only give Hermia four days to consider of it, and at the end of that time, if she still refused to marry Demetrius, she was to be put to death.

When Hermia was dismissed from the presence of the duke, she went to her lover, Lysander, and told him the peril she was in, and that she must either give him up and marry Demetrius, or lose her life in four days.

Lysander was in great affliction at hearing these evil tidings; but recollecting that he had an aunt who lived at some distance from Athens, and that at the place where she lived the cruel law could not be put in force against Hermia (this law not extending beyond the boundaries of the city), he proposed to Hermia that she should steal out of her father's house that night, and go with him to his aunt's house, where he would marry her. "I will meet you," said Lysander, "in the wood a few miles without the city; in that delightful wood where we have so often walked with Helena in the pleasant month of May."

To this proposal Hermia joyfully agreed; and she told no one of her intended flight but her friend Helena. Helena (as maidens will do foolish things for love) very ungenerously resolved to go and tell this to Demetrius, though she could hope no benefit from betraying her friend's secret but the poor pleasure of following her faithless lover to the wood; for she well knew that Demetrius would go thither in pursuit of Hermia.

The wood in which Lysander and Hermia proposed to meet was the favourite haunt of those little beings known by the name of *Fairies*.

Oberon the king, and Titania the queen of the fairies, with all their tiny train of followers, in this wood held their midnight revels.

Between this little king and queen of sprites there happened, at this time, a sad disagreement: they never met by moonlight in the shady walks of this pleasant wood but they were quarrelling, till all their fairy elves would creep into acorn-cups and hide themselves for fear.

The cause of this unhappy disagreement was Titania's refusing to give Oberon a little changeling boy, whose mother had been Titania's friend; and upon her death the fairy queen stole the child from its nurse, and brought him up in the woods.

The night on which the lovers were to meet in this wood, as Titania was walking with some of her maids of honour, she met Oberon attended by his train of fairy courtiers.

"Ill met by moonlight, proud Titania," said the fairy king. The queen replied, "What! Jealous Oberon, is it you? Fairies, skip hence; I have forsworn his company!"—"Tarry, rash fairy!" said Oberon: "am not I thy lord? Why does Titania cross her Oberon? Give me your little changeling boy to be my page."

"Set your heart at rest," answered the queen; "your whole fairy kingdom buys not the boy of me." She then left her lord in great anger. "Well, go your way," said Oberon: "before the morning dawns I will torment you for this injury."

Oberon then sent for Puck, his chief favourite and privy councillor.

Puck (or, as he was sometimes called, Robin Goodfellow) was a shrewd and knavish sprite, that used to play comical pranks in the neighbouring villages—sometimes getting into the dairies and skimming the milk, sometimes plunging his light and airy form into the butter-churn, and while he was dancing his fantastic shape in the churn, in vain the dairymaid would labour to change her cream into butter: nor had the village swains any better success; whenever Puck chose to play his freaks in the brewing copper, the ale was sure to be spoiled. When a few good neighbours were met to drink some comfortable ale together, Puck would jump into the bowl of ale in the likeness of a roasted crab, and when some old goody was going to drink he would bob against her lips, and spill the ale over her withered chin; and presently after, when the same old dame was gravely seating herself to tell her neighbours a sad and melancholy story, Puck would slip her three-legged stool from under her, and down toppled the poor old woman, and then the old gossips would hold their sides and laugh at her, and swear they never wasted a merrier hour.

"Come hither, Puck," said Oberon to this little merry wanderer of the night. "Fetch me the flower which maids call 'Love in Idleness'; the juice of that little purple flower laid on the eyelids of those who sleep will make them, when they awake, dote on the first thing they see. Some of the juice of that flower I will drop on the eyelids of my Titania when she is asleep, and the first thing she looks upon when she opens her eyes she will fall in love with, even though it be a lion or a bear, a meddling monkey or a busy ape; and before I will take this charm from off her sight, which I can do with another charm I know of, I will make her give me that boy to be my page."

Puck, who loved mischief to his heart, was highly diverted with this intended frolic of his master, and ran to seek the flower; and while Oberon was waiting the return of Puck, he observed Demetrius and Helena enter the wood: he overheard Demetrius reproaching Helena for following him, and after many unkind words on his part, and gentle expostulations from Helena, reminding him of his former love and professions of true faith to her, he left her (as he said) to the mercy of the wild beasts, and she ran after him as swiftly as she could.

When Puck returned with the little purple flower, Oberon said to his favourite, "Take a part of this flower: there has been a sweet Athenian lady here who is in love with a disdainful youth; if you find him sleeping, drop some of the love-juice in his eyes, but contrive to do it when she is near him, that the first thing he sees when he awakes may be this despised lady. You will know the man by the Athenian garments which he wears." Puck promised to manage this matter very dexterously, and then Oberon went, unperceived by Titania, to her bower, where she was preparing to go to rest. Her fairy bower was a bank, where grew wild thyme, cowslips, and sweet violets under a canopy of woodbine, musk-roses, and eglantine. There Titania always slept some part of the night; her coverlet, the enamelled skin of a snake, which, though a small mantle, was wide enough to wrap a fairy in.

He found Titania giving orders to her fairies how they were to employ themselves while she slept.

When the fairies had sung their queen asleep they left her, to perform the important services she had enjoined them. Oberon then softly drew near his Titania, and dropped some of the love-juice on her eyelids.

But to return to Hermia, who made her escape out of her father's house that night to avoid the death she was doomed to for refusing to marry Demetrius. When she entered the wood, she found her dear Lysander waiting for her, to conduct her to his aunt's house; but before they had passed half through the wood, Hermia was so much fatigued that Lysander, who was very careful of this dear lady, who had proved her affection for him even by hazarding her life for his sake, persuaded her to rest till morning on a bank of soft moss, and lying down himself on the ground at some little distance, they soon fell fast asleep. Here they were found by Puck, who, seeing a handsome young man asleep, and perceiving that his clothes were made in the Athenian fashion, and that a pretty lady was sleeping near him, concluded that this must be the Athenian maid and her disdainful lover whom Oberon had sent him to seek;

and he naturally enough conjectured that, as they were alone together, she must be the first thing he would see when he awoke; so without more ado he proceeded to pour some of the juice of the little purple flower into his eyes. But it so fell out that Helena came that way, and, instead of Hermia, was the first object Lysander beheld when he opened his eyes; and, strange to relate, so powerful was the love-charm that all his love for Hermia vanished away, and Lysander fell in love with Helena.

Thus this misfortune happened. Helena, as has been before related, endeavoured to keep pace with Demetrius when he ran away so rudely from her; but she could not continue this unequal race long, men being always better runners in a long race than ladies. Helena soon lost sight of Demetrius, and as she was wandering about, dejected and forlorn, she arrived at the place where Lysander was sleeping. "Ah!" said she, "this is Lysander lying on the ground: is he dead or asleep?" Then, gently touching him, she said, "Good sir, if you are alive, awake." Upon this Lysander opened his eyes, and (the love-charm beginning to work) immediately addressed her in terms of extravagant love and admiration, telling her she as much excelled Hermia in beauty as a dove does a raven, and that he would run through fire for her sweet sake, and many more such lover-like speeches. Helena, knowing Lysander was her friend Hermia's lover, and that he was solemnly engaged to marry her, was in the utmost rage when she heard herself addressed in this manner, for she thought (as well she might) that Lysander was making a jest of her. "Oh!" said she, "why was I born to be mocked and scorned by everyone?" In great anger, she ran away; and Lysander followed her, quite forgetful of his own Hermia, who was still asleep.

When Hermia awoke, she was in a sad fright at finding herself alone. She wandered about the wood, not knowing what was become of Lysander, or which way to go to seek for him. In the meantime Demetrius, not being able to find Hermia and his rival Lysander, and fatigued with his fruitless search, was observed by Oberon fast asleep. Oberon had learnt, by some questions he had asked of Puck, that he had applied the love-charm to the wrong person's eyes, and now, having found the person first intended, he touched the eye-lids of the sleeping Demetrius with the love-juice, and he instantly awoke; and the first thing he saw being Helena, he, as Lysander had done before, began to address love speeches to her; and just at that moment Lysander, followed by Hermia (for through Puck's unlucky mistake it was now become Hermia's turn to run after her lover), made his appearance; and then Lysander and Demetrius, both speaking together, made love to Helena, they each one under the influence of the same potent charm.

The astonished Helena thought that Demetrius, Lysander, and her once dear friend Hermia were all in a plot together to make a jest of her.

Hermia was as much surprised as Helena: she knew not why Lysander and Demetrius, who both before loved her, were now become the lovers of Helena; and to Hermia the matter seemed to be no jest.

The ladies, who before had always been the dearest of friends, now fell to high words together.

While Helena and Hermia were speaking to each other, Demetrius and Lysander left them, to fight together in the wood for the love of Helena.

When they found the gentlemen had left them, they departed, and once more wandered weary in the wood in search of their lovers.

As soon as they were gone, the fairy king, who with little Puck had been listening to their quarrels, said to him, "This is your negligence, Puck; or did you do this wilfully?" "Believe me, king of shadows," answered Puck, "it was a mistake: did not you tell me. I should know the man by his Athenian garments? However, I am not sorry this has happened, for I think their jangling makes excellent sport."—"You heard," said Oberon, "that Demetrius and Lysander are gone to seek a convenient place to fight in. I command you to overhang the night with a thick fog, and lead these quarrelsome lovers so astray in the dark that they shall not be able to find each other. Counterfeit each of their voices to the other, and with bitter taunts provoke them to follow you, while they think it is their rival's tongue they hear. See you do this till they are so weary they can go no farther; and when you find they are asleep, drop the juice of this other flower into Lysander's eyes, and when he awakes he will forget his new love for Helena, and return to his old passion for Hermia; and then the two fair ladies may each one be happy with the man she loves, and they will think all that has passed a vexatious dream. About this quickly, Puck, and I will go and see what sweet love my Titania has found."

Titania was still sleeping, and Oberon, seeing a clown near her who had lost his way in the wood, and was likewise asleep: "This fellow," said he, "shall be my Titania's true-love"; and, clapping an ass's head over the clown's, it seemed to fit him as well as if it had grown upon his own shoulders. Although Oberon fixed the ass's head on very gently, it awakened him, and rising up, unconscious of what Oberon had done to him, he went towards the bower where the fairy queen slept.

"Ah! What angel is that I see?" said Titania, opening her eyes, and the juice of the little purple flower beginning to take effect: "are you as wise as you are beautiful?"

"Why, mistress," said the foolish clown, "if I have wit enough to find the way out of this wood, I have enough to serve my turn."

"Out of the wood do not desire to go," said the enamoured queen. "I am a spirit of no common rate. I love you. Go with me, and I will give you fairies to attend upon you." She then called four of her fairies: their names were Peaseblossom, Cobweb, Moth, and Mustard-seed.

"Attend," said the queen, "upon this sweet gentleman; hop in his walks, and gambol in his sight: feed him with grapes and apricots, and steal for him the honey-bags from the bees. Come, sit with me," said she to the clown, "and let me play with your amiable hairy cheeks, my beautiful ass! and kiss your fair large ears, my gentle joy!"

When the fairy king saw the clown sleeping in the arms of his queen, he advanced within her sight, and reproached her with having lavished her favours upon an ass.

This she could not deny, as the clown was then sleeping within her arms, with his ass's head crowned by her with flowers.

When Oberon had teased her for some time, he again demanded the changeling boy, which she, ashamed of being discovered by her lord with her new favourite, did not dare to refuse him.

Oberon, having thus obtained the little boy he had so long wished for to be his page, took pity on the disgraceful situation into which, by his merry contrivance, he had brought his Titania, and threw some of the juice of the other flower into her eyes; and the fairy queen immediately recovered her senses, and wondered at her late dotage, saying how she now loathed the sight of the strange monster.

Oberon likewise took the ass's head from off the clown, and left him to finish his nap with his own fool's head upon his shoulders.

Oberon and his Titania being now perfectly reconciled, he related to her the history of the lovers, and their midnight quarrels; and she agreed to go with him, and see the end of their adventures.

The fairy king and queen found the lovers and their fair ladies, at no great distance from each other, sleeping on a grass plot: for

Puck, to make amends for his former mistake, had contrived with the utmost diligence to bring them all to the same spot, unknown to each other; and he had carefully removed the charm from off the eyes of Lysander with the antidote the fairy king gave to him.

Hermia first awoke, and finding her lost Lysander asleep so near her, was looking at him and wondering at his strange inconstancy. Lysander presently opening his eyes, and seeing his dear Hermia, recovered his reason which the fairy charm had before clouded, and with his reason his love for Hermia; and they began to talk over the adventures of the night, doubting if these things had really happened, or if they had both been dreaming the same bewildering dream.

Helena and Demetrius were by this time awake, and a sweet sleep having quieted Helena's disturbed and angry spirits, she listened with delight to the professions of love which Demetrius still made to her, and which, to her surprise as well as pleasure, she began to perceive were sincere.

These fair night-wandering ladies, now no longer rivals, became once more true friends; all the unkind words which had passed were forgiven, and they calmly consulted together what was best to be done in their present situation. It was soon agreed that, as Demetrius had given up his pretensions to Hermia, he should endeavour to prevail upon her father to revoke the cruel sentence of death which had been passed against her. Demetrius was preparing to return to Athens for this friendly purpose, when they were surprised with the sight of Egeus, Hermia's father, who came to the wood in pursuit of his runaway daughter.

When Egeus understood that Demetrius would not now marry his daughter, he no longer opposed her marriage with Lysander, but gave his consent that they should be wedded on the fourth day from that time, being the same day on which Hermia had been condemned to lose her life; and on that same day Helena joyfully agreed to marry her beloved and now faithful Demetrius.

The fairy king and queen, who were invisible spectators of this reconciliation, and now saw the happy ending of the lovers' history brought about through the good offices of Oberon, received so much pleasure, that these kind spirits resolved to celebrate the approaching nuptials with sports and revels throughout their fairy kingdom.

LITTLE BROTHER AND SISTER

By JACOB *and* WILHELM GRIMM

This story of bewitched pools and of spells cast by a stepmother who was a witch with an ugly one-eyed daughter of her own is another tale in which the power of true love proves too strong for the forces of evil and dark deceit. Only after long and painful separation were the brother and sister truly united, but they were happy because the spells and bewitchment had in no way lessened their deep affection for each other.

THERE was once a little Brother who took his Sister by the hand, and said, "Since our own dear mother's death we have not had one happy hour; our stepmother beats us every day, and, if we come near her, kicks us away with her foot. Our food is the hard crusts of bread which are left, and even the dog under the table fares better than we, for he often gets a nice morsel. Come, let us wander forth into the wide world."

So the whole day long they travelled over meadows, fields, and stony roads, and when it rained the Sister said, "It is heaven crying in sympathy."

By evening they came into a large forest, and were so wearied with grief, hunger, and their long walk that they laid themselves down in a hollow tree and went to sleep. When they awoke the next morning the sun had already risen high in the heavens, and its beams made the tree so hot that the little boy said to his Sister, "I am so thirsty, if I knew where there was a brook I would go and drink. Ah! I think I hear one running"; and so saying, he got up, and, taking his Sister's hand, they went in search of the brook.

The wicked stepmother, however, was a witch, and had witnessed the departure of the two children; so, sneaking after them secretly, as is the habit of witches, she had enchanted all the springs in the forest.

Presently they found a brook which ran trippingly over the pebbles, and the Brother would have drunk out of it, but the

Sister heard how it said, as it ran along, "Who drinks of me will become a tiger!"

So the Sister exclaimed, "I pray you, Brother, drink not, or you will become a tiger, and tear me to pieces!" So the Brother did not drink, although his thirst was so great, and he said, "I will wait till the next brook."

As they came to the second, the Sister heard it say, "Who drinks of me becomes a wolf!" The Sister ran up crying, "Brother, do not, pray do not drink, or you will become a wolf and eat me up!" Then the Brother did not drink, saying, "I will wait until we come to the next spring, but then I must drink. You may say what you will; my thirst is much too great."

Just as they reached the third brook the Sister heard the voice saying, "Who drinks of me will become a fawn—who drinks of me will become a fawn!" So the Sister said, "Oh, my Brother! do not drink, or you will be changed to a fawn, and run away from me!" But he had already kneeled down and drunk of the water, and, as the first drops passed his lips, his shape became that of a fawn.

At first the Sister cried over her changed little Brother, and he wept too, and kneeled by her very sorrowful; but at last the maiden said, "Be still, dear little Fawn, and I will never forsake you"; and, undoing her golden garter, she put it round his neck, and weaving rushes, made a white girdle to lead him with. This she tied to him, and, taking the other end in her hand, she led him away, and they travelled deeper and deeper into the forest.

After they had walked a long distance they came to a little hut, and the maiden, peeping in, found it empty, and thought, "Here we can stay and dwell."

Then she looked for leaves and moss to make a soft couch for the Fawn; and every morning she went out and collected roots and berries and nuts for herself, and tender grass for the Fawn, which he ate out of her hand, and played happily around her. In the evening, when the Sister was tired and had said her prayers, she laid her head upon the back of the Fawn, which served for a pillow, on which she slept soundly. Had but the Brother regained his own proper form, their life would have been happy indeed.

Thus they dwelt in this wilderness, and some time had elapsed when it happened that the King of the country held a great hunt in the forest; and now resounded through the trees the blowing of horns, the barking of dogs, and the lusty cries of the hunters, so that the little Fawn heard them, and wanted very much to join.

"Ah!" said he to his Sister, "let me go to the hunt; I cannot restrain myself any longer." And he begged so hard that at last she consented.

"But," said she to him, "return again in the evening, for I shall shut my door against the wild huntsmen, and, that I may know you, do you knock and say, 'Sister, let me in,' and if you do not speak I shall not open the door."

As soon as she had said this, the little Fawn sprang off, quite glad and merry in the fresh breeze. The King and his huntsmen perceived the beautiful animal, and pursued him; but they could not catch him, and when they thought they had him for certain, he sprang away over the bushes and got out of sight.

Just as it was getting dark he ran up to the hut, and, knocking, said, "Sister mine, let me in." Then she undid the little door, and he went in, and rested all night long upon his soft couch.

The next morning the hunt was commenced again, and as soon as the little Fawn heard the horns and the tally-ho of the sportsmen he could not rest, and said, "Sister dear, open the door; I must be off." The Sister opened it, saying, "Return at evening, mind, and say the words as before."

When the King and his huntsmen saw again the Fawn with the golden necklace, they followed him close, but he was too nimble and quick for them. The whole day long they kept up with him, but towards evening the huntsmen made a circle round him, and one wounded him slightly in the foot behind, so that he could only run slowly.

Then one of them slipped after him to the little hut, and heard him say, "Sister dear, open the door," and saw that the door was opened and immediately shut behind. The huntsman, having observed all this, went and told the King what he had seen and heard, and he said, "On the morrow I will once more pursue him."

The Sister, however, was terribly frightened when she saw that her Fawn was wounded, and, washing off the blood, she put herbs upon the foot, and said, "Go and rest upon your bed, dear Fawn, that the wound may heal." It was so slight that the next morning he felt nothing of it and when he heard the hunting cries outside he exclaimed, "I cannot stop away—I must be there, and none shall catch me so easily again!" The Sister wept very much, and told him, "Soon they will kill you and I shall be here all alone in this forest, forsaken by all the world: I cannot let you go."

"I shall die here in vexation," answered the Fawn, "if you do not; for when I hear the horn I think I shall jump out of my skin."

The Sister, finding she could not prevent him, opened the door with a heavy heart, and the Fawn jumped out, quite delighted, into the forest. As soon as the King perceived him, he said to his huntsmen, "Follow him all day long till the evening, but let no one do him an injury." When the sun had set the King asked his huntsmen to show him the hut, and as they came to it he knocked at the door, and said, "Let me in, dear Sister."

Then the door was opened, and, stepping in, the King saw a maiden more beautiful than he had ever before seen. She was frightened when she saw not her Fawn but a man step in who had a golden crown upon his head.

But the King, looking at her with a friendly glance, reached her his hand, saying, "Will you go with me to my castle, and be my dear wife?" "Oh, yes," replied the maiden; "but the Fawn must go too: him I will never forsake." The King replied, "He shall remain with you as long as you live, and shall want for nothing." In the meantime the Fawn had come in, and the Sister, binding the girdle to him, again took it in her hand, and led him away with her out of the hut.

The King took the beautiful maiden upon his horse and rode to his castle, where the wedding was celebrated with great splendour, and she became Queen, and they lived together a long time; while the Fawn was taken care of, and lived well, playing about the castle garden.

The wicked stepmother, however, on whose account the children had wandered forth into the world, supposed that long ago the Sister had been torn to pieces by the wild beasts, and the little Brother hunted to death in his Fawn's shape by the hunters. As soon, therefore, as she heard how happy they had become, and how everything prospered with them, envy and jealousy were roused in her heart and left her no peace; and she was always thinking in what way she could work misfortune to them.

Her own daughter, who was as ugly as night, and had but one eye, for which she was continually reproached, said, "The luck of being a queen has never yet happened to me."

"Be quiet now," said the old woman, "and make yourself contented: when the time comes I shall be at hand."

As soon, then, as a beautiful little boy was born, which happened when the King was out hunting, the old witch took the form of a chambermaid, and got into the room where the Queen was lying, and said to her, "The bath is ready, which will restore you and give you fresh strength; be quick, before it gets cold." Her daughter being at hand, they carried the weak Queen between them into the room, and laid her in the bath, and then, shutting the door to, they ran off; but first they had made up an immense fire in the stove, which must soon suffocate the young Queen.

When this was done the old woman took her daughter, and, putting a cap on her, laid her in the Queen's place. She gave her, too, the form and appearance of the real Queen as far as she could; but she could not restore the lost eye, and, so that the King might not notice it, she turned her upon that side where there was no eye.

When he came home at evening and heard that a son was born to him, he was much delighted, and prepared to go to his wife's bedside to see how she did; so the old woman called out in a great hurry, "For your life, do not undraw the curtains; the Queen must not yet see the light, and must be kept quiet." So the King went away.

When midnight came and everyone was asleep, the nurse, who sat by herself, wide awake, near the cradle in the nursery, saw the door open and the true Queen come in. She took the child in her arms and rocked it a while, and then, shaking up its pillow, laid it down in its cradle, and covered it over again. She did not forget the Fawn either, but, going to the corner where he was, stroked his back, and then went silently out at the door.

In the morning the nurse asked the guards if anyone had passed into the castle during the night, but they answered, "No, we have seen nobody." For many nights afterwards she came constantly, and never spoke a word; and the nurse saw her always, but she would not trust herself to speak about it to anyone.

When some time had passed away, the Queen one night began to speak, and said:

"How fares my child, how fares my fawn?
Twice more will I come, but never again."

The nurse made no reply, but, when she had disappeared, went to the King and told him all. The King exclaimed, "Oh, heavens! what does this mean? The next night I myself will watch by the child."

In the evening he went into the nursery, and about midnight the Queen appeared, and said:

"How fares my child, how fares my fawn?
Once more will I come, but never again."

And she nursed the child as she was used to do, and then disappeared. The King dared not speak; but he watched the following night, and this time she said:

"How fares my child, how fares my fawn?
This time have I come, but never again."

At these words the King could hold back no longer, but sprang up, and said, "You can be no other than my dear wife!" Then she answered, "Yes, I am your dear wife!" and at that moment her life was restored by God's mercy, and she was again as beautiful and charming as ever. She told the King the fraud which the witch and her daughter had practised upon him, and he had them both tried and sentence pronounced against them. The daughter was taken into the forest, but the old witch was burned. And as soon as she was reduced to ashes the little Fawn was unbewitched, and received again his human form; and the Brother and Sister lived happily together to the end of their days.

ENTER AN ANGEL

By CHARLES READE

Mr. Triplet, an unsuccessful dramatist, attempts to dash off a comedy for Mrs. Woffington, a popular actress and the toast of London. However, he finds that his invalid wife and brood of hungry children with classical names do not make for peace of mind. He calls on heaven to send an angel to help him, and an angel duly appears, accompanied by Pompey, her small black servant. This story is taken from "Peg Woffington."

JAMES TRIPLET, water in his eye, but fire in his heart, went home. Arrived there, he anticipated curiosity by informing all hands he should answer no questions. Only in the intervals of a work, which was to take the family out of all its troubles, he should gradually unfold a tale, verging on the marvellous—a tale whose only fault was, that fiction, by which alone the family could hope to be great, paled beside it. He then seized some sheets of paper, fished out some old dramatic sketches, and a list of *dramatis personæ*, prepared years ago, and plunged into a comedy.

"Wife!" said Triplet, "don't put me into a frame of mind in which successful comedies are not written." He scribbled away; but his wife's despondency told upon the man of disappointments. Then he stuck fast; then he became fidgety.

"Do keep those children quiet!" said the father.

"Hush, my dears," said the mother; "let your father write. Comedy seems to give you more trouble than tragedy, James," added she soothingly.

"Yes," was his answer. "Sorrow comes somehow, more natural to me; but for all that I have got a bright thought, Mrs. Triplet. Listen all of you. You see, Jane, they are all at a sumptuous banquet, all the *dramatis personæ*, except the poet."

Triplet went on writing, and reading his work out: "music, sparkling wine, massive plate, rosewater in the hand-glasses, soup, fish—shall I have three sorts of fish? I will; they are cheap in this market. Ah! Fortune, you wretch, here at least I am your master, and I'll make you know it—venison," wrote Triplet with a malicious grin, "game, pickles and provocatives in the centre of the table, then up jumps one of the guests, and says he——"

"Oh dear, I am so hungry."

This was not from the comedy, but from one of the boys.

"And so am I," cried a girl.

"That is an absurd remark, Lysimachus," said Triplet, with a suspicious calmness.

"How can a boy be hungry three hours after breakfast?"

"But, father, there was no breakfast for breakfast."

"Now I ask you, Mrs. Triplet," appealed the author, "how am I to write comic scenes if you let Lysimachus and Roxalana here, put the heavy business in every five minutes?"

"Forgive them; the poor things are hungry."

"Then let them be hungry in another room," said the irritated scribe. "They shan't cling round my pen, and paralyze it just when it is going to make all our fortunes; but you women," snapped Triplet the Just, "have no consideration for people's feelings. Send them all to bed; every man jack of them!"

Finding the conversation taking this turn, the brats raised an unanimous howl.

Triplet darted a fierce glance at them. "Hungry, hungry," cried he; "is that a proper expression to use before a father who is sitting down here all gaiety (scratching wildly with his pen) and hilarity, (scratch) to write a com—com——" he choked a moment; then in a very different voice, all sadness and tenderness, he said: "Where's the youngest—where's Lucy? As if I didn't know you are hungry."

Lucy came to him directly. He took her on his knee, pressed her gently to his side, and wrote silently. The others were still.

"Father," said Lucy, aged five, the germ of a woman, "I am not tho very hungry."

"And I am not hungry at all," said bluff Lysimachus, taking his sister's cue; then, going upon his own tact, he added: "I had a great piece of bread and butter yesterday!"

"Wife, they will drive me mad!" and he dashed at the paper.

The second boy explained to his mother, *sotto voce:* "Mother, he *made* us hungry out of his book."

"It is a beautiful book," said Lucy. "Is it a cookery book?"

Triplet roared, "Do you hear that?" inquired he, all trace of ill-humour gone.

"Ah!" sighed he, "if my friend Mrs. Woffington would but drop these stupid comedies and take to tragedy, this house would soon be all smiles."

"Oh, James!" replied Mrs. Triplet, almost peevishly, "how can you expect anything but fine words from that woman. You won't believe what all the world says. You will trust to your own good heart."

"I haven't a good heart," said the poor, honest fellow. "I spoke like a brat to you just now."

"Never mind, James," said the woman; "I wonder how you put up with me at all—a sick, useless creature. I am such a weight round your neck."

The man made no answer, but he put Lucy gently down, and went to the woman, and took her forehead to his bosom, and held it there; and after a while, returned with silent energy to his comedy.

"Play us a tune on the fiddle, father."

"Ay, do husband. That helps you often in your writing."

Lysimachus brought him the fiddle, and Triplet essayed a merry tune; but it came out so doleful, that he shook his head, and laid the instrument down. Music must be in the heart, or it will come out of the fingers—notes, not music.

"No," said he; "let us be serious and finish this comedy slap off. Perhaps it hitches because I forgot to invoke the comic muse. She must be a black-hearted jade, if she doesn't come with merry notions to a poor devil, starving in the midst of his hungry little ones."

"We are past help from heathen goddesses," said the woman. "We must pray to heaven to look down upon us and the children."

The man rose, and flung his pen upon the floor.

"Have we given honesty a fair trial—yes or no?"

"No!" said the woman, without a moment's hesitation; "not till we die, as we have lived. Heaven is higher than the sky; children," said she, "the sky is above the earth, and heaven is higher than the sky; and Heaven is just."

"I suppose it is so," said the man, a little cowed by her. "Everybody says so. I think so, at bottom, myself; but I can't see it. I want to see it, but I can't!" cried he, fiercely. "Have my children offended Heaven? They will starve—they will die! If I was Heaven, I'd be just, and send an angel to take these children's part. They cried to me for bread—I had no bread; so I gave them hard words. The moment I had done that, I knew it was all over. God knows, it took a long while to break my heart; but it is broken at last; quite, quite broken!"

And the poor thing laid his head upon the table, and sobbed, beyond all power of restraint. The children cried round him, scarce knowing why; and Mrs. Triplet could only say, "My poor husband!" and prayed and wept upon the couch where she lay.

It was at this juncture that a lady, who had knocked gently and unheard, opened the door, and with a light step entered the apartment; but no sooner had she caught sight of Triplet's anguish, than saying hastily, "Stay, I forgot something," she made as hasty an exit.

This gave Triplet a moment to recover himself; and Mrs. Woffington, whose lynx-eye had comprehended all at a glance, and who had determined at once what line to take, came flying in again, saying:

"Wasn't somebody inquiring for an angel? Here I am. See, Mr. Triplet," and she showed him a note, which said, 'Madame, you are an angel.' "From a perfect stranger," explained she; "so it must be true."

"Mrs. Woffington," said Mr. Triplet to his wife.

Mrs. Woffington planted herself in the middle of the floor, and with a comical glance, setting her arms akimbo, uttered a shrill whistle.

"Now you will see another angel—there are two sorts of them."

Pompey came in with a basket: she took it from him.

"Lucifer, avant!" cried she, in a terrible tone, that drove him to the wall; "and wait outside the door," added she, conversationally.

"I heard you were ill, ma'am, and I have brought you some physic—black draughts from Burgundy"; and she smiled. And recovered from their first surprise, young and old began to thaw beneath that witching, irresistible smile. "Mrs. Triplet, I have come to give your husband a sitting; will you allow me to eat my little luncheon with you? I am so hungry." Then she clapped her hands, and in ran Pompey. She sent him for a pie she professed to have fallen in love with at the corner of the street.

"Mother," said Alcibiades, "will the lady give me a bit of her pie?"

"Hush! you rude boy!" cried the mother.

"She is not much of a lady if she does not," cried Mrs. Woffington. "Now, children, who helps me to lay the cloth?"

"I!"

"And I!" (The children run to the cupboard.)

MRS. TRIPLET (half rising): "Madam, I—can't think of allowing you."

MRS. WOFFINGTON replied: "Sit down, madam, or I must use brute force. If you are ill, be ill—till I make you well. Twelve plates, quick! Twenty-four knives, quicker! Forty-eight forks, quickest!" She met the children with the cloth and laid it; then she met them again and laid knives and forks, all at full gallop, which mightily excited the bairns. Pompey came in with the pie, Mrs. Woffington took it and set it before Triplet.

MRS. WOFFINGTON: "Your coat, Mr. Triplet, if you please."

MR. TRIPLET: "My coat, madam!"

MRS. WOFFINGTON: "Yes, off with it—there's a hole in it—and carve." Then she whipped to the other end of the table and stitched like wild-fire. "Eat away, children! now is your time, when once I begin, the pie will soon end; I do everything so quick."

ROXALANA: "The lady sews quicker than you, mother."

WOFFINGTON: "Bless the child, don't come so near my sword-arm; the needle will go into your eye, and out at the back of your head."

This nonsense made the children giggle.

"The needle will be lost—the child no more—enter undertaker—house turned topsy-turvy—father shows Woffington to the door—off she goes with a face as long and dismal as some people's comedies—no names—crying fine cha-ney oran-ges."

The children, all but Lucy, screeched with laughter.

Lucy said, gravely:

"Mother, the lady is very funny."

"You will be as funny, when you are as well paid for it."

This just hit poor Trip's notion of humour; and he began to choke, with his mouth full of pie.

"James, take care," said Mrs. Triplet, sad and solemn.

James looked up.

"I am sure, James," said the poor, good, lackadaisical woman, "if I don't laugh, it is not for want of the will. I used to be a very hearty laugher," whined she; "but I haven't laughed this two years."

"Oh, indeed!" said the Woffington. "Then the next two years you shall do nothing else."

"Ah, madam!" said Triplet. "That passes the art, even of the great comedian."

"Does it?" said the actress, coolly.

LUCY: "She is not a comedy lady. You don't ever cry, pretty lady?"

WOFFINGTON (ironically): "Oh! of course not."

LUCY (confidentially): "Comedy is crying. Father cried all the time he was writing his one."

Triplet turned as red as fire.

"Hold your tongue," said he; "I was bursting with merriment. Wife, our children talk too much; they put their noses into everything, and criticise their own father."

"Unnatural offspring!" laughed the visitor.

"And when they take up a notion, Socrates couldn't convince them to the contrary. For instance, madam, all this morning they thought fit to assume that they were starving."

"So we were," said Lysimachus, "until the angel came; and the devil went for the pie."

"There—there—there! Now, you mark my words; we shall never get that idea out of their heads——"

"Until," said Mrs. Woffington, lumping a huge cut of pie into Roxalana's plate, "we put a very different idea into their stomachs." This and the look she cast on Mrs. Triplet, fairly caught that good, though sombre personage. She giggled; put her hand to her face, and said: "I'm sure I ask your pardon, ma'am?"

It was no use; the comedian had determined they should all laugh, and they were made to laugh. Then she rose, and showed them how to drink healths *à la Française*; and keen were her little admirers, to touch her glass with theirs. And the pure wine she had brought did Mrs. Triplet much good, too; though not so much as the music and sunshine of her face and voice. Then, when their stomachs were full of good food, and the soul of the grape tingled in their veins, and their souls glowed under her great magnetic power, she suddenly seized the fiddle, and showed them another of her enchantments. She put it on her knee, and played a tune that would have made gout, cholic, and phthisick dance upon their last legs. She played to the eye as well as to the ear, with such a smart gesture of the bow, and such a radiance of face as she looked at them, that whether the music came out of her wooden shell, or her horsehair wand, or her bright self, seemed doubtful. They pranced on their chairs; they could not keep still. She jumped up; so did they. She gave a wild Irish horroo. She put the fiddle in Triplet's hand.

"The wind that shakes the barley, ye divil!" cried she.

Triplet played like Paganini, or an intoxicated demon. Woffington covered the buckle in gallant style; she danced, the children danced. Triplet fiddled and danced, and flung his limbs in wild dislocation; the wine-glasses danced; and last, Mrs. Triplet was observed to be bobbing about on her sofa, in a monstrous absurd way, droning out the tune, and playing her hands with mild enjoyment, all to herself. Woffington pointed out this pantomimic soliloquy to the two boys, with a glance full of fiery meaning. This was enough: with a fiendish yell, they fell upon her, and tore her, shrieking, off the sofa. And lo! when she was once launched, she danced up to her husband, and set to him with a meek deliberation, that was as funny as any part of the scene. So then the mover of all this slipped on one side, and let the stone of merriment roll—and roll it did; there was no swimming, sprawling, or irrelevant frisking; their feet struck the ground for every note of the fiddle, pat as its echo, their faces shone, their hearts leaped, and their poor frozen natures came out, and warmed themselves at the glowing melody; a great sunbeam had come into their abode, and these human motes danced in it.

The wonder of these worthy people soon changed to gratitude. Mrs. Woffington stopped their mouths at once.

"No, no!" cried she; "if you really love me, no scenes: I hate them. Tell these brats to kiss me, and let me go."

The children needed no bidding; they clustered round her, and poured out their innocent hearts as children only do.

"I shall pray for you after father and mother," said one.

"I shall pray for you after daily bread," said Lucy, "because we were *tho* hungry till you came!"

"My poor children!" cried Woffington, and sensitive to children, she fairly melted as she embraced them.

MAMA ROSA HOLDS COURT

By W. H. G. KINGSTON

The narrator of this story is a young Englishman who has gone to South America. In the city of Lima, in Peru, he discovers the slave queen of the Mandingoes, old Mama Rosa, who holds her court regularly with all the dignity and solemnity befitting her regal status. But, like Cinderella, when the court is over, she returns to her young charges, for she is a children's nurse. This story is taken from "Manco, the Peruvian Chief."

THE Indians who reside in Lima endeavour to imitate the Spanish creoles in dress and manners. They are chiefly engaged in making gold and silver lace, and other delicate gold work; while some are tailors and vendors of fruit, flowers, and vegetables.

The African negroes are numerous, and, though slaves, are well treated by their masters. Those of the same tribe or nation find each other out, and form a sort of club or association, called a *confradia.* They generally hold their meetings in the suburbs on a Sunday afternoon. At the time I speak of, there was an old slave-woman who had lived in a family for nearly fifty years, and who was the acknowledged queen of the Mandingoes. She was called Mama Rosa; and I remember seeing her seated at the porch of her master's house, when a number of her black subjects who were passing knelt before her, and kissing her hand in a true loyal fashion, asked her blessing. Her mistress had given her a silver sceptre, and the young ladies of the family would lend her jewels, artificial flowers, and other ornaments; bedecked in which, on certain days, she would be carried off by her subjects in great state, her sceptre borne before her, to the house of the *confradia,* where a throne was prepared to receive her. Here she held a regular court, when as much respect was shown her as to any sovereign in Europe.

While strolling out in the afternoon, I happened to pass the abode of Mama Rosa, the black queen of the Mandingoes. A large crowd of negroes were assembled before the door, decked in all the finery they could command. They wore garments of all fashions and of every gay-coloured hue imaginable—the women with wreaths of flowers round their heads, and necklaces of coral and beads on their necks and arms. There were silk coats a century old, and round jackets, and shirts, blue, red, yellow, and white; and naval and military uniforms curiously altered to suit the taste of the wearer—not an uncommon mode of wearing trousers being round the neck instead of on the legs, with the upper part hanging down the back, and the lower on either side in front like a shawl. Some acted the part of guards of honour, and others appeared as ministers of state. A select body bore a sort of palanquin, or litter, which they placed before the door till Mama Rosa descended into the street, when she was conducted with great ceremony to her seat in it. She was very old and ugly; but her subjects did not love her the less for that. Her dress was resplendent with flowers and jewels, and all the ornaments she could hang about herself.

A band was in attendance, the instruments of which were somewhat curious. The most important was a drum, made of a section of the trunk of a tree, with the skin of a kid drawn over one end. Another was a bow, the string being of catgut, which was struck with a small cane. A third was the jaw-bone of an ass with the teeth loose in the socket, and which, when struck by the hand, made a capital rattle. If there was not much harmony in the music, there was plenty of noise, which was not a little increased by the voices of a party of singers, who frisked about before the sovereign's state carriage as she advanced. The sceptre-bearer stepped out with her majesty's insignia of office in his arms, looking back as he did so to ascertain that the queen was following. Her people shouted, the palanquin-bearers moved on, the band struck up a negro sort of *God Save the Queen*, and away they all went towards the quarters of the *confradia*. I followed to see the end of the ceremony. After passing through a number of narrow and somewhat dirty streets, with the houses built of bamboo and mud, we reached the palace, for so I may call it. The hall was of good size, and the walls were ornamented with what I suppose were intended for likenesses of other sable monarchs. If they were correct, I am compelled to own that the royal Rosa's predecessors, both ladies and gentlemen, were a very ugly set of personages. The band played louder, and the people shouted more vehemently, as her majesty ascended the throne at the end of the hall. She seemed perfectly at home, and sat down with right royal dignity.

The sceptre-bearer presented the sceptre. She seized it in her right hand and waved it around to command silence. Her ministers of state formed on either side of the throne, and doffed their cocked hats, or straw hats, or hats with three corners, or their red caps, or whatever covering adorned their heads. She then made them a speech, but as I did not know a word of the Mandingo language, I was not much the wiser for it. When it was concluded, her Chancellor of the Exchequer made a report of the financial condition of her kingdom, while her Home Secretary described the good behaviour of her subjects, and her Minister for Foreign Affairs assured her that she was on good terms with all her neighbours. This part of the business being concluded, they squatted down about the throne, and, filling their pipes with tobacco, began to smoke; while her other subjects, one by one, stepped forward, and, dropping on both knees, each one gave her hand a kiss, not bashfully, as if they were afraid of it, but with a hearty smack, which sounded through the hall. Her ancient majesty in return bestowed a blessing on them, and told them all to behave well; and especially to be contented with their lot, if their masters and mistresses treated them kindly. After the speech, all the people shouted, and the musicians struck up a magnificent flourish with the drums, and the bows, and the jaw-bones of the asses; and if there was not much harmony, there was a great deal of enthusiasm. Several slaves then stepped forward, and preferred complaints against their masters for ill-treatment.

The queen listened to them attentively, and, I thought, seemed to judge their cases very judiciously. To some she replied, that it was through their own neglect of their duty that they had been punished. Others she advised to bear their ill-treatment patiently, and to endeavour, by zeal and attention to the wishes of their masters, to soften their tempers, and to gain their goodwill; but there were two or three who had been treated so barbarously and unjustly, that she promised them that the *confradia* should make every effort to purchase their freedom.

"You shall be freed," she observed; "but remember, you will have to work as hard as you have ever before done, to repay the *confradia* the money they have advanced for your emancipation."

These were not exactly her words, but what she said was to this effect.

The serious business of the day being over, the negroes and negresses set to work to dance; and though I cannot speak much of the grace they exhibited, I never saw any human beings frisk and jump about with so much agility. Who would have thought they were for the most part slaves, groaning under their chains? Never did dancers enter more thoroughly into the spirit of dancing. The black beaux did not waste their time in talking or doing the amiable to their sable partners; nor did the latter seem to expect any such attention—they came to dance, and their great aim seemed to be to get through as much of it as the time would allow. As I looked on I could scarcely refrain from rushing into the sable throng, and joining them in their frisks and jumps; though, I dare say, had I done so, they would have considered me a very contemptible performer. At length the queen's chamberlain clapped his hands, and gave notice that the court must break up, as her majesty was desirous of retiring to attend to her duties in putting to bed the children of her mistress to whom she was nurse. The bearers of her palanquin came forward, the queen stepped into it, the sceptre-bearer marched before it, the band struck up their loudest tune, the people shouted till they were hoarse, and the procession returned in due state to old Mama Rosa's abode; where, like Cinderella when the clock had struck twelve, she was again converted into the old negro nurse.

A MOUNTAIN CHALET

By FREDERIC W. FARRAR

Edward Kennedy and Violet, the sister of his best friend at college, Julian Home, go with Julian and other friends from their Swiss hotel to the top of the Schilthorn, a mountain popular with tourists. On the way back Edward and Violet become separated from the others in the party. They lose their way and are overtaken by a sudden mountain storm. In the gloom they perceive a light, and the lost travellers arrive at a mountain chalet, or hut, where they meet a strange reception, and where Edward's vigilance is more than justified by what happens. This story is taken from "Julian Home."

WHILE Kennedy walked on with Violet in silence more sweet than speech, they fell into a dreamy mood, and wandered on half oblivious of things around them, while deeper and deeper the shades of twilight began to cast their gloom over the hills.

"Look, Violet, I mean Miss Home; the moon is in crescent, and we shall have a pleasant evening walk, won't it be delightful?"

"Yes," she murmured; but neither of them observed that the clouds were gathering thick and fast, and obscured all except a few struggling glimpses of scattered stars.

They came to a sort of stile formed by two logs of wood laid across the gap in a stone wall, and Kennedy, vaulting over it, gave her his hand.

"Surely," she said, stopping timidly for a moment, "we did not pass over this in coming, did we?"

Kennedy looked back. "No," he said, "I don't remember it; but no doubt it has been put up merely for the night to prevent the cattle from going astray."

They went forward, but a deeper and deeper misgiving filled Violet's mind that they had chosen a wrong road.

"I think," she said with a fluttered voice, "that the path looks much narrower than it did this morning. Do you see the others?"

They both strained their eyes through the gloom, now rendered more thick than ever by the dark driving clouds, but they could see no trace of their companions, and though they listened intently, not the faintest sound of voices reached their eager ears.

They spoke no word, but a few steps farther brought them to a towering rock around the base of which the path turned, and then seemed to cease abruptly in a mass of loose shale. It was too clear now. They had lost their road and turned, whilst they were indulging those golden fancies, into a mere cattle-path worn by the numerous herds of goats and oxen, the music of whose jangling bells still came to them now and then in low sweet snatches from the pastures of the valley and hill.

What was to be done? They were alone amid the all but unbroken silence and the eternal solitudes of the now terrible mountain. The darkness began to brood heavily above them; no one was in sight, and when Kennedy shouted there was no answer, but only an idle echo of his voice. Sheets of mist were sweeping round them, and at length the gusts of wind drove into their faces cold swirls of splashing rain.

"Oh, Mr. Kennedy, what can we do? Do shout again."

Once more Kennedy sent his voice ringing through the mist and darkness, and once more there was no answer, except that to their now excited senses it seemed as if a scream of mocking laughter was carried back to them upon the wind. And clinging tightly to his arm, as he wrapped her in his plaid to shelter her from the wet, she again cried, "Oh, Edward, what must we do?"

Even in that fearful situation—alone on the mountain, in the storm—he felt within him a thrill of strength and pleasure that she called him Edward, and that she clung so confidently upon his arm.

"Dare you stay here, Violet," he asked, "while I run forward and try to catch some glimpse of a light?"

"Oh, I dare not, I dare not!" she cried. "You might miss your way in coming back to me, and I should be alone."

Thunder began to growl, and while the sounds of it were beaten back with long, loud, hollow buffetings from the rocks on every side, the blue and winged flash of lightning glittered before their eyes, cleaving a rift with dazzling and vivid intensity amid the purple gloom.

"Stay here but one instant, Violet—Miss Home," he said; "I will climb this rock to see if any light is near."

He bounded actively up the rock, reckless of danger, and gazed from the summit into the night. For a second another flash of lightning half blinded him with its lurid glare, but when he was again accustomed to the darkness he saw a dull glimmer in the distance, and supposing it to come from the hotel, sprang down the rock again to Violet's side.

"This way," he said, "dear Violet; I see a light, and from the

direction of it, I think it must be from our hotel. Keep up courage, and we shall soon reach it."

Dangerous as it was to hurry over the wet and slippery shale, and down the steep sides of the rugged hill, Kennedy half drew, half carried her along with swift steps towards the place from which the dim light still seemed to allure them by its wavering and uncertain flicker. The light came from the ragged windows of an old tumbledown tenement, built of pine-boards which the sun had dried and charred until they looked black and strained and forbidding. Going up the rotten wooden steps to the door, and looking through the broken windows, Kennedy saw two men seated, smoking, with a flaring tallow candle between them.

"Must we go in there?" asked Violet; and Kennedy observed how her arm and the tones of her voice were trembling with agitation.

"Isn't it better than staying out in this dreadful storm?" said Kennedy. "The Swiss are an honest people, and I dare say these are herdsmen who will gladly give us food and shelter."

Their voices had roused the inmates of the chalet, and both the men jumped up from their seats, while a large and fierce dog also shook himself from sleep, and gave a low deep growl.

Kennedy knocked at the door. A gruff voice bade him enter; and as he stepped over the threshold the dog flew at him with an angry bark. Violet uttered a cry of fear, and Kennedy struck the dog a furious blow with the nobbed end of his alpenstock, which for the moment stunned the animal, while it drew down on the heads of the tired and fainting travellers some very rough expostulations.

"Can you give us shelter?" said Kennedy, who spoke German with tolerable fluency. "We have lost our way, and cannot stay out in this storm."

The man snarled an affirmative, and Violet observed with a shudder that he was an ill-looking, one-eyed fellow, with villainy stamped legibly on every feature. The other peasant looked merely stolid and dirty as he sat heavily in his place without offering to stir.

"Can't you give us some food, or at any rate some milk? We have been to the top of the Schilthorn, and are very tired."

The man brought out a huge coarse wooden bowl of goat's milk, and some sour bread; and feeling in need of food, they tried to eat and drink. While doing so, Kennedy noticed that Violet gave a perceptible start; and looking up, observed the one eye of their grim entertainer intently fixed on the gold watch-chain which hung over his silk jersey. He stared the man full in the face, finished his meal, and then asked for a candle to show the lady to her room.

"No light but this," said the Cyclops, as Kennedy mentally named him.

"Then you must lend me this."

And taking it without more ado, he went first to the cupboard from which the milk had been produced, where, seeing another dip, he coolly took it, lighted it, and pushed open the creaking door which opened on the close, damp closet which the man had indicated as the only place where Violet could sleep.

This room opened on another, rather larger; and here, putting the candle on the floor, for the room (if room it could be called) was destitute of all furniture, he spread his plaid on the ground over some straw, and said:

"Try to sleep here, Miss Home, till morning. I will keep watch in the outer room."

He shut the door, went back to the two men, looked full at them both, and, leaving them their candle, returned to the closet, where, fastening the door with his invaluable alpenstock, he sat on the ground by the entrance of Violet's room.

He felt a conviction that they had fallen into bad hands. The man's anger had first been stirred by the severe wound which Kennedy had in self-defence inflicted on the dog, and now there was too much reason to dread that his cupidity had been excited by the sight of the gold chain, and by Violet's ornaments, which gave promise that he might by this accident gain a wealthy prize.

After an interval of silence, during which he perceived that they listened at his door and were deceived by his measured breathing into a notion that he was asleep, he noticed that they put out the candle, and continued to whisper in low thick voices. He was very, very weary, his head nodded many times, and more than once he was afraid that sleep would overcome him, especially as he dared not stir or change his position; but the thought of Violet's danger, and the blaze of the lightning mingled with the yell of the wind, kept him watchful, and he spent the interminable moments in thinking how to act when the attack came.

At last, about an hour and a half after he had retired, he heard the men stir, and with a thrill of horror he detected the sound of guns being loaded. Violet's candle was yet burning, as he perceived by the faint light under her door, so he wrote on a leaf of his pocket-book in the dark, "Don't be afraid, Violet, whatever you may hear; trust in God," and noiselessly pushed it under the crevice of the door into her room.

The muffled footsteps approached, but he never varied the sound of his regular breathing. At last came a push at the door, followed by silence, and then the whisper, "He has fastened it." Still he did not stir till he observed that they were both close against the door, and were preparing to force it open. Then, guided by a swift instinctive resolution, he determined to trust to the effects of an unexpected alarm. Noiselessly moving his alpenstock, he suddenly and with all his force dashed the door open, shouted aloud, and with his utmost violence swung round the heavy iron spike. A flash, the report of a gun, and a yell of anguish instantly followed; and as Violet, in terror and excitement, threw open her door the light which streamed from it showed Kennedy in a moment that the foremost villain, startled by the sudden opposition, had accidentally fired off his gun, of which the whole contents had lodged themselves in the shoulder of his comrade. This second man had also armed himself with a chamois-gun, which slipped out of his hands as he fell wounded to the ground. Springing forward, Kennedy wrenched it out of his relaxing grasp, and presented it full at the head of the other, who, half stunned with the blow he had received from the heavy iron-shod point of the ashen alpenstock, was crouching for concealment in the corner of the chalet.

"Violet," he said, "all is now safe. These wretches are disarmed; if you like to take shelter here till the morning, I can secure you from any further attack. If you stir but an inch," he continued, addressing the unwounded man, "I will shoot you dead. Lay down your gun."

The man's one eye glared with rage and hatred, but Kennedy still held the loaded gun at his head, and he was forced sullenly to obey. Kennedy put his foot upon the gun, and was in perplexity what to do next, fearing that the wounded peasant, who was moaning heavily, might nevertheless spring at him from behind, and also momentarily dreading an attack from the dog, who kept up a sullen growl.

"Let us leave this dreadful place," said Violet, who, pale but undaunted at the horrors of the scene, had taken refuge by Kennedy's side.

"Dare you pick up and carry the gun?" he asked. "It would be dangerous to leave it in their hands."

Violet picked it up, where it lay under his feet, and then glided rapidly out of the chalet, while Kennedy slowly followed, never once taking his eye from his crouching antagonist. Before he stepped into the open air he said to the men, "If I hear but one footstep in pursuit of us, I will shoot one of you dead."

"Oh, what a relief to be in the open air once more!" said Violet as she grasped Kennedy's arm, and he cautiously led her down a rude path which was faintly marked a few hundred yards from the lonely cottage where they had been. "Are we safe now, do you think?"

"Yes, quite safe, Violet, I trust. They will not dare pursue me now that their guns are gone, and I have this loaded one in my hand."

"Dear, brave Mr. Kennedy. How shall I ever thank you enough for having saved my life so nobly? If you had not been so strong and watchful we should both have now been killed."

"I would die a thousand deaths," he whispered, "to save you from the least harm, Violet. But you are tired, you must rest here till the dawn. Sit under this rock, and cover yourself with my plaid. I will keep watch still."

She sat down wearily, and her head sank upon the rock. The storm was over: the thunder was still muttering like a baffled enemy in the distance, but the wind, after its late fury, was sobbing gently and fitfully like a repentant child. The rock gave her shelter, and after her fatigue and agitation she was sleeping peacefully, while Kennedy bowed down his head, and thanked God for the merciful protection which He had extended to them.

He had not been seated long when his eye caught the light of torches being waved at a distance in the direction of the hotel. In an instant he felt sure that Julian was come out to search for them, and, gently awakening Violet, he told her with a thrill of joy that help was at hand. The torches drew nearer the place where they were seated, and he raised a joyous shout. As yet they were too far off to hear him, but suddenly it occurred to him to fire his gun. The flash and echoing report attracted their notice; the torches grew rapidly nearer; he could almost see the dark figures of those who carried them; and now in answer to his second shout came the hurried sound of familiar voices.

THE ROAD TO LEYDEN

By ROBERT LOUIS STEVENSON

David Balfour is on his way to take up his studies in the Netherlands, and on board the good ship "Rose," which brought him to Holland from his native Scotland, he has spent a deal of his time with Catriona Drummond, on her way to meet her father after the disastrous rising of the Forty-five. They arrive in Rotterdam after it is clear that Catriona's father has failed to meet her as arranged, and young David realizes that he is the only friend she has in a strange land. Further, a pickpocket leaves them no choice but to tramp to Leyden, where David has arranged for credit. So they start their long walk on a night of black frost. This story is taken from "Catriona."

THE rattel-wagon, which is a kind of a long wagon set with benches, carried us in four hours of travel to the great city of Rotterdam. It was long past dark by then, but the streets pretty brightly lighted and thronged with wild-like, outlandish characters. I made the best face I could, for the lass's sake and my own credit; but the truth is I felt like a lost sheep, and my heart beat in my bosom with anxiety. Once or twice I inquired after the harbour or the berth of the ship *Rose*. A little after we issued forth upon an open place along the harbour.

"We shall be doing now," cries I, as soon as I spied masts. "Let us walk here by the harbour. We are sure to meet some that has the English, and at the best of it we may light upon that very ship."

We did the next best, as happened; for, about nine of the evening, whom should we walk into the arms of but Captain Sang? He told us they had made their run in the most incredible brief time, the wind holding strong till they reached port; but which means his passengers were all gone already on their further travels. It was the more gratifying to find the man friendly and wishful to assist. He made it a small affair to find some good plain family of merchants, where Catriona might harbour till the *Rose* was loaden; declared he would then blithely carry her back to Leith for nothing and see her safe; and in the meanwhile carried us to a late ordinary for the meal we stood in need of. He seemed extremely friendly, as I say, but what surprised me a good deal, rather boisterous in the bargain; and the cause of this was soon to appear. For at the ordinary, calling for Rhenish wine and drinking of it deep, he soon became unutterably tipsy. I had no resource but carry her suddenly away.

She came out of that ordinary clinging to me close. "Take me away, David," she said. "*You* keep me. I am not afraid with you."

"And have no cause, my little friend!" cried I, and could have found it in my heart to weep.

"Where will you be taking me?" she said again. "Don't leave me at all events—never leave me."

"Where am I taking you indeed?" says I, stopping, for I had been staving on ahead in mere blindness. "I must stop and think. But I'll not leave you, Catriona; the Lord do so to me, and more also, if I should fail or fash you."

She crept closer in to me by way of a reply.

"Here," I said, "is the stillest place that we have hit on yet in this busy byke of a city. Let us sit down here under yon tree and consider of our course."

That tree (which I am little like to forget) stood hard by the harbour side. It was a black night, but lights were in the houses, and nearer hand in the quiet ships; there was a shining of the city on the one hand, and a buzz hung over it of many thousands walking and talking; on the other, it was dark and the water bubbled on the sides. I spread my cloak upon a builder's stone, and made her sit there; she would have kept her hold upon me; but I wanted to think clear, disengaged myself, and paced to and fro before her, in the manner of what we call a smuggler's walk, belabouring my brains for any remedy. By the course of these scattering thoughts I was brought suddenly face to face with a remembrance that, in the heat and haste of our departure, I had left Captain Sang to pay the ordinary. At this I began to laugh out loud, for I thought the man well served; and at the same time, by an instinctive movement, carried my hand to the pocket where my money was. My purse was gone.

"You will have thought of something good," said she, observing me to pause.

At the pinch we were in, my mind became suddenly clear as a perspective glass, and I saw there was no choice of methods. I had not one doit of coin, but in my pocket-book I had still my letter on the Leyden merchant; and there was now but the one way to get to Leyden, and that was to walk on our two feet.

"Catriona," said I, "I know you're brave and I believe you're strong—do you think you could walk thirty miles on a plain road?" We found it, I believe, scarce the two thirds of that, but such was my notion of the distance.

"David," she said, "if you will just keep near, I will go anywhere and do anything. The courage of my heart, it is all broken. Do not be leaving me in this horrible country by myself, and I will do all else."

"Can you start now and march all night?" said I.

"I will do all that you can ask of me," she said, "and never ask you why."

I had matters to consider, and the first of these was to get clear of that city on the Leyden road. It proved a cruel problem; and it may have been one or two at night ere we had solved it. Once beyond the houses, there was neither moon nor stars to guide us; only the whiteness of the way in the midst and a blackness of an alley on both hands. The walking was besides made most extraordinary difficult by a plain black frost that fell suddenly in the small hours and turned that highway into one long slide.

"Well, Catriona," said I, "here we are like the king's sons and the old wives' daughters in your daft-like Highland tales. Soon we'll be going over the '*seven bens, the seven glens, and the seven mountain moors.*'" Which was a common byword or overcome in those tales of hers that had stuck in my memory.

"Ah," says she, "but here are no glens or mountains! Though I will never be denying but what the trees and some of the plain places hereabouts are very pretty. But our country is the best yet."

"I wish we could say as much for our own folk," says I.

"I will never complain of the country of my friend," said she, and spoke it out with an accent so particular that I seemed to see the look upon her face.

I caught in my breath sharp and came near falling (for my pains) on the black ice.

"I do not know what *you* think, Catriona," said I, when I was a little recovered, "but this has been the best day yet! I think shame to say it, when you have met in with such misfortunes and disfavours; but for me, it has been the best day yet."

"It was a good day when you showed me so much love," said she.

"And yet I think shame to be happy too," I went on, "and you here on the road in the black night."

"Where in the great world would I be else?" she cried. "I am thinking I am safest where I am with you."

It was an eerie employment to walk in the gross night, beholding only shadows and hearing nought but our own steps.

Before the day peeped, came on a warmish rain, and the frost was all wiped away from among our feet. I took my cloak to her and sought to hap her in the same; she bade me to keep it.

"Indeed and I will do no such thing," said I. "Here am I, a great, ugly lad that has seen all kinds of weather, and here are you a tender, pretty maid! My dear, you would not put me to a shame?"

Without more words she let me cover her; which as I was doing in the darkness, I let my hand rest a moment on her shoulder, almost like an embrace.

"You must try to be more patient of your friend," said I.

I thought she seemed to lean the least thing in the world against my bosom, or perhaps it was but fancy.

"There will be no end to your goodness," said she.

We went on again in silence; and the happiness that was in my heart was like a fire in a great chimney.

The rain passed ere day; it was but a sloppy morning as we came down into the town of Delft. The red-gabled houses made a handsome show on either hand of a canal; the servant lassies were out slestering and scrubbing at the very stones upon the public highway; smoke rose from a hundred kitchens; and it came in upon me strongly it was time to break our fasts.

"Catriona," said I, "I believe you have yet a shilling and three baubees?"

"Are you wanting it?" said she, and passed me her purse. "I am wishing it was five pounds! What will you want it for?"

"And what have we been walking for all night, like a pair of waif Egyptians?" says I. "Just because I was robbed of my purse and all I possessed in that unchancy town of Rotterdam. I will tell you of it now, because I think the worst is over, but we have still a

good tramp before us till we get to where my money is, and if you would not buy me a piece of bread, I were like to go fasting."

She looked at me with open eyes. By the light of the new day she was all black and pale for weariness, so that my heart smote me for her. But as for her, she broke out laughing.

"My torture! Are we beggars, then?" she cried. "You too? Oh, I could have wished for this same thing! And I am glad to buy your breakfast to you. But it would be pleisand if I would have had to dance to get a meal to you! For I believe they are not very well acquainted with our manner of dancing over here, and might be paying for the curiosity of that sight."

I could have kissed her for that word, not with a lover's mind, but in a heat of admiration. For it always warms a man to see a woman brave.

We got a drink of milk from a country wife but new come to the town, and in a baker's a piece of excellent, hot, sweet-smelling bread, which we ate upon the road as we went on. That road from Delft to the Hague is just five miles of a fine avenue shaded with trees, a canal on the one hand, on the other excellent pastures of cattle. It was pleasant here indeed.

"And now, Davie," said she, "what will you do with me at all events?"

"It is what we have to speak of," said I, "and the sooner yet the better. I can come by money in Leyden; that will be all well. But the trouble is how to dispose of you until your father come. I thought last night you seemed a little sweir to part from me?"

"It will be more than seeming, then," said she.

"You are a very young maid," said I, "and I am but a very young callant. This is a great piece of difficulty. What way are we to manage? Unless, indeed, you could pass to be my sister?"

"And what for no?" said she, "if you would let me!"

"I wish you were so, indeed!" I cried. "I would be a fine man if I had such a sister. But the rub is that you are Catriona Drummond."

"And now I will be Catrine Balfour," she said. "And who is to ken? They are all strange folk here."

"If you think that it would do," says I. "I own it troubles me. I would like it very ill, if I advised you at all wrong."

"David, I have no friend here but you," she said.

"The mere truth is, I am too young to be your friend," said I. "I am too young to advise you, or you to be advised. I see not what else we are to do, and yet I ought to warn you."

"I will have no choice left," said she. "I am cast upon your hands like a sack of barley meal, and have nothing else to think of but your pleasure. If you will have me, good and well. If you will not"—she turned and touched her hand upon my arm—"David, I am afraid," said she.

"No, but I ought to warn you," I began; and then bethought me that I was the bearer of the purse, and it would never do to seem too churlish. "Catriona," said I, "don't misunderstand me: I am just trying to do my duty by you, girl! Here am I going alone to this strange city, to be a solitary student there; and here is this chance arisen that you might dwell with me a bit, and be like my sister: you can surely understand this much, my dear, that I would just love to have you?"

"Well, and here I am," said she. "So that's soon settled."

I know I was in duty bounden to have spoke more plain. I know this was a great blot on my character, for which I was lucky that I did not pay more dear. The truth is, I could see no other feasible method to dispose of her. And I dare say inclination pulled me very strong.

A little beyond the Hague she fell very lame and made the rest of the distance heavily enough. Twice she must rest by the wayside, which she did with pretty apologies, calling herself a shame to the Highlands and the race she came of, and nothing but a hindrance to myself. It was her excuse, she said, that she was not much usel with walking shod. I would have had her strip off her shoes and stockings and go barefoot. But she pointed out to me that the women of that country, even in the landward roads, appeared to be all shod.

"I must not be disgracing my brother," said she, and was very merry with it all, although her face told tales of her.

There is a garden in that city we were bound to, sanded below with clean sand, the trees meeting overhead, some of them trimmed, some pleached, and the whole place beautified with alleys and arbours. Here I left Catriona, and went forward by myself to find my correspondent. There I drew on my credit, and asked to be recommended to some decent, retired lodging. My baggage not being yet arrived, I told him I supposed I should require his caution with the people of the house; and explained that, my sister being come for a while to keep house with me, I should be wanting two chambers. This was all very well; but the trouble was that Mr. Balfour in his letter of recommendation had condescended on a great deal of particulars, and never a word of any sister in the case. I could see my Dutchman was extremely suspicious; and viewing me over the rims of a great pair of spectacles—he was a poor, frail body, and reminded me of an infirm rabbit—he began to question me close.

Here I fell in a panic. Suppose he accept my tale (thinks I), suppose he invite my sister to his house, and that I bring her. I shall have a fine ravelled pirn to unwind, and may end by disgracing both the lassie and myself. Thereupon I began hastily to expound to him my sister's character. She was of a bashful disposition, it appeared, and so extremely fearful of meeting strangers that I had left her at that moment sitting in a public place alone. And then, being launched upon the stream of falsehood, I must do like all the rest of the world in the same circumstance, and plunge in deeper than was any service; adding some altogether needless particulars of Miss Balfour's ill-health and retirement during childhood. In the midst of which I awoke to a sense of my behaviour and was turned to one blush.

The old gentleman was not so much deceived but what he discovered a willingness to be quit of me. But he was first of all a man of business; and knowing that my money was good enough, however it might be with my conduct, he was so far obliging as to send his son to be my guide and caution in the matter of a lodging. This implied my presenting of the young man to Catriona. The poor, pretty child was much recovered with resting, looked and behaved to perfection, and took my arm and gave me the name of brother more easily than I could answer her. But there was one misfortune: thinking to help, she was rather towardly than otherwise to my Dutchman. And I could not but reflect that Miss Balfour had rather suddenly outgrown her bashfulness. And there was another thing, the difference of our speech. I had the Low Country tongue and dwelled upon my words; she had a hill voice, spoke with something of an English accent, only far more delightful, and was scarce quite fit to be called a deacon in the craft of talking English grammar; so that, for a brother and sister, we made a most uneven pair. But the young Hollander was a heavy dog, without so much spirit in him as to remark her prettiness, for which I scorned him. And as soon as he had found a cover to our heads, he left us alone, which was the greater service of the two.

THE HUMAN ODDITY

By JONATHAN SWIFT

Lemuel Gulliver, an intrepid voyager and discoverer of unusual lands and peoples, is left on the strange island of Brobdingnag by some mischance, and found by a farmer who is a giant. Adopted by the giant's family as a strange pet, he receives many kindnesses from the young daughter of the household, as related in "Gulliver's Travels," from which this story is taken. But one day the farmer realizes he can make great profit by exhibiting his curious midget in this land of giants, and then Gulliver grows weary of his new life.

MY mistress had a daughter of nine years old, a child of toward parts for her age, very dexterous at her needle, and skilful in dressing her baby. Her mother and she contrived to fit up the baby's cradle for me against night: the cradle was put into a small drawer of a cabinet, and the drawer placed upon a hanging-shelf, for fear of the rats.

This was my bed all the time I stayed with those people, though made more convenient by degrees, as I began to learn their language, and make my wants known. This young girl was so handy, that after I once or twice pulled off my cloaths before her she was able to dress and undress me, though I never gave her that trouble when she would let me do either myself. She made me seven shirts, and some other linen, of as fine cloth as could be got, which indeed was coarser than sack-cloth; and these she constantly washed for me with her own hands.

She was likewise my schoolmistress to teach me the language: When I pointed to anything, she told me the name of it in her own tongue, so that in a few days I was able to call for whatever I had a mind to. She was very good-natured, and not above forty foot high, being little for her age. She gave me the name of Grildrig, which the family took up, and afterwards the whole kingdom. The word imports what the Latins call *nanunculus*, the Italians *homunceletino*, and the English mannikin.

To her I chiefly owe my preservation in that country: we never parted while I was there. I called her my *glumdalclitch*, or little nurse: and I should be guilty of great ingratitude if I omitted this honourable mention of her care and affection towards me, which I heartily wish it lay in my power to requite as she deserves, instead of being the innocent but unhappy instrument of her disgrace, as I have too much reason to fear.

It now began to be known and talked of in the neighbourhood, that my master had found a strange animal in the field about the bigness of a *splacknuck*, but exactly shaped in every part like a human creature; which it likewise imitated in all its actions: seemed to speak in a little language of its own, had already learned several words of theirs, went erect upon two legs, was tame and gentle, would come when it was called, do whatever it was bid, had the finest limbs in the world, and a complexion fairer than a nobleman's daughter of three years old.

Another farmer who lived hard by, and was a particular friend of my master, came on a visit on purpose to inquire into the truth of this story. I was immediately produced, and placed upon a table, where I walked as I was commanded, drew my hanger, put it up again, made my reverence to my master's guest, asked him in his own language how he did, and told him he was welcome, just as my little nurse had instructed me.

The man, who was old and dim sighted, put on his spectacles to behold me better, at which I could not forbear laughing very heartily, for his eyes appeared like the full moon shining into a chamber at two windows. Our people, who discovered the cause of my mirth, bore me company in laughing, at which the old fellow was fool enough to be angry and out of countenance.

He had the character of a great miser, and to my misfortune he well deserved it by the cursed advice he gave my master to shew me as a sight upon a market day in the next town, which was half an hour's riding, about two and twenty miles from our house. I guessed there was some mischief contriving when I observed my master and his friend whispering long together, sometimes pointing at me; and my fears made me fancy that I overheard and understood some of their words. But the next morning Glumdalclitch, my little nurse, told me the whole matter, which she had cunningly picked out from her mother.

The poor girl laid me on her bosom, and fell a weeping with

shame and grief. She apprehended some mischief would happen to me from rude, vulgar folks, who might squeeze me to death or break one of my ribs by taking me in their hands. She had also observed how modest I was in my nature, how nicely I regarded my honour, and what an indignity I should conceive it to be exposed for money as a public spectacle to the meanest of the people.

She said her papa and mamma had promised that Grildrig should be hers, but now she found they meant to serve her as they did last year, when they pretended to give her a lamb, and yet, as soon as it was fat, sold it to a butcher. For my own part, I may truly affirm that I was less concerned than my nurse.

I had a strong hope, which never left me, that I should one day recover my liberty; and as to the ignominy of being carried about for a monster, I considered myself to be a perfect stranger in the country, and that such a misfortune could never be charged upon me as a reproach if ever I should return to England; since the King of Great Britain himself, in my condition, must have undergone the same distress.

My master, pursuant to the advice of his friend, carried me in a box the next market day to the neighbouring town, and took along with him his little daughter, my nurse, upon a pillion behind him.

The box was close on every side, with a little door for me to go in and out, and a few gimlet-holes to let in air. The girl had been so careful to put the quilt of her baby's bed into it, for me to lie down on. However, I was terribly shaken and discomposed in this journey, though it were but of half an hour. For the horse went about forty foot at every step, and trotted so high, that the agitation was equal to the rising and falling of a ship in a great storm, but much more frequent. Our journey was somewhat further than from London to St. Alban's.

My master alighted at an inn which he used to frequent; and after consulting a while with the inn-keeper, and making some necessary preparations, he hired the *grultrud*, or crier, to give notice through the town of a strange creature to be seen at the Sign of the Green Eagle, not so big as a *splacknuck* (an animal in that country very finely shaped, about six foot long), and in every part of the body resembling a human creature, could speak several words, and perform a hundred diverting tricks.

I was placed upon a table in the largest room of the inn, which might be near three hundred foot square. My little nurse stood on a low stool close to the table, to take care of me, and direct what I should do.

My master, to avoid a crowd, would suffer only thirty people at a time to see me. I walked about on the table as the girl commanded: she asked me questions as far as she knew my understanding of the language reached, and I answered them as loud as I could. I turned about several times to the company, paid my humble respects, said they were welcome, and used some other speeches I had been taught. I took up a thimble filled with liquor which Glumdalclitch had given me for a cup, and drank their health. I drew out my hanger, and flourished with it after the manner of fencers in England. My nurse gave me part of a straw, which I exercised as a pike, having learned the art in my youth.

I was that day shewn to twelve sets of company, and as often forced to go over again with the same fopperies, till I was half dead with weariness and vexation. For those who had seen me made such wonderful reports that the people were ready to break down the doors to come in. My master for his own interest would not suffer anyone to touch me except my nurse; and, to prevent danger, benches were set round the table at such a distance as put me out of everybody's reach.

However, an unlucky schoolboy aimed a hazel-nut directly at my head, which very narrowly missed me; otherwise, it came with so much violence that it would have infallibly knocked out my brains, for it was almost as large as a small pumpion: but I had the satisfaction to see the young rogue well beaten, and turned out of the room.

My master gave public notice that he would show me again the next market-day, and in the meantime he prepared a more convenient vehicle for me, which he had reason enough to do—for I was so tired with my first journey and with entertaining company for eight hours together, that I could hardly stand upon my legs or speak a word.

It was at least three days before I recovered my strength; and that I might have no rest at home, all the neighbouring gentlemen from an hundred miles round, hearing of my fame, came to see me at my master's house. There could not be fewer than thirty persons with their wives and children (for the country was very populous); and my master demanded the rate of a full room whenever he showed me at home, although it were only to a single family: so that for some time I had but little ease every day of the week (except Wednesday, which is their sabbath) although I were not carried to the town.

My master finding how profitable I was like to be, resolved to carry me to the most considerable cities of the kingdom. Having therefore provided himself with all things necessary for a long journey and settled his affairs at home, he took leave of his wife, and upon the 17th of August, 1703, about two months after my arrival, we set out for the metropolis, situated near the middle of that empire and about three thousand miles distant from our house. My master made his daughter Glumdalclitch ride behind him.

She carried me on her lap in a box tied about her waist. The girl had lined it on sides with the softest cloth she could get, well quilted underneath, furnished it with her baby's bed, provided me with linen and other necessaries, and made everything as convenient as she could. We had no other company but a boy of the house, who rode after us with the luggage.

My master's design was to shew me in all the towns by the way, and to step out of the road for fifty or an hundred miles, to any village or person of quality's house where he might expect custom.

We made easy journeys of not above seven or eightscore miles a day: for Glumdalclitch, on purpose to spare me, complained she was tired with the trotting of the horse. She often took me out of my box at my own desire, to give me air, and shew me the country, but always held me fast by a leading-string.

We passed over five or six rivers many degrees broader and deeper than the Nile or the Ganges; and there was hardly a rivulet so small as the Thames at London Bridge. We were ten weeks in our journey, and I was shown in eighteen large towns besides many villages and private families.

On the 26th day of October we arrived at the metropolis, called in their language *Lorbrulgrud*, or Pride of the Universe. My master took a lodging in the principal street of the city, not far from the royal palace, and put out bills in the usual form, containing an exact description of my person and parts.

He hired a large room between three and four hundred foot wide. He provided a table sixty foot in diameter, upon which I was to act my part, and palisadoed it round three foot from the edge, and as many high, to prevent my falling over. I was shown ten times a day to the wonder and satisfaction of all people.

I could now speak the language tolerably well, and perfectly understood every word that was spoken to me. Besides, I had learned their alphabet, and could make a shift to explain a sentence here and there; for Glumdalclitch had been my instructor while we were at home, and at leisure hours during our journey. She carried a little book in her pocket, not much larger than a Sanson's atlas; it was a common treatise for the use of young girls, giving a short account of their religion; out of this she taught me my letters, and interpreted the words.

MABEL MEETS THE PATHFINDER

By J. FENIMORE COOPER

Mabel Dunham, her seafaring uncle, and two Indians set out to reach a fort on Lake Ontario, where Mabel's father, a soldier, awaits them. It is a long journey through forests and over large rivers, and the father, anxious for the safety of his daughter, sends the famous hunter known as Hawkeye to the redskins and Pathfinder to the soldiers and rangers of the woods to find and aid the travellers. It is Mabel who goes forward alone when the party sights the smoke of a paleface camp-fire. This story is taken from "The Pathfinder."

FOUR persons had managed to ascend a pile of trees, that had been uptorn by a tempest, to catch a view of the objects that surrounded them. They were all wayfarers in the wilderness. Two of the party, indeed—a male and female—belonged to the native owners of the soil, being Indians of the well-known tribe of the Tuscaroras; while their companions were—a man, who bore about him the peculiarities of one who had passed his days on the ocean; and his female associate, who was a maiden of a class in no great degree superior to his own, though her youth, sweetness of countenance, and a modest but spirited mien, lent that character of intellect and refinement which adds so much to the charm of beauty in the sex. On the present occasion, her full blue eye reflected the feeling of sublimity that the scene excited, and her pleasant face was beaming with the pensive expression with which all deep emotions, even though they bring the most grateful pleasure, shadow the countenances of the ingenuous and thoughtful.

And truly the scene was of a nature deeply to impress the imagination of the beholder. Towards the west, in which direction the faces of the party were turned, the eye ranged over an ocean of leaves, glorious and rich in the varied and lively verdure of a generous vegetation, and shaded by the luxuriant tints which belong to the forty-second degree of latitude.

It was the vastness of the view, the nearly unbroken surface of verdure, that contained the principle of grandeur.

"Uncle," said the wondering but pleased girl, addressing her male companion, whose arm she rather touched than leaned on, to steady her own light but firm footing, "this is like a view of the ocean you so much love!"

"So much for ignorance and a girl's fancy, Magnet"—a term of affection the sailor often used in allusion to his niece's personal attractions; "no one but a child would think of likening this handful of leaves to a look at the real Atlantic. You might seize all these tree-tops to Neptune's jacket, and they would make no more than a nosegay for his bosom."

"More fanciful than true, I think, Uncle. Look thither; it must be miles on miles, and yet we see nothing but leaves! What more could one behold if looking at the ocean?"

"More!" returned the uncle, giving an impatient gesture with the elbow the other touched, for his arms were crossed, and the hands were thrust into the bosom of a vest of red cloth, a fashion of the times—"more, Magnet? Say, rather, What less? Where are your combing seas, your blue water, your rollers, your breakers, your whales, or your waterspouts, and your endless motion, in this bit of forest, child?"

"And where are your tree-tops, your solemn silence, your fragrant leaves, and your beautiful green, Uncle, on the ocean?"

"Tut, Magnet; if you understood the thing, you would know that green water is a sailor's bane. He scarcely relishes a greenhorn less."

"But green trees are a different thing. Hist! That sound is the air breathing among the leaves!"

"You should hear a nor'-wester breathe, girl, if you fancy wind aloft. Now, where are your gales, and hurricanes, and trades, and levanters, and such-like incidents, in this bit of forest? And what fishes have you swimming beneath yonder tame surface?"

"That there have been tempests here, these signs around us plainly show; and beasts, if not fishes, are beneath those leaves."

"I do not know that," returned the uncle, with a sailor's dogmatism. "They told us many stories at Albany of the wild animals we should fall in with, and yet we have seen nothing to frighten a seal. I doubt if any of your inland animals will compare with a low-latitude shark."

"See!" exclaimed the niece, who was more occupied with the sublimity and beauty of the "boundless wood" than with her uncle's arguments; "yonder is a smoke curling over the tops of the trees. Can it come from a house?"

"Ay, ay; there is a look of humanity in that smoke," returned the old seaman, "which is worth a thousand trees. I must show it to Arrowhead, who may be running past a port without knowing it. It is probable there is a caboose where there is a smoke."

As he concluded, the uncle drew a hand from his bosom, touched the male Indian, who was standing near him, lightly on the shoulder, and pointed out a thin line of vapour which was stealing slowly out of the wilderness of leaves, at a distance of about a mile, and was diffusing itself in almost imperceptible threads of humidity in the quivering atmosphere.

The quick eye of the Tuscarora instantly caught a sight of the smoke; and for full a minute he stood, slightly raised on tiptoe, with distended nostrils, like the buck that scents a taint in the air, and a gaze as riveted as that of the trained pointer while he waits his master's aim. Then falling back on his feet, a low exclamation, in the soft tones that form so singular a contrast to its harsher cries, in the Indian warrior's voice, was barely audible; otherwise, he was undisturbed.

"There must be Oneidas, or Tuscaroras, near us, Arrowhead," said Cap, addressing his Indian companion by his conventional English name; "will it not be well to join company with them, and get a comfortable berth for the night in their wigwam?"

"No wigwam there," Arrowhead answered, in his unmoved manner—"too much tree."

"But Indians must be there—perhaps some old messmates of your own, Master Arrowhead."

"No Tuscarora—no Oneida—no Mohawk—paleface fire."

"The devil it is! Well, Magnet, this surpasses a seaman's philosophy: we old seadogs can tell a lubber's nest from a mate's hammock; but I do not think the oldest admiral in his Majesty's fleet can tell a king's smoke from a collier's."

The idea that human beings were in their vicinity, in that ocean of wilderness, had deepened the flush on the blooming cheek and brightened the eye of the fair creature at his side; but she soon turned with a look of surprise to her relative, and said hesitatingly —for both had often admired the Tuscarora's knowledge, or, we might almost say, instinct:

"A paleface's fire! Surely, Uncle, he cannot know *that*!"

"Ten days since, child, I would have sworn to it; but now I hardly know what to believe. May I take the liberty of asking, Arrowhead, why you fancy that smoke now, a paleface's smoke and not a redskin's?"

"Wet wood," returned the warrior, with the calmness with which the pedagogue might point out an arithmetical demonstration to his puzzled pupil. "Much wet—much smoke; much water—black smoke."

"But, begging your pardon, Master Arrowhead, the smoke is not black, nor is there much of it. To my eye, now, it is as light and fanciful a smoke as ever rose from a captain's tea-kettle, when nothing was left to make the fire but a few chips from the dunnage."

"Too much water," returned Arrowhead, with a slight nod of the head. "Tuscarora too cunning to make fire with water! Paleface too much book, and burn anything; much book, little know."

"Well, that's reasonable, I allow. He means that as a hit at your reading, Magnet; for the chief has sensible notions of things in his own way. How far now, Arrowhead, do you make us, by your calculation from the bit of a pond that you call the Great Lake, and towards which we have been so many days shaping our course?"

The Tuscarora looked at the seaman with quiet superiority as he answered, "Ontario, like heaven; one sun, and the great traveller will know it."

"Well, I have been a great traveller, I cannot deny; but of all my v'y'ges this has been the longest, the least profitable, and the farthest inland. If this body of fresh water is so nigh, Arrowhead, and so large, one might think a pair of good eyes would find it out; for, apparently, everything within thirty miles is to be seen from this lookout."

"Look!" said Arrowhead, stretching an arm before him with quiet grace—"Ontario!"

"Uncle, you are accustomed to cry 'Land ho!' but not 'Water

ho!' and you do not see it," cried the niece, laughing, as girls will laugh at their own idle conceits.

"How now, Magnet? Dost suppose that I shouldn't know my native element if it were in sight?"

"But Ontario is not your native element, dear Uncle; for you come from the salt water, while this is fresh."

"That might make some difference to your young mariner, but none to the old one. I should know water, child, were I to see it in China."

"Ontario!" repeated Arrowhead, with emphasis, again stretching his hand towards the north-west.

The Tuscarora now gave a quiet inclination of his head, and the whole party descended from the roots of the uptorn tree in silence. When they had reached the ground, Arrowhead intimated his intention to go towards the fire, and ascertain who had lighted it, while he advised his wife and the two others to return to a canoe which they had left in the adjacent stream, and await his return.

"Why, Chief, this might do on soundings, and in an offing where one knew the channel, but in an unknown region like this I think it unsafe to trust the pilot alone too far from the ship; so, with your leave, we will not part company."

"What my brother want?" asked the Indian gravely, though without taking offence at a distrust that was sufficiently plain.

"Your company, Master Arrowhead, and no more. I will go with you and speak these strangers."

The Tuscarora assented without difficulty, and again he directed his patient and submissive little wife, who seldom turned her full rich black eye on him but to express equally her respect, her dread, and her love, to proceed to the boat. But here Magnet raised a difficulty. Although spirited, and of unusual energy under circumstances of trial, she was but woman; and the idea of being entirely deserted by her two male protectors, in the midst of a wilderness that her senses had just told her was seemingly illimitable, became so keenly painful that she expressed a wish to accompany her uncle.

"The exercise will be a relief, dear sir, after sitting so long in the canoe," she added, as the rich blood slowly returned to a cheek that had paled, in spite of her efforts to be calm; "and there may be females with the strangers."

"Come then, child; it is but a cable's length, and we shall return an hour before the sun sets."

With this permission, the girl, whose real name was Mabel Dunham, prepared to be of the party; while the Dew-of-June, as the wife of Arrowhead was called, passively went her ways towards the canoe, too much accustomed to obedience, solitude, and the gloom of the forest, to feel apprehension.

The three who remained now picked their way around its tangled maze, and gained the margin of the woods.

The Indian turned. "The Salt-water"—for so the Indian styled his companion—"all eye now; no tongue."

"He means, Uncle, that we had needs be silent; perhaps he distrusts the persons we are about to meet."

"Ay, 'tis an Indian's fashion of going to quarters. You perceive he has examined the priming of his rifle, and it may be as well if I look to that of my own pistols."

Without betraying alarm at these preparations, to which she had become accustomed by her long journey in the wilderness, Mabel followed with a step as elastic as that of the Indian, keeping close in the rear of her companions. For the first half-mile, no other caution beyond a rigid silence was observed; but as the party drew nearer to the spot where the fire was known to be, much greater care became necessary.

The forest, as usual, had little to intercept the view, below the branches, but the tall, straight trunks of trees. These columns of trees, however, often served to conceal the adventurer, the hunter, or the foe; and as Arrowhead swiftly approached the spot where his practised and unerring senses told him the strangers ought to be, his footstep gradually became lighter, his eye more vigilant, and his person was more carefully concealed.

"See, Salt-water," said he exultingly, pointing through the vista of trees, "paleface fire!"

"Arrowhead is but half right!" whispered Mabel; "for there are two Indians, and only one white man."

"Palefaces," said the Tuscarora, holding up two fingers; "red man," holding up one.

"He must be right, Uncle; for his eye seems never to fail. But it is now urgent to know whether we meet as friends or foes. They may be French."

"One hail will soon satisfy us on that head. Stand you behind this tree, Magnet, lest the knaves take it into their heads to fire a broadside without a parley, and I will soon learn what colours they sail under."

The uncle had placed his two hands to his mouth, to form a trumpet, and was about to give the promised hail, when a rapid movement from the hand of Arrowhead defeated the intention by deranging the instrument.

"Red man, Mohican," said the Tuscarora—"good; palefaces, Yengeese."

"These are heavenly tidings," murmured Mabel, who little relished the prospect of a deadly fray in that remote wilderness. "Let us approach at once, dear Uncle, and proclaim ourselves friends."

"Good," said the Tuscarora; "red man cool, and know; paleface hurried, and fire. Let the squaw go."

"What! Send little Magnet ahead as a look-out while two lubbers like you and me lie to to see what sort of a landfall she will make! If I do, I——"

"It is wisest, Uncle," interrupted the generous girl, "and I have no fear. No Christian, seeing a woman approach alone, would fire upon her; and my presence will be a pledge of peace. Let me go forward, as Arrowhead wishes, and all will be well. We are as yet unseen, and the surprise of the strangers will not partake of alarm."

"Good," returned Arrowhead, who did not conceal his approbation of Mabel's spirit.

"It has an unseamanlike look but being in the woods, no one will know it. If you think, Mabel——"

"Uncle, I know. There is no cause to fear for me; and you are always nigh to protect me."

"Well, take one of the pistols, then——"

"Nay, I had better rely on my youth and feebleness," said the girl, smiling, while her colour heightened under her feelings. "Among Christian men, a woman's best guard is her claim to their protection. I know nothing of arms, and wish to live in ignorance of them."

The uncle desisted; and after receiving a few cautious instructions from the Tuscarora, Mabel rallied all her spirit, and advanced alone towards the group seated near the fire. Although the heart of

the girl beat quick, her step was firm, and her movements, seemingly, were without reluctance. A deathlike silence reigned in the forest, for they towards whom she approached were too much occupied in appeasing their hunger to avert their looks for an instant from the important business in which they were all engaged. When Mabel, however, had got within a hundred feet of the fire, she trod upon a dried stick, and the trifling noise produced by her light footstep, caused the Mohican, as Arrowhead had pronounced the Indian to be, and his companion, whose character had been thought so equivocal, to rise to their feet as quick as thought. Both glanced at the rifles that leaned against a tree; and then each stood without stretching out an arm, as his eyes fell on the form of the girl. The Indian uttered a few words to his companion, and resumed his seat and his meal, as calmly as if no interruption had occurred. On the contrary, the white man left the fire and came forward to meet Mabel.

The latter saw, as the stranger approached, that she was about to be addressed by one of her own colour, though his dress was so strange a mixture of the habits of the two races that it required a near look to be certain of the fact. He was of middle age; but there was an open honesty, a total absence of guile in his face, which otherwise would not have been thought handsome, that at once assured Magnet she was in no danger. Still she paused.

"Fear nothing, young woman," said the hunter, for such his attire would indicate him to be; "you have met Christian men in the wilderness, and such as know how to treat all kindly who are disposed to peace and justice. I am a man well known in all these parts, and perhaps one of my names may have reached your ears. By the Frenchers and the redskins on the other side of the Big Lakes I am called La Longue Carabine; by the Mohicans, a just-minded and upright tribe, what is left of them, Hawk-eye; while the troops and rangers along this side of the water call me Pathfinder, inasmuch as I have never been known to miss one end of the trail when there was a Mingo, or a friend who stood in need of me at the other."

This was not uttered boastfully, but with the honest confidence of one who well knew that by whatever name others might have heard of him, he had no reason to blush at the reports. The effects on Mabel was instantaneous. The moment she heard the last sobriquet, she clasped her hands eagerly and repeated the word "Pathfinder!"

"So they call me, young woman, and many a great lord has got a title that he did not half so well merit; though, if truth be said, I rather pride myself in finding my way where there is no path than in finding it where there is. But the regular troops are by no means particular, and half the time they don't know the difference between a trail and a path, though one is a matter for the eye, while the other is little more than scent."

"Then you are the friend my father promised to send to meet us?"

"If you are Sergeant Dunham's daughter, the great Prophet of the Delawares never uttered more truth."

"I am Mabel; and yonder, hid by the trees, are my uncle, whose name is Cap, and a Tuscarora called Arrowhead. We did not hope to meet you until we had nearly reached the shores of the lake."

"I wish a juster-minded Indian had been your guide," said Pathfinder; "for I am no lover of the Tuscaroras, who have travelled too far from the graves of their fathers always to remember the Great Spirit; and Arrowhead is an ambitious chief. Is the Dew-of-June with him?"

"His wife accompanies us, and a humble and mild creature she is."

"Ay, and true-hearted; which is more than any who know him will say of Arrowhead. Well, we must take the fare that Providence bestows while we follow the trail of life. I suppose worse guides might have been found than the Tuscarora, though he has too much Mingo blood for one who consorts altogether with the Delawares."

"It is then, perhaps, fortunate we have met," said Mabel.

"It is not misfortunate, at any rate; for I promised the sergeant I would see his child safe to the garrison, though I died for it. We expected to meet you before you reached the falls, where we have left our own canoe; while we thought it might do no harm to come up a few miles, in order to be of service if wanted. It is lucky we did, for I doubt if Arrowhead be the man to shoot the current."

"Here come my uncle and the Tuscarora, and our parties can now join."

As Mabel concluded, Cap and Arrowhead, who saw that the conference was amicable, drew nigh; and a few words sufficed to let them know as much as the girl herself had learned.

UNCLE REMUS TELLS TALES

By JOEL CHANDLER HARRIS

Miss Sally's little boy is fond of going down to the cabin of Uncle Remus, and listening to the strange tales of other days told by the old darky. In "Uncle Remus," from which this story is taken, Brer Rabbit is a rather unusual hero, and his adventures and pranks never fail to arouse the interest of Miss Sally's little boy, or of countless other children who read them.

IT had been raining all day, so that Uncle Remus found it impossible to go out. The storm had begun, the old man declared, just as the chickens were crowing for day, and it had continued almost without intermission. The dark grey clouds had blotted out the sun, and the leafless limbs of the tall oaks surrendered themselves drearily to the fantastic gusts that drove the drizzle fitfully before them. The lady to whom Uncle Remus belonged had been thoughtful of the old man, and 'Tildy, the house-girl, had been commissioned to carry him his meals. This arrangement came to the knowledge of the little boy at supper-time, and he lost no time in obtaining permission to accompany 'Tildy.

Uncle Remus made a great demonstration over the thoughtful kindness of Miss Sally.

"If she isn't one blessed white woman," he said, in his simple, fervent way, "then there isn't one of them around in these parts."

With that he addressed himself to the supper, while the little boy sat by and eyed him with that familiar curiosity common to children. Finally the youngster disturbed the old man with an inquiry:

"Uncle Remus, do geese stand on one leg all night, or do they sit down to sleep?"

"To be sure they do, honey; they sit down just as you do. Of course, they don't cross their legs," he added cautiously, "because they sit down flat-footed."

"Well, I saw one the other day, and he was standing on one foot, and I watched him and watched him, and he kept standing there."

"As to that," responded Uncle Remus, "they might stand on one foot and drop off to sleep and forget themselves. These geese," he continued, wiping the crumbs from his beard with his coat-tail, "are mighty curious fowls; they are mighty curious. In olden times they were among the big-bugs, and in those days when old Miss Goose gave a dinner all the quality was there. And they weren't stuck up either, because with all their fine style, Miss Goose wasn't too proud to take in washing, so she made money and got sleek and fat.

"That is the way matters stood when one day Brer Fox and Brer Rabbit were sitting up at the cotton-patch, one on one side of the fence, and the other on the other side, going on with one another, when all of a sudden they heard something—*blim, blim, blim!*

"Brer Fox asked what that noise was, and Brer Rabbit replied that it was old Miss Goose down at the spring. Then Brer Fox asked what she was doing, and Brer Rabbit said that she was battling clothes."

"Battling clothes, Uncle Remus?" said the little boy.

"That is what they called it in those days, honey. In these times they rub clothes on boards which have furrows in them, but in those days they just took the clothes and laid them out on a bench, and caught hold of the battling-stick and hammered the stuffing out of them.

"When Brer Fox heard that old Miss Goose was down there dabbling in soap-suds and washing clothes, he licked his lips, and declared that one of these long-come-shorts he would call and pay his respects. The minute he said that, Brer Rabbit knew that something was up, and he said to himself that he had better be by and have some fun while it was going on. Presently Brer Fox said to Brer Rabbit that he was obliged to be moving towards home, and with that they both said good-bye.

"Brer Fox set out to find his family, but Brer Rabbit slipped round and called on old Miss Goose. Old Miss Goose was down at the spring washing, and boiling, and battling clothes, but Brer Rabbit marched up and asked her how she was, and then she asked Brer Rabbit how he was.

" 'I'd shake hands with you, Brer Rabbit,' said she, 'but they are full of suds.'

" 'That doesn't matter, Miss Goose,' said Brer Rabbit, 'as long as your will's good.' "

"A goose with hands, Uncle Remus!" the little boy exclaimed.

"How do you know that a goose hasn't hands?" Uncle Remus inquired, with a frown. "Have you been sleeping with old man Know-all? A little more and you will be telling me that snakes haven't feet, and yet if you take and lay a snake down here before the fire, the feet will come out before your eyes."

Uncle Remus paused here, but presently continued:

"After old Miss Goose and Brer Rabbit had passed the time of day with each other, Brer Rabbit asked her how she was in those days, and Miss Goose said that she was very poorly.

" 'I'm getting stiff and I'm getting clumsy,' said she, 'and more than that, I'm getting blind. Just before you came along, Brer Rabbit, I dropped my spectacles in the tub, and if you had come along about that time, I declare I should have taken you for that nasty, audacious Brer Fox, and it would have been a born blessing if I hadn't scalded you with a pan of boiling suds. I'm so glad I found my spectacles that I don't know what to do,' said old Miss Goose.

"Then Brer Rabbit said that as Sis Goose had mentioned Brer Fox's name, he had something to tell her, and then he told her how Brer Fox was going to call on her.

" 'He's coming,' said Brer Rabbit, 'he's coming, sure enough, and when he comes it will be just before day.'

"With that, old Miss Goose wiped her hands on her apron, and put her spectacles up on her forehead, and looked as if she had trouble on her mind.

" 'Laws-a-mercy!' said she, 'supposing he comes, Brer Rabbit! what am I going to do? And there isn't a man about the house neither.'

"Then Brer Rabbit shut one eye, and said:

" 'Sis Goose, the time is come when you must roost high, because if you don't roost high you are done for.'

"Then old Miss Goose asked Brer Rabbit what she should do, and he told her that she must go home and tie up a bundle of the white folks' clothes, and put them on the bed. Then she must fly up on a rafter, and let Brer Fox grab the clothes and run off.

"Old Miss Goose said that she was much obliged, and she took her things and waddled off home. That night she did as Brer Rabbit said with the bundle of clothes, and then she sent down word to Mr. Dog, and Mr. Dog came down and said that he would sit up with her.

"Just before day, there came Brer Fox creeping up. The door opened when he gave it a slight push, and on the bed he saw something white which he took for Miss Goose, so he grabbed it and ran. Just about that time Mr. Dog sailed out from under the house, and if Brer Fox hadn't dropped the clothes he would have been caught. From that, word went around that Brer Fox had been trying to steal Miss Goose's clothes, and he came perilously near losing his standing. To this day," Uncle Remus continued, preparing to fill his pipe, "Brer Fox believes that Brer Rabbit was the occasion of Mr. Dog being in the neighbourhood at that time of night, and Brer Rabbit hasn't denied it. The bad feeling between Brer Fox and Mr. Dog started then and there, and it has gone on until now they don't get in smelling distance of each other unless there is a row."

There was a pause after the story of old Miss Goose. The culmination was hardly sensational enough to win the hearty applause of the little boy, and this fact appeared to have a depressing influence upon Uncle Remus. As he leaned slightly forward, gazing into the depths of the great fireplace, his attitude was one of pensiveness.

"I expect I have worn out my welcome at the big house," he said, after a while. "I am almost certain I have," he continued, setting himself resignedly in his deep-bottomed chair, "because the last time I was there I had my eye on Miss Sally nearly the whole of the time, and when you see Miss Sally bustling around arranging things on the mantelshelf, bouncing the chairs around, and brushing up dust where there isn't any dust, and flying around singing louder than usual, then I know I've done something to annoy her."

"Why, Uncle Remus!" exclaimed the little boy, "Mamma was just glad I was feeling so good."

"It might have been that," the old man remarked, in a tone that was far from implying conviction. "If it wasn't that, then she was getting tired of seeing me lounging around up there night after night; and if it wasn't that, then she was waiting for a chance to lecture your pa. Oh, I knew Miss Sally long before your pa knew her!" exclaimed Uncle Remus, in response to the astonishment depicted upon the child's face; "I've known her since she was so high, and during all that time I haven't seen a more outspoken white woman than Miss Sally.

"But that's all neither here nor there. You can now run down here just as you used to do, and we can sit here and tell tales to amuse ourselves just as we used to do before you got that splinter in your foot.

"I remember one time"—with an infectious laugh—"when old Brer Rabbit got Brer Fox in almost worse trouble than a man has ever got in yet. That was when he made a fool of him about the horse. Haven't I ever told you about that? But no matter if I have. Hoecake isn't well done until it has been turned over a couple of times.

"Well, after Brer Fox had rested from keeping out of the way of Mr. Dog, and was able to catch his breath, he said to himself that he would pay out old Brer Rabbit if it took a month; and that too on top of all the experience he had had with him. Brer Rabbit managed to get wind of this, and, one day, while he was going along wondering how he could hold his own with Brer Fox, he saw a great big horse lying stretched out on his side in the field. He crept up to see if the horse were dead. He crept up, and he crept round, and presently he saw the horse switch his tail, and then Brer Rabbit knew that he wasn't dead. With that, Brer Rabbit ran back to the big road, and almost the first man he saw go by was Brer Fox, so Brer Rabbit ran after him, and shouted:

"'Brer Fox! O Brer Fox! Come back! I have some good news for you. Come back, Brer Fox,' said he.

"Brer Fox turned around, and when he saw who was calling him he came galloping back, because it seemed that this was as good a time as any to nab Brer Rabbit; but before he got near enough to seize him, Brer Rabbit said:

"'Come on, Brer Fox! I have found a place where you can lay in enough fresh meat to last you well till the middle of next year.'

"Brer Fox asked whereabouts, and Brer Rabbit said over there in the field. Brer Fox asked what it was, and Brer Rabbit said that it was a whole horse lying on the ground where they could catch him and tie him. With that Brer Fox said he would come, and so they set off.

"When they got there, sure enough, there lay the horse stretched out in the sun, fast asleep, and then Brer Fox and Brer Rabbit had a dispute about how they were going to fasten the horse so that he couldn't get loose. One said one way and the other said another way, and there they went at it, until after a while Brer Rabbit said:

" 'The only plan I know, Brer Fox, is for you to get down there and let me tie you to the horse's tail, and then, when he tries to get up, you can hold him down. If I were a big man like you, you might tie me to that horse's tail, and if I didn't hold him down, then Joe's dead and Sal's a widow. I know well that you can hold him down,' said Brer Rabbit, 'but still, if you are afraid, we had better drop the idea, and work out some other plan.'

"Brer Fox was rather doubtful about this, but he had to look big before Brer Rabbit, so he agreed to the plan. Then Brer Rabbit tied Brer Fox to the horse's tail, and after he had got him tied there hard and fast, he stepped back, put his hands akimbo, and said:

" 'If ever there was a horse caught, then we have caught this one. It does look as if we had put the bridle on the wrong end, but I'll warrant that Brer Fox has got enough strength to hold him,'

"With that, Brer Rabbit cut a long switch and trimmed it, and when he had finished it he stepped up and gave the horse a rap—*pow*! The horse was so surprised at such goings-on that he made one jump, and landed on his feet. When he did that, there was Brer Fox dangling in the air. Brer Rabbit darted out of the way, and shouted:

" 'Hold him down, Brer Fox! Hold him down! I'll stand here and see fair play. Hold him down, Brer Fox! Hold him down!'

"Of course, when the horse felt Brer Fox hanging there on to his tail, he thought that something curious was the matter, and this made him jump and rear all the more. He shook Brer Fox just like a rag in the wind, and Brer Rabbit jumped and shouted:

" 'Hold him down, Brer Fox! Hold him down! You've got him now, sure enough! Keep your grip and hold him down!'

"The horse jumped and humped, and ripped and reared, and

snorted and cavorted, but still Brer Fox hung on, and still Brer Rabbit skipped around and shouted:

"'Hold him down, Brer Fox! You've got him so that he can't escape. Hold him down, Brer Fox!'

"By and by, when Brer Fox got a chance, he shouted back:

"'How in the name of goodness am I going to hold the horse down unless I can get my claws in the ground?'

"Then Brer Rabbit stood back a little farther and shouted a little louder:

"'Hold him down, Brer Fox! Hold him down! You've got him now, sure enough! Hold him down!'

"Presently the horse began to kick with his hind-legs, and before long he gave Brer Fox a blow in the stomach that fairly made him shriek. Then he kicked him again, and this time he broke the cord and sent Brer Fox a-whirling. Brer Rabbit kept on jumping and shouting:

"'Hold him down, Brer Fox!'"

"Was the fox killed, Uncle Remus?" asked the little boy.

"He wasn't exactly killed, honey," replied the old man, "but he was next door to it. He was all broken up, and while he was getting well it seemed to cross his mind that Brer Rabbit had played another game on him."

"What did Brother Rabbit do after that?" the little boy asked presently.

"Now, then, you don't want to push old Brer Rabbit too close," replied Uncle Remus significantly. "He is a very tender-footed creature, and the more you push him the farther he'll leave you."

There was prolonged silence in the old man's cabin, until, seeing that the little boy was growing restless enough to cast several curious glances in the direction of the tool-chest in the corner, Uncle Remus lifted one leg over the other, scratched his head reflectively, and began:

"At one time, honey, after Brer Rabbit had been tramping around hunting for some salad for his dinner, he found himself in the neighbourhood of Mr. Man's house, and he passed along until he came to the garden-gate. Near the gate he saw Little Girl playing around in the sand. When Brer Rabbit looked between the garden railings and saw the greenstuff, his mouth began to water. Then he walked up to Little Girl, pulled his forelock, bowed, scraped his foot, and talked most politely:

"'How do you do, Little Girl?' said Brer Rabbit; 'how are you?'

"Then the Little Girl said, 'How do you do?' and she asked Brer Rabbit how he was. Brer Rabbit declared that he was very poorly, and then he asked her if she was the Little Girl whose pa lived in the big white house, and the Little Girl said she was. Brer Rabbit said that he was very glad, because he had been there to see her pa, and that he had sent him to tell the Little Girl that she must open the garden-gate so that Brer Rabbit could get some greenstuff. Then the Little Girl ran around and opened the gate. With that Brer Rabbit hopped in, got a fine feed of greens, and hopped out again. When he was going he made a bow and told the Little Girl that he was obliged, and after that he set out for home.

"The next day Brer Rabbit hid himself until he saw the Little Girl come out to play. Then he put up the same tale, and walked off with another fine feed of greens. He kept on doing this, until presently Mr. Man began to miss his greens. He kept on missing them, until he got to accusing everybody on the place of taking them, and when that came to pass the Little Girl said:

" 'My goodness, Pa! you told Mr. Rabbit to come and make me let him in the garden after some greens, and hasn't he come and asked me, and haven't I let him in?'

"Mr. Man had to think a long time before he saw how the land lay. Then he laughed, and told the Little Girl that he had quite forgotten about Mr. Rabbit. Then he said to her:

" 'The next time Mr. Rabbit comes, let him in, and then run as fast as you can and tell me, because I have some business with him that must be attended to.'

"Sure enough, next morning, there was the Little Girl playing around, and there came Brer Rabbit after his allowance of greens. He was ready with the same tale, and then the Little Girl let him in and ran up to the house, saying:

" 'Oh, Pa! Pa! Oh, Pa! Brer Rabbit is in the garden now! Here he is, Pa!'

"Then Mr. Man rushed out, grabbed up a fishing-line that was hanging on the back porch, and made for the garden. When he got there, there was Brer Rabbit trampling on the strawberry-bed and crushing the tomatoes. When Brer Rabbit saw Mr. Man, he squatted down behind a cabbage leaf, but it wasn't any use. Mr. Man had seen him, and before you could count eleven he had got old Brer Rabbit tied hard and fast with the fishing-line. After he had got him tied safely, Mr Man stepped back and said:

" 'You have fooled me many times, but this time you are mine. I'm going to take you and give you a thrashing, and then I'm going to skin you and nail your hide to the stable-door. To make sure that you get the right kind of thrashing, I'll just step up to the house and fetch the little red cowhide, and then I can warm your jacket.'

"Then Mr. Man called to the Little Girl to watch Brer Rabbit while he was gone.

"Brer Rabbit said nothing, but Mr. Man had only just gone out of the gate when he began to sing. In those days Brer Rabbit was a singer, I can tell you," continued Uncle Remus, with unusual emphasis, "and when he tuned up to sing he made the other creatures hold their breath."

"What did he sing, Uncle Remus?" asked the little boy.

"If I haven't forgotten that song," said Uncle Remus, looking over his spectacles at the fire, with a curious air of attempting to remember something, "it ran something like this:

"The jay-bird hunted the sparrow's nest,
The bee-martin sailed all 'round;
The squirrel, he shouted from the top of the tree,
Mr. Mole, he stayed in the ground;
He did and he stayed till the dark dropped down—
Mr. Mole, he hid in the ground."

"When the Little Girl heard that, she laughed and asked Brer Rabbit to sing some more, but Brer Rabbit gave a cough, and declared that he was very hoarse somewhere down in his windpipe. The Little Girl persuaded and persuaded, and presently Brer Rabbit declared that he could dance even better than he could sing. Then the Little Girl asked him to dance, and Brer Rabbit said how in the name of goodness could a man dance while he was tied up in that way. The Little Girl said that she could untie him, and Brer Rabbit said that he didn't care if she did. With that the Little Girl reached down and untied the fishing-line, and Brer Rabbit stretched himself and looked around."

Here Uncle Remus paused and sighed, as though he had relieved his mind of a great burden. The little boy waited for a few minutes for the old man to resume, and finally he asked:

"Did the rabbit dance, Uncle Remus?"

"Who? Him?" exclaimed the old man, with a queer affectation of elation. "Bless your heart, honey! Brer Rabbit gathered up his feet under him, he danced out of that garden, and he danced home. He did that! Surely you don't expect that an old hand who had had so much experience as Brer Rabbit was going to stay there and let Mr. Man sacrifice him? *Shoo!* Brer Rabbit danced, but he danced home. Do you hear me?"

THE TRIALS OF AN AUNT

By JOHN HABBERTON

Young Mrs. Burton has agreed to look after her two young nephews, Budge and Toddie, for a short while, and she soon finds their high spirits, curiosity, and natural sense of adventure rather wearing for her nerves. The youngsters are two healthy American children with a talent for getting first into mischief, then arguing their way out of chastisement. Their Aunt Alice, one rather feels, is to be pitied. This story is taken from "Other People's Children."

MRS. Burton rose from her chair, brought from a closet in the dining-room a couple of pieces of cake, and gave one to each boy, saying:

"It isn't that Aunt Alice cares so much for her cake, dears, that she doesn't like you to have it between meals, but because it is bad for little boys to eat such heavy food excepting at their regular meals. There are grown people who were once happy little children, but now they are very cross all the while because their stomachs are all disordered by eating when they should not, and eating things which are richer and heavier than their bodies can use."

"Well," said Budge, crowding the contents of his mouth into his cheeks, "can we eat something plainer an' lighter to mix up with 'em inside us? I should think charlotte russe or whipped cream would be about the thing; shall I ask the cook to fix some?"

"No," said Mrs. Burton, in haste. "Exercise would be better than anything else. I think you had better take a walk."

"Up to Hawkshnesht Rock?" suggested Toddie.

"Oh, yes!" exclaimed Budge. "An' you come with us, Aunt Alice."

Mrs. Burton could not decline; and soon the trio were on the road, Mrs. Burton walking leisurely on the turf by the side, while the boys ploughed their way through the dust of the middle of the road, pretending to be horses and succeeding so far as to create a dust cloud which no team of horses could have excelled.

"Boys, boys!" shouted Mrs. Burton. "Is no one going to be company for me?"

"Oh—*I'll* be your gentleman," said Budge.

"I'll help," said Toddie, and both boys hurried to their aunt's side.

"Little boys," said Mrs. Burton gently, "do you know that your mamma and papa have to pay a high price for the fun you have in kicking up dust? Look at your clothes; they must be sent to the cleaner's before they will ever again be fit to wear where respectable people can see you."

"Then," said Budge, "they're just right to give to poor little boys, and just think how glad they'll be. I guess they'll thank the Lord 'cause we ran in the dust."

"The poor little boys would have been just as glad to have had them while they were clean," said Mrs. Burton, "and the kindness would have cost your papa and mamma no more."

"Well, then—then—then I guess we'd better talk about something else," said Budge, "an' go 'long froo the woods instead of in the road. Oh—h—h!" continued Budge, kicking through some grass under the chestnut-trees by the roadside, "here's a chestnut! Is it chestnut-time again already?"

"Oh, no, that's one of last year's nuts," said Mrs. Burton.

"H'm!" exclaimed Budge; "I ought to have known that; it's dreadfully old-fashioned."

"Old-fashioned!" exclaimed Mrs. Burton.

"Why, yes; it's full of wrinkles, don't you see? like the face of Mrs. Paynter, an' you say *she's* old-fashioned."

"Aunt Alice," said Toddie, "birch-trees izh the only kind that wearzsh Sunday clothes, ain't they? Theyzh always all in white, like me and Budgie, when we goes to Sunday school. Gwacious!" exclaimed Toddie, as he leaned against one of the birches and examined its outer garments. "Thezh Sunday trees are awful funny—thish one is singin' a song! Dzust come—hark!"

Though somewhat startled at the range of Toddie's imagination, and wondering what incentive it had on the present occasion, Mrs. Burton approached the tree, and solved the mystery by hearing the breeze sighing softly through the branches. Then she told Toddie what caused the sound, and the young man replied: "Oh! Then it's the Lord come down to sing in it 'cauzh it's got Sunday clothes on. Thatsh it, izhn't it?"

"Oh, no, Toddie; the wind is only the wind," said Mrs. Burton.

"Why, *I* always fought it wazh the Lord a-talkin' when the wind blowed. I guesh somebody tolded me so 'cauzh I fought that before I had many uvver finks."

Up the mountain road leisurely sauntered Mrs. Burton, while her nephews examined every large stone boulder, tree, and hole in the ground. This passion for investigation was finally rewarded, for, as Toddie poked a stick into a hole at the root of a tree, a little snake came out, and seemed disposed to defend his domicile.

Toddie ran shrieking to his aunt, while Budge belaboured the reptile vigorously with his own stick until it was dead.

"Ah—h—h—h!" screamed Toddie. "The hateful fing! Why don't snakesh come an' offer little boysh apples, like that one did in Adam's garden, 'stead of scarin' 'em most to deff?"

"Because snakes don't like little boys to bother them," said Mrs. Burton, trying to comfort the frightened child.

"If he would only teach me to run along the ground on my tummuk like *he* does, I wouldn't care," said Toddie. "Why don't he git dirty when he runs? See how clean and white he is along the bottom side of him. I wiss we'd asked him how he keeps so clean 'fore Budgie killed him."

"Why, snakes can't talk, Toddie!" said Mrs. Burton.

"Can't they?" asked Toddie. "That garden-snake did."

"*He* was somebody else—Satan was in him," said Mrs. Burton.

"Did he get inside of the snake so's to play in the dust without gettin' his clothes dyty?" asked Toddie.

"No. He did it to make trouble," said Mrs. Burton.

"Shouldn't fink he'd *want* to make any crubble," said Toddie, "when he could have such fun wrigglin' around!"

The top of the hill was gained at last, and, with a long-drawn "Oh!" both boys sat down upon stones and gazed in delight at the extended scene before them. Budge at last broke the silence by asking:

"Aunt Alice, don't you 'spose our friends up in heaven is lookin' at all these towns, an' hills, an' rivers, an' things, just like we are?"

"Very likely, dear," said Mrs. Burton.

"Well, then, they can see a good deal further than we can. Do our spirits have new eyes put in 'em when they get up to heaven?"

"I don't know how that is," said Mrs. Burton. "Perhaps they only have their sight made better."

"Why, does spirits take their old eyes wif' 'em to hebben, an' leave all the rest part of 'em in the deader?" asked Toddie.

Mrs. Burton realised that she had been too hasty in assuming knowledge of spiritual physiognomy, and she endeavoured to retract by saying:

"Spiritual eyes and bodily eyes are different.'

"Does dust and choochoo cinders ever get into spirit eyes, an' make little boy andzels cry, and growed-up andzels say swear wordsh?" asked Toddie.

"Certainly not," said Mrs. Burton. "There's no crying or swearing in heaven."

"Then what does angels do with the water that comes in their eyes when they hear music that makes 'em feel as if wind was blowin' froo 'em?" asked Budge.

Mrs. Burton endeavoured to change the subject of conversation to one with which she was more familiar, by asking him if he knew that there were hills a hundred times as high as Hawksnest Rock.

"Goodness, no!" exclaimed the child. "Why, I should think you could look right *into* heaven from the tops of them; can't you?"

"No," said Mrs. Burton, with some impatience at the result of her attempt. "Besides, their tops are covered with snow all the time, and nobody can get up to them."

"Then the little boy andzels can play snowball on 'em wifout no cross man's comin' up an' sayin' 'Don't!'" said Toddie.

Mrs. Burton tried again.

"Just see how high that bird is flying," said she, pointing to a hawk who was soaring far above the hill.

"Yes," said Budge. "*He* can go up into heaven whenever he wants to, can't he, 'cause he's got wings: I don't know why birds have got wings and little boys haven't."

"Little boys are already hard enough to find when they're wanted," said Mrs. Burton. "If they had wings they'd always be out of sight. But what makes you little boys talk so much about heaven to-day?"

"Oh, 'cause we're up so much closer to it, I suppose," said Budge, "when we're on a high hill like this."

"Don't you think it must be nearly lunch-time?" asked Mrs. Burton, using, in despair, the argument which had seldom failed with healthy children.

"Certainly," said Budge. "I always do. Come on, Tod. Let's go the shortest way."

The shortest way was by numerous short cuts, with which the boys seemed perfectly acquainted. One of these, however, was by a very steep incline, and Budge, perhaps snuffing the lunch afar off, descended so rapidly that he lost his balance, fell forward, tried to recover himself, failed, and slipped rapidly through a narrow path which finally ended in a gutter traversing it.

"Ow!" remarked the young man as he picked himself up, and relieved himself of a mouthful of mud. "Did you see my back come up an' me walk down the mountain on my mouth? I think a snake would be ashamed of himself to see how easy it was. I didn't try a bit—I just went slip, slop, bunk! to the bottom."

"An' you didn't get scolded for dytyin' your clothes, either," said Toddie.

The subject of dirt upon juvenile raiment began to trouble the mind of Mrs. Burton. Could it be possible that children had a natural right to dirtier clothing than adults, and without incurring special blame? Again Mrs. Burton went into a study of the brownest description, while the children improved these moments of preoccupation to do all sorts of things which would have seemed dreadful to their aunt, but were delightful to themselves. At length, however, they reached the Burton lunch-table, and managed a series of rapid disappearances for whatever was upon it.

"Aunt Alice," said Budge, after finishing his meal, "what are you going to do to make us happy this afternoon?"

"I think," said Mrs. Burton, "I shall allow you to amuse yourselves. I shall be quite busy superintending the baking. Our cook has only lately come to us, you know, and she may need some help from me."

"Do you know, Aunt Alice," said Budge, "that *we* can bake? We can—real nice. We've helped mamma make pies an' cakes lots of times, only hers are big ones an' ours are baby ones."

"I suppose I am to construe that remark as a hint that you would like to help *me*?" said Mrs. Burton. "If you will do only what you are told, you may go to the kitchen with me; but listen—the moment you give the cook or me the least bit of trouble, out you shall go."

"Oh, goody, goody!" shouted Toddie. "An' can we have tea-parties on the kitchen-table as fast as we bake our fings?"

"I suppose so," said Mrs. Burton.

"Come on, come on!" exclaimed Toddie. "My hands won't be still a bittie, I wants to work so much. How many kindsh of pies is you goin' to make?"

"None at all," said Mrs. Burton.

"Gwacious!" exclaimed Toddie. "I shouldn't fink you'd call it bakin'-day then. Izhn't you goin' to make noffin' but ole nasty bread?"

"Perhaps I can find a way for you to make a little cake—some buns, say," remarked Mrs. Burton, relenting.

"Well, that would be *kind* o' bakin'-day like; but my hands is gettin' still again awful fasht."

Mrs. Burton led the way to the kitchen, and the preparation of the staff of life was begun by the new cook, with such assistance as could be rendered by a small boy wedged closely under each elbow, and two inquiring faces hanging over the very edge of the bread-pan.

"*That* don't look very cakey," remarked Budge. "She ain't put any powder into it."

"This kind of bread needs no powder," said Mrs. Burton. "Baking-powders are used only in tea-biscuits."

"When tea-biscuits goes in the oven they is little bits of flat fings," remarked Toddie—"theysh little bits of flat fings, but when they comes out they's awful big an' fat. What *makes* 'em bake big?"

"That's what the powder is put in for," said Mrs. Burton. "They'd be little hard, tasteless things if it weren't for the powder. Bridget, just work some sweetening with a little of the dough, so the boys can have some buns."

Both boys escorted the cook to the pantry for sugar, and back again to the table, and got their noses as nearly as possible under the roller with which the sugar was crushed, and they superintended the operation of working it into the dough, and then Mrs. Burton found some very small pans in the centre of which the boys put single buns which they were themselves allowed to shape.

"Stop, Toddie!" exclaimed Mrs. Burton, suddenly noticing that Toddie was shaping his dough by rolling it vigorously between his hands, as little boys treat clay while attempting to make marbles. "If you press your dough as hard as that, you may feel certain that it will never bake light in the world."

Then some of the little pans were placed in the vacant space in the oven, and during the next fifteen minutes Mrs. Burton was implored at least twenty times to see if they weren't almost done. When, finally baked, Toddie's were as small as bullets and about as hard.

"Put some powder in the rest of them," pleaded Toddie.

"I'm sure it wouldn't do the slightest bit of good," said Mrs. Burton.

Further entreaties led to a conflict between will and authority, after which Toddie sulked and finally disappeared, carrying one of his precious pans with him. When after a few moments he returned the baking was done, and the oven door was open.

"I'zhe a'-goin to bake this uvver one *any*how," said Toddie, putting the single remaining pan into the oven and closing the door. "Say, Aunt Alice," he continued, his good nature returning. "Now fix that tea-party we was goin' to have wif our own fings. *You* can come to the table wif us if you want to."

Suddenly a loud report, like the shot of a gun, startled the party, a piece of the stove flew violently across the room and broke against the wall, the stove-lids shivered violently and the doors fell open, the poker, which had lain on the stove, danced frantically, and a small pan of some sort of fat—such as some cooks have an insane fancy to be always doing something with, but never do it—was shaken over, and its burning contents began to diffuse a sickening odour. The cook dropped upon her knees and crossed herself; the party arose, Budge roaring, Toddie screaming, and Mrs. Burton very pale, while the cook remarked:

"Holy Mudther! The watherback's busted!"

Mrs. Burton disengaged herself from her tightly clinging nephews, and approached the range cautiously. There was no sign

of water, and the back of the range was undisturbed; even the fire was not disarranged.

"It isn't the water-back," said Mrs. Burton, "nor the fire. What *could* it have been?"

"An' I belave, mum," said the cook, "that 'twas the dhivil, savin' yer prisince; an', saints presarve us! I've heerd at home as how he hated these new ways of cookin', because dhere was no foire-place for him to sit in the corner of, bad luck to him! It was the dhivil, sure, mum," repeated the cook, crossing herself again. "Did iver ye schmell the loike av that?"

Mrs. Burton snuffed the air, and sure enough, in spite of the loathsome odour of burning grease, she detected a strong sulphurous smell.

"An' he went and tookted my last bun wif him, too," complained Toddie, who had been cautiously approaching the oven in which he had placed his pan, "*Bad* ole debbil! I fought he didn't have noffin' but roasted people at hizh tea-parties!"

The whole party was too much agitated and mystified to pursue their investigations further. The fire was allowed to die out, Mrs. Burton hurried upstairs and to the front of the house with the children, while the cook craved and received permission to make an immediate call upon her spiritual adviser.

Mr. Burton, on his way home, was met by his wife and nephews, and heard a tale which had now reached blood-curling proportions. His descent to the scene of the disaster was reluctantly consented to by his wife; but he was unable to discover the cause of the accident, and he succeeded in getting his hands most shockingly dirty. He hurried to wash them, and a moment after he roared from the head of the stairs: "Boys, which of you have been up here to-day?"

There was no response for a moment; then Budge shouted: "Not me."

Mrs. Burton looked enquiringly at Toddie, noting which, the young gentleman averted his eyes. Then Mr. Burton hurried downstairs, looked at both boys, and asked: "What did you meddle with my powder-flask for, Toddie?"

"Why—why—why," stammered Toddie. "Aunt Alice wouldn't put no powder in my buns to make 'em light after I rolled 'em heavy—said 'twouldn't do 'em no good. But my papa says 'taint never no harm to try, so I dzust wented and gotted some powder out of your brass bottle that's hangin' on your gun, and I didn't say nuffin' to anybody, 'cauzh I wanted to s'prise 'em. An' while I was waiting for it to get done bad ole debbil came an' hookted it. Guesh it must have been real good else he wouldn't have tookted it, 'cauzh he's such a smart fief he can steal the nicest fings he wantsh—whole cake-shop windows full."

"How did you mix it with the dough?—how much did you take?" demanded Mrs. Burton.

"Didn't mixsh it at all," said Toddie; "dzush pourded it on the pan azh full azh I could. You'd fink I'd *have* to if you tried to eat one of my buns that didn't have no powder in. Gwacious! *wasn't* they hard? I couldn't bite 'em a bit—I dzust had to swallow 'em whole."

"Umph!" growled Mr. Burton. "And do you know who the devil—the *little* devil was that——"

"Harry!" remonstrated Mrs. Burton.

"Well, my dear, the truth appears to be just this: your nephew——"

"*Your* nephew, Mr. Burton!"

"Well, my—*our* nephew put into the oven this afternoon about enough of gunpowder to charge a six-pounder shell, and the heat gradually became too much for it."

Toddie had listened to this conversation with an air of anxious inquiry, and at last timidly asked:

"Wazhn't it the right kind of powder? I fought it wazh, 'cauzh it makes everyfing else light when it goezh off."

"Do you suppose your method of training will ever prevail against that boy's logic, my dear?" asked Mr. Burton. "And if it won't, what will?"

"I won't put so much in nexsht time," said Toddie, "'cauzh 'tain't no good to try a fing an' then have the tryin' stuff go an' take the fing all away from you an' get so mad as to break stoves to bits an' scare little boysh an' Aunt Alishes most to deff."

MIDNIGHT TROUBLE

By SAMUEL LOVER

After a fight with Dick Dawson, in which he had taken a drubbing, Handy Andy ran home to his mother's cabin for rest and refuge. But true to his singular fate, which seemed to be to find trouble at every move he made, even sleeping under a bed in which his mother and Cousin Oonah slumbered was sufficient to get Andy Rooney into further hot water. He finished the night even less happy than he had begun it. This story is taken from "Handy Andy."

WHEN Handy Andy ran to his mother's cabin, to escape from the fangs of Dick Dawson, there was no one within: his mother being digging a few potatoes for supper from the little ridge behind her house, and Oonah Riley, her niece—an orphan girl who lived with her—being up to Squire Egan's to sell some eggs; for round the poorest cabins in Ireland you scarcely ever fail to see some ragged hens, whose eggs are never consumed by their proprietors, except, perhaps, on Easter Sunday, but sold to the neighbouring gentry at a trifling price.

Andy cared not who was out, or who was in, provided he could only escape from Dick: so without asking any questions, he crawled under the wretched bed in the dark corner, where his mother and Oonah slept, and where the latter, through the blessed influence of health, youth, and an innocent heart, had brighter dreams than attended many a couch whose downy pillows and silken hangings would more than purchase the fee-simple of any cabin in Ireland. There Andy, in a state of utter exhaustion from his fears, his race, and his thrashing, soon fell asleep, and the terrors of Dick the Devil gave place to the blessing of the profoundest slumber.

Quite unconscious of the presence of her darling Andy was the widow Rooney as she returned from the potato ridge into her cabin; depositing a *skeough* of the newly dug esculent at the door, and replacing the spade in its own corner of the cabin. At the same moment Oonah returned, after disposing of her eggs, and handed the threepence she had received for them to her aunt, who dropped them into the deep pocket of blue striped tick which hung at her side.

"Take the pail, Oonah, *ma chree*, and run to the well for some wather to wash the pratees, while I get the pot ready for bilin' them; it wants scourin', for the pig was atin' his dinner out iv it, the craythur!"

Off went Oonah with her pail, which she soon filled from the clear spring; and placing the vessel on her head, walked back to the cabin with that beautiful erect form, free step, and graceful swaying of the figure so peculiar to the women of Ireland and the East, from their habit of carrying weights upon the head. The potatoes were soon washed; and as they got their last dash of water in the *skeough*, whose open wickerwork let the moisture drain from them, up came Larry Hogan, who, being what is called "a civil spoken man," addressed Mrs. Rooney in the following manner;

"Them's purty pratees, Mrs. Rooney; God save you, ma'am!"

"'Deed an' they are—thank you kindly, Mr. Hogan; God save you and yours too! And how would the woman that owns you be?"

"Hearty, thank you."

"Will you step in?"

"No, I'm obliged to you—I must be aff home wid me; but I'll just get a coal for my pipe, for it wint out on me awhile agone with the fright."

"Well, I've heer'd quare things, Larry Hogan," said Oonah, laughing and showing her white teeth; "but I never heer'd so quare a thing as a pipe goin' out with the fright."

"Oh, how sharp you are!—takin' one up afore they're down."

"Not afore they're down, Larry: for you said it."

"Well, if I was down, you were down *on* me; so you are down too, you see. Ha, ha! And afther all now, Oonah, a pipe is like a Christian in many ways: sure it's made o' clay like a Christian, and has the spark o' life in it, and while the breath is in it the spark is alive; but when the breath is out of it the spark dies, and then it grows cowld like a Christian; and isn't it a pleasant companion like a Christian?"

"Faix, some Christians isn't pleasant companions at all!" chimed in Mrs. Rooney sententiously.

"Well, but they ought to be," said Larry; "and isn't a pipe sometimes cracked like a Christian, and isn't it sometimes choked like a Christian?"

"Oh, choke you and your pipe together, Larry! Will you never have done?" said the widow.

"The most improvinist thing in the world is smokin'," said Larry, who had now relit his pipe, and squatted himself on a three-legged stool beside the widow's fire. "The most improvinist in the world—(paugh!)"—and a parenthetical whiff of tobacco-smoke curled out of the corner of Larry's mouth—"is smokin'; for the smoke shows you, as it were, the life o' man passin' away like a puff—(paugh!)—just like that; and the tibakky turns to ashes like his poor perishable body; for as the song says:

"Tibakky is an Indian weed
Alive at morn and dead at eve;
It lives but an hour,
Is cut down like a flower.
Think o' this when you're smoking tiba-akky."

And Larry sung the ditty as he crammed some of the weed into the bowl of his pipe with his little finger

"Why, you're as good as a sarmint this evenin', Larry," said the widow, as she lifted the iron pot on the fire.

"There's worse sarmints nor that, I can tell you," rejoined Larry, who took up the old song again:

"A pipe it larns us all this thing—
'Tis fair without and foul within,
Just like a sowl begrim'd with sin.
Think o' this when you're smoking tiba-akky!"

Larry puffed away silently for a few minutes, and when Oonah had placed a few sods of turf round the pot in an upright position, that the flame might curl upward round them, and so hasten the boiling, she drew a stool near the fire, and asked Larry to explain about the fright.

"Why, I was coming up by the crossroad there, when what should I see but a ghost."

"A ghost!" exclaimed the widow and Oonah, with suppressed voices and distended mouth and eyes.

"To all appearances," said Larry; "but it was only a thing was stuck in the hedge to freken whoever was passin' by; and as I kem up to it there was a groan, so I started, and looked at it for a minit, or thereaway; but I seen what it was, and threwn a stone at it, for fear I'd be mistaken: and I heer'd tittherin' inside the hedge, and then I knew 'twas only devilment of someone."

"And what was it?" asked Oonah.

"'Twas a horse's head, in throth, with an owld hat on the top of it, and two buck-briars stuck out at each side, and some rags hanging on them, and an owld breeches shakin' undher the head: 'twas just altogether like a long pale-face man, with high shouldhers and no body, and very long arms and short legs: faith, it frightened me at first!"

"And no wondher," said Oonah. "Dear, but I think I'd lose my life if I seen the like!"

"But sure," said the widow, "wouldn't you know that ghosts never appears by day?"

"Ay, but I hadn't time to think o' that, bein' taken short wid the fright—more betoken, 'twas the place the murdher happened in long ago."

"Sure enough," said the widow. "God betune us and harm!" and she marked herself with the sign of the cross as she spoke; "and a terrible murdher it was," added she.

"How was it?" inquired Oonah, drawing her seat closer to her aunt and Larry.

The boiling-over of the pot recalled them to a sense of the business that ought to be attended to at the moment, and Larry was invited to take share of the potatoes. This he declined; declaring, as he had done some time previously, that he must "be off home." The widow returned to the fireside and was silent, while Oonah looked by the light of a candle into the boiling pot, to ascertain if the potatoes were yet done, and cast a fearful glance up the wide chimney as she withdrew from the inspection.

"I wish Larry did not tell us such horrid stories," said she, as she laid the rushlight on the table; "I'll be dhramin' all night o' them."

"Ate your supper, child, ate your supper," said her aunt, giving the example, which was followed by Oonah; and after the light meal their prayers were said, and perchance with a little extra devotion, from their pecular state of mind: then to bed they went. The rushlight being extinguished, the only light remaining was that shed from the red embers of the decaying fire, which cast so uncertain a glimmer within the cabin that its effect was almost worse than utter darkness to a timid person: for any object within its range assumed a form unlike its own, and presented some fantastic image to the eye; and as Oonah, contrary to her usual habit, could not fall asleep the moment she went to bed, she could not resist peering forth from under the bedclothes through the uncertain gloom, in a painful state of watchfulness, which became gradually relaxed into an uneasy sleep.

The night was about half spent when Andy began to awake; and as he stretched his arms, and rolled his whole body round, he struck the bottom of the bed above him in the action and woke his mother. "Dear me," thought the widow, "I can't sleep at all tonight," Andy gave another turn soon after, which roused Oonah. She started, and, shaking her aunt, asked her, in a low voice if it was she who kicked her, though she scarcely hoped an answer in the affirmative, and yet dared not believe what her fears whispered.

"No *acushla*," whispered the aunt.

"Did *you* feel anything?" asked Oonah, trembling violently.

"What do you mane, *alanna*?" said the aunt.

Andy gave another roll. "There it is again!" gasped Oonah; and in a whisper scarcely above her breath she added, "Aunt—there's someone under the bed!"

The aunt did not answer: but the two women drew closer together and held each other in their arms, as if their proximity afforded protection. Thus they lay in breathless fear for some minutes, while Andy began to be influenced by a vision, and soon an odd word began to escape from the dream.

"There are two of them!" whispered Oonah.

"Screech!" said her aunt.

"I can't," said Oonah.

Andy was quiet for some time, while the women scarcely breathed.

"Suppose we get up, and make for the door?" said the aunt.

"I wouldn't put my foot out of the bed for the world," said Oonah. "I'm afeared one o' them will catch me by the leg."

"Howld him; howld him!" grumbled Andy.

"I'll die with the fright, Aunt! I feel I'm dying! Let us say our prayers, Aunt, for we're going to be murdhered!" The two women began to repeat with fervour their *aves* and *paternosters*, while at this immediate juncture, Andy's dream having borne him to the dirty ditch where Dick Dawson had pommelled him, he began to vociferate, "Murder, murder!" so fiercely that the women screamed together in an agony of terror, and, "Murder, murder!" was shouted by the whole party, for, once the widow and Oonah found their voices, they made good use of them. The noise awoke Andy, who had had, be it remembered, a tolerably long sleep by this time: and he having quite forgotten where he had lain down, and finding himself confined by the bed above him, and smothering for want of air, with the fierce shouts of murder ringing in his ear, woke in as great a fright as the women in the bed, and became a party in the terror he himself had produced; every plunge he gave under the bed inflicted a poke or a kick on his mother and cousin, which was answered by a cry of "Murder!"

"Let me out—let me out, Misther Dick!" roared Andy. "Where am I at all? Let me out!"

"Help! help! murdher!" roared the woman.

Andy scrambled from under the bed, half awake, and frightened by the darkness and the noise, which was now increased by the barking of the cur-dog.

"Hie at him, Coaly!" roared Mrs. Rooney. "Howld him! howld him!"

Now as this address was often made to the cur respecting the pig, when Mrs. Rooney sometimes wanted a quiet moment in the day, and the pig didn't like quitting the premises, the dog ran to the corner of the cabin where the pig habitually lodged, and laid hold of his ear with the strongest testimonials of affection, which polite attention the pig acknowledged by a prolonged squealing, that drowned the voices of the women and Andy together; and now the cocks and hens that were roosting on the rafters of the cabin were startled by the din, and the crowing and the flapping of the frightened fowls, as they flew about in the dark, added to the general uproar and confusion.

"A—h!" screamed Oonah, "take your hands off me!" as Andy getting from under the bed, laid his hand upon it to assist him, and caught a grip of his cousin.

"Who are you at all?" cried Andy, making another claw, and catching hold of his mother's nose.

"Oonah, they're murdhering me!" shouted the widow.

The name of Oonah, and the voice of his mother, recalled his senses to Andy, who shouted, "Mother, Mother! what's the matter?" A frightened hen flew in his face and nearly knocked Andy down. "Bad cess to you," cried Andy. "What do you hit me for?"

"Who are you at all!" cried the widow.

"Don't you know me?" said Andy.

"No, I don't know you; by the vartue o' my oath, I don't; and I'll never swear again you, jintlemen, if you lave the place and spare our lives!"

Here the hens flew against the dresser, and smash went the plates and dishes.

"Oh, jintlemen dear, don't rack and ruin me that way; don't destroy a lone woman."

"Mother, Mother, what's this at all? Don't you know your own Andy?"

"Is it you that's there?" cried the widow, catching hold of him.

"To be sure it's me," said Andy.

"You won't let us be murdhered, will you?"

"Who'd murdher you?"

"Them people that's with you." Smash went another plate. "Do you hear that?—they're rackin' my place, the villains!"

"Divil a one's wid me at all!" said Andy.

"I'll take my oath there was three or four under the bed," said Oonah.

"No one but myself," said Andy.

"Are you sure?" said his mother.

"Cock sure!" said Andy, and a loud crowing gave evidence in favour of his assertion.

"The fowls is going mad," said the widow.

"And the pig's distracted," said Oonah.

"No wonder! The dog's murdherin' him," said Andy.

"Get up and light the rushlight, Oonah," said the widow; "you'll get a spark out o' the turf cendhers."

"Some o' them will catch me, maybe," said Oonah.

"Get up, I tell you!" said the widow.

Oonah now arose and groped her way to the fireplace where, by dint of blowing upon the embers and poking the rushlight among the turf ashes, a light was at length obtained. She then returned to the bed, and threw her petticoat over her shoulders.

"What's this at all?" said the widow, rising and wrapping a blanket round her. "Look under the bed, Oonah."

Oonah obeyed, and screamed and ran behind Andy. "There's another here yet!" said she.

Andy seized the poker, and, standing on the defensive, desired the villain to come out: the demand was not complied with.

"There's nobody there," said Andy.

"I'll take my oath there is," said Oonah; "a dirty blackguard, without any clothes on him."

"Come out, you robber!" said Andy, making a lunge under the truckle.

A grunt ensued, and out rushed the pig, who had escaped from the dog—the dog having discovered a greater attraction in some fat that was knocked from the dresser, which the widow intended for the dipping of rushes in; but the dog being enlightened to his own interest without rushlights, and prefering mutton fat to pig's ear, had suffered the grunter to go at large, while he was captivated by the fat. The clink of a three-legged stool the widow seized to the rescue was a stronger argument against the dog than he was prepared to answer, and a remnant of fat was preserved from the rapacious Coaly.

"Where's the rest o' the robbers?" said Oonah. "There's three o' them, I know."

"You're dhramin'," said Andy. "Divil a robber is here but myself."

"And what brought you here?" said his mother.

"I was afeared they'd murdher me!" said Andy.

"Murdher!" exclaimed the widow and Oonah together, still startled by the very sound of the word. "Who do you mane?"

"Misther Dick," said Andy.

"Aunt, I tell you," said Oonah, "this is some more of Andy's blundhers. Sure Misther Dawson wouldn't be goin' to murdher anyone; let us look round the cabin, and find out who's in it, for

I won't be aisy ontil I look into every corner, to see there's no robbers in the place: for I tell you again, there was three o' them undher the bed."

The search was made, and the widow and Oonah at length satisfied that there were no midnight assassins there with long knives to cut their throats; and then they began to thank God that their lives were safe.

"But, oh! look at my chaynee!" said the widow, clasping her hands, and casting a look of despair at the shattered delf that lay around her; "look at my chaynee!"

"And what was it brought *you* here!" said Oonah, facing round on Andy, with a dangerous look, rather, in her bright eye. "Will you tell us that—what was it?"

"I came to save my life, I tell you," said Andy.

"To put us in dhread of ours, you mane," said Oonah. "Just look at the *omadhaun* there," said she to her aunt, "standin' with his mouth open, just as if nothin' happened, and he after frightening the lives out of us."

"Thrue for you, *alanna*," said her aunt.

"And would no place sarve you indeed, but undher our bed, you vagabone?" said his mother, roused to a sense of his delinquency; "to come in like a merodin' villain as you are, and hide under the bed, and frighten the lives out of us, and rack and ruin my place!"

" 'Twas Misther Dick, I tell you," said Andy.

"Bad scran to you, you unlucky hangin' bone thief!" cried the widow, seizing him by the hair, and giving him a hearty cuff on the ear, which would have knocked him down, only that Oonah kept him up by an equally well-applied box on the other.

"Would you murdher me?" shouted Andy, as he saw his mother lay hold of the broom.

"Aren't you afther frightenin' the lives out of us, you dirty, good-for-nothing, mischief-making——"

On poured the torrent of abuse, rendered more impressive by a whack at every word. Andy roared, and the more he roared the more did Oonah and his mother thrash him.

HELPING HANDS

By ELIZABETH GASKELL

Miss Matilda Jenkyns was ruined financially when her bank suddenly stopped making payments, and this rather shy and timid middle-aged lady was faced with the hard choice of finding a way to provide a living. Fortunately her sweet nature had won for her a number of true friends, who in her need were eager to extend helping hands, as related by Mary Smith, her companion in the old Rectory. This story is taken from "Cranford."

THE next morning news came, both official and otherwise, that the Town and County Bank had stopped payment. Miss Matty was ruined.

She tried to speak quietly to me; but when she came to the actual fact that she would have but about five shillings a week to live upon, she could not restrain a few tears.

"I am not crying for myself, dear," said she, wiping them away; "I believe I am crying for the very silly thought of how my mother would grieve if she could know; she always cared for us so much more than for herself. But many a poor person has less, and I am not very extravagant, and, thank God, when the neck of mutton, and Martha's wages, and the rent are paid, I have not a farthing owing. Poor Martha! I think she'll be sorry to leave me."

Miss Matty smiled at me through her tears, and she would fain have had me see only the smile, not the tears.

It was an example to me, and I fancy it might be to many others, to see how immediately Miss Matty set about the retrenchment which she knew to be right under her altered circumstances.

Martha opened the door, her face swollen with crying. As soon as she saw me she burst out afresh, and taking hold of my arm she pulled me in, and banged the door to, in order to ask me if indeed it was all true that Miss Matty had been saying.

"I'll never leave her! No; I won't. I telled her so, and said I could not think how she could find it in her heart to give me warning. I could not have had the face to do it, if I'd been her. I might ha' been just as good for nothing as Mrs. Fitz-Adam's Rosy, who struck for wages after living seven years and a half in one place. I said I was not to go and serve Mammon at that rate; that I knew when I'd got a good missus, if she didn't know when she'd got a good servant——"

"But, Martha," said I, cutting in while she wiped her eyes.

"Don't 'but, Martha' me," she replied to my deprecatory tone.

"Listen to reason——"

"I'll not listen to reason," she said, now in full possession of her voice, which had been rather choked with sobbing. "Reason always means what someone else has got to say. Now I think what I've got to say is good enough reason; but reason or not, I'll say it, and stick to it. I've money in the Savings Bank, and I've a good stock of clothes, and I'm not going to leave Miss Matty. No, not if she gives me warning every hour in the day!"

She put her arms akimbo, as much as to say she defied me; and, indeed, I could hardly tell how to begin to remonstrate with her, so much did I feel that Miss Matty, in her increasing infirmity, needed the attendance of this kind and faithful woman.

"Well——" said I at last.

"I'm thankful you begin with 'well'! If you'd ha' begun with 'but,' as you did afore, I'd not ha' listened to you. Now you may go on."

"I know you would be a great loss to Miss Matty, Martha——"

"I telled her so. A loss she'd never cease to be sorry for," broke in Martha triumphantly.

"Still, she will have so little—so very little—to live upon, that I don't see just now how she could find you food—she will even be pressed for her own. I tell you this, Martha, because I feel you are like a friend to dear Miss Matty, but you know she might not like to have it spoken about."

Apparently this was even a blacker view of the subject than Miss Matty had presented to her, for Martha just sat down on the first chair that came to hand, and cried out loud (we had been standing in the kitchen).

At last she put her apron down, and looking me earnestly in the face, asked, "Was that the reason Miss Matty wouldn't order a pudding to-day? She said she had no great fancy for sweet things, and you and she would just have a mutton chop. But I'll be up to her. Never you tell, but I'll make her a pudding, and a pudding she'll like, too, and I'll pay for it myself; so mind you see she eats it. Many a one has been comforted in their sorrow by seeing a good dish come upon the table."

I was rather glad that Martha's energy had taken the immediate and practical direction of pudding-making, for it staved off the quarrelsome discussion as to whether she should or should not leave Miss Matty's service. She began to tie on a clean apron, and otherwise prepare herself for going to the shop for the butter, eggs, and what else she might require. She would not use a scrap of the articles already in the house for her cookery, but went to an old tea-pot in which her private store of money was deposited, and took out what she wanted.

I found Miss Matty very quiet, and not a little sad; but by and by she tried to smile for my sake. It was settled that I was to write to my father, and ask him to come over and hold a consultation, and as soon as this letter was despatched we began to talk over future plans.

Teaching was, of course, the first thing that suggested itself. If Miss Matty could teach children anything, it would throw her among the little elves in whom her soul delighted. I ran over her accomplishments. Once upon a time I had heard her say she could play *Ah! vous dirai-je, maman?* on the piano, but that was long, long ago; that faint shadow of musical acquirement had died out years before. She had also once been able to trace out patterns very nicely for muslin embroidery, by dint of placing a piece of silver paper over the design to be copied, and holding both against the window-pane while she marked the scollop and eyelet-holes. But that was her nearest approach to the accomplishment of drawing, and I did not think it would go very far.

What she piqued herself upon, as arts in which she excelled, was making candle-lighters, or "spills" (as she preferred calling them), of coloured paper, cut so as to resemble feathers, and knitting garters in a variety of dainty stitches. I had once said, on receiving a present of an elaborate pair, that I should feel quite tempted to drop one of them in the street, in order to have it admired; but I found this little joke (and it was a very little one) was such a distress to her sense of propriety, and was taken with such anxious, earnest alarm, lest the temptation might some day prove too strong for me, that I quite regretted having ventured upon it. A present of these delicately wrought garters, a bunch of gay "spills," or a set of cards on which sewing-silk was wound in a mystical manner, were the well-known tokens of Miss Matty's favour. But would anyone pay to have their children taught these arts? or, indeed, would Miss Matty sell, for filthy lucre, the knack and the skill with which she made trifles of value to those who loved her?

No! there was nothing she could teach to the rising generation of Cranford, unless they had been quick learners and ready imitators of her patience, her humility, her sweetness, her quiet contentment with all that she could not do. I pondered and pondered until dinner was announced by Martha, with a face all blubbered and swollen with crying.

I had forgotten to tell Miss Matty about the pudding, and I was afraid she might not do justice to it, for she had evidently very little appetite this day; so I seized the opportunity of letting her into the secret while Martha took away the meat. Miss Matty's eyes filled with tears, and she could not speak, either to express surprise or delight, when Martha returned bearing it aloft, made in the most wonderful representation of a lion *couchant* that ever was moulded. Martha's face gleamed with triumph as she set it down before Miss Matty with an exultant "There!" Miss Matty wanted to speak her thanks, but could not; so she took Martha's hand and shook it warmly, which set Martha off crying, and I myself could hardly keep up the necessary composure. Martha burst out of the room, and Miss Matty had to clear her voice once or twice before she could speak. At last she said, "I should like to keep this pudding under a glass shade, my dear!" and the notion of the lion *couchant*, with his currant eyes, being hoisted up to the place of honour on a mantelpiece, tickled my hysterical fancy, and I began to laugh, which rather surprised Miss Matty.

"I am sure, dear, I have seen uglier things under a glass shade before now," said she.

So had I, many a time and oft, and I accordingly composed my countenance (and now I could hardly keep from crying), and we both fell to upon the pudding, which was indeed excellent—only every morsel seemed to choke us, our hearts were so full.

We had too much to think about to talk much that afternoon. It passed over very tranquilly. But when the tea-urn was brought in a new thought came into my head. Why should not Miss Matty sell tea—be an agent to the East India Tea Company which then existed? I could see no objections to this plan, while the advantages were many—always supposing that Miss Matty could get over the degradation of condescending to anything like trade. Tea was neither greasy nor sticky—grease and stickiness being two of the qualities which Miss Matty could not endure. No shop-window would be required. A small, genteel notification of her being licensed to sell tea would, it is true, be necessary, but I hoped that it could be placed where no one would see it. Neither was tea a heavy article, so as to tax Miss Matty's fragile strength. The only thing against my plan was the buying and selling involved.

While I was giving but absent answers to the questions Miss Matty was putting—almost as absently—we heard a clumping sound on the stairs, and a whispering outside the door, which indeed once opened and shut as if by some invisible agency. After a little while Martha came in, dragging after her a great tall young man, all crimson with shyness, and finding his only relief in perpetually sleeking down his hair.

"Please, ma'am, he's only Jem Hearn," said Martha, by way of an introduction; and so out of breath was she that I imagine she had had some bodily struggle before she could overcome his reluctance to be presented on the courtly scene of Miss Matilda Jenkyns' drawing-room.

"And please, ma'am, he wants to marry me off-hand. And please, ma'am, we want to take a lodger—just one quiet lodger, to make our two ends meet; and we'd take any house conformable; and, oh dear, Miss Matty, if I may be so bold, would you have any objections to lodging with us? Jem wants it as much as I do." [To Jem] —"You great oaf! why can't you back me!—But he does want it all the same, very bad—don't you, Jem?—only, you see, he's dazed at being called on to speak before quality."

"It's not that," broke in Jem. "It's that you've taken me all on a sudden, and I didn't think for to get married so soon—and such quick words does flabbergast a man. It's not that I'm against it, ma'am" (addressing Miss Matty), "only Martha has such quick ways with her when once she takes a thing into her head; and marriage, ma'am—marriage nails a man, as one may say. I dare say I shan't mind it after it's once over."

"Please, ma'am," said Martha—who had plucked at his sleeve, and nudged him with her elbow, and otherwise tried to interrupt him all the time he had been speaking—"don't mind him, he'll come to; 'twas only last night he was an-axing me, and an-axing me, and all the more because I said I could not think of it for years to come, and now he's only taken aback with the suddenness of the joy; but you know, Jem, you are just as full as me about wanting a lodger." (Another great nudge.)

"Ay! if Miss Matty would lodge with us—otherwise I've no mind to be cumbered with strange folk in the house," said Jem, with a want of tact which I could see enraged Martha, who was trying to represent a lodger as the great object they wished to obtain, and that, in fact, Miss Matty would be smoothing their path and conferring a favour, if she would only come and live with them.

Miss Matty herself was bewildered by the pair; their, or rather Martha's, sudden resolution in favour of matrimony staggered her, and stood between her and the contemplation of the plan which Martha had at heart. Miss Matty began:

"Marriage is a very solemn thing, Martha."

"It is indeed, ma'am," quoth Jem. "Not that I've no objections to Martha."

"You've never let me a-be for asking me for to fix when I would be married," said Martha—her face all a-fire, and ready to cry with vexation—"and now you're shaming me before my missus and all."

"Nay, now! Martha, don't ee! don't ee! only a man likes to have breathing-time," said Jem, trying to possess himself of her hand, but in vain. Then seeing that she was more seriously hurt than he had imagined, he seemed to try to rally his scattered faculties, and with more straightforward dignity than, ten minutes before, I should have thought it possible for him to assume, he turned to Miss Matty, and said, "I hope, ma'am, you know that I am bound to respect everyone who has been kind to Martha. I always looked on her as to be my wife—some time; and she has often and often

spoken of you as the kindest lady that ever was; and though the plain truth is, I would not like to be troubled with lodgers of the common run, yet if, ma'am, you'd honour us by living with us, I'm sure Martha would do her best to make you comfortable; and I'd keep out of your way as much as I could, which I reckon would be the best kindness such an awkward chap as me could do."

Miss Matty had been very busy with taking off her spectacles, wiping them, and replacing them; but all she could say was, "Don't let any thought of me hurry you into marriage: pray don't. Marriage is such a very solemn thing!"

"But Miss Matilda will think of your plan, Martha," said I struck with the advantages that it offered, and unwilling to lose the opportunity of considering about it. "And I'm sure neither she nor I can ever forget your kindness; nor your's either, Jem."

"Why, yes, ma'am! I'm sure I mean kindly, though I'm a bit fluttered by being pushed straight ahead into matrimony, as it were, and mayn't express myself conformable. But I'm sure I'm willing enough, and give me time to get accustomed; so, Martha, wench, what's the use of crying so, and slapping me if I come near?"

This last was *sotto voce* and had the effect of making Martha bounce out of the room, to be followed and soothed by her lover. Whereupon Miss Matty sat down and cried very heartily.

The next morning, very early, I received a note from Miss Pole, so mysteriously wrapped up, and with so many seals on it to secure secrecy, that I had to tear the paper before I could unfold it. And when I came to the writing I could hardly understand the meaning, it was so involved and oracular. I made out, however, that I was to go to Miss Pole's at eleven o'clock; the number *eleven* being written in full length as well as in numerals, and *A.M.* twice dashed under, as if I were very likely to come at eleven at night, when all Cranford was usually a-bed and asleep by ten. There was no signature except Miss Pole's initials reversed, P. E.; but as Martha had given me the note, "with Miss Pole's kind regards," it needed no wizard to find out who sent it; and if the writer's name was to be kept secret, it was very well that I was alone when Martha delivered it.

I went as requested to Miss Pole's. The door was opened to me by her little maid Lizzy in Sunday trim, as if some grand event was impending over this work-day. And the drawing-room upstairs was arranged in accordance with this idea. The table was set out with the best green card-cloth, and writing materials upon it. On the little chiffonier was a tray with a newly decanted bottle of cowslip wine, and some ladies'-finger biscuits. Miss Pole herself was in solemn array, as if to receive visitors, although it was only eleven o'clock. Mrs. Forrester was there, crying quietly and sadly, and my arrival seemed only to call forth fresh tears. Before we had finished our greetings, performed with lugubrious mystery of demeanour, there was another rat-tat-tat, and Mrs. Fitz-Adam appeared, crimson with walking and excitement. It seemed as if this was all the company expected; for now Miss Pole made several demonstrations of being about to open the business of the meeting, by stirring the fire, opening and shutting the door, and coughing and blowing her nose. Then she arranged us all round the table, taking care to place me opposite to her; and last of all, she inquired of me if the sad report was true, as she feared it was, that Miss Matty had lost all her fortune?

Of course, I had but one answer to make.

"Miss Smith," she continued, addressing me (familiarly known as "Mary" to all the company assembled, but this was a state occasion), "I have conversed in private—I made it my business to do so yesterday afternoon—with these ladies on the misfortune which has happened to our friend, and one and all of us have agreed that while we have a superfluity, it is not only a duty, but a pleasure—a true pleasure, Mary!"—her voice was rather choked just here and she had to wipe her spectacles before she could go on—"to give what we can to assist her—Miss Matilda Jenkyns. Only in consideration of the feelings of delicate independence existing in the mind of every refined female we wish to contribute our mites in a secret and concealed manner, so as not to hurt the feelings I have referred to. And our object in requesting you to meet us this morning is that, believing you are the daughter—that your father is, in fact, her confidential adviser, in all pecuniary matters, we imagined that, by consulting with him, you might devise some mode in which our contribution could be made to appear the legal due which Miss Matilda Jenkyns ought to receive from—— Probably your father, knowing her investments, can fill up the blank."

Miss Pole concluded her address, and looked round for approval and agreement.

Now I saw why papers, pens, and ink were provided. Every lady wrote down the sum she could give annually, signed the paper, and sealed it mysteriously. If their proposal was acceded to, my father was to be allowed to open the papers, under pledge of secrecy. If not, they were to be returned to their writers.

When the ceremony had been gone through, I rose to depart; and promised all sorts of things in my anxiety to get home to Miss Matty, who might well be wondering what had become of me—absent from her two hours without being able to account for it. She had taken very little notice of time, however, as she had been occupied in numberless little arrangements preparatory to the great step of giving up her house.

Old hoards were taken out and examined as to their money value which luckily was small, or else I don't know how Miss Matty would have prevailed upon herself to part with such things as her mother's wedding-ring, the strange uncouth brooch with which her father had disfigured his shirt-frill, etc. However, we arranged things a little in order as to their pecuniary estimation, and were all ready for my father when he came the next morning.

I am not going to weary you with the details of all the business we went through; and one reason for not telling you about them is, that I did not understand what we were doing at the time, and cannot recollect it now. Miss Matty and I sat assenting to accounts, and schemes, and reports, and documents, of which I do not believe we either of us understood a word; for my father was clear-headed and decisive, and a capital man of business, and if we made the slightest inquiry, or expressed the slightest want of comprehension, he had a sharp way of saying, "Eh? eh? it's as clear as daylight. What's your objection?" And as we had not comprehended anything of what he had proposed, we found it rather difficult to shape our objections; in fact, we never were sure if we had any.

The lunch—a hot savoury mutton-chop, and a little of the cold loin sliced and fried—was brought in. Every morsel of this last dish was finished, to Martha's great gratification. Then my father bluntly told Miss Matty he wanted to talk to me alone.

I gave her a hearty kiss, and ran after my father. The result of our conversation was this. If all parties were agreeable, Martha and Jem were to be married with as little delay as possible, and they were to live on in Miss Matty's present abode; the sum which the Cranford ladies had agreed to contribute annually being sufficient to meet the greater part of the rent, and leaving Martha free to appropriate what Miss Matty should pay for her lodgings to any little extra comforts required. I then alluded to my idea that she might add to her small income by selling tea; and, to my surprise, (for I had nearly given up the plan), my father grasped at it with all the energy of a tradesman. I evidently rose in his estimation for having made this bright suggestion. I only hoped we should not both fall in Miss Matty's.

When we came to the proposal that she should sell tea, I could see it was rather a shock to her; not on account of any personal loss of gentility involved, but only because she distrusted her own powers of action in a new line of life, and would timidly have preferred a little more privation to any exertion for which she feared she was unfitted. However, when she saw my father was bent upon it, she sighed, and said she would try; and if she did not do well, of course, she would give it up. One good thing about it was, she did not think men ever bought tea; and it was of men particularly she was afraid. They had such sharp loud ways with them; and did up accounts, and counted their change so quickly! Now, if she might only sell comfits to children, she was sure she could please them!

FIFTY FAMOUS STORIES *for* GIRLS

In the same Series

Fifty Famous Stories for Boys
Fifty Famous Animal Stories